MENU FOR ROMANCE

MENU FOR
ROMANCE

LOVE HEATS UP FOR THE
CHEF AND THE PARTY PLANNER

KAYE DACUS

BARBOUR
PUBLISHING

ISBN 978-1-60260-455-1

Scripture quotations are taken from the New American Standard Bible, © 1960, 1962, 1963, 1968, 1971, 1972, 1973, 1975, 1977, 1995 by The Lockman Foundation. Used by permission.

This book is a work of fiction. Names, characters, places, and incidents are either products of the author's imagination or used fictitiously. Any similarity to actual people, organizations, and/or events is purely coincidental.

Published by Barbour Publishing, Inc., P.O. Box 719, Uhrichsville, OH 44683, www.barbourbooks.com

Our mission is to publish and distribute inspirational products offering exceptional value and biblical encouragement to the masses.

 Member of the
Evangelical Christian
Publishers Association

Printed in the United States of America.

DEDICATION:

To the real-life Corie, Lori, and Pam—wonderful sisters-of-the-heart who're always there for me.

ACKNOWLEDGMENTS:

This book wouldn't be here if it weren't for my brilliant agent, Chip MacGregor, and my incomparable editor, Rebecca Germany. My sincerest thanks to both of you for believing in me. Most sincere thanks go to my copyeditor, Becky Fish. Thanks for everything you do! As always, my deepest gratitude goes to my family who are my biggest supporters and greatest fans. And greatest of all, praises to God for granting me the desire of my heart: the opportunity to stay home and write.

CHAPTER 1

*H*appy New Year!"

Her thirty-fourth New Year and still no kiss at the stroke of midnight. . .or any other day or time. Meredith Guidry stood in the doorway leading into Vue de Ciel—the cavernous, sky-view event venue at the top of the tallest building in downtown Bonneterre, Louisiana—and swallowed back her longing as she watched hundreds of couples kiss.

A short burst of static over the earpiece startled her out of her regrets.

"Mere, we're going to set up the coffee stations and dessert tables." The executive chef's rich, mellow voice filled her ear.

She clicked the button on the side of the wireless headset. "Thanks, Major." Turning her gaze back to the main room, she tapped the button again. "Let's slowly start bringing the houselights back up. I want us at full illumination around twelve thirty." She strolled into the ballroom, the floor now covered with shiny metallic confetti, the hundreds of guests milling about wishing each other a happy New Year. Out on the dance floor, a large group of men stood swaying, arms about shoulders, singing "Auld Lang Syne" at the top of their lungs, accompanied by the jazz band.

"Let's make sure tables are bussed." Pressing her finger to the earpiece to speak over the network made her feel like those secret service agents in the movies who were always talking into their shirt cuffs. "I'm seeing several tables with empty plates and glasses."

She kept to the perimeter of the room, doing her best to blend in with the starlit sky beyond the glass walls, barely repressing the feeling of being the loner, the schoolgirl no one else paid any attention to. . . the woman no man ever gave a second glance.

"You look like a kid staring through a candy store window, wishing you could go inside."

Meredith's heart thumped at the sudden voice behind her. She turned. Major O'Hara grinned his lopsided grin, his chef's coat nearly fluorescent with its pristine whiteness.

"How're you holding up?" He squeezed her shoulder in a brotherly way, his indigo eyes gentle.

She sighed. "You know me—I operate on pure adrenaline at these things no matter how little sleep I've gotten the night before. So long as I stay busy and don't slow down, the fatigue can't catch up with me."

"And stopping to grab a bite to eat would have meant slowing down?"

"Yep."

Coldness embraced her shoulder when Major lifted his hand away. "I set aside a few take-home boxes for you—and Anne. I told her I'd be sure to save a little of everything."

Anne. Meredith's cousin and best friend. Her inspiration and mentor. Owner of a stellarly successful wedding- and event-planning business, Happy Endings, Inc. And friends with Major O'Hara on a level Meredith could never attain.

"If you see George, tell him I've been experimenting with that plum pudding recipe he gave me. I'll need his expert opinion before I can officially add it to my repertoire."

"I'll tell him—but you see him more often than I do."

"Yeah, I guess so. I'm glad we convinced Anne to fall in love with him. Finally, having another man's opinion when we're all working an event together." He winked.

Meredith quickly turned her eyes toward the milling crowd so he wouldn't see how he affected her. It would only embarrass him—and mortify her.

He tweaked her chin. "Come on. Back to work for the bosses."

Over the next hour, Meredith poured herself into her work to try to keep exhaustion at bay. The last few guests meandered out just after one thirty. Meredith turned on all of the lights, their glare on the glass walls and ceiling nearly blinding her. She tasked her staff to stack chairs, pull linen from tables, and clear the room.

She directed the sorting of the rented decorations and materials into different dump sites around the room. Early Tuesday morning she would meet all of the vendors here to have their stuff carted away so the building maintenance staff could get in for a final cleaning before resetting the room for lunch service.

"Miss Guidry, are these your shoes?" Halfway across the room, one of the black-and-white-clad workers held aloft a pair of strappy, spike-heeled sandals. Meredith's medium-height, pointy-toed brown pumps rubbed her feet in a couple of places after six hours—but nothing like the pain those sandals would have caused.

"Lost and found," she called over the music throbbing through the room's built-in PA system. Not what she would choose to listen to, but it kept the staff—mostly college students—happy and working at a brisk clip. That made three pairs and two stray shoes, five purses, sixteen cellular phones, and one very gaudy ruby ring—and those were only the items Meredith had seen herself. Her assistant would be fielding phone calls for days.

Vacuum cleaners roared to life—a wonderful sound, as it meant they were getting close to quitting time. A couple of guys loaded the last of the large round tables onto a cart and wheeled it down the hall to the freight elevator, followed by several more pushing tall stacks of dark blue upholstered chairs on hand trucks.

Vue de Ciel expanded in all directions around her. She hugged her arms around her middle. She'd survived another New Year's Eve Masked Ball—and the eight hundred guests seemed to have enjoyed themselves immensely. Hopefully her parents would deem it a success.

The soprano of flatware, alto of china, tenor of voices, and bass rumble of the dish sterilizers created a jubilant symphony that thrilled Major O'Hara's heart.

Simply from the questions the food-and-wine columnist from the *Reserve* had asked, the review in the morning newspaper wouldn't be good. It would be glowing.

"Chef, stations are clean, ready for inspection." Steven LeBlanc, sous chef, wiped his hands on the towel draped over his shoulder. Though Steven's white Nichols State University T-shirt was sweat-soaked—much like Major's own University of Louisiana–Bonneterre tribute—the kid's blond hair still stood stiff and tall in mini spikes all over his head.

Major hadn't yet been able to find anything that would keep his own hair from going curly and flopping down onto his forehead in the heat and humidity of a working kitchen. Yet asking Steven for hair-styling tips—Major grunted. He'd rather slice his hand open and stick it in a vat of lemon juice.

He followed Steven through the kitchen, inspecting each surface and utensil, releasing some of the staff to clock out, pointing out spots missed to others.

"Civilian in the kitchen," rang out from one of the line cooks.

Meredith, stately and graceful, light hair set off to perfection by her brown velvet dress—like strawberries served with chocolate ganache—swept into the kitchen, drawing the attention of every man present. If she knew she had that effect on his crew, she would laugh her head off and call them all nuts.

"I'm ready to release my staff, unless you need any help in here." Meredith came over and leaned against the stainless-steel counter beside him. She even smelled vaguely of strawberries and chocolate— or maybe that was just his imagination.

He cleared his throat. "I think we've got it covered."

"Dish-washing station cleared, Chef!"

"See?" He grinned at her.

She graced him with a full smile then covered her mouth as a yawn overwhelmed her. "I'll let my guys go, then." She pressed her hands to the base of her neck and rolled her head side to side. "I've got to run down to my office to get my stuff."

"Why don't I meet you at your office, since I have to come downstairs anyway?"

"Don't be ridiculous. I'll be fine—"

"Mere. Stop. I will come to your office to walk you to your car. You're lucky I'm not insisting on driving you home myself."

Her nutmeg eyes flickered as if she were about to argue; then her smile returned. "Thank you, Major. I'd appreciate that."

Good girl. "That wasn't too hard, was it?" He limited himself to once again laying his hand on her shoulder instead of pulling her into a hug. "Go on. I'll make sure all the rest get clocked out and then shut everything down for the night."

Meredith nodded and departed. Major rounded up the last few stragglers and watched them run their cards through the computerized time clock. Returning their "Happy New Year" wishes, he ducked into his office at the rear of the kitchen, grabbed his dry-cleaning bag along with his duffel, turned off his computer and light, and locked the door.

The brass nameplate winked in the bright kitchen light. MAJOR O'HARA, EXECUTIVE CHEF. He grimaced. What pride he'd taken eight years ago when Mr. Guidry had offered him the position— saving Major years of working his way up the chain of command in restaurants.

He heaved the two bags over his shoulder. Meredith's parents had been better to him than he deserved, had given him the flexibility in his schedule to take care of family matters no other employer would have given. They had also given him their blessing—their encouragement—to strike out on his own, to open the restaurant

11

he'd dreamed of since working for Meredith's aunt in her catering company throughout high school and college. The restaurant he'd already have if it weren't for his mother.

Major shut down the houselights, guilt nipping at his heels. Ma couldn't help the way she was. The mirrored elevator doors whispered shut, and he turned to stare out the glass wall overlooking downtown Bonneterre from twenty-three floors above.

His descent slowed then stopped. The doors slid open with a chime announcing his arrival on the fifth floor. Before he could turn completely around, Meredith stepped into the elevator.

"How long were you standing in the hall waiting for one of these doors to open?"

Meredith busied herself with pushing the button for the basement parking garage. "Not long."

"*Not long*," he imitated the super-high pitch of her voice. "You've never been a good liar, Mere."

"Fine." She blew a loose wisp of hair out of her eyes. "I was out there a couple of minutes. I didn't want you to have to wait for me. Happy?"

"Not in the least. But I appreciate your honesty." Due to the tenseness around her mouth, he changed the subject. "Your mom invited me to drop by their New Year's open house. You going?"

Meredith shook her head. "No." The simple answer held a magnitude of surprise.

"She said she had something she wanted to talk to me about."

The porcelain skin between Meredith's brows pinched. "Hmm. No—I don't usually go over for the open house, just for our family dinner later. Instead, I'm fixing to go home, sleep for a few hours, and then head over to the new house. I'm planning to get the paint stripped from all the woodwork in the living room and dining room tomorrow."

"In one day?" Major grunted. Meredith's *new* house was anything but: a one-hundred-year-old craftsman bungalow everyone had tried to talk her out of buying. "Wouldn't you rather relax on your holiday?"

"But working on the house is relaxing to me. Plus, it gives me a good excuse to go off by myself all day and be assured no one's going to disturb me."

The elevator doors opened to the dim, chilly underground parking garage. Major took hold of Meredith's arm and stopped her from exiting first. He stepped out, looked around, saw nothing out of the ordinary, then turned and nodded to her. "Looks safe."

"Of course it's safe. You lived in New York too long." She walked out past him.

"Meredith, Bonneterre isn't the little town we grew up in anymore. Even before Hurricane Katrina, it was booming." He stopped her again, planted his hands on her shoulders, and turned her to face him. "Please don't ever take your safety for granted. Not even here in the garage with security guards on duty. If anything happened to you. . ."

Meredith blushed bright red and dropped her gaze.

"Look, I don't mean to alarm you. But in this day and age, anything could happen." He kept hold of her a moment longer, then let go and readjusted the straps of the bags on his shoulder.

Meredith released a shaky breath. "So, what are you going to do on your day off?"

"Watch football." He winked at her over his shoulder as he approached her Volvo SUV. The tinted windows blocked him from seeing inside. Perhaps he had lived in New York too long. But Bonneterre had changed even in the eight years he'd been back. Crime rates had risen along with the population. And he would have done this for any other lady of his acquaintance, wouldn't he?

He heard the lock click and opened the driver's-side door for her—taking a quick peek inside just to make sure that the boogey man wasn't hiding in the backseat.

"Oh, honestly!" Meredith playfully pushed him out of the way and, shaking her head, opened the back door and heaved her large, overstuffed briefcase onto the seat.

Major moved out of the way for her to get in. "Drive safely, okay?"

KAYE DACUS

"I always do."

"Call me when you get home. Nuh-uh. No arguments. If you don't want to call, just text message me—all right?—once you're in your apartment with the door locked."

"Hey, who died and made you my keeper?" Meredith laughed.

He didn't let his serious expression crack. "Just call me safety obsessed."

"Okay, Major Safety Obsessed." She leaned into his one-armed hug then settled into the driver's seat. "Thank you for your concern. I will text you as soon as I arrive safely home, am safely in my house, with my door safely locked."

He closed the car door and waved before walking over to Kirby, his beaten-up old Jeep, a few spaces down. As he figured, Meredith waited to back out until he was in with the engine started. He followed her out of downtown and waved again as they parted ways on North Street.

A few fireworks flickered in the distance against the low-hanging clouds. He turned the radio on and tuned it to the southern gospel station. Always keyed-up after events, he sang the high-tenor part along with the Imperials. Though it had taken him a while to build the upper range of his voice—having always sung baritone and bass before—when he, George Laurence, Forbes Guidry, and Clay Huntoon started their own quartet, Major had been the only one who could even begin to reach some of the high notes. Sometimes it was still a strain, but he practiced by singing along with the radio as loudly as he could to keep his voice conditioned.

When he pulled into the condo complex parking lot, his cell phone chimed the new text message alert. He shook his head. Of course she texted instead of calling. He pulled the phone out of the holster clipped to his belt and flipped it open to read the message:

SAFELY HOME. : -)
HAPPY NEW YEAR
MERE

While Kirby's engine choked itself off, Major typed out a return message:

> *HOME TOO*
> *SWEET DREAMS*
> *MO'H*

The phone flashed a confirmation that the message was sent, and he holstered it. Grabbing his black duffel from the back, he left the orange dry-cleaning bag to drop off at the cleaners Tuesday.

To blow off some steam and try to relax enough to fall asleep, he turned on the computer and played a few rounds of Spider Solitaire. About an hour later, his whole body aching, eyes watering from yawning every other minute, he grabbed a shower before turning in. At thirty-eight years old, he shouldn't feel this out of shape—of course, if he still made time to go to the gym every day and didn't enjoy eating his own cooking as much as he did, he probably wouldn't be this out of shape. He weighed as much now as he had playing middle linebacker in college—except twenty years ago, it had all been muscle.

But who trusted a skinny chef anyway?

Thunder grumbled, and rain pattered against the window. Major kicked at the comforter that had become entangled in his legs during the night and rolled over to check the time.

Eight thirty. What a perfect day to don ratty old sweats, sit in the recliner watching football on the plasma TV, and eat junk food.

If he had a plasma TV. Or any junk food in the condo.

Alas, though, he'd promised Mrs. Guidry he would drop by. Best check the schedule of games, see which he cared least about, and make the visit then. He pulled on the ratty old sweats and an equally ratty ULB T-shirt, though. As he passed down the short hallway, he tapped the temperature control on the thermostat up a couple of degrees to knock a little of the chill out of the air.

His stomach growled in concert with the thunder outside. The tile in the kitchen sent shockwaves of cold up his legs. Shifting from foot to foot, he yanked open the dryer door, dug through the clothes in it, and found two somewhat matching socks. Sometimes having the laundry hookups here did come in handy, even though they took up more than a third of the space in the small galley kitchen.

The fridge beckoned. Not much there—maybe he should hit the grocery store on the way back from the Guidrys' open house.

Half an hour later, with the Rose Bowl Parade providing ambiance, he sank into his recliner and dug into an andouille, shrimp, potato, mushroom, red pepper, onion, jack cheese, and bacon omelet spread with Creole mustard on top.

Maybe he should consider making a New Year's resolution to cut back on calories this year. What was missing? Oh yeah, the grits. He'd left the bowl sitting by the stove.

Halfway to the kitchen to retrieve the rest of his breakfast, the phone rang. He unplugged it from the charger as he passed by.

"Hello?"

"Mr. O'Hara, this is Nick Sevellier at Beausoleil Pointe Center." Major stopped. So did his heart.

"I'm sorry to bother you on a holiday, sir, but your mother has had an episode. She's asking for you."

CHAPTER 2

$\mathcal{M}$eredith poured herself another mug of coffee. The machine might have cost only twenty dollars, but it sure did keep the liquid hot. Careful not to jiggle the tray table when she replaced the carafe, she blew through the steam rising from the cup and turned to survey her house.

She thrilled at the thought: *her* house. She owned it. She'd dreamed of owning a craftsman bungalow ever since she could remember. Now that Anne and George were getting married, they wanted to convert the three-story Victorian from apartments—where Meredith, Anne, and Meredith's sister Jenn lived—back to a single-family home. Ready to get out of such close proximity to anyone—even family—Meredith decided to buy a house. She hadn't been looking a week when she found this one.

From the outside, she'd been afraid she wouldn't be able to afford it—the previous owner had restored the exterior and landscaped the front yard to complement it. Inside was a totally different story.

Meredith sipped her coffee and leaned against the door frame between the dining room and kitchen. Pipes stuck out of the wall where the sink should have been. A few remnants of cabinets hung from the walls, and the plywood subfloor moaned and bowed whenever she walked across it.

Her parents had tried to talk her out of it. The previous owner had gone into foreclosure trying to restore the house for resale. But Meredith didn't mind the gutted kitchen, nor the bare bulbs swinging from wires in every room. She'd be able to fix up the inside exactly how she wanted.

But not if she just stood around looking at it.

Jazz music echoed through the house from the radio. The two large space heaters worked overtime to chase away the damp chill of New Year's Day. Meredith slipped on her safety goggles and mask, opened the can of paint stripper, and started on the built-in bookcase in the living room. Between the music and the vision of what the house would eventually look like, she lost herself in the project.

She'd just started the fourth shelf when her phone's earpiece beeped. She grabbed it from the mantel and stuck it in her ear. "Hello?"

"Hey, it's Anne." Her cousin yawned. "Sorry. What time did you get in last night? I never even heard you drive up."

"After two o'clock."

"And you're already out and about?"

"You know how it is when days off are few and far between."

"Ah. You're at the new house."

"Right you are, my dear."

Anne yawned again. "It's not even nine yet. Did you sleep at all?"

"A few hours." Meredith continued stripping the absolutely gross, moss-colored paint from the original, hand-detailed woodwork beneath.

"It can't be healthy for you to get only five or six hours of sleep a night."

Meredith let out a derisive snort. "And I'm hearing this from the woman who doesn't sleep at all during wedding season?"

The thunder outside nearly drowned out Anne's chuckle. "Point taken. Anyway, that's not why I called. I'm looking at the Style section of the newspaper. Looks like you really outdid yourself last night."

Tingles of trepidation and pride danced up and down Meredith's skin. "The article is good?"

"Article? Try the whole section! Looks like the writers had the time of their lives. All of the quotes from guests are glowing. And the food reviewer couldn't find enough adjectives to describe Major's food."

"Good. Mom and Dad will be happy." Meredith released her breath and rolled her head to try to ease the tension in her neck.

"Of course they will. Their oldest daughter is the best event planner in town."

"Second best."

"Oh no," Anne disagreed. "I left Boudreaux-Guidry because all those huge events daunted me. I'd never have been able to pull off a party like that."

"Oh, spare me. You did last summer—or have you already forgotten the wedding and reception you put together for the most popular movie star in the country?"

"But you and Major really helped me out with that. Take the compliment, Meredith. I wouldn't say it if I didn't mean it."

Why did Anne's praise make Meredith feel like a complete fraud? "Well, thanks, I guess."

"You're welcome. I'll leave the paper on your kitchen table before I go."

"Wedding today?" Meredith started on the fifth shelf.

"Yeah. And I'd better get a move on."

"Okay—oh, Major sent some leftovers home for you and George. They're in my fridge. I wrote your name on them so they wouldn't get mixed in with all the other boxes I have in there."

"I'll get them. Thanks. And thank Major for me, too."

Meredith put the earpiece back on the mantel. She tried not to imagine what Anne would think of the interior of the fridge. Hardly a day passed when Meredith didn't bring home at least one Styrofoam box filled with a more-than-ample serving of the lunch entrée from Vue de Ceil.

She knelt to work on the cabinets below the open shelves. Until now she hadn't thought about missing her afternoon visit from Major. He'd started bringing her a box of lunch-service leftovers every day

19

about a year ago—after she accidentally confessed to almost always eating out because she hated to cook. Every day around three o'clock, her pulse quickened, and she had to stop herself from rushing to the restroom to reapply her lipstick, fix her hair, and make sure she looked her best for him.

Heart racing as it did whenever she expected his appearance, she sank back onto her heels. She had to get over this. Eight years was way too long to carry a torch for someone who'd shown no indication he had any interest in her other than friendship.

Her earpiece beeped again. She took a deep breath to try to settle her emotions then stood to retrieve the phone. "Hello?"

"Hey, it's me." Her older brother's voice filled her ear.

"Hey, Forbes."

"I didn't wake you, did I?"

"Nope—I've been at the new house for a while. You and the boys having fun at the lake?" Her brothers always spent New Year's Eve at their family's lake house on Larto Lake.

"Yep, though it's been really wet and cold. But the fish are biting, which makes it all worthwhile. We'll be headed back to town around noon, and then we'll go over to watch football with Dad."

Watching football with her father and four brothers was something that Meredith usually dropped everything to do. "Aw, that sounds like fun."

"But not as fun as whatever construction project you're doing today?" The tone of amusement in Forbes's voice came across as almost patronizing. Along with their parents, Forbes had been very vocal in his disapproval of Meredith's purchase of the house.

"Exactly. I'll miss y'all, but this is where I want to be." *So please don't make a fuss and try to convince me to come over.*

"Okay. Well, if you decide to knock off early, there might be an inch of sofa for you."

"I'll keep that in mind."

"You are planning on coming over for family dinner tonight, right?" Forbes asked.

"Of course. Why?"

"I just wanted to make sure. Um. . .there might be a non–family member there tonight as well."

"Is Marci's boyfriend coming?"

Her brother paused a little longer than necessary.

"Oh, Forbes!" She groaned. "Please tell me he isn't going to propose to her in front of the whole family."

"He'll be okay."

"It's not *him* I'm worried about. Marci came to me a couple of weeks ago, worried about whether or not he's the right one for her. If he does this in front of all of us, she's going to feel obligated to say yes, just so she doesn't disappoint us or hurt him."

"You're not giving her enough credit, Mere. Or him. I've talked to Shaun at length. He really does love Marci and will provide her with a good life."

"You've talked. . . Did you talk him into doing it this way?"

"No." A little sharpness crept into Forbes's voice. "Look. I realize you still haven't forgiven me for what you think was my interference with Anne and George's relationship—"

"Forbes, you told George to lie to her—not once, but twice. She was so angry with him she almost let him walk away forever."

"Whatever happened last summer is between them and me." Forbes's voice strained with forced softness. "Besides, I don't really think you're upset with me."

Meredith's annoyance started turning to anger. "Are you a psychologist now? Is that something they taught you in law school?"

"Whoa there, girl! I'm not trying to psychoanalyze you. I just wonder if the idea of a sister who's ten years younger than you getting married first is the main issue."

"You don't seem to have a problem with it. She's only twenty-four!" Meredith slammed the scraper on the floor and paced the living room. "She isn't finished with her bachelor's degree yet. How can she be thinking about getting married when she can't even commit to a major?"

"Uh-huh."

Frustration, disappointed hopes, self-recrimination for her still-single status wrapped around her chest in tight bands, cutting off her air. Her head spun for a moment. She hadn't wanted to admit it, but she could no longer deny the fact that there was something wrong with her. Why else would she still be single at thirty-four?

She took a deep breath and tried to gather up the shattered pieces of her emotions, then let out a bitter laugh. "I guess I should thank you for the forewarning. Now I won't have a meltdown like this tonight."

"You're welcome." Forbes spoke with a gentle laugh.

"I'll get home in time to make sure Jenn is ready to go at six."

"Great. I'm going to let you go then."

"I'm sorry I yelled at you."

"I'm sorry I deliberately provoked you."

In spite of the remaining tightness in her chest, Meredith smiled. "Yeah, well, I guess I can forgive you. I love you."

"I love you, too, Sis."

When the call ended, she tossed the earpiece back onto the mantel, wishing she hadn't answered—but also grateful she knew what was coming. She grabbed her coat and trudged out to the back porch, where she sank onto the wet top step, the rain having momentarily paused. The old cypress boards sagged, just like her spirits.

"Lord, what's wrong with me?" She glared up at the dark clouds. "Why is it that a twenty-four-year-old without a clue can find a man who'll love her, and I haven't been able to get a guy to take me out on a date even once in my life? Why is it that the two men I've fallen in love with haven't even noticed?"

Wrapping her arms around her legs, she rested her forehead on her knees. "It's not fair. I've been asking You ever since I turned fifteen for a boyfriend—for a husband ever since I turned twenty. What have I done so wrong that You've kept that from me?"

A large raindrop plastered hair to the top of her head. The cold water running down her neck made her feel even worse, adding insult to injury. She scooted back up the porch to lean against the house wall and pulled her coat closer. Driving rain sliced the air, eliminating her view of the tree-lined fence at the back of her half-acre lot. The squeaky moan of the floorboards did nothing to help her mood—one more thing that needed to be fixed.

She was just like this house. The part the world saw was complete, pulled together, polished; but inside, everything was a mess. The difference was that she could fix the house.

Lightning streaked, followed by booming thunder, the sky nearly black, water forming in vast pools in low-lying places in the yard. The porch boards moaned—no, that wasn't possible. She wasn't moving. Something else was making the noise.

The pounding rain nearly deafened her. She leaned over and pressed her ear to the crack between two floorboards.

Was that something whimpering? She crawled to the edge of the porch and leaned over, her head and shoulders instantly soaked. The trellis that enclosed the area under the porch broke away easily.

With one hand trying to keep her hair out of her eyes, the other sinking into the mud to keep her balance, Meredith hung half off the porch, trying to see under it.

No good—too dark.

She pushed herself up, and not caring about the rivulets of water—and mud—she tracked in, she ran into the dining room. From the bottom drawer of her tool chest, she grabbed the giant flashlight.

Back outside, she once again leaned over the edge of the decking. She flicked on the high-powered beam and swept it slowly from one side to the other—

There. Light reflected in two small eyes. Too big to be a rat, not close enough together to be a possum—or were they? No, the rounded shape of the shivering body was wrong.

Though the edge of the porch dug into her diaphragm, Meredith whistled. "Come 'ere," she called in a high-pitched voice.

The shape moved—Meredith nearly lost her balance in surprise.

"Come on. That's it. I'm not going to hurt you." She ignored the water running up her face, filling her nose, and stinging her eyes but kept offering encouragement until she could finally see the puppy clearly.

A few long moments brought it close enough for her to make a grab for it—Meredith landed shoulders-first flat out on her back in the grass, face fully exposed to the drowning rain. And now she had a cold nose whuffling in her ear.

She grabbed the squatter, mud squishing between her fingers. Numb, soaked, and trembling, she struggled to her feet, puppy clenched firmly before her, and went inside.

"Look at the pair of us! Good thing we've got hot water, huh?" The heavy pup nearly wagged itself out of her grip. In the utility room, she set him down in the deep sink and hosed him off with the sprayer—revealing what looked like a puppy that was mostly black Lab, though his gangly legs, large muzzle, and huge feet indicated he had some other, bigger breed in his blood, too.

The caked mud and dirt gone, fur soaked down smooth, she could see the poor little guy's ribs and hip bones. "I'll bet you're hungry."

The tail thumped against the side of the sink. Meredith grabbed a towel off the stack of old ones she kept there for emergencies and did her best to wrap up the little bundle of energy. She carried him into the living room, dragged a drop cloth over in front of the space heater with her foot, and sat down to towel-dry the dog.

The towel proved too tempting, and the puppy grabbed a corner and started to play tug-of-war with her. After unsuccessfully trying to get him to behave, she finally gave in and just played with him.

Once they'd both stopped shivering, Meredith walked over to the small, dormitory-style fridge in the dining room. She crouched in front of it and, keeping the puppy at bay, pulled out the half loaf of bread. "I don't know if you'd be able to eat roast beef." She pushed the Vue de Ceil box back into the fridge, took out a slice of bread, and put the rest of it away.

After nearly snapping her fingers off the first couple of tries, she finally convinced him to take the bits of bread politely from her fingers. She held him over the utility sink to let him lap water from the faucet, then put him down.

She followed him around as he explored all the rooms in the house. After about twenty minutes, he curled up on the drop cloth in front of the space heater, heaved a huge yawn, and fell asleep.

Meredith shook her head and glanced at the ceiling. "If this is Your idea of a joke, God, I'm not laughing. I asked for a husband, not a dog."

CHAPTER 3

"I want grandchildren, Major."

Major tucked the blanket around his mother's legs in the recliner. Her private room in the assisted-living facility was as homey as they could make it. "Ma, let's just concentrate on getting you better."

"I am better. My boy's here." She reached over and patted his cheek with her smooth, dry fingers. Though not quite sixty, his mother's hard life showed in her sunken, dark-circled eyes and white hair.

He sank into the chair he'd pulled over beside her recliner. "You're sure there was no episode?"

"That little boy just panicked. He's an intern. He doesn't know anything."

"He said you were pacing the hall and yelling and wouldn't stop when the nurse asked you to return to your room." Major leaned forward, elbows propped on his knees.

"I was bored."

"You were bored."

"It's boring here, if you haven't noticed, son. Everyone who lives here is crazy—there's no one to carry on a conversation with."

No, no, no. She couldn't want to move again. Beausoleil Pointe Center was the only assisted-living center for the psychologically challenged in this part of the state—over the last eight years, she'd lived in every other inpatient facility in the parish that would take psychiatric patients; she'd either demanded to be taken home, or Major had been told by the staff he had to remove her. If it happened again, he'd be forced to look at properties in Shreveport or Baton Rouge, both about two hours away. Which would mean moving. Leaving behind his friends, his job. And his dreams of possibly opening his restaurant this year—or ever—would vanish.

He clenched his fists and pressed them against the tops of his legs. "I thought you liked it here. Every time I come, you're always in the lounge playing Rook or gossiping with the other ladies. Aren't they your friends?"

"Yeah—the crazy ones." She smiled, her blue eyes twinkling. "Crazy—I guess that's me, too, or I wouldn't be here, would I?"

Major shook his head and swallowed hard. "You're not crazy. You're schizophrenic. It's nothing to be ashamed of. You've always done the best you could for me." The words oozed with thick bitterness in his mouth. He hated feeling this way, hated resenting the fact that her illness kept him from pursuing his goals, from making his dreams reality.

"Sometimes I think I am crazy. Sometimes when the meds wear off and the hallucinations creep in. . ." She took hold of his hand. "Maybe I didn't. . .take my pills last night like I should have."

Truth. Finally. "Maybe?"

"I wanted to watch Dick Clark on TV. The meds make me sleepy—they want us all doped up and asleep by eight o'clock. But it was New Year's Eve. I always watch Dick Clark on New Year's Eve. Although some young kid was on with him, and I didn't like him at all. Looked like he was up to something. I think he's trying to take that show away from Mr. Clark."

"Well, Dick Clark is getting awfully old now. He needs help with that show. What did you do with the meds, Ma?"

"But I've *always* watched Dick Clark on New Year's Eve—since Guy Lombardo went off. Talk about a great musician. That Guy Lombardo was something. Good-lookin', too, before he got so old.

Why don't you like Guy Lombardo, Major?"

"I like Guy Lombardo just fine, but he died when I was just a kid. Ma, what did you do with your pills last night?"

"I think Dick Clark may have died a few years ago and was reanimated by scientists in some kind of experiment."

"Ma—what?" Major rubbed his palms up and down his face.

"Well, you know they do it for commercials all the time— Fred Astaire and Frank Sinatra. Natalie Cole did a duet with her reanimated father. And they brought back the popcorn guy, too— that Knickerbocker guy."

"Redenbacher. And they're not reanimated. They just use old footage of them and splice it into the new stuff—Mother, quit trying to throw me off the subject." He paused for a moment to try to take the anger out of his voice. "What did you do with your meds last night?"

"I wanted to watch Dick Clark."

"Yes. I got that part." Inside, Major shouted with frustration.

She held her left hand out in front of her, forefinger and thumb pinched together. "Plop." She opened her fingers. "Dropped them in the commode and flushed them away. Let the fishes go to sleep early on New Year's Eve."

He dropped his head into one hand and rubbed his eyes with the other so hard he saw white dots.

"But then when the nurse came to check on me later and saw I wasn't asleep, she told me that I had to turn the TV off. Well, no one tells me to turn off Guy—Dick—whoever it was. But I wasn't watching that anymore because there was a John Wayne movie on another channel, and I really wanted to watch that. They don't understand about John Wayne here. Can you make sure they understand about John Wayne?"

He raised his head to look at her again. If it had been John Wayne they'd tried to take her away from, her reaction was starting to make more sense. "I'll make sure they understand. What did you do then?"

The papery skin between her barely there eyebrows furrowed. "I went out into the hall to find her supervisor, but then that little boy came and tried to tell me I was disturbing all the other patients. I told him they were all so doped up that none of them would hear me."

"What little boy?"

"That Nick kid. He says he's a doctor, but he can't be old enough to shave yet. Not like my Major." She patted the top of his head.

"Ma, you can't do this anymore. If you don't take your meds on your own, you know what's going to happen, don't you?"

Her thin lips twisted into a grimace. "They'll start observing me while I take them. Danny, I don't want them to do that."

His stomach lurched. She hadn't called him Danny in years. Not since just before the first time she set fire to their apartment when he was in high school.

"Why aren't you home watching football? Isn't that what you usually do on New Year's?"

"Yeah, Ma. I'm here because they called me to say you had an episode, remember?" He rubbed his forehead, a headache coming on like an iron rod being shoved through his temples.

"Well I didn't. And I'm not going to. I took my meds like a good girl this morning. So, get. I know you worked hard all weekend. And I've got a date in a little while, anyway."

Major snapped his head up. "A *date*?"

She grinned. "Gotcha. The girls and I are going down to the kitchen to watch that new young cook fix our dinner—he's almost as cute as you, hon. He told us he might let us help."

"No handling anything hot."

"I'm not a child, Major Daniel Xavier Kirby O'Hara."

Major allowed himself a measure of relief. She hadn't been able to remember his full name in a while—at least not with all the names in order—so she must be doing okay. "No, but the last time you were in a kitchen and paying more attention to the cute cook. . ."

"You drove me to distraction with everything you were telling me to do. I forgot the burner was turned on. But it's healed okay." She held her left hand out, palm up.

He took hold of her fingertips and pulled her hand forward to kiss the burn scar. "Try not to forget this time, please? I don't want to have to leave my football game in the middle to rush back out here because you've set your hair on fire, okay?"

She leaned forward and gripped his cheeks between her thumb and forefinger, pushing his lips into a pucker. "Don't give me ideas. Now, get out of here." She kissed him. "Go live your life."

"Do you want me to put a movie on for you before I go?" he asked through her pinch.

She released his face. "Yeah. *Flying Leathernecks*—no, *Fort Apache*—no, wait. . .*North to Alaska*."

He knelt by the small TV stand, hand hovering over the DVDs. "Are you sure? *North to Alaska*?"

"Yes, definitely. *North to Alaska*. That's what was on last night that they wouldn't let me watch."

He put the disc in, stood, and headed for the door. She was better at handling the remotes than he was. "I'll see you Wednesday night."

"Are you ever going to find a girlfriend and bring her out here to meet me? I want grandchildren."

Major leaned his head back and started to smack the door frame, then stopped himself and slowly lowered his palm to press against it. "We're not having this discussion again today."

His stomach roiled. He couldn't tell his mother he was in love with someone, because he couldn't bring himself to tell the object of his affection about his mother and her condition. That was a burden no one would choose to bear and something he wouldn't wish on his worst enemy.

"You're thirty-eight, son. It's time for you to find a girl and marry her. But bring her here before you propose. I want to tell you if I like her or not."

Weary to his soul, Major leaned his forehead against the back of his hand. "Yes, Ma."

The intro music for the movie started playing. "You're still here," she singsonged.

He straightened. "I'm going. I love you."

"I know. Me, too."

He closed the door of his mother's room and made his way down the wood-floored hall to the nurse's station that looked more like a concierge desk at a five-star hotel in Manhattan. "I need to speak with. . ." He pulled the crumpled envelope out of his pocket and smoothed it. "I need to see Nick Sevellier."

"Yes, Mr. O'Hara. I'll page him."

Major crossed to the common room, where he had a clear line of sight to the desk, and sank onto one of the plush sofas. He slouched down, leaned his head back against the cushion, and covered his eyes with his right hand. This was definitely not how he'd expected to spend the morning.

"Mr. O'Hara?"

He uncovered his eyes and stood. Ma had been right—the young man in front of him couldn't be old enough to be responsible for patient care, could he? Aside from the fact the kid wasn't even as tall as Meredith—and she must be about five-seven—the wire-rim glasses he wore did nothing to add maturity to his baby face.

"Yes. I'm Major O'Hara."

"Sorry—Major, sir."

Major eased his stance. "No, it's not a title. It's just my first name."

"Oh." The kid set his miniature laptop computer on the coffee table and seemed to relax a little. "I'm Nick Sevellier. Let's sit."

Major resumed his place on the couch but leaned forward, elbows on knees again, hands clasped.

"You've seen your mother?"

"Yeah, I've been with her for about an hour. She told me she didn't take her meds last night. No insult meant, but how long have you been working here?"

Sevellier's mouth twisted into a wry smile. "Everyone asks that. I know I look like Doogie Howser, but I really am old enough to be almost finished with my med school internship. I've been here since August. I was assigned to your mother's case a few weeks ago when the other intern rotated out."

"And what have you observed?"

"That she seems to be handling the medications and managing her condition quite well. That's probably why I panicked last night. I was so sure that no one could go as long as her charts indicated without having an episode." Sevellier picked up the laptop, slid a stylus out of the side of it, and began tapping things on the screen. "How did she appear to you this morning?"

"A bit disoriented—some of her thought processes were disjointed. But nothing I haven't witnessed before."

Sevellier typed something into the computer. "You're her only family?"

Major nodded. "She was a single mom—a great one."

"How old was she when she first started exhibiting symptoms?"

"I was just a kid—so she was in her late twenties or early thirties."

"And she was in and out of the hospital?"

"Not in the beginning." Major reclined against the back of the sofa. If Doogie wanted to know the whole history, they might be here awhile. "She had her first real psychotic break when I was in high school. She was committed to Central State Hospital over in Pineville. Since then, she's been in and out of residential programs, until eight years ago when she finally agreed she needed to move to an assisted-living facility."

The kid doctor didn't look up from the notes he was making. "What precipitated that decision?"

Major crossed his arms. "She set fire to her condo, and several other residents of the complex were injured. It wasn't the first fire she'd set."

"She was living alone?"

Here it came. The accusation. How could he have left her alone to fend for herself when he knew how bad off she was? "I was working in New York at the time. She'd been taking her meds and going to therapy regularly. But I moved back immediately afterward. I tried taking care of her myself for several months, but it didn't work."

Sevellier nodded as if gaining new understanding. "I see. She's come a long way since then."

"There is something you should know—and it's supposed to be in her charts. She is sort of obsessed with John Wayne movies. That was why she had. . .why she was such a problem last night. It wasn't just that she hadn't taken her meds; it was because she was watching a John Wayne movie. She doesn't like to be interrupted when she's watching one of those."

"I see." Sevellier typed some more. "But if she'd taken her meds, it wouldn't have been a problem?"

Major bit the inside of his cheek. These guys never really understood her. "Probably not, because she would have been asleep before the movie came on. But I'm telling you, she's watching one right now. If you want to see how she reacts to having her John Wayne time interrupted, be my guest."

"I. . .uh. . .I don't think we need to upset her again. I've noted it on her chart." He stood and extended his right hand. "It was nice to meet you, Mr. O'Hara."

Major rose and shook the kid's hand. "You, too. Please don't hesitate to call me if anything like this happens again."

"Will do." Sevellier moved away then turned back. "Oh, I hear congratulations are in order."

Major frowned. "For what?"

"You mother has been telling everyone for weeks that her son is getting married."

Ma! "She's mistaken—she just wishes I would get married and is trying to force me into it."

"Oh." Doogie Howser blushed. "Sorry."

"No problem."

Major shrugged into his coat and exited the center into the frigid, pouring rain. He pulled the collar up around his ears and ran toward Kirby. His cell phone vibrated against his waist, and as soon as he climbed into the vehicle, he unholstered the phone and flipped it open. "Hello?"

"Hey, Major. It's Forbes."

His best friend's voice came as a welcomed relief. "Hey. What's up?"

"Wondered if you might have time to get together one day this week."

His mind still occupied with his mother and her issues, Major couldn't think clearly. "I think I should be able to get free one day, now that Steven's handling lunch service. But I'll have to check my calendar once I get back to the office tomorrow to let you know for sure."

"Okay. Good. I've been reviewing the paperwork you gave me on your restaurant idea, and I wanted to talk to you about it."

No more bad news. Not today. Major slumped forward until his forehead pressed against the top of the steering wheel. "My restaurant proposal?"

"Yeah. I don't really want to get into it over the phone. Let's just try to get together as soon as possible next week."

"Sure. I'll shoot you an e-mail tomorrow to let you know when."

"You all right?"

"Just exhausted. You know, the event last night. . ." He wasn't really lying to his friend—just not divulging the truth.

"Why don't you come over and watch football with us this afternoon—Dad and the boys and me—over at Mom and Dad's house?"

"Thanks for the invite, but. . .I'll be at the open house for a few minutes; then I'm going to head home for some peace and quiet."

"I gotcha. I'll talk to you later."

After they disconnected, Major tossed the phone into the passenger seat. "Lord, why did I get out of the bed today?"

Chapter 4

*Y*ou'd better not mess up my car, buddy-boy."

The puppy thumped its tail a couple of times against the floor then put its head back on its paws. The veterinarian at the quick clinic had said the little guy would be out of it from some of the shots.

Meredith pulled her jacket over her almost-dry hair and dashed across the small lot to the store's front door.

"We close for lunch in thirty—oh, hey, Glamour Girl." The proprietor rounded the sales counter and shook Meredith's hand. "To what do we owe the honor of your visit today?"

One of the things she loved about Robichaud's Hardware was the fact that no one cared if she arrived in paint-splattered clothes, wearing no makeup, and looking no better than that puppy had when she'd pulled him out from under the porch.

"Since you're having your big New Year's Day sale, I figured I'd come in and clean you out of the rest of that paint stripper. And I need some wood epoxy, as well. Same aisle?"

"You know where stuff is in here better than I do, gal." He handed her a shopping basket. "If you think of anything else you need, or if I don't have exactly what you're looking for back there, give me a holler."

"Thanks, Rob. Will do." Meredith dropped her wallet and keys into the basket and headed for the painting supplies section in the back of the store. Her work boots thudded slightly on the wide-plank pine floor.

She breathed deeply and let it out as a sigh. The smell of wood and metal and turpentine and hard work welcomed and embraced her. She was certain she could get what she needed at the warehouse-like home improvement center a few miles closer to the house, but she preferred the sounds, scents, and service she experienced here.

She grabbed the last two one-gallon cans of the gel-style solvent she liked best for removing old paint and moved down the aisle to the display of all the caulks, glues, and epoxies. The few products that she needed to look at were, naturally, on the bottom shelf. She set the heavy basket on the floor and crouched down to read the labels.

In the stillness, the front-door bell chimed faintly, followed by Rob's echoing voice calling out that the store would be closing for lunch in twenty minutes. Meredith turned her attention back to the product labels, not wanting to leave her leather seats at the mercy of the puppy any longer than necessary.

The light above her dimmed. She glanced up—and nearly lost her balance.

"Do you need help finding something, miss?" The man who asked towered over her.

She jumped to her feet, balancing the can, bottle, and tube of epoxy in her hands. "No, thank you. I'm just reading to try to see which one I want to buy." The can shifted and her fingers spasmed and cramped trying to keep hold of it—to no avail.

Before it could fall, the giant with curly dark hair caught it. "Whoops. Don't want that falling and popping open. We might be stuck here forever." He had a jaw like a sledge hammer and a grin like a teen idol.

She shook her head. So he was good-looking—so what? "Thanks."

"You're buying wood epoxy?" His gray eyes twinkled.

"Yes." She shifted the tube and bottle into her left hand and reached for the can.

He didn't immediately let go, a crease forming between his thick brows. "Are you sure this is what you're looking for?"

Annoyance prickled up Meredith's spine. "Unless you know of something else I can use to fill in years' worth of wear and tear in my woodwork."

"If it's molding or baseboards, you'd be better off just replacing the piece of trim completely."

She pulled a little harder and finally succeeded in getting him to let go of the can. "If they weren't period and prohibitively expensive to replace, I might consider it. But I can't replace all of the moldings, baseboards, and cabinets in a craftsman house."

His brows elevated in tandem with his low whistle. "A craftsman—not the cedar-sided one over on Destrehan Place?"

She stepped back, hugging the epoxies to her. "Yes."

"Whaddya know? A buddy of mine owned it—bought it to flip right before the market crashed. I helped him as much as I could with the exterior. We'd just started on the interior when he ran out of money."

"As in, y'all ripped the kitchen out completely without any means of putting another one in?" The corners of Meredith's mouth twitched.

The six-and-a-half-foot-tall giant rubbed his hand over his short curls. "Yeah," he drawled. "I told him not to do that until he knew for sure he could get another line of credit. You—" He regarded her curiously. "You aren't actually living in that house with no kitchen, are you?"

Meredith smiled at him for the first time since the conversation began. "No. I'm not currently living in the house. But at the rate I'm making progress, it's not going to be in much better shape when I do need to move in a few months from now."

"Lease on your current place ending?" He motioned for the bottle and tube she held, took them at her nod, and set them back on the shelf.

"Sort of." More like Anne and George would be returning from their honeymoon to England and wanting to get started on restoring the Victorian.

"So are you thinking about hiring a contractor?" He rested his elbow against the second shelf as if settling in for a long chat.

Who was this guy? "Yeah, I'm thinking about it. Why—do you know one?"

His full lips split into a smile, revealing too-white-to-be-natural teeth. He reached into the pocket of his denim shirt and produced a business card.

Meredith read it—then did a double take.

"What's wrong?"

"Nothing. I just didn't read your card right the first time." She looked up at him. At his quizzical look, she decided to confess. "I've just never actually met anyone named Ward before."

"I know—it's odd, isn't it? But Edward's a family name, and my parents didn't want me being 'Eddie the fourth.' I've never seen it anywhere else as a first name."

"You've never heard of Ward Bond?" She slipped the card into her pocket.

Ward Breaux shook his head. "No. Who's he?"

Meredith's jaw unhinged momentarily. "*The Searchers? Rio Bravo? The Quiet Man?*" At the title of each film, the contractor shook his head. "Surely, you've at least seen *Fort Apache?*"

"Um. . .if those are westerns, I can guarantee you I've never seen them."

"They're not just westerns, they're John Wayne classics—Ward Bond costarred in all of those and a bunch more with John Wayne."

"Well, there you go." Ward winked at her. "I've never seen a John Wayne movie."

"Never? Oh, you don't know what you're missing. *Fort Apache* and *She Wore a Yellow Ribbon* are my two favorite movies."

Ward's eyes crinkled a bit at the corners when he smiled. "Then I guess I'll have to watch them sometime if they're your favorites."

Movement behind him caught Meredith's attention, and she bent to grab her basket. "Sorry, Rob. I'm ready—" She glanced askance at Ward and held up the can in her hand. "At least, I think I am."

"That's the putty I always use." Ward turned toward Rob. "I'll be done by the time you finish ringing up Miss. . . ?" He swung his head around, brows raised.

Her skin tingled at the way his dark lashes perfectly framed his gray eyes. "Meredith Guidry."

"Miss Guidry."

Meredith tried her best not to look back as she followed Rob to the sales counter. She nearly bounced on each step, buoyed by high spirits. Never before had a man flirted with her like that.

After handing her check card to Rob, she pulled a business card out of her wallet. She stared at it a moment. MEREDITH E. GUIDRY, EXECUTIVE DIRECTOR, EVENTS & FACILITIES MANAGEMENT. Her title always made her feel pretentious, though she supposed it did reflect her real job better than "the event planner," which is what most people called her. She signed her receipt and willed Rob to move slower in bagging her purchases.

Her heart jangled like a cartoon telephone when footsteps approached from behind. She drew in a calming breath. Strange. In the eight years since she'd first met Major, she'd never experienced this level of attraction toward anyone else. Maybe she was finally getting over him.

She handed Ward her business card while Rob scanned Ward's three cans of primer.

"Impressive." Ward's flirtatious gaze made her almost want to forgive him for having been so condescending to her a few minutes ago. "Never would have expected someone as young as you to be such a bigwig with a company as huge as B-G Enterprises. You must be good at what you do."

Rob's chuckle brought flames of embarrassment to Meredith's cheeks. All of a sudden, all she could think of was her grubby appearance. Who was she kidding, thinking that a man like Ward Breaux was flirting with her?

"E-mail or call me, and we can set up a time for you to come by the house to look it over and then review my plans so that you can start putting together a bid." She grabbed her bags off the counter. "Thanks, Rob. Happy New Year."

She didn't usually take the coward's way out, but she pretended not to hear Ward calling for her to *wait up* and ran through the rain to her SUV.

The puppy awoke with a yip when the can of epoxy fell off the seat and bumped him.

"Oh, goodness—I'm so sorry." She leaned over the console and rubbed his head before returning the can to its bag and putting the supplies on the floor behind her seat. One glance at the rearview mirror showed Ward exiting the store. Stomach churning, Meredith started the engine and pulled out of the parking lot.

"Stupid, stupid, stupid. How could I be so dense as to think he was flirting with me for any reason other than wanting my business?"

The rain slapped the windshield all the way back to the house, doing nothing to improve her mood. She sat for a moment after parking under the protection of the carport.

He probably hadn't seen her as anything more than a potential client. How many people had she sucked up to in the past, believing they could potentially become clients? But she couldn't deny that while the delusion lasted, she had felt the stirrings of attraction toward him.

Maybe, just maybe, she was finally recovering from her eight-year affliction—the affliction that went by the name Major O'Hara.

Cars—mostly expensive, foreign models—lined the street of the upscale subdivision. Major parked a few houses down from the Guidrys', pulled his coat collar up, and ran through the rain to the cover of their wide, wraparound porch.

He reached the front steps at the same time as a pair of other guests—familiar looking and smart enough to be carrying a huge black and red umbrella. One of Major's part-time staff opened the door and grinned at him, dressed in the standard black pants and white tuxedo shirt all servers at B-G events wore.

Major stepped aside for the woman to enter first. As she passed, the small dog draped across her arm snapped and growled at him. Behind her, folding the umbrella, the man rolled his eyes and sighed—and Major finally recognized him. Gus McCord, Bonneterre's new mayor. Major hadn't realized how short the man was. He always looked much taller on TV.

When the mayor drew even with Major, he extended his right hand. "Sorry about the dog. She can't go anywhere without that thing. You look familiar, but I can't place you."

"Major O'Hara, sir." Major returned the politician's firm, brief grip.

The quick processing of Major's name registered in Mayor McCord's brown eyes. "You played football with my son at ULB."

Major reined in his surprise. "Yes, sir. He was a couple years ahead of me."

"And now you're the most popular chef in Beausoleil Parish—if not all of Louisiana." Mr. McCord handed his dripping umbrella to the doorman.

Maybe Major shouldn't have voted for the other guy last fall. "Mr. and Mrs. Guidry would be pleased to hear you say so."

"I'll be sure to tell them, then." Mr. McCord motioned Major to enter ahead of him.

Major stopped just inside the door, awestruck. He didn't know much about architecture, but this house reminded him of the big plantation houses down on the river he'd seen on school fieldtrips. The dark-wood-floored entryway echoed with a hum of voices coming from all around. To his left, the walnut and green library featured a large, round table laden with a display of fruit, guests hovering around it like hummingbirds in a flower garden.

For a moment, professional jealousy reared up in his chest. Why hadn't they asked him to cater? Then, before the envy could take full root, he spotted Maggie Babineaux, Mairee Guidry's sister—the caterer who'd taught Major more about food service than they'd ever imagined teaching in culinary school. She waved at him but didn't break away from her conversation. He waved in return.

To his right, circulating around the twenty-person dining table piled high with exquisite displays of pastries, he recognized a few people—the mayor's wife and her little dog, the state senator for Beausoleil Parish, the pastor of Bonneterre Chapel. . .who motioned Major into the room.

"We've missed you the last couple of Sundays." Pastor Kinnard shifted his plate and extended his right hand.

Major smiled and shook hands with him. "I've missed everyone, too, but I was filling in for the chaplain out at. . .one of the nursing homes."

Reverend Kinnard nodded. "When are you boys going to sing for us again?"

Major shrugged. "Everything's been so crazy with the holidays and then with the Christmas musical before that—we haven't practiced in months."

"Three weeks enough notice?"

To pull together four professional workaholics to learn the intricate harmonies of a southern gospel song and have it memorized? "Shouldn't be a problem—oh, but I think Forbes said something about going to a conference in Baton Rouge in a couple of weeks, so let me check with him—and George and Clay—and I'll try to let you know by Wednesday."

"Sounds good—ah, Mairee, no doubt you're here for our chef extraordinaire."

Average height, like Meredith, with dark auburn hair, Mairee Guidry entered the dining room with a majestic air. "I hate to steal him away, Frank, but I do have some business to discuss with everyone's favorite chef." She hooked her arm through Major's and, though ever polite, steered him through the crowd without interruption.

She led him up the back staircase from the kitchen. "I know you probably want to get home and relax on your day off." She pushed open a set of double doors at the end of the hall. "So I'll keep this as short as possible."

The study was at least the size of Major's living room and

bedroom combined. Mairee led him to a raised area in a bay window and motioned for him to take one of the wing chairs while she enthroned herself in the other.

"How's your mother?" she asked, settling back as if ready for a long chat.

"She's fine. I just came from seeing her, actually."

Mairee's eyes flickered to the door. "Oh, good, Lawson—there you are."

Discomfort settled in Major's gut. What in the world would they want to talk to him about that they couldn't do at the office? He blanched. *Please, Lord, don't let anyone have come down with food poisoning last night!* But Mairee had told him early yesterday evening she wanted him to come by today.

He stood and offered the chair to Lawson, but Meredith's father waved him off and pulled one of the ottomans beside Mairee's chair.

Mairee folded her hands in her lap. "I know you've got to be wondering why we asked you to meet with us today, outside of business hours."

Major nodded and swallowed, trying to ease the dryness in his throat.

"We wanted to discuss your future with Boudreaux-Guidry Enterprises. Your annual appraisal is coming up in a couple of weeks, and Lawson and I wanted to take some time to talk to you about your goals and plans for the future."

Rubbing his tongue hard against the backs of his teeth, Major nodded again, flickering a glance at Lawson then back at Mairee. Meredith looked more like her father than her mother.

"You told us a long time ago that one of your dreams is to open a restaurant here in Bonneterre." Mairee uncrossed and recrossed her ankles, leaning forward slightly. "We have recently purchased a bundle of properties in the Warehouse District—all of which has been rezoned to commercial and retail space. You may or may not have heard that we have just contracted with another company to develop the area into a village square–style shopping area—boutiques, specialty stores, high fashion, and the like."

The knot in Major's stomach stopped twisting.

Lawson took over. "One of the properties in the parcel was a cafeteria. It's a separate building with a large industrial kitchen. While it would need a complete overhaul, we believe you're up to the task."

His heart tripped and fell into his feet, then leaped back up into his throat. "Me? You want me to overhaul the cafeteria?"

Lawson chuckled. "No. Not a cafeteria. A restaurant. *Your* restaurant. Well, technically, we would own most it—but with an investment, you'll be a co-owner in addition to being executive chef. And over time, we expect you to buy us out of it—even if it's just 10 or 20 percent at a time—until it truly is your restaurant."

Investment. He prayed he had enough money saved. So long as nothing happened with Ma anytime soon, he could be on the road toward becoming the restaurateur he had always dreamed of being.

Mairee laid her hand on her husband's arm. "We don't need to get into all of the business details right now—Forbes will take care of that. What we do want is for you to take some time to think about this. You'd still be working for us—drawing a salary—and we would need you to continue to oversee the event catering division. I know that will put quite a strain on your time, but no one ever said opening a restaurant would be easy."

"No, ma'am, no one ever did." Major's heart pounded so hard, he could feel it in the tip of his nose.

Lawson stood and stepped over to the large writing desk nearby, returning with a thick manila folder. "Forbes is handling all of the legalities—the restaurant will be incorporated separately from B-G Enterprises. I believe he's already called you to set up an appointment."

Rising from the chair, Major took the folder with trembling hands. "Yes, sir."

"We don't expect you to make this decision quickly or without a lot of thought," Mairee said. "In fact, if you said yes today, I would withdraw the offer because you hadn't thought through all of the pros and cons. We do ask for an answer by Easter, though. Groundbreaking is scheduled for the first week of May."

Lawson extended his right hand to Major. "We want you to know that if you feel this isn't the right time for you to take on something like this, we'll still consider ourselves fortunate to have the best chef in the Gulf South working for us at B-G."

Hand so numb he barely felt the pressure from Lawson's, Major thanked his employers.

"Will you stay a little while?" Mairee asked, standing. "Several people hoped to see you to compliment you on last night's food." She raised her brows.

Networking—one of the most important skills he'd learned about the food service industry. Personal relationships with the right people could ensure a restaurant's success. "Of course I'll stay awhile."

Mairee beamed. "Come along, then. I believe I saw Kitty McCord looking at you with adoring eyes just before we came up."

He followed his employers downstairs. No sooner had he cleared the bottom step than a woman dressed in pink tweed took hold of his arm.

"Major O'Hara, isn't it?"

"Yes, Mrs. McCord." Major eyed her little dog speculatively, but for the moment it appeared calm.

"Just call me Kitty. I'm sorry I didn't recognize you when we came in. When Gus told me who you were, I just had to find you to tell you how fabulous the food was last night—though really I should be reprimanding you, making me have to start the New Year off with a resolution to lose the ten pounds I know I put on with all of your wonderful dishes."

"Thank you."

"Now, come with me. There are a few people I want to introduce you to."

Feeling very much like the dog clasped in her other arm, Major allowed himself to be led around the Guidrys' home and introduced like a prized pet to Mrs. McCord's friends.

"Were you responsible for last night?" the state senator's wife asked. "That was one of the most wonderful galas I've ever attended—and we've been to ever so many in Baton Rouge and New Orleans."

"I wish I could claim full responsibility, ma'am, but that praise rightfully goes to Meredith Guidry, the executive director of events. She planned and organized everything." He wished Meredith were here, listening to the accolades. She tended to be too hard on herself, taking a few minor complaints to heart and not enjoying the copious amounts of praise for her events.

"Yes. . .Meredith. Bless her heart. I met with her the other day to start planning Easter in the Park. I never would have guessed she'd be capable of pulling off an event like last night, though. She must rely greatly on you." Mrs. McCord's simpering voice and flirtatious expression were repeated by the retinue of ladies circled around him.

Major stiffened, and the tiny hairs at the back of his neck prickled. "Actually, Mrs. McCord, the truth of the matter is that we all rely on Meredith more than we should. She's such an organizational genius that all I have to do is show up and follow her plan to make everything go smoothly."

"Hmm." Kitty McCord's smile tightened. Before she could say more, a commotion caught her attention. "Oh, here's someone you *must* meet."

Major turned to look the same direction and quickly closed his eyes against a blinding beam of light. He blinked a couple of times and finally was able to open them enough to see the source—a large TV camera.

The mayor's wife held her hands out toward an exotic young woman with dark hair and features. "Alaine Delacroix, what a surprise to see you here." The two women exchanged a kiss on the cheek.

"Mrs. McCord, how lovely to see you. Might I impose on you for an interview?"

"Naturally, you know how much I love talking to you." Mrs. McCord clamped her hand around the reporter's elbow. "But first, there's someone I want to introduce to you."

Major's skin tingled as the two women drew closer, even with as much as he tried to quell the purely epicurean reaction to the younger one. What man wouldn't react to such a beautiful creature?

"Alaine, this is Major O'Hara. He's the chef responsible for the New Year's Eve Ball."

The young woman shook hands with him. "Alaine Delacroix, Channel Six News. I would love to get an interview with you, Mr. O'Hara. Would you have time this afternoon?"

Held enthralled by Alaine Delacroix's chocolate eyes, Major swallowed a couple of times. "I. . .yes, I'm. . .I have time."

Alaine's full lips split into a smile revealing perfect, dazzlingly white teeth.

"Did I hear someone say something about Major being interviewed for Alaine's show?" Mairee Guidry joined the cluster of women. She gave Major a significant look. "What a wonderful opportunity."

Major wiped his clammy palms on his khakis, unsure of how he'd gotten himself into this situation. Yes, being featured on a news show would be great publicity for B-G Enterprises—and potentially for the restaurant—but that kind of publicity would only lead to people asking questions, finding out about his background. . .about his mother.

He cleared the rising apprehension from his throat. "Yes, it would be a wonderful opportunity." Collecting himself, he gave a slight bow. "Ladies, it was a delight to meet you. Ms. Delacroix, I just recalled a previous engagement, so I won't be able to do that interview right now—" Catching sight of Mairee's raised eyebrow, he fished into his back pocket, slid a business card out of his wallet, and handed it to the reporter. "But do call me sometime, and we'll reschedule."

Alaine's fingers brushed his as she took the card, sending quivers of sensation up his arm. "I will call you tomorrow morning, Major O'Hara."

Major excused himself, retrieved his coat from the kid at the door, and barely waited for the door to close behind him before he took off toward Kirby at a full-out run. The cold rain in his face helped calm him, and by the time he reached the Jeep, his thoughts had stopped swirling. He hadn't had a reaction like that to a woman's mere presence in. . .ever. Now that he was away from her, shame over his reaction seeped through him. He'd foresworn dating, realizing that he'd never be able to saddle a woman he loved with his life—between the hours he worked and never knowing when the day might come that his mother would have a complete psychotic break.

Meredith's image slipped into his mind. Of any woman he knew, she was the only one who would understand his life, the only one who gave him a sense of fulfillment, of companionship. She wouldn't care about his hours—she worked longer than he did and spent the rest of her time refurbishing that house—but still, the specter of her reaction when she found out about Ma turned his stomach.

Kirby's engine roared to life. No. He couldn't do that to Meredith. She deserved better, better than the pittance of a life he could offer her. Major would have to settle for finding fulfillment in work—in opening a restaurant.

CHAPTER 5

After a day of falling in the mud, scraping paint, and hauling in a twenty-pound bag of puppy food, Meredith stood in the shower for several minutes, letting the hot, pulsating water work on her sore muscles. On the other side of the shower curtain, snuffling sounds and nails clicking on tile kept her well aware of the fur ball's movements around the small bathroom.

"I still can't believe I let myself think that guy was interested in me."

The puppy barked in response to her voice. Meredith smiled and worked honeysuckle-scented shampoo into her hair. "Maybe it is a good thing I found you, if you're going to talk back to me. Now people won't think I'm quite as crazy when I talk to myself out loud. I just don't know if I'm ready for a dog."

Meredith nearly tripped over the puppy when she got out of the shower. She pushed him back with her foot to keep his claws from her bare legs. His wagging tail caused his whole body to wriggle. How could she give up such unadulterated, uninhibited love? "Okay. I'll put signs up, and if no one has contacted me in a week or so, I'll take them down and you can stay with me."

She took extra time styling her shoulder-length hair and applying makeup. Even though she would only be with her parents and siblings, if she showed up the way she preferred—jeans, sweatshirt, and well-worn work boots—Mom wouldn't speak to her all night. But Meredith would definitely hear about it in undertones and insinuations all day tomorrow.

Her sisters could wear designer jeans and nice tops. But none of them worked for Mom and Dad. Meredith bypassed the closet full of denim and comfortable clothes and went instead to the closet holding her more expensive, work-appropriate attire.

After twenty minutes, she sank onto the side of the bed amid a pile of tops and pants. She hated feeling like she had to be "on" all the time around her family. But it kept at bay the whispers and hints that her choice in casual clothes might have something to do with why she was still single.

"What will I be most comfortable in?" she asked the clothes now strewn across her bed.

She chose her utilitarian black slacks—the size twelves that were somewhat loose in the waist—and a light turquoise cashmere twinset with a little beading around the neck. She stepped into her favorite loafer-style black pumps and turned to admire the look in the antique cheval mirror. Knowing Mom, she'd be dressed similarly.

"No, no, no!" She pushed the puppy away with one foot as he pounced on the hem of her pant leg. "If you're going to stay with me, you're going to have to learn better manners than that!"

Unabashed, he sat and hunched over to scratch at his new collar.

"Get used to it, bubba. Come on. We'd better take you out before it's time to go."

Pleased with his performance outside, she took him back into the bathroom, where she picked up the rug and draped it over the shower curtain rod. In its place, she put down a triple layer of newspaper and an old towel for him to sleep on.

As soon as she closed the door, he cried and whined his displeasure. She ignored him.

With the lint roller in hand and balancing on one foot so she could get the dog hair off the hem of her pant leg, she buzzed the intercom to Jenn's apartment.

"What?" Her sister's voice crackled through the speaker.

"You about ready to go?"

"It's only—crimenetly. I didn't realize it was already six. I'll be down in five minutes."

"Jenn. You know how I hate—"

"Being late. I know. But everyone will blame me, not you."

Eight minutes later, Jenn clattered downstairs and entered without knocking. "Wow, Mere, you're awfully dressed up." Jenn, of course, looked fabulously stylish in her dark indigo jeans with penny loafers and a bright green turtleneck sweater.

Meredith quirked the corner of her mouth in a grimace. "You know how it is with Mom."

"Yeah, I know. She gives you a hard time. But that's only when you show up in the rattiest stuff you own—" Jenn cocked her head. "What in the— Is that a *dog* I hear?"

"A puppy. Come on—I'll tell you about him in the car."

"I want to see him." Jenn barreled through the apartment and opened the bathroom door before Meredith could stop her.

"He's so *cute!*" Jenn's voice reached the extreme high pitch usually brought on by a baby sighting. She crouched and scooped up the puppy. "Let's take him over to Mama and Daddy's."

"No. Jenn, look—you already have fur all over your sweater. Can you imagine how Mom would react if he had an accident in the house?"

Jenn's expression shouted incredulity. She stood and tucked the squirming pup under her arm. "Mom loves dogs. She's the one who kept Daddy from getting rid of Jax, even after Jax completely lost control of his bladder. He's coming." Jenn marched past. "Why you've gotten it in your head that they're going to disapprove of everything you do or say..."

Because I'm the only sap who went into the family business. Well, that wasn't true. Rafe had worked for their parents for a couple of years, flying one of the corporate jets. But he didn't have to work with them day in and day out—and he'd left the company late last year to

51

work for a charter airline.

The only reason Meredith had seven siblings was because her parents thought that all of them would run B-G so they could retire early. With a master's degree in art history, Meredith hadn't really had any job options other than going to work as an assistant event planner ten years ago.

Sometimes she wished she'd been brave enough to pursue her dream of working in home design, but as that had not been deemed a viable job choice by her parents—

"Hey! We going or what?" Jenn stepped back into the apartment.

"Coming." Meredith grabbed her keys and wallet off the table and followed her sister outside.

"Can we take your car?" Jenn asked, walking around to the passenger side of the SUV. "The 'Stang's top is still leaking."

Meredith rounded the tail end of Jenn's classic Mustang, already expecting to be the one driving. She climbed into the Volvo and started the engine.

"So, how'd you end up with this little guy?" Jen nuzzled the puppy, who joyously licked her chin.

Meredith buckled her seat belt and pulled out of the driveway, relating what had happened. By the time she parked under one of the centuries-old oak trees in front of their parents' house, she'd gotten to the part about taking the pup to the quick clinic at the pet store.

"Yeah? Well I think I'd be kinda wiggly, too, if someone was trying to stick a thermometer there." Jenn cooed gibberish at the dog and climbed out of the vehicle, tucking the puppy under her raincoat for the dash to the front porch.

Sighing, Meredith popped open her umbrella and followed her sister up the sidewalk.

With the exception of all the furniture still being shoved up against the walls in the front rooms, little evidence remained of the hundreds of people who'd likely crowded the house for most of the day.

The front door opened behind her, and she turned. Forbes closed his umbrella and stowed it in the rack beside the door. She waited for him; he hooked his arm around her neck and kissed her temple.

"Did you have a good day?" He eased the headlock and settled his arm across her shoulders as they strolled down the hall.

"Yep—well, for the most part. My stupid brother provoked me into an argument this morning."

He squeezed his arm tightly around her neck again. "I apologized."

She nudged his side with her knuckles; he released her and danced away, squirming. "I know. And you were right—it was better for me to find out ahead of time instead of being blindsided by it. Did you forewarn Jenn, too?"

"Uh. . .no. You know she can't keep a secret to save her life."

Meredith wrinkled her nose. "She might not take it as well as I did."

"I know. But we'll cross that bridge—"

"There you two are." Mom greeted them as soon as Meredith and Forbes entered the kitchen. She looked Meredith over from head to toe. "Do you have a date after this or something?"

Meredith glanced at Forbes, in his form-fitting black turtleneck and jeans, then back at their mother—also in jeans. She plastered on a smile. "Oh, I thought I'd try to make everyone else feel completely *under*dressed for a change." Would she ever be able to do *anything* right when it came to her parents?

"Well, come on and get some food."

As in years past, almost every inch of counter space in the generously sized kitchen was covered with trays and pans of food. Growing up, Meredith and her siblings had always looked forward to dinner on New Year's Day because they got to eat the leftovers from the open house—including as much dessert as they wanted.

Family members milled about, filling plates, while some had already migrated into the great room beyond the kitchen's breakfast bar.

Rafe vacated the rocking chair and offered it to Meredith. "Don't want you getting your fancy duds messed up." Though his voice lilted with teasing humor, his eyes held sympathy and understanding.

"Thanks."

At her youngest sisters' high-pitched voices, she looked across the room and saw them feeding bits of Aunt Maggie's gourmet food to the puppy. Her brothers were more interested in the football game on the flat-panel TV mounted above the crackling fireplace—even Forbes seemed to be getting involved in the game between two teams from faraway colleges no one in this family had ever cared about before.

Finally, at eight o'clock, Meredith's father turned off the TV. "Well, here we are, at the start of another year. This time we have a new face with us." He motioned toward Marci's boyfriend with an outstretched hand. "Welcome, Shaun. I'm not sure if Marci explained exactly what it is that we do here on New Year's."

"Yes, sir, sort of like what most families do at Thanksgiving."

"Right—except we're giving our goal for the upcoming year and what we intend to do to reach it. Last year I believe Forbes went first?" Lawson shot a raised-brow glance at his oldest son.

"Yes, sir."

"Then it's youngest to oldest this year. Tiffani, take it away."

As her youngest sister started talking about her upcoming semester at college and grades and school projects, Meredith mentally rehearsed her goal: finishing renovations on the house and getting moved and settled in. No, it wasn't creative or soul-searching, but really, what else did she have in her life?

An image of Major flickered in her mind's eye. She wished she had Major in her life—more than as just an infatuation that wouldn't go away. She forced her mind to replace his image with one of Ward Breaux. Had he been flirting with her before he knew she might need a contractor? Sure, he'd been a little condescending, but he'd seen her as a woman, not as "just one of the guys" as most of the other men she'd ever known did.

Jonathan and Kevin gave their goals—both also talking mostly about college. When Marci's turn came, Meredith set her own relationship musings aside and paid attention. Marci launched into her goal—changing her major to nursing and, in another two years, finally finishing school.

"That's an admirable goal, Marci. You know we'll support you no matter what career path you choose." Dad's eyes twinkled, and the corners of his mouth twitched. Like Jenn, he was horrible at keeping secrets. "Shaun, would you like to participate?"

Though almost thirty years old, Shaun squirmed like a schoolboy in the principal's office. "I'm really happy to have been included in your family's tradition." His gaze darted around the room, but he didn't make eye contact with anyone. Seated on the floor in front of her, he turned to face Marci and raised up onto one knee. "Marci, we've been together for four years now. I can't imagine spending my life without you by my side. Will you marry me?"

Marci shrieked a yes. Meredith swallowed and blinked hard.

Jenn fled the room.

Meredith groaned. Not good. Fortunately, Marci and Shaun were too preoccupied with each other to notice Jenn's reaction. Meredith dabbed the corners of her eyes with a napkin and stood, waving her mother back down. "Let me."

She passed through the kitchen and down the main hallway, calling her sister's name. She followed the sound of sobbing to the powder room under the elaborate staircase. She knocked softly. "Jenn?"

"Go away."

"Jennifer." Meredith tapped on the door again.

"Go away! I don't want to talk about it, okay?"

"Do you want me to go get your stuff and tell the family you're sick and we're going home?"

A long pause. "No."

"Then talk to me. You can't stay in there all night."

The doorknob rattled and clicked; Jenn didn't come out, though. Meredith pulled the door open. "May I come in?"

Jenn perched on the closed commode, elbows on knees, weeping into a wad of toilet paper.

Meredith closed the door behind her and leaned against the edge of the pedestal sink.

"It's not fair," Jenn wailed.

"What? That Marci's engaged? Or that she's twenty-four and engaged?"

Jenn moaned into her fistful of tissue.

"Look, I understand—"

"How could you possibly understand what I'm feeling?"

Meredith rocked back, the words hitting her like a sucker punch to the gut. "Wait just a minute. You haven't forgotten that I'm almost three years older than you, have you? And that I'm having to figure out how to accept the fact that my sister who is *ten* years younger than me just got engaged?"

"But you've never been in love—you've never even dated! How could you understand what this means to me? I've been trying for half my life to find what Marci found with her first boyfriend."

Meredith separated the hurt and anger Jenn's words caused from the need to counsel her sister through this emotional crisis. She'd deal with her own emotions later. "Just because I've never dated doesn't mean I've never been in love."

Once again the specter of Major flickered in Meredith's mind, but she shoved the thought aside. "When I was in college, I fell in love with someone who didn't return my feelings, and I had to stand by and watch him marry a girl who was supposed to be a friend of mine: my roommate, who knew I was in love with him. So how do you think it makes me feel to know my younger sister has found something I'm still searching for? Something I've been searching for longer than you? How do you think I feel every time a handsome, interesting man asks you for a date? Or when Rafe doesn't come to Thursday night dinner because he's on a date? Or being maid of honor for Anne?"

Jenn sniffed, but her sobs subsided.

"We can't begrudge Marci the fact that she found the love of her life at a young age. We both know all she's ever wanted out of life is to be a wife and mother—yes, I know you want that, too. But you and

I both had aspirations for our education and for careers. Look at how successful you've been with the restaurant. Do you think you could have done that with a husband and babies to take care of?"

"But I've been praying so hard for God to send me my husband. What's wrong with me?"

Meredith moved to kneel in front of her sister—after shifting the rug closer with her foot—and rubbed Jenn's upper arms. "Remember that just because it seems like God isn't giving us the main desire of our hearts doesn't mean He's not working in other areas of our lives—blessing us in ways we can't see because we're focusing so hard on the one thing we want but don't have."

"How can you be so calm about this?" Jenn grabbed a fresh wad of toilet paper and patted her face dry.

"Because I've had all day to think about it."

"Forbes?"

"Forbes."

Jenn rolled her eyes. "I swear he knows everything everyone in this family is going to do three days before we know we're going to do it."

The continued celebration of Marci's engagement created enough chaos that only their parents, Forbes, and Rafe looked at Meredith and Jenn in concern when they returned.

Though she smiled and laughed, Jenn remained subdued for the rest of the evening, cuddling the puppy on her lap. As they walked out, Forbes wrapped his arm around Jenn's shoulders and leaned his head close to hers. Rafe came up beside Meredith and encircled her waist in a quick half hug and walked with her toward the front door.

"Crazy, huh?"

"What do you mean?" Meredith tilted her head to study her younger brother's profile. Though he would turn twenty-nine in a few weeks, she could still trace elements of the pudgy-faced, red-haired little boy.

"I mean that Marci is the first one of us to get married. I always figured it would be Jenn."

Rafe's words pressed salt into the gaping emotional wound Jenn's had ripped open. "Gee, thanks."

"Oh, come on, you know what I mean—Jenn had her first serious boyfriend when she was barely fifteen."

"The first one Mom and Dad knew about, you mean."

"Yeah." Rafe opened the door.

Meredith shivered in the cold, damp air and buttoned her jacket.

"She's taking this kinda hard, isn't she?" He nodded toward Jenn and Forbes, standing next to Meredith's SUV. Jenn hugged the puppy to her, like a shipwreck survivor hanging onto a buoy.

"She'll get over it—as soon as she finds a new boyfriend. And that won't take long." But Meredith wasn't certain about herself. She'd known a day would come when her younger siblings started getting married, but she hadn't expected to still be single when it happened.

"So long as she doesn't make any rash decisions, like eloping with the next guy who asks her out."

Meredith laughed and dug her keys out of her purse. She used the key fob remote to unlock her car. "You know Forbes would never let any of us make a rash decision about anything."

"He's so. . .I don't know, anal retentive or obsessive-compulsive or something. He needs serious psychological profiling."

"I think all they'd be able to tell us is that he's a massive control freak."

"Y'all talking about me?" Forbes turned to face them while opening the car door for Jenn. "Because there's only one control freak allowed in this family." He waggled his eyebrows.

"Rafe, are you in town Thursday?" Jenn settled the puppy on the floor while she fastened her seat belt.

"I think I get in late in the afternoon, so I should be there for dinner." He blew her a kiss then hugged Meredith.

"Fly carefully."

"I always do." Rafe clasped hands with Forbes then trotted off to his classic red Corvette in the driveway.

Forbes closed Jenn's door then walked around the SUV to stand with Meredith. "What're you thinking about?"

She couldn't bring herself to admit to her emotional turmoil over tonight's events, not even to Forbes. "Just stuff."

"Marci-related stuff?"

"Yeah—sort of." She leaned against the door—then regretted it when the beaded raindrops soaked through her jacket.

"You want to share?"

Tell Major's best friend in the world that she'd had a crush on Major for eight years? "I don't think so."

He reached over and squeezed her shoulder. "I think it would be good for you—you know how you get when you keep things bottled up too long."

"I'll take it out on the house." She sighed. "Are you coming to dinner Thursday night?"

"Of course. I have to be there to orchestrate my siblings' and cousins' lives, control freak that I am." He opened her door and waited until she was in with her seat belt fastened before closing her door, then waved as she drove away.

Jenn stayed quiet on the fifteen-minute drive home, staring out the window and slowly stroking the sleeping puppy in her lap. Approaching the large Victorian—one of the largest on the block of turn-of-the-twentieth-century houses in Bonneterre's garden district—Meredith could see lights on in the second-floor windows. Once in the driveway, she recognized the dark Buick parked behind Anne's convertible.

George was over—probably for dinner and a movie...with a little work mixed in, now that he was officially Anne's business partner as well as her fiancé.

Melancholy caught in Meredith's throat. She was tired of praying the same prayer Jenn had lamented earlier: *When, oh Lord, will it be* my *turn?* At least Jenn dated—a lot. Meredith didn't even have that opportunity. Even if she weren't in love with Major, she never seemed to meet eligible men anymore. None of the single guys at church had ever shown the least interest in her; they'd always vied for Jenn's attention. Meredith had even tried the online dating thing. But whenever she started getting close with someone, a feeling of dread—of wrongness—overwhelmed her, and she withdrew.

"Can I keep the puppy with me tonight?" Jenn asked as she trudged across the back deck.

"Sure. You'll need to let him run around the yard before you take him inside, though, since he hasn't been out for a while."

"I know how to take care of a puppy."

Meredith forgave her sister's snappish tone and bade Jenn good night. Meredith didn't bother turning on the lights but felt her way through the dark apartment to her bedroom. She changed into her favorite pajamas—an old Bonneterre High School T-shirt and stretchy cotton-knit shorts—and climbed into bed.

The tears she'd been fighting all evening welled up and overflowed onto her pillow. She couldn't deny it anymore—Major would never return her feelings. She had to move on, find someone new.

Meredith turned on her back and stared at the shadowy ceiling. Though she'd told her family her goals about the house, a new, more important goal begged to be made, to be spoken aloud.

"Lord, my real New Year's resolution is that I won't still be single by this time next year."

CHAPTER 6

*G*reat spread this morning, Major. I meant to tell you earlier."

Major accepted Lawson Guidry's proffered hand, his stomach twisting. "Thank you, sir." He hadn't slept much this week, visions of and plans for the restaurant running constantly through his mind. This morning he'd given up on sleep around three o'clock and been at work at four, half an hour early, to prepare breakfast for Mr. Guidry's weekly prayer breakfast.

"What brings you down here at this time of the afternoon?" the older man asked.

Major looked beyond Mr. Guidry toward the offices at the end of the hallway. "I came down to bring Meredith's takeaway box for her dinner, but she's not in her office. I need to talk to her." At her father's raised-brow look, Major quickly added, "About my part of the financial report on the New Year's event." Which was sort of true, though what he needed to ask her about could be done over the phone.

Maybe he read too much into Mr. Guidry's expression, but he was pretty sure Meredith's dad didn't believe him. "She had to go out to meet clients at Lafitte's Landing—probably won't be back for a while."

"Oh. Okay. I'll catch her later, then."

"Don't you have an interview scheduled for this afternoon anyway?"

Major checked his watch. "Yes, sir. I guess I'd better get back up to the kitchen, since that's where I told them to meet me."

"You'll have to let us know how it goes." Lawson raised his hand palm forward, his own unique good-bye wave. "I'd wish you luck, but you don't need it."

"Thank you, sir." Major nodded his farewell, then booked it back to the elevator and returned to the twenty-third floor.

Several kitchen and service staff stood facing him when the doors opened.

"Bye, Chef."

"Have a great afternoon, Mr. O'Hara."

"See ya tomorrow, Chef."

He tossed a good-bye over his shoulder as he exchanged places with them, then headed across the expanse of Vue de Ceil to the kitchen on the opposite side. Vacuums' whines filled the cavernous space, run by two of the waiters, both of whom had changed from their black pants and white button-downs into droopy jeans and sweatshirts.

In the kitchen, only Steven and the sauté chef and two dishwashers remained. Steven and his second-in-command hovered over the whiteboard, which they'd taken down and laid on the long prep table in the middle of the room, discussing tomorrow's lunch menu and assigning components to the various staff who would be here.

Major stepped into his office and closed the door. He opened the wardrobe behind his desk, planning to wear his white chef's jacket for the interview—but it wasn't there. He smacked his forehead. He'd dropped it off at the dry cleaner Tuesday and had meant to pick it up after the prayer breakfast this morning.

He swapped his navy polo for the burgundy tunic and watched himself in the mirror on the back of the armoire's door as he buttoned the double-breasted placket. Hmm. Must have shrunk when he had it cleaned. At least, he didn't remember the buttons around his gut pulling like that last time he'd worn it.

He sat down at the desk to write a note reminding himself to go to the cleaners tomorrow. The computer dinged, indicating a new e-mail received. Meredith usually checked her e-mail regularly when offsite, so maybe she'd finally decided to respond to him.

But the message was from Anne Hawthorne to set up a time to discuss the menu for her rehearsal dinner and wedding reception. He flagged it for follow-up later, then scanned the rest of the unread messages in his inbox. None from GUIDRY, MEREDITH.

If he didn't know better, he'd think she was avoiding him.

The five-minute warning of the time scheduled for the interview popped up on the screen. He quickly straightened up his desk, though that consisted of making sure the stapler and tape dispenser were at a perfect right-angle to the desk blotter and that the blotter lay exactly one inch—as measured by the tip of his thumb—from the edge of the desk.

Back out in the kitchen, the dish sanitizers had stopped rumbling, and a solitary Steven was hanging the whiteboard back on the wall.

"Everyone else gone?" Major paused to glance over tomorrow's menu.

"Yes, Chef. I'm about to call it a day, too, unless you need me for something." He glanced pointedly at Major's attire.

Have Steven hanging around for the interview? "No. It's already after four o'clock. Go on home."

"Thanks. I'll see you tomorrow." Steven slung his denim chef's jacket over his shoulder, tucked his knife case under his arm, and swaggered from the kitchen.

Major gave him half a minute's head start then stepped out into the warehouse-sized, sky-view room. Just as one set of elevator doors closed behind Steven, another set opened.

Though he thought he'd prepared for it, the sight of Alaine Delacroix once again disarmed him. No woman had the right to be so distractingly beautiful. She held the door while the burly guy with her muscled out a large duffel bag and a couple of equipment cases.

Major jogged over. "Can I help with any of that?"

The guy looked up at him, apparently offended. "Naw, man. I can get it."

"Chef O'Hara, it's good to see you again." Alaine extended her hand.

Heat rushed into Major's face when he took her hand in his enormous paw and tried not to hurt her. "Ms. Delacroix. Welcome to Vue de Ceil." He swept his arm toward the room.

Alaine strolled past him. "It looks so different. I've only been here at night—and with five or six hundred other people, like at New Year's."

More like eight or nine hundred, but who was counting? He followed her. Alaine Delacroix was the kind of woman who could be admired from afar but not someone Major had any interest in getting to know better on a personal level.

Not like Meredith. He didn't have to worry about hurting Meredith on the rare occasion that called for him taking her hand in his—which he wished happened more often. He also didn't feel like a prepubescent boy at his first school dance around Meredith the way he did right now. And to put final nails in the coffin in which he would bury his reaction to Alaine, he decided he much preferred strawberry blonds with nutmeg-colored eyes to brunettes with eyes so dark he couldn't distinguish the pupil from the iris.

". . .your office?" Alaine stopped in the middle of the room and turned to face him, those dark brown eyes gazing at him askance.

What about his office? Oh, the interview. "Right through here."

He led her down the service corridor and pushed open the ENTER ONLY door into the kitchen, motioning for her to pass through ahead of him—and for the overloaded cameraman to do the same.

"Wow. I've seen some professional kitchens on TV before, but this one takes the cake." Alaine ran her hand along the stainless-steel countertops. "Nelson, we'll want to get some footage of this kitchen. In fact—" She whirled around to look at both men. "I know we discussed filming the cooking segments in the executive kitchen downstairs, but I wonder now if maybe we should do it up here."

Nelson thunked the equipment cases down on the floor and crossed his arms. "I'd have to see the other space to find out which one'll be easier to light."

Alaine returned to her perusal of the kitchen. "Mrs. Guidry said they'll help us out with getting some new lights installed if our portables won't be sufficient."

Major felt as if he'd walked into the middle of a movie. "Cooking segments? I wasn't supposed to have prepared a cooking exhibition for today, was I?"

"No, no. Your weekly guest spot for my show."

"Oh." Now he really needed to talk to Meredith. It wasn't like her not to tell him when she made decisions that impacted his work. And even if the decision had come from farther up the food chain, the least Meredith could have done was to give him a heads-up. She was his *boss* after all.

"After we finish the interview, can you show us the other kitchen?"

"Sure." That would give him a good excuse to see if Meredith was back yet and talk to her. He had to talk through this restaurant thing with someone. He couldn't talk to Forbes—Forbes was representing his parents in the business deal. Meredith was the only other person he trusted.

Then why can't I bring myself to tell her about Ma?

He pushed the wayward thoughts aside and led Alaine and Nelson into his office. He'd think about his relationship issues with Meredith later. Much, much later.

"Hey, kiddo. Good meeting this afternoon?"

Meredith looked up from her computer at her dad's voice. "Yeah. I think we've got that wedding reception in the bag."

"How much are they wanting to spend?"

"At least six figures."

"That's my girl."

Yep. That's when her parents were proud of her: whenever she brought more money into the company coffers. "It's not signed yet."

"I'll put the pressure on the father of the bride—I'm playing golf with him Saturday morning. You hooked the fish; I'll just reel it in." He leaned his shoulder against the doorjamb. "Major was down here a little while ago looking for you. Said he needed to talk to you."

Meredith's insides cringed, but she kept her expression neutral. "Yeah, I've got a couple of e-mails from him that I haven't gotten around to yet—it's been such a busy week."

"Well, before you talk to him, there's something you should know." Her father rubbed the back of his neck. "Your mother and I offered to become investors in a restaurant with Major. He'd still work for you as the head of the catering division while the restaurant is in the start-up phase. But as soon as it opens, he'd be running the restaurant full-time."

Meredith took several deep breaths to try to settle her churning stomach. Major was going to leave B-G? She wouldn't get to see him every day. She might not see him ever again.

But you're supposed to be getting over him, remember? Maybe this is God's way of helping with that goal.

She cleared her throat. "I see. I guess I'll have to ask him to help me find a replacement executive chef."

"He hasn't accepted the offer yet, and we're not pushing him to make the decision quickly. Let him get through the Hearts to HEARTS banquet."

"Sounds reasonable." Meredith dug her thumbnail into the opposite palm. "Anything else?"

"He said he needed to talk to you about the financial report for New Year's Eve, too." Dad gave her his stop-sign farewell wave. "See you tomorrow. Don't work too late."

"'Night, Daddy." As soon as he disappeared, she rubbed her forehead. Her head—and heart—split in two: one part of her wanting to be happy that both she and Major would have a chance to move on, move forward; the other part mourning the loss of what she'd always wished would happen.

Major's Jeep—that old green thing he called Kirby—had still been in the garage when she'd driven in a few minutes ago. Steeling herself to see him for the first time since making her New Year's resolution, she left the B-G corporate offices and got onto the elevator before second thoughts hit.

The orange, red, purple, and navy of sunset gave Vue de Ceil the aura of a cathedral. She paused for a moment just to appreciate the view.

Is this a sign, Lord? A sign that I'm doing the right thing by letting go of my childish crush on him? Of course it was. As was the fact that he would leave B-G to start a restaurant, and she'd rarely—if ever—see him again.

She entered the kitchen through the EXIT ONLY door, since it was closest—and then stopped. Voices came from Major's office. His, followed by—a woman's. Meredith took a step back, bumped the door, and covered her mouth with her hand. He was up here alone with a woman?

He said something; then both he and the unknown female laughed. The refrigerators and other equipment in the kitchen made too much noise for Meredith to clearly make out the words, and through the cracked-open door, she could see only the corner of the wardrobe that stood behind his desk.

Though she gulped, her lungs wouldn't fill with air. What more sign did she need to prove Major did *not* return her feelings and that it was time for her to move on?

Dazedly, she backed out through the door and somehow ended up at the elevators. When she'd voiced her resolution, it hadn't seemed like it would be hard—at least not *this* hard. But as her mother would say, *a goal that's easily attained doesn't bring the satisfaction that comes through sacrifice, hard work, and sometimes even tears.*

She held her breath to keep the tears at bay, staring out over the darkening city as the glass elevator descended. She refused to go through the pain she'd experienced in college. At least she was fairly certain that Major wasn't about to marry one of her closest friends as Brent had.

Back in her office, she sat down to work on her report—after all, the more she could get done now, the less she'd have to take home over the weekend. But the tinkling laughter of the mystery woman continued ringing in Meredith's head.

Who was she? What was it about this other woman that caught Major's attention—what quality Meredith didn't have?

Okay, stop. She had to concentrate on the report. See, this was why it was good she didn't have a relationship with someone she worked with. If she got this distracted by his having a conversation with another woman, what would she be like if Major actually returned her feelings—if they were dating?

Her head started throbbing, so she turned to grab a soda out of the mini-fridge. She'd just laid her hand on the neck of the last bottle when the Styrofoam carryout box caught her eye. Major's bold scrawl across the top of it sent chill bumps down the back of her neck:

Meredith—sorry I keep missing you. Hope you enjoy. I think this is one of your favorite meals.

M O'H

A raft of tears flooded her eyes, but she blinked hard to make them go away. She jumped when her cell phone buzzed against her waist and began trilling her general ringtone. An unfamiliar number scrolled across the screen.

With a deep breath, followed by clearing her throat, she clicked the appropriate button and pressed the device to her ear. "This is Meredith Guidry."

"Well, hello there, Meredith Guidry," came a deep voice. "This is Ward Breaux. You didn't answer the e-mail I sent earlier in the week, so I figured I'd give you a call."

Yeah, she'd been meaning to get around to reading that e-mail. "Hey, Ward. I guess you want to talk about my house, huh?"

"That wasn't my primary reason for calling, no." The humor that filled his voice conjured an image of him towering over her, giving her that grin and looking at her with flirtatious eyes. "I was hoping

I could take you out for dinner tonight."

"Tonight?" Thursday. Dinner with the other unmarried adult cousins and siblings. "I can't tonight. I already have plans."

"Tomorrow then."

She pulled the phone away, stared at it in astonishment, and put it back to her ear. "Hold on. Let me check my calendar." She already knew what it would show her. No event tomorrow night that she needed to be at—the event planners were doing that—which meant that her Friday night might include going upstairs to watch a movie with Anne and George if they weren't going out.

"Am I freaking you out by moving too fast?" Ward's voice tingled on her skin like ice chips followed by a warm shower.

"No—not at all." She was freaked out by someone she'd only met four days ago calling her and asking her out for a date, since it had never happened to her. She tried to swallow the knot of nerves blocking her air passage. "It looks like I'm free tomorrow night."

"Great. Why don't I pick you up at your office—say around five thirty? Or is that too late for a Friday evening?"

Meredith pulled a pen from under the untidy stack of papers beside the computer and started drawing question marks on the back of a legal pad. "Sure. Five thirty. Here. Sounds fine."

"I hope you like jazz music. I know the greatest little club down on the river. I thought maybe we could get dinner in downtown and then drive over to Town Square, stroll along the Riverwalk, and then sit and have coffee and listen to some jazz."

The word *JAZZ* appeared in big, bold letters under her pen. "I love jazz. And if you're talking about the Savoy, I've been wanting to go there since they opened."

"Excellent. I'll see you at five thirty tomorrow evening, then. I can't wait."

"Me, too." She repeated his "Bye-bye now" farewell and hung up. She tapped the phone to her chin and glanced around the office, looking for some confirmation of what had just occurred.

Aside from the fact that for the last three months she'd been trying to think of some way to invite Major to go to the Savoy with her, she was excited about tomorrow night. The idea of going out with someone she didn't know the first thing about—well, she knew he was a contractor, so didn't know the second thing about—frightened her a little. But not as much as the blind dates Jenn wanted to set her up on.

Besides, if she was going to end her single status by this time next year, how else did she expect that to happen?

She leaned back in her chair and stared up at the ceiling. "Lord, please let him be a nice, normal, Christian guy—with no weird fetishes or obsessions. And if You could keep him from getting distracted by an attractive woman while we're on our date, I would so appreciate it."

CHAPTER 7

$\mathcal{M}$ajor filled the thermal carafe with chicory-flavored dark roast, covered the platter holding warm croissants, strawberries and raspberries, bacon, shelled hard-boiled eggs, and a large ramekin of honey butter—everything he'd watched Meredith pile onto her plate the last time he'd seen her at one of her father's prayer breakfasts—and added them to the rolling service cart. Preparing a meal for someone he was mad at always helped him overcome the feelings and approach the situation in a positive frame of mind.

The silverware rattled against the porcelain plates when the cart's wheels bumped over the threshold of the freight elevator. He checked his watch again: 7:53. As long as she hadn't decided to come in early this morning, he should be able to get everything set up on the small conference table in her office before she arrived.

With a grinding squeal and an unnerving bounce, the elevator stopped on the fifth floor. He swiped his security card on the reader beside the door directly across the hall. Dark quiet enveloped the smaller-scale kitchen—the place Alaine Delacroix decided would be *just perfect* for the cooking segments on her midday news show. The segments Meredith had never told him about.

He rubbed his tongue against the backs of his teeth. Maybe Meredith had a good reason for why she'd failed to tell him she'd volunteered him to do a weekly cooking demonstration in addition to his regular job. His *full-time* job at which he worked nearly fifty hours a week—even longer when gearing up for big events, like the upcoming Hearts to HEARTS banquet.

The soft wheels of the cart whispered across the wood floor in the executive dining room and hallway. Meredith's office door stood open, and the lights were still off. Good. She wasn't here yet.

He glanced around as he raised the dimmer switch to bring the lights up. The dark wood along the curved juncture of wall and ceiling, copper ceiling tiles, cream walls, and dark-wood floors made the room look like a Boston cream pie. His stomach rumbled. But the rest of the office—he cringed. Unkempt stacks of paperwork sat on her desk. She'd obviously done some work at the small round table, too, because the vase of bright pink flowers sat near the far edge, as if shoved aside.

Three minutes until eight o'clock. He moved the vase to the center of the table then set out the plates, napkins, silverware, and cups and saucers. He measured distances between utensils and china using his fingers—the way Maggie Babineaux had taught him—then stepped back to make sure everything looked uniform and symmetrical.

"What's this?"

His stomach jumped at Meredith's voice. He stepped aside so she had an unhindered view of the tablescape. "Breakfast."

The shoulder strap of her overloaded briefcase fell from her shoulder into the crook of her elbow. She jolted to the side from the shift in weight, then hugged her arms around an opaque garment bag. "Breakfast?"

"Yes. You know, the meal that one usually eats first thing in the morning. Which for you typically consists of a child's-size box of Cheerios, dry, and possibly a tub of applesauce, if you get around to eating it, with several cups of coffee, I believe."

"What—do you have a nanny cam in here somewhere to keep up with my eating habits?" She smiled, but wariness still filled her eyes. She hung the garment bag on the coat hook on the back of the door then went around her desk, divested herself of her briefcase and purse, and turned on her computer.

"No, we've just had enough early morning meetings for me to observe the fact that you take a very haphazard approach to breakfast." He clasped his hands behind his back to try to stop the itching sensation in his fingers from wanting to go to her desk and straighten up all of the paper stacks, line up the several sticky notes on the edge of her computer monitor, and close the partially opened file drawer in the credenza behind her desk. The office hadn't looked this disheveled when he dropped off her dinner box yesterday afternoon.

"Do we—are we supposed to be meeting this morning?" She grabbed her thick leather planner out of her briefcase and flipped it open on top of the papers strewn over her desk blotter.

"No, but I saw on the computer that you don't have any meetings this morning—at least Outlook showed your time as free—and I hoped to be able to get half an hour with you."

Being in the same room with Meredith made yesterday's frustration with her evaporate. The dark gray suit she wore high-lighted her figure to perfection—making him wonder what was in the hanging bag on the back of the door.

"Are you working an event tonight?"

"Tonight? No. Pam and Lori are overseeing a couple of functions—I thought they'd worked out the catering with your staff." Concern troubled her usually calm, golden brown eyes.

"Yes, I have staff assigned to both events. I just saw you'd brought extra clothes and wondered..." His thought drifted off when Meredith turned deep red.

"Oh, that." Her voice squeaked. "I have plans after work and didn't want to spend the evening in a suit."

Major stopped rubbing his tongue against his teeth and caught the inside of his cheek between them instead. Plans? A *date*? With whom?

"So what did you want to meet with me about?" She carried a legal pad and pen over to the conference table.

"Meet? Right. Why don't you get started serving your plate." He picked up the carafe and poured coffee for both of them.

"This looks wonderful, Major. Thanks for thinking of it." She sat down and draped the cloth napkin over her lap.

He cut open a croissant, slathered it with honey butter, arranged a layer of raspberries on one half, then replaced the top.

"A raspberry sandwich?" Meredith grinned at him as she layered her bread with bacon and the egg she'd just sliced. "Not a bad idea."

Of course she had a date tonight. Any man would have to be an idiot to pass up the chance to date Meredith Guidry. *Call me an idiot, then*. "Something I picked up from my roommate during culinary school."

"How's the week been? Sorry I've been missing you, but clearing everything up after the New Year's gala and trying to get things going for the H to H banquet have kept me running." Meredith took a big bite out of her bacon and egg sandwich.

Major hid his amusement. One thing he'd always appreciated about Meredith was the gusto with which she ate—no pretense, no falsely dainty bites, just a sheer enjoyment of the food in front of her. He washed down his raspberry croissant with a slug of coffee then gave her a recap of everything the catering division had done that week.

Meredith refilled both coffee cups. The recap of the catering division's week turned into a discussion of the New Year's Eve gala and what they could improve upon next year.

But I might not be here next year.

The last bite of his sandwich stuck in his throat. That was something he hadn't taken into consideration about the restaurant deal: not working with Meredith day in and day out. But *not* seeing her every day might help him stick to his resolve of never dragging her into the uncertainty of his life, the fear that at any time a call would come that his mother'd had a psychotic break and would have to be removed from the assisted-living facility and find a new place.

"So are you going to tell me what you wanted to meet with me about?" Meredith rested her elbows on the edge of the table and cradled her coffee cup in both hands.

He pushed his plate back, grateful for the derailment of his train of thought. "I guess you know that I had an interview with Alaine Delacroix from Channel Six yesterday."

"Alaine Delacroix? The girl who does that talk show at noon? Interviewed you?" Meredith's brows flattened into a frown.

Major didn't know what to make of her response. "Yeah. Apparently she's going to be doing a story on the Hearts banquet and wanted to interview me about that, and the New Year's gala. And she also wanted to talk to me about the cooking segment."

"The cooking segment?" Meredith almost dropped her coffee and set it down quickly. "What cooking segment?"

He rubbed his forehead. Obviously she was as much in the dark as he'd been. "You didn't know that I'm apparently supposed to be doing a weekly cooking demonstration for Alaine Delacroix's show?"

She shook her head. "This is the first I've heard about it."

"Oh." His heart twisted at the pained expression that filled Meredith's eyes—and the knowledge that he'd probably just put her in a very awkward position. "I thought maybe, since the catering division falls under your department. . ." Shame sloshed around in his gut at the memory of the accusatory anger he'd held toward her since yesterday.

"Catering does, yes. But you know that my parents sometimes like to make decisions without department directors' input." Meredith didn't pull her gaze away from her clasped hands.

He opened his mouth then clamped it shut. Asking Meredith if she really thought her parents did that with any of their other executive directors probably wasn't the best direction to take the conversation. He wanted to apologize, to take back the knowledge he'd just thrust upon Meredith that her parents didn't respect her authority and position. But once the soup was spilled, there was no getting it back into the pot.

"I'll talk to my mom and pass along whatever details she can give me." Meredith's soft voice and the weariness in her eyes when she finally looked up tugged at Major's heart. He wanted to reach over and hug her, wanted to express the sentiments he'd kept bottled up for years, wanted to make her a permanent fixture in his life.

But she deserved better. She deserved more than what he could offer her. She deserved a man who could devote his whole attention to her, who hadn't been a coward and hidden his schizophrenic mother from her.

"Is there something else on your mind?" Meredith asked.

He frowned and stared into the little bit of coffee remaining in his cup. "I had a meeting with your parents Monday. They want me to consider investing in a restaurant with them."

With what looked like a conscious effort, the remnants of her earlier frown disappeared. "Dad told me yesterday. It's a great opportunity for you. When would it happen?"

"I'm not sure. Forbes and I are supposed to be setting up a meeting to discuss the details." Major checked the carafe to see how much coffee remained before offering it to Meredith, but she waved him off.

"I knew this would happen eventually. You're too good to be kept from the general public by catering B-G events for the rest of your life."

"Thanks."

"It kills me to say this, but you have to do it. You've been wanting to open a restaurant for so long."

Major leaned back and hooked his arm around the top of the vacant chair beside him, all the fear and doubt that had kept him awake at night returning. "Meredith, you're one of the closest friends I have. I can't tell your parents or Forbes this, but I don't know what to do. I'm afraid."

An odd expression crossed her face before sympathy replaced it. "Afraid of what?"

"Failure. Of disappointing your parents. Of disappointing all those VIPs I met at your folks' house Monday."

The corner of her mouth quirked up. "And you've never worried about that here? I'm jealous."

Through the jocularity of her tone, her words hit home. "I guess. . .I guess because here I've always been working on someone else's orders—working someone else's plan—I've never had the sense of being completely responsible for the success or failure of an event. Not the way I would be as the person in charge of everything at a restaurant."

Meredith didn't say anything for a long moment. "This is probably going to sound like a patronizing question, but have you prayed about it?"

"Nonstop since I left their house."

"What is God telling you to do?"

"I'm not sure. A verse keeps running through my head, but I'm not sure how to interpret it."

"What verse?" She stood and crossed to her desk and sat at the computer.

" 'For to everyone who has, more shall be given, and he will have an abundance; but from the one who does not have, even what he does have shall be taken away.' I think it's in Matthew somewhere." He moved around and leaned against the edge of the desk where he could see her screen. He recognized the Web site she accessed—he used it all the time when it was his turn to lead Bible study, or when he filled in for the chaplain out at Beausoleil Pointe Center.

"Matthew 25:29, to be exact. It's in the parable of the talents—where the master gave each of three slaves some money. . . ."

"Two went out and doubled what they received; the third hoarded his and did nothing useful with it." Major dragged his fingers through his hair. "So is God telling me that if I don't take this opportunity, I'm acting like that third slave who risked nothing?"

Meredith turned to face him. "In my experience, faith is a lot like the money Jesus was talking about. Unless you use it—unless you invest it in some worthy endeavor—it will never grow. It'll never do you any good." She looked back at the screen. "Did you read this verse—15?"

" 'To one he gave five talents, to another, two, and to another, one, each according to his own ability. . . .'"

"'According to his own ability.'" Meredith repeated. "Do you think maybe *that's* what God is trying to tell you? He is rewarding your ability and wants you to go out and invest that reward?"

He squeezed her shoulders. "Thanks." His phone beeped, and he angled it from his belt to see the screen. "That's Steven wondering where I am."

"Reports by noon?"

"I'll send everything to your assistant." He loaded up the remnants of their breakfast onto the cart and departed—but turned to take one last look over his shoulder from the door.

Meredith sat at her desk, face buried in her hands.

His insides twisted around all that food he'd just eaten, hating himself for having caused pain to the woman he desired to please above all else.

Meredith pounded the backspace key on the computer's keyboard. She'd made the same spelling mistake five times while typing the memo that would go to her parents along with the spreadsheet her assistant was even now finalizing. Her brain buzzed with everything Major had told her this morning, and her emotions swung from despair at the thought of Major leaving B-G to start a restaurant to frustration and anger that her parents—Mom, most likely—had once again made a major decision that would impact one of the divisions in Meredith's department without alerting Meredith first.

She had no delusions that her parents would seek her advice or input on something like asking Major to appear on TV weekly, adding to his already overloaded schedule. But they could have at least informed her of their decision ahead of time so she didn't come across looking like such a complete imbecile in front of Major.

"Oh, for mercy's sake!" She smacked the edge of her keyboard with the heels of her hands when she misspelled the seafood vendor's name a sixth time.

"Everything okay, Meredith?" Corie, her administrative assistant, hesitated in the doorway, a thick folder in her hands.

"Just frustrated with myself." Meredith turned away from the computer and reached for the bottle of soda that usually sat next to her phone—but she hadn't replenished her stock yesterday. "What's up?"

Corie crossed the office and extended the folder. "I finished the spreadsheet and e-mailed it to you. Here's all the receipts and invoices."

"Does that include everything from catering?" Meredith took the file and set it on her desk without looking at it. Though just seven months out of college, Corie was the most efficient and organized assistant Meredith had ever had.

"Yes. Major got everything to me this morning."

"And the payroll report?"

"Included."

"Really? I was expecting to have to get on the phone with HR this afternoon and pull rank to get the information from them before deadline." Finally, something was going right today.

Corie filled her in on everything she'd done to get the report finished before the end of the day so Meredith could take it home to work on over the weekend.

"Good job. I owe you lunch big-time." Meredith glanced at the clock. "It's four o'clock. All I have left is to finish the memo, so if you don't have anything else you need to do today, why don't you go ahead and knock off early."

"Thanks, boss!" Corie bounced out of the office.

Once more, Meredith reached for the soda bottle, only to find empty air. "Good grief." She dug into her purse and pulled out a handful of coins.

"Did I miss something?" Corie asked when Meredith came out of the office.

"Nope. I just need a Coke."

"I can go get it for you." The assistant put her tote down on her desk.

"That's sweet. But you go on home. I'm perfectly capable of going down to the shop and getting a drink." No way was Meredith going to become one of those spoiled executives whose assistant did nothing but get her coffee, pick up her dry cleaning, and answer her phone—like her mother's executive assistant.

"I'll walk down with you."

On the five-flight trek down the stairs, at Meredith's inquiry, Corie talked about her plans for the weekend, which included a trip to Baton Rouge for a concert of some band Meredith had never heard of. Once they reached the first floor, Meredith bade the girl farewell and crossed the large, atrium-style lobby to the coffee shop–newsstand–convenience store.

"Afternoon, Miss Guidry."

She greeted the cashier and made a beeline for the refrigerated cases at the back of the small shop. She vacillated between ginger ale and root beer and finally chose Cherry Coke instead, figuring the caffeine would help with the dull headache she'd been trying to ignore all day. Plus, she wasn't sure how late she'd be out tonight, so the boost might be helpful.

She paid and headed back toward the bank of elevators—but was diverted when she saw one of her building maintenance managers and a couple of his guys at the security desk. When she joined them, the manager explained that several complaints had been made about trip-and-fall accidents on the twelfth floor near where new tenants were remodeling their office space.

Meredith tucked the information away to ask about in the facilities staff meeting on Monday if the manager forgot to mention it.

Back in her office, fortified with caffeine and sugar, Meredith returned to the report, recapping everything that happened from planning through execution of the New Year's Eve gala. Finally, at a quarter of five, she e-mailed the memo and spreadsheet to herself at home, then stuffed the folder of receipts and invoices into her bag.

She switched over to her e-mail program. . .and groaned. More than a hundred unread e-mails just since lunchtime. She scanned the subject lines. Nothing vitally important that couldn't wait until Monday. She shut down the computer and reached for the phone.

As she took a long swig of soda while listening to her twelve new voicemail messages, her eye caught on the garment bag hanging from the coat hook on the back of the door. Her stomach gave a little flip. In half an hour, Ward Breaux would arrive to take her on a date. A *date*.

She wrote down the messages on the page for Monday in her planner. Finished with those, she scanned the sticky notes scattered around her desk and stuck to the sides of her computer monitor. Half of them referenced completed projects, so she threw them away. The rest she stuck to the appropriate pages in her planner to deal with next week.

The phone rang, and she picked it up without looking at the caller ID window. "Events and Facilities Management. This is Meredith Guidry."

"Well, hello there, Meredith Guidry." Ward Breaux's voice sent goosebumps racing down Meredith's arms. "I just wanted to give you a heads-up that I left my job site earlier than I thought, so I'm probably going to be there about ten or fifteen minutes early. I hope that doesn't mess up your schedule."

She glanced at her watch. "No, I was just wrapping things up, as a matter of fact."

"Great. I'll see you in a few minutes then."

As soon as she hung up, Meredith jumped up from her desk and closed her door so she could change clothes. The dress was something Anne had talked her into buying a couple of years ago, and it had hung in Meredith's closet ever since. The chocolate brown matte-silk sheath topped with a three-quarter sleeve bolero had a very 1940s vibe to it, which was the only reason she'd been cajoled into buying it. Her round-toed brown pumps had a similar retro feel to them. She hoped she didn't look like she was wearing a costume.

Hanging the gray tweed suit in the garment bag, Meredith slipped into the marble and cherry powder room that connected her office with her mother's. She added a little makeup—but didn't go for the full war paint that she wore for formal events—and let her hair down from the clip she'd pulled it back with at the height of her frustration this afternoon.

The intercom on her phone buzzed. She jogged over to grab the receiver.

"Miss Guidry, there's a Ward Breaux here to see you."

"Yes, thank you. I'll be out in a moment."

Heart trying to make a jailbreak through her rib cage, she grabbed the small purse she'd tucked into her larger bag that morning, draped her burgundy wool car coat over her arm, and left the security of her office.

Most of the lights were out except for in the main hallway and the reception area, which the girls were getting ready to close down. Standing with his hands clasped behind his back, engrossed in the images of all the Boudreaux-Guidry properties mounted on the wall, was Ward Breaux. His charcoal overcoat made him look even larger than she remembered, and instead of the jeans and boots she'd seen him in before, dark pants and shiny black shoes showed beneath the hem of the coat.

She stopped, stomach knotted, and nearly turned tail and ran back to her office. No. She could do this. She *needed* to do this.

"Ward." Could she have sounded more breathless? She moved forward and extended her right hand. "It's good to see you again."

"Meredith." His grin was somewhat lopsided. She hadn't noticed that before. His large hand wrapped around hers, not in a businesslike handshake, but as if he were going to raise it to kiss the back of it. "When I met you, I thought you were beautiful. But I was wrong. You're gorgeous."

Her toes curled in their cramped confines. Heat prickled her face, knowing the two receptionists were gawking at them. "Thanks."

"Ready to go?" He turned and swept his arm toward the main doors.

"Yes." She allowed him to take her coat and assist her into it, and her breathing hitched when he settled his hand in the middle of her back to walk her to the door. Deep smile lines appeared in his cheeks when she looked up at him.

The front door swung open before they got to it. Meredith stopped, mortified.

Of anyone who could possibly walk through those doors at five twenty on a Friday evening, why, oh why, did it have to be Major O'Hara?

CHAPTER 8

$\mathcal{M}$ajor stopped and did a double take of the couple standing in front of him. Some guy had his arm around Meredith—who looked absolutely stunning. Something hot and sticky and. . .and. . .green oozed through every piece of Major's being.

She had the decency to blush almost as dark red as her coat. "Major? Did you need something?"

The temptation to hide the Styrofoam box behind his back and make up some other excuse for his presence made his hand start to shake. How could he have forgotten she'd mentioned she had plans tonight?

"I—one of the sauté chefs didn't show up, so we got into the weeds this afternoon, and I forgot. . ." He held up the box. "I forgot to bring you a dinner box."

"Oh." An expression that looked quite close to pity flickered across Meredith's face. She glanced at her companion then back at Major. "It'll keep till Monday, won't it?"

He was the biggest idiot in the world. "Yeah. . .yes, it should. I'll put it in the fridge in the executive kitchen just to make sure it stays cold enough."

"Thanks. I have so many meetings on Monday, it'll be nice to know I don't have to worry about scrounging up lunch." She twisted the shoulder strap of her briefcase with her left hand.

When Meredith again glanced at the man beside her, Major turned his attention in that direction as well. Because he was six foot one, not many men made Major feel short—but this guy did. He towered over Meredith, even in her high heels, by almost a foot.

"I'm sorry. I should have introduced you. Major, this is Ward Breaux. Ward—Major O'Hara, B-G's executive chef."

The curly-haired giant didn't even have the decency to take his left arm from around Meredith when he shook Major's hand.

"So, how do you two know each other?" Major cringed, but the words were out of his mouth before he could stop them.

"I had the very good fortune of running into Meredith at the hardware store on New Year's Day. I knew it must be fate—how often does a guy run into a gorgeous lady like this buying wood epoxy on a holiday?" Breaux smiled down at Meredith with a proprietary gleam in his dark eyes.

Molten heat roiled in Major's stomach. "Really?"

Meredith cleared her throat. "Ward is a contractor. He's going to give me a bid for finishing the work on my house."

"Oh." That didn't explain why Meredith was wearing a silk dress and looking like a movie star.

"Yes—but I do have to admit, I'm much more interested in the *owner* of the house right now." The interloper glanced at his watch—and returned his arm around Meredith's waist. "If we're going to make our six o'clock reservations, we should go."

"I'll put this away for you." Major wanted to draw her into his arms and show his previous claim but settled for giving her the warmest smile he could muster. "I'll see you Monday."

"Bye."

He turned when he reached the executive dining room, hoping to see Meredith watching him with longing in her gaze. But she and Breaux were already disappearing through the frosted-glass doors.

"Stupid, stupid, stupid, stupid," he mumbled, making his way through the dining room by the dim light from the cityscape beyond the windows. In the kitchen, he felt his way along in the dark until he found the handle on the door of the reach-in refrigerator.

The reception lobby was dark when he came out, and he had to unlock the doors to exit. He fished his keys out of his pocket and locked up before heading toward the elevators. They took too long, so he opted for the stairs instead.

He should have been happy for Meredith finding time to date, having a social life, allowing room for romance in her busy schedule. But seeing her with another man only made Major want to make her part of his life all the more.

Who was he kidding? He'd seen the amount of work she was taking home with her to do this weekend. If he had the added pressure of getting a restaurant started, not only would his social life become nearly nonexistent, but what little personal time he might have would need to be spent with Ma. He had to let go of Meredith.

Knowing his brain wasn't going to easily let go of the image of Meredith with the Jolly Green Giant, he pointed Kirby toward Beausoleil Pointe Center.

The receptionists greeted him by name at the front desk, and many of the residents did the same as he made his way to Ma's apartment. When she didn't answer the door, he walked down the hall to the common room.

"Major, what are you doing here?" Ma looked up from her hand of cards when he approached her table.

"I came to see you."

"Today isn't your regular day to come. I'm busy. You'll have to come back another day."

After all these years, his mother telling him to go away shouldn't have stung like it did. But after being rejected by Meredith a little while ago, albeit in a roundabout fashion, it hurt that the person he was giving Meredith up for didn't want to see him either.

"Fine. You know how to reach me if you change your mind."

He trudged back out to the Jeep and squealed the tires a bit pulling out of the parking lot. If he were already running a restaurant, he'd be there on a Friday night and not worrying about how the two women in his life didn't want him. He also wouldn't have to face the fact that he'd done such a good job of keeping everyone out of his personal affairs that he found himself in this situation.

Would it really be so terrible if Meredith knew about Ma?

Major's mind went back to the last time his mother had a real, full-blown schizophrenic episode. He shuddered. Yes, it really would be so terrible if Meredith had to witness that. Just like the few other women he'd dated, if she found out, she would look at him in disgust, wondering when that was going to happen to him—and then hightail it out of there. And he wouldn't blame her. There were times he wished he could do the same.

He stopped at the international market on the way home and picked up a bunch of random, interesting ingredients. Back at the condo, he put *The Fighting Seabees* DVD on and started cooking—thinking about and planning for what he might put on the menu of his restaurant.

The opportunity offered by the Guidrys looked more and more like the only future Major had.

"You've hardly touched your *cordero*."

Meredith cut another small piece of the braised lamb. Cooked with honey, garlic, and onions, and topped with crumbled Cabrales cheese, the strong flavors burst in her mouth. But nerves kept her from enjoying it as she should.

She set her fork and knife on the edge of the plate and raised her napkin to wipe her mouth. "I think I ate too much of the tapas. Of course, they gave me enough of this"—she indicated the large lamb chop atop a mound of garlic mashed potatoes—"to feed three people." And plenty to take a sample to Major, who always liked trying new dishes.

Her chest once again felt like it would cave in at the memory of the look on Major's face when he'd seen her with Ward. Had she imagined the flicker of jealousy in his eyes?

Ward waved the server over and asked for a takeaway box. "And two flans for dessert with *café con leche*." He gave Meredith a slow smile.

She couldn't help but smile back at him, though his high-handed manner was starting to grate on her nerves a bit. Just because they were in a Spanish restaurant and he spoke the language didn't mean she couldn't order for herself.

Nevertheless, it was kind of charming and old-fashioned in its way. And if she were out with Major, she'd allow him to order for her. But of course, she had good reason to trust Major implicitly when it came to food.

"You were telling me about your college major," Ward reminded her.

"Art history. I specialized in the arts and crafts movement."

"Thus your love of the craftsman style of architecture?"

"Yes. I've wanted a craftsman bungalow since I was a little girl." She grinned. "And now I have one."

"One that isn't livable." His dark brows arched over gray eyes twinkling with amusement.

His flirtatiousness had made her uncomfortable at the beginning of the meal, but now she rather enjoyed the focused attention. "But you're going to help me remedy that, aren't you?"

"I'll do my best."

"I do have one request—I'd like to ask Major O'Hara to help with the kitchen design. He worked with the architects who designed the kitchens at B-G—the large one for Vue de Ceil and the smaller executive kitchen—and I've seen some of his ideas for his dream home kitchen that I hope to incorporate in my house." Of course, when she'd originally come up with this idea, it had been with the thought in mind that the kitchen might one day be his, if he ever woke up and realized she was in love with him.

No. She couldn't allow herself to think like that anymore. He'd had eight years. She couldn't waste any more time on him.

"That's an excellent idea. When we get to that point, I'll be happy to work with him." Ward looked down at his buzzing phone.

Meredith grimaced but quickly schooled her expression. While Ward hadn't actually answered his cell phone during dinner, several times he'd looked down when it vibrated to see who was calling him. She'd have to check with Anne and Jenn, but she was under the impression that proper etiquette was to turn one's cell phone off when out on a date. That's why hers was currently just a deadweight in the bottom of her purse.

He glanced across at her. Some of what she was thinking must have shown in her expression.

"Sorry. I'll turn this off. I'm such a phone addict, it's hard for me to ignore it." He looked up and leaned back when the server brought their desserts.

The baked custard with the burnt-sugar syrup was almost as good as Anne's favorite dessert—crème brûlée—but not quite as good as cheesecake. She savored each bite slowly.

"If you majored in art history, how did you end up becoming a big-time corporate executive? I mean, I know it's your parents' company and all, but it seems like you'd have gone into some kind of design work, or maybe become curator at an art gallery."

"I thought about that—actually, I minored in interior design as an undergrad." She put her spoon down after about half of the rich dessert. "When I finished my master's degree, I was ready to get out of Mom and Dad's house, to live on my own. But the part-time job I had at the city art museum wasn't enough to pay rent and utilities and buy groceries."

She tried not to stare at the way Ward's long, tapered fingers curled around his spoon. She could get used to eating out with him.

Clearing her throat, she continued. "At that time, my cousin Anne was the event planner for B-G—and the company was much smaller then with just a couple of event venues. But they'd just acquired Lafitte's Landing, which almost doubled the amount of work Anne had to do, so she needed an assistant. And I needed a full-time job."

"And your cousin. . .she doesn't work there anymore?"

"She started her own wedding- and event-planning business

almost six years ago. As the only person left in the department, I was promoted."

"Now you're an executive director." He spooned up the last bit of syrup on his plate. "And from your title, it sounds like you do a whole lot more than planning events."

"Yeah." Meredith let out a sardonic chuckle. "I do a lot of paperwork."

"That's not what I meant, and you know it."

"It's my job. I do what's required of me." *And I try to live with the fact that my parents have no respect for my title or authority.*

"So the reason you bought a house that's gutted inside is because you wanted to get back to your first love—designing?"

She shrugged. "I guess that had something to do with it. I love renovation projects. I've done most of the interior renovations in the triplex."

"Triplex?"

"Where I live. About a year ago, Anne bought the old Victorian where we live—it's split into three apartments. She and my sister Jenn and I have lived in those apartments for five or six years." She sipped the café con leche—rich, bitter coffee tempered by scalded milk.

"You live with your cousin and your sister; you work for your parents. Do you ever get away from your family?"

"Get away from them?" She thought about the glorious hours she'd spent at her house Monday, relieved that after Anne's and Forbes's phone calls, everyone had left her alone. "Not very often. But I have a large family—immediate and extended—and we're all very close to each other."

"I'll bet I could beat you on family size. I'm one of six." Ward pushed his dessert plate aside and lifted the delicate china cup. It could have looked awkward in his large, calloused fingers, but he moved with grace, making it look as if he was accustomed to such finery.

"I have four brothers and three sisters." She pursed her lips together, daring him to challenge her, ready to pull out a family photo to prove it.

"You've got me there. Do they all live in town?"

"Every single one."

"Let me guess. You're the oldest?"

"Second. I have one older brother."

"And does he work for your parents' company as well?"

"No. He's a lawyer."

"A respectable choice if he wasn't going to go into the family business." He swirled the liquid in his cup. "You said your sister lives with you. I guess she's next oldest to you?"

"We don't actually live *together*—we do have separate apartments." Which was a good thing, given Jenn's penchant for not picking up after herself.

"Let me guess—doctor?"

Meredith laughed at the image of Jenn dealing with sick people. "Restaurateur. She owns The Fishin' Shack down in Comeaux."

"I've heard about that place. You'll have to take me there sometime."

Ward continued questioning her about her family until he'd heard what each of her brothers and sisters did, about Marci's engagement, and what Meredith knew of the plans for Anne's wedding.

When the bill arrived, Meredith reached for her purse.

"What are you doing?" Ward asked, his thick, dark brows drawn together.

"I...I guess I'm just used to going out with friends and having to pay my own way."

"If you haven't already figured it out, Meredith, I'm sort of an old-fashioned guy. Which means that when I ask a lady out on a date, I pick up the tab." He slipped a platinum card into the bill folder and laid it on the edge of the table.

A few minutes later, Ward helped her back into her coat and escorted her from the restaurant, carrying her takeaway box for her.

On the drive to Town Square, Meredith turned the tables on him and questioned him about his siblings, learning that two of his brothers worked in the construction business with him—one as a painting contractor, one as an electrician.

The Savoy was pretty crowded when they got there. She followed Ward through the forest of bodies, glad for his large size, as people tended to get out of his way. He left her at the table to go get beverages.

Meredith shrugged out of her coat and draped it across the back of her chair, glad to have a moment to reflect and regroup.

She liked Ward, was enjoying the evening with him. But being completely honest with herself, the chemistry just wasn't there. His lopsided grin didn't make her heart zing the way the faintest hint of a dimple in Major's cheek could.

Maybe it was just a matter of time. She'd known Major a lot longer. Maybe Ward just needed to grow on her.

She frowned at a sudden thought. She'd known Major for almost a decade, Ward for less than a week. Yet she already knew more about Ward's family than she knew about Major's. The only thing she knew for sure about Major was that he'd been raised by a single mother. She assumed he was an only child, since he never mentioned brothers or sisters. But he never really mentioned his mother, either, so she couldn't be sure. She knew his mom was still living—she'd overheard Forbes asking Major about his mother awhile back.

Maybe they'd had a falling-out. Maybe he didn't really see or talk to her anymore. Her heart ached for him and made her want to include him in her family all the more.

"Here you go. One Sprite with a twist of orange." Ward set her glass down on the table. "You looked so serious just a second ago. Everything okay?"

"Thanks. Yes, everything's fine. Just thinking about. . .a friend who isn't as fortunate as we are to have big, close-knit families." She took a large gulp of the soda, enjoying the tangy taste and the slight burn of the fizz going down her throat.

"There is a downside to families like ours." Ward twisted the cap off his bottle of sparkling water.

"What's that?"

"They're always in our business. You know, I didn't tell my brothers why I needed to leave the job site early this afternoon. I knew if I told them I was going on a date with a girl I picked up at the hardware store, there wouldn't have been an end to the grief they would have given me."

Meredith laughed. "I know exactly what you mean. I had dinner with some of my siblings and cousins last night, and there was no way I was going to tell them about tonight. Especially my older brother."

"Protective?"

"Yes—and somewhat high-handed. If he can't control something, he doesn't like it one bit."

Ward grinned, showing his perfect, ultrawhite teeth. "I think that's an affliction all oldest brothers have. I'm that way with my siblings—especially my sisters."

"It's one thing to be protective, but Forbes is actually a genuine control freak. I could tell you stories about him that would make you reconsider classing yourself in the same category with him as an oldest brother." Guilt over bad-mouthing her brother rushed in. "Now, don't get me wrong; I love my brother dearly—"

Ward leaned forward and caressed her cheek, stopping her excuse—and all coherent thought. "I understand."

Meredith sat frozen, mesmerized by the warmth in Ward's eyes. What was it about chemistry she'd been thinking a few minutes ago?

"Well, well, well. What's this?"

The all-too-familiar voice drew her out of her entrancement. She looked over Ward's shoulder and cringed to see Forbes, one hand on his hip, an inquisitive light in his eyes.

Ward turned to look.

No way to get out of the situation now. "Ward Breaux, this is my older brother, Forbes Guidry."

Ward stood and shook Forbes's hand enthusiastically. "We've just been talking about our families. It's wonderful to meet you. Won't you join us?"

Meredith's stomach felt as if it was about to reject that huge, expensive dinner she'd just eaten.

"Thank you, but no. I'm entertaining clients tonight. I just thought I'd come over and say hello."

"Hello, Forbes," Meredith said. "Good-bye."

He had the audacity to wink at her.

CHAPTER 9

"Can I catch a ride with you to church this morning?" Jennifer helped herself to a large mug of coffee.

"Hey—I haven't had any of that yet!" Meredith reached for the cup, but her sister twirled to keep it out of her reach. Typical.

"You can make more."

"I don't know how you're going to survive when we don't live in the same house." Meredith tightened the belt of her robe and crossed her arms.

Holding the cup to her lips, Jenn blew across the surface of the steaming liquid, sending a few drops of it over the opposite side. "I'll have you know I signed a lease on a house—not an apartment mind you—a house less than half a block from the restaurant."

Meredith stopped halfway through grabbing a napkin from the holder on the table and sank into the nearest chair. "You're moving to Comeaux?"

Jenn shrugged and slurped the coffee. "Why not? I'm at the restaurant eighty or so hours a week. It's wasteful for me to be driving the twenty or thirty miles back to an apartment in Bonneterre when I can walk to work. And the rent's a lot cheaper down there, too."

For all that Meredith had enjoyed teasing her sister over the past few months about how lost Jenn would be without being able to raid Meredith's or Anne's kitchens or catch a ride somewhere with one of them, she hadn't really thought through how *she* would feel without her sister so close by. They'd shared a room until Meredith was eighteen and moved into the dorms at college.

She swallowed hard against the emotion swelling in her throat. "When are you going to move?"

"The house won't be ready until March first. But I'm going to rent a storage unit down there and go ahead and start packing up books and stuff that I'm not using right now. That way I don't have quite as much to do when the time comes. What about you? Are you really going to hire someone to finish that house of yours?"

Meredith shook off the melancholy and crossed the small kitchen to the coffeepot. She poured what was left into her mug then started another half pot brewing. She added flavored, powdered creamer to her cup and stared into it as she stirred and the liquid turned a kind of grayish brown. She smirked, remembering the last time Major had seen her use powdered creamer in her coffee. He'd looked like he was about to be sick or cry—or both.

"Mere?"

"Who—oh, yeah, I've found a contractor."

Ward Breaux's darkly handsome features replaced Major's in her mind's eye. She'd had a surprisingly good time Friday night, and he'd been everything she'd always imagined a romantic date would be. As they said good-bye at her SUV in the parking garage, her heart had raced—with nervous energy only, she was certain—when for a moment she thought he was going to try to kiss her.

She touched the back of her right hand where his lips had landed instead.

"Are you even awake this morning?"

An oven mitt smacked the back of Meredith's head and knocked loose the towel wrapped around her wet hair. "Cut it out, will ya? I just have a lot on my mind." She turned and leaned her hip against the cabinet.

"So can I?" Jenn stood with her hand on the knob of the door out to the common stairwell.

"Can you what?"

Her younger sister heaved a dramatic sigh. "Look, I'm sorry I took your coffee—obviously you need it more than I do this morning. Can I get a *ride* with you to *church?*"

"Yeah. Of course. But if you're not down here ready to walk out the door at nine o'clock, I'm leaving without you."

"You say that every time, and you never do," Jenn called over her shoulder, leaving Meredith's door standing open.

"And every time, we walk in late wherever we're going." Meredith closed the door and sent up a quick prayer that Jenn would be better about closing doors—and locking them—when she lived by herself. Sometimes Meredith was amazed that Jennifer was thirty-two and owned a successful business instead of still seventeen and playing her way through high school.

She poured a full, fresh cup of coffee and carried it with her—but stopped in the middle of the living room. Jenn hadn't said anything to indicate she'd heard about Meredith's date Friday. More than twenty-four hours was usually ample time for everyone in the family to find out what one of their siblings had been up to.

Maybe, for once in his life, Forbes had decided to allow Meredith to have some semblance of a private life. He'd left the Savoy much earlier than Meredith and Ward had, and surprisingly, her brother hadn't called or e-mailed about it yesterday.

Worries about what Forbes might say to the rest of the family plagued her as she finished getting ready for church. Finally, dressed in a tailored suede jacket over a brown tweed skirt, she retrieved her Bible from the nightstand and took it and the pumps she'd worn Friday night into the kitchen.

A bowl of cereal and another cup of coffee later, she sat at the kitchen table, staring at the clock on the back of the stove as the minutes ticked away. At 8:55 she returned to the bathroom to brush her teeth and put lipstick on. At nine o'clock on the nose, she stepped into her shoes, grabbed her Bible and purse, and walked out to the SUV.

It only took ten minutes to get to church, and Sunday school never started at nine fifteen like it was supposed to. But she was tired of Jenn's taking advantage of her. Just like everyone else did.

At five minutes after nine when Jenn still hadn't appeared, Meredith started the engine. Movement caught her eye, and she waved at George, who pulled his car up behind Anne's on the parking apron. Anne appeared almost immediately, and they were off.

She shifted into reverse, feeling guilty that she was about to leave her sister behind. But Jenn had her own car; and since it wasn't raining, the fact that the ragtop leaked shouldn't be an issue.

Besides, what message was she sending Jenn if she didn't follow through on her threat? Jenn treated Meredith just like their parents did. They made decisions and just expected Meredith to go gladly along with them.

She backed out and drove away.

No more. She liked making people happy, but she wasn't going to let anyone walk all over her any longer. Not Mom and Dad. Not Jennifer. And not Major O'Hara.

Jenn didn't show up for Sunday school but caught Meredith in the vestibule outside the sanctuary before worship service.

"I can't believe you left without me."

Meredith raised her brows. "I warned you I would."

"But you didn't mean it. I was counting on you to call me, or else I wouldn't have gone back to bed."

"I guess you have less than two months to acclimate yourself to getting up and out the door on Sundays. Don't forget, it's going to take you half an hour to get here after you move."

Jenn rolled her eyes and flounced away like a petulant teen.

Forbes intercepted Jenn and gave her one of his headlock hugs, greeting her with a, "Hey, kiddo."

Jenn launched into blaming Meredith for making her late, and it looked like Forbes would take Jenn's side—as usual.

Meredith shook her head and moved into the sanctuary to the

opposite side from where she usually sat with her brother and sister in the midst of the singles group. Until now, she hadn't realized how juvenile Forbes's standard greeting for his sisters appeared.

A rustling beside Meredith caught her attention. Anne, followed by George, sidled in and sat beside her.

"Everything okay?" Anne didn't hug her, headlock her, kiss her, or touch her in any way.

Meredith appreciated it. "Just needed a break from the sibs."

Across the large sanctuary, Meredith's brothers and sisters gathered with the rest of the single adults and college students. Though some of the other people did hug each other in greeting, they were quick, almost perfunctory gestures.

"Anne, is my family abnormally touchy-feely?"

"What?"

"Do you think that my brothers and sisters are too physically affectionate?"

"You make it sound like something bad."

Meredith combed her teeth over her bottom lip but stopped when she tasted lipstick. "That's not what I mean."

Anne cast a sidelong glance at George—her fiancé sat a modest few inches away from her, and though his arm rested along the back of the pew behind Anne, it wasn't as if he really had his arm *around* her.

"Yeah," Anne drawled the syllable out. "You and the rest of your siblings tend to be a little more touchy-feely than what makes some people comfortable. But y'all practically lived on top of each other most of your lives. It was bound to make you extremely close and comfortable with your lack of personal space, or it could have made you hate each other and never want to be near each other once you grew up and left the house."

"I think it's why they have no respect for me," Meredith murmured.

"What do you mean? Of course they respect you."

Meredith gave her cousin her most exasperated look. "No, they don't. Everyone takes advantage of me. And it's because of what you said: no boundaries." She had to raise her voice slightly as the organist began playing the prelude. "How can my parents take me seriously as an executive in the company when Rafe comes in and tackles me on the sofa in front of them? Or Jenn makes me her alarm clock and chauffeur?"

The organ's bellowing almost drowned out the end of Meredith's question. She leaned closer to her cousin. "None of them treat you that way. And when you were in charge, Mom and Dad would never have made decisions affecting our department without discussing it with you first."

Anne reached over and laid her hands atop Meredith's balled fists. "I'm sorry you feel that way. Why don't we plan dinner early this week, and we can talk about it and figure out what you can do."

Anne's calm acceptance of what Meredith said reassured her, and Meredith stood to sing the first hymn with a lighter heart.

When the service ended, Meredith lagged behind the rest of her relatives, debating whether or not to skip the weekly gathering of the full extended family. But making the decision to stand up to her parents and siblings and then hiding from them seemed counterintuitive.

Aunt Maggie and Uncle Errol's house rang with voices when Meredith entered. All of the single and young adult cousins would be out in the sunroom. Meredith detoured into the kitchen where her grandmother, aunts, Anne, and a few older cousins and cousins' wives put final preparations on dinner. If any of them were surprised by Meredith's offer to help, they didn't let on.

Once seated at the enormous table, which fit everyone over college age, Meredith glanced around at her immediate family members with new eyes. Sunday dinner with the entire Guidry clan was a given—just like going to church or going to school when they were growing up. There were a few times Meredith had wished it otherwise: most especially her first few years out of college and in the singles group at church, when every week she turned down the invites to go out to lunch with them. Eventually, the invitations stopped.

She couldn't remember the last time she'd participated in a social activity that didn't consist of mainly her relatives. Ward's question Friday rang in her head. *Do you ever get away from your family?*

"Hey, earth to Meredith."

She snapped out of her thoughts when Marci poked her shoulder. The men had already cleared the table and disappeared into the kitchen to wash the dishes.

"It's your turn." Marci pushed her auburn hair back with her left hand, her engagement ring catching the light.

"My—oh. I had a rather uneventful week after the New Year's Eve gala was over. Lots of paperwork to do. Nothing exciting."

"Yeah, except leaving people stranded when they're counting on you for a ride." Jenn could pout with the best—worst?—of them.

Meredith tried to laugh it off. "Don't be so melodramatic. You have a car; you weren't stranded."

"The roof leaks—I told you."

"It isn't raining—" Frustration bubbled up in Meredith's chest, but she did her best to squelch it. Arguing with her sister over something so stupid wouldn't help gain her family's respect.

She turned to face her grandmother again. "Anyway, nothing too exciting." Should she tell them about Ward?

Marci's glittering diamond hinted that Meredith would come across as desperately trying to one-up her younger sister if she blurted out, "I went on my first real date ever."

Meredith refolded her napkin and set it on the table. "A friend and I went to the Savoy Friday night."

"The new jazz club?" Across the table, Anne leaned forward, blue eyes dancing. "George and I have been talking about going. How was it?"

Perfect, until Forbes showed up. "Great. Their house band could give anyone in New Orleans a run for their money. I'd never heard of the headline act, but they were great, too."

"Next time you go, let me know—George and I might tag along with you."

A double date? Meredith considered the possibility but dismissed it pretty quickly. Until she knew Ward better—and her tummy tingled at the idea—it might be nice to keep at least that small part of her life private. Because once everyone found out about him, they would bombard her with questions and would want her to bring him to Thursday night supper or Sunday dinner so they all could meet him.

Before she could think of an excuse to leave the table, the male members of the family returned, signaling it was time to head home. She'd just started to push her chair back and disappear in the general melee, but the chair bumped into something and wouldn't budge.

Hands clamped onto her shoulders in a squeeze. She hunched her shoulders and pulled away, slipping sideways from the chair to stand up.

A confused frown formed an upside-down Y between Forbes's eyebrows. "What's with you today?"

"I don't know what you're talking about." Meredith skirted around her brother and tried to escape. She made it to the quiet of the front foyer before Forbes caught up with her.

"Meredith, stop."

"Please don't tell me what to do." She hooked her arm through her purse straps and dug out her keys.

"I'm not trying to order you around. I just want to find out why you're mad at the world today."

She sighed. No one in the family—least of all control-freak Forbes—would easily understand her sudden need for privacy. "Just because I don't feel like being touched doesn't mean I'm angry. I simply need my personal space."

Forbes folded his arms. "Personal space I can understand. But running off this morning after you told Jenn she could ride to church with you?"

"Forbes, she's thirty-two years old! She's not a teenager anymore. And she needs to start taking responsibility for her own life and for getting herself the places she needs to go."

"This doesn't sound like you, Mere."

"Well, it is me. Or at least the me I am when I'm not trying to be the person everyone else thinks I *should* be."

One of Forbes's brows arched up. "No one has ever asked you to be something you're not."

Meredith matched his crossed-arm stance. "Really? Then why is Mom still mad that I bought a house that needed to be renovated— and that I chose to do it myself?" Moisture burned her eyes, but she blinked it away. "No one in this family really knows me, knows who I am—except Anne—and I'm tired of having to hide behind this veneer of the perfect daughter, the one who never stands up for herself, the one who always defers to someone else's decision or opinion." She caught her breath before she hyperventilated. "I'm tired of constantly trying to please everyone else. And I know that sounds selfish, and maybe I am. But that's what's 'up' with me today."

Sadness filled her brother's blue-gray eyes. "I wish you'd said something before you got to the point where this has hurt you so much." He reached for her, but Meredith stepped back.

The hurt expression that replaced the sadness nearly made Meredith feel guilty. "I'm sorry, but I need space. I need time—time away from being with the family every waking minute—to figure out who I really am, to figure out what it is I truly want out of life."

Forbes looked as if he wanted to argue, but he restrained himself at great effort. "I understand. And I'll try to cover for you with the family while you sort things through. But I hope you know that I'm here for you—for the *real* you—no matter what. You can tell me anything."

"Thanks." She smiled, keeping her lips pressed tightly together to keep the bottom one from quivering. Not wanting to leave things between them quite so tense, she cast around for something to lighten the mood.

Of course.

"Oh, and I'd like to also thank you for not saying anything to the family about Friday night. I already know that rumors are going to get around at the office—since he picked me up there and several people saw him." Including Major, which still wrenched Meredith's heart. "But I'd rather not have the family know just yet that I went out on a date."

Forbes tried his best to look offended. "I? You think that I would immediately run off and tell everyone that I caught you out on a date with someone we've never met before?" Humor danced around his mouth. "I'll make you a deal. You tell me all about him, and I'll keep it to myself until you're ready for the family to know."

She sighed and shook her head. Change wasn't going to come easily. She just hoped she was up for the challenge.

CHAPTER 10

"*P*lease tell me my face isn't really that puffy."

"No, Chef."

"Of course not, Chef."

Somehow, Major didn't believe Steven and Jana's denials. There, for all of Bonneterre to see, his pudgy face filled the TV screen. Sure, the antique-reproduction wardrobe behind him looked good. The bright lights hadn't washed him out as much in the burgundy coat as it would have if he'd worn the white one, but he couldn't deny that he looked like a chipmunk on an acorn binge.

"I don't think I can watch the rest of this. Y'all can stay and watch the whole thing, but don't forget, we have lunch service going on right now."

Eyes glued to the TV, his sous chef and head server waved him out of his own office.

"You can handle it, boss." Steven moved from the edge of the desk into Major's chair without even looking at him.

Indeed, the kitchen and waitstaff had Monday lunch service well under control. Major headed out into the main room and walked from table to table, chatting with regulars and introducing himself to those he'd never met before. News about this year-old project seemed to be spreading around downtown, and people working in nearby buildings had started coming to Vue de Ceil for weekday lunches, since they would probably never get another chance to see the famed event venue. After all, this was where local-boy-turned-movie-star Cliff Ballantine had held his wedding reception last year.

Not only was Major happy his idea had proved a good one, making him look even better to the Guidrys, but he was happy that it had allowed people like Steven and Jana—who'd been his most loyal part-timers—to work for him full-time instead of just when he needed them for events. And the Guidrys had been happy to put Vue de Ceil to use five days a week, instead of having it sitting empty for weeks and even months at a time.

If only he could have this kind of success in the restaurant's first year. His stomach twisted. That had been a line of questioning he hadn't expected from Alaine Delacroix last week. Obviously, Mrs. Guidry had filled the reporter in on every aspect of it except one: that Major hadn't officially accepted the offer yet.

A flicker of light to his left caught his attention. One set of the reflective elevator doors slid open to reveal Anne Hawthorne, along with several other people—including Meredith. Major tugged the hem of his coat to straighten it and resisted the urge to run his fingers through his hair.

In a bright blue sweater, Meredith reminded him of a soothing waterfall. He tried to smile at her when she looked over at him; she smiled back but glanced away again quickly. Avoiding her at church yesterday had been easy, since he always went to the early service and a late Sunday school class; and looking at her now, he couldn't help but see her standing next to that guy Friday night, dressed to the nines and looking too beautiful for words.

He met them at the perimeter of the room.

"As you can see," Meredith told the potential clients, "Vue de Ceil definitely has enough capacity to host your event, with room to seat everyone at four- and eight-person tables, if that's what you want." She barely spared Major a glance, as if embarrassed to meet his eye again.

Anne stepped forward. "This is Major O'Hara, executive chef for all events held at Boudreaux-Guidry properties." Anne introduced her clients—a bride who appeared to be hardly out of high school, along with her parents, future mother-in-law, and a couple of grandmothers.

"Oh yes! I was at the New Year's ball just a few days ago," the future mother-in-law gushed. "What a wonderful spread of food. If that's the quality we can look forward to, I definitely recommend this place."

"Thank you, ma'am." Why wouldn't Meredith look at him? "It's my goal to try to serve the best food possible at every event—to make it delicious and memorable."

"That's just what we want," said the mother of the bride. She turned to Anne. "When do you think we can get this booked and set up the menu?"

Anne raised her eyebrows in question to Meredith.

"We can go back down to my office now and look at dates for your event. Once we have that scheduled, Chef O'Hara will develop several sample menus for you to choose from. After that, we'll set up a tasting."

This seemed to please everyone, and Meredith herded them back to the elevator.

"Are we still on for two o'clock tomorrow afternoon?" Anne asked, slowly bringing up the rear of the group.

"Yeah." Major frowned. Something was definitely wrong with Meredith. Was she afraid he was going to ask her about her date Friday? "I'll bring the cost analyses for the menus we talked about."

Anne nodded. "All right. I'll see you then." She glanced over her shoulder at Meredith, who was engrossed in listening to something one of the grandmothers said. "Yes, we have a lot to talk about." The elevator whisked her away before Major could ask her to clarify that last statement.

Shaking his head, he went back to the kitchen. Steven and Jana came out of his office laughing, though their amusement died as soon as they saw him.

"Great interview, Chef." Steven smirked.

Jana elbowed Steven hard enough to send him off balance. "It was a good interview. But why didn't you tell us you're starting a restaurant?"

Major groaned. So much for asking Alaine not to include that part in what she aired. "It's not a done deal. I'm still thinking about it."

"What's to think about?" Jana's eyes widened. "Chef, it's a great opportunity. You'd be wonderful at running a restaurant. And there are a lot of folks here who'd love to work in a restaurant owned by you."

Major studied Steven's face. Was his second in command thinking about the day when he'd be running this kitchen? A chill ran down Major's spine at the thought. Though Steven was a good chef, his people-management skills left a lot to be desired.

He looked back at Jana. In a restaurant environment, she could make three or four times as much money as she did working this lunch service every day. Everyone in the industry knew that people didn't spend as much or tip as well at lunch as they did for supper— even when ordering off the same menu. Yes, he would definitely take Jana with him.

"As I said, nothing has been decided yet. Believe me, when the decision is made, y'all will be amongst the first to know." He stepped aside. "Now, please get back to work so I don't have to fire you for slacking off."

Sitting at his desk, Major stared at the blank TV screen, wondering if he really wanted to watch the recording of the program when he got home tonight. Just what had he gotten himself into, agreeing to appear on television? Not just the interview, but every week. Would the potential for publicity really be worth the public humiliation?

"Hey. I'm not late am I?"

Meredith jumped at Major's voice, her pen striking a blue mark across the page before her. "N–no. I'm just making a list of everything we need to get done today."

A soft smile hinted at his dimples; Meredith ignored her squirmy stomach—just as she tried to ignore the fact that the dark green shirt he wore made his eyes a vivid violet-blue.

"So, what's on the agenda?"

What? Oh, right. Meeting. "Hearts to HEARTS: menu and final food budget, staffing requirements, space planning. . ." She let her voice drift when her mother appeared in the doorway.

"Oh good, Major, you're here already. Would you both step into my office?"

"Of course." Meredith glanced at Major, who looked as if he shared her confusion. She took her pen and legal pad with her. At the threshold to her mother's elaborate office, Meredith hesitated, and Major bumped into her.

One of the most beautiful women she'd ever seen sat in front of her mother's desk. Black hair lay tumbled in voluptuous curls around the woman's shoulders—the kind of curls Meredith had prayed for every time she'd subjected her own poor fine, limp hair to perms back in her teens.

Pushing envy aside, she slapped a smile on, armed herself with professional confidence, and strode into the office. The woman stood and extended her right hand.

"Alaine Delacroix," Mom said, beginning the introduction, "this is Meredith Guidry, our executive director of events and facilities."

"It's very nice to meet you." The name clicked in Meredith's memory. "Alaine Delacroix—from Channel Six?"

Perfect, full lips parted to reveal dazzling white teeth. "Yes. It's nice to meet you, too. I've heard so many wonderful things about you—about how you're practically a miracle worker when it comes to planning these social events everyone wants to attend."

Dreaded heat tingled in Meredith's cheeks. She hated that compliments still made her blush at her age.

Alaine looked over Meredith's shoulder, and her nearly black eyes sparkled like diamond-studded onyx. "Hello, Chef."

Meredith's heart crashed into an iceberg and succumbed to

hypothermia. Stepping aside, she avoided looking at Major, not wanting to see the drool hanging from his mouth at the reporter's overly warm greeting. She followed her mother to the table and sat.

Ever the gentleman, Major waited to sit until all three ladies had taken their places.

"Alaine is here"—Mom looked from Major to Meredith— "because she has come up with an idea that I'm really excited about. Alaine, why don't you explain it?"

"I'd be happy to, Mrs. Guidry."

"Oh, please, it's Mairee."

Alaine's smile beamed at Mom. Meredith thought she might be ill. She could handle when her mom turned on the fake charm for gold key clients. But she wasn't sure she could stomach these two women fawning over each other.

"The idea actually came to me because of meeting you, Chef O'Hara." The dark eyes twinkled at Major again. "I thought it would be a good idea to create a news special on all of the planning that goes into the Hearts to HEARTS banquet. Kind of like the shows they do on the food channel—but not just about the food. About everything that goes into the event."

"That's where you come in, Meredith." Mom leaned forward, more excited than she'd been when Meredith landed the contract for Senator Kyler's inauguration ball. "Alaine is going to set up a time to talk to you so you can explain everything you've already done. And she's brought her cameraman with her today so that they can observe your planning meeting."

Meredith balled her hands together in her lap and tried to maintain a neutral expression. "I'll do whatever I can to help." A reporter following her around, scrutinizing every decision she made? Great. Just great.

"Now, Major, the other part involves you," Mom continued. "Alaine is to be given access to the kitchen during the week before the event so she can get footage of y'all making everything, so you'll need to let her know that schedule. Oh, and you two still need to work out the schedule for the weekly cooking segment on her program."

Meredith swallowed hard, gritting her teeth against the desire to ask why she'd ever been made an executive director if Mom and Dad were going to continue making these kinds of decisions without consulting her. Meredith was beginning to believe Anne hadn't been completely honest about why she'd decided to leave B-G and start her own business.

"Major, if you can come back when you and Meredith finish your meeting, we'll discuss the details." Mom placed her palms flat on the tabletop and stood. "I know you have a lot of work to do, so I'll let you get to it. Alaine, Major, if you'll go ahead, I need a few words with Meredith."

Partially out of her chair, Meredith sank back into it, pulse thudding. Had she not done a good enough job hiding her reactions to her mother's pronouncements?

Mom made sure the door closed firmly behind Alaine and Major before rejoining Meredith at the table. "I have a couple of questions now that I've had time to dig into your report." She flipped open her thick planner.

Meredith cringed. If Mom took the time to write everything down, this would be no quick chat.

"First, you sort of glazed over this in our meeting earlier, but the final financial report. . . I noticed the expenditure was nearly twenty percent below last year's. What happened?"

Any other employer would have been praising Meredith for saving the company money, not questioning her as if she'd done something wrong. "I spent a lot more time this year negotiating rates and working out trade agreements."

"No cutting corners anywhere? Nothing that takes advantage of anyone?"

Disbelief and shock pulled at Meredith's bottom jaw, and she stared at her mother. "I would never compromise my integrity—nor B-G's—like that."

"Calm down. I'm not saying you did. I was just confused by how the final number could have been that much lower." Mom looked back down at her list, asked about some of the complaints detailed in the report: valet parking attendants too slow; tables bussed too fast; band too loud; lights too dim—"Pretty much the same complaints as at every event, so just keep working on that."

Same complaints. . .probably by the same people. Meredith scrawled something illegible on her notepad as if taking it seriously.

Mom studied her notes for a moment then closed the planner. "It's come to my attention that you've been keeping something from me."

Ward. Of course. The receptionists had no doubt blabbed about his coming here to pick her up. She hated the idea that her personal life was fodder for watercooler gossip around the office. But she also knew her mother's way of getting information out of people. "What are you talking about?"

"Jenn told me you've hired a contractor for your house."

Defensive words gathered in a ball in the back of Meredith's throat. "What? Oh, yeah—well, I haven't officially hired him. I ran into him at the hardware store last Monday and asked for a bid."

"I can't tell you what a relief that is to me." Mom smiled—the first real smile she'd shown since Meredith entered the room. "I probably haven't told you, but the only reason I counseled you against buying that house is because I thought you would be stubborn and insist on doing everything yourself. I can't wait to see it when it's finished."

Relief tripped up Meredith's thoughts. "Thanks, Mom."

"You're welcome. Now, best not keep Alaine and Major waiting any longer."

"Right." Meredith took her notepad and returned to her own office, smiling. But her good mood vanished as soon as she walked in. Alaine sat in Meredith's regular place at the table, having what looked like an intimate conversation with Major.

"How's that? Can you see both of our faces?" Alaine asked.

The guy behind the camera gave a thumbs-up, and Alaine stood. "Oh, Meredith, I didn't hear you come in. We're ready to get started whenever you are." Alaine waved Meredith toward the table. Toward *Meredith's* table in *Meredith's* office.

Meredith turned around, pretending to look for something on her desk. She closed her eyes and drew a deep breath, reaching as far down inside as she could to draw upon whatever confidence she could find in this situation. She couldn't let this woman's beauty and command of the situation rob her of what little professionalism she had left. She caught sight of the tube of her favorite tinted lip balm next to her phone and quickly swiped a little on.

"We're mostly here to get footage of you two working together. That will become part of a montage with a voice-over, most likely. Meredith, if you don't mind, after you're finished, I'd love to do an on-camera interview with you to get caught up on everything you've already done."

"I don't mind." Good. Her voice hadn't sounded as if she'd been inhaling helium. She took her seat and avoided making eye contact with Major. She couldn't let him see how much this was getting to her.

"Remember, just pretend like we're not even here."

"Right." Meredith scooted her stack of files closer. "Okay. Menu and final food budget. . ."

Even though Major seemed to have no problem ignoring Alaine and the camera and the big, fuzzy microphone catching every word they uttered, Meredith had never been so uncomfortably aware of her body in her life: her hands, her legs—should she cross them or just her ankles?—her facial expressions, her posture.

"Next week, the board and Mrs. Warner are coming in for the tasting so we can finalize the menu." Great. Now she was saying things Major already knew because she was thinking about that microphone hovering below the edge of the table. "What have you decided to make?"

Major pulled out a stapled-together packet and handed it to her. "Everything we discussed, and I added a few things at your suggestion."

Beyond the camera, Alaine Delacroix scribbled something on her steno pad.

"Uh, okay. Great." Meredith hadn't been this nervous since the oral presentation of her master's thesis. Major handed her another piece of paper. She read, scrawled in his bold handwriting, *Hang in there, you're doing fine.*

Some of the anxiety ebbed away. She looked up in time to see a bead of sweat trace its way down his hairline and along his jaw then disappear under his shirt collar. The confirmation that Major wasn't as cool and collected as he appeared filled Meredith with the first traces of genuine confidence. She delved into his tasting menu, and soon she had almost forgotten anyone but she and Major were in the room.

When they turned to determining how many staff Major would need—kitchen porters, servers, cleanup crew—Meredith went to the small fridge built into the wall unit behind her desk and retrieved four bottles of water. Without interrupting Major's monologue of calculations, she gave Alaine and the cameraman two of the bottles and the third to Major.

"Thanks." He opened it and took a long swallow. "So that's two servers per table of ten, one per eight-top, and one per two four-tops."

"And we need to get them all to bring in their black pants a couple of days ahead of time to make sure none of them are stained or faded and that we don't end up with anyone in chinos again." The cold water soothed the dryness of nerves and extensive talking in Meredith's throat.

"Agreed." He made a note in his binder. "And as soon as Jana gets the schedule confirmed, I'll have her get the sizes to Corie so we can make sure we get the shirts ordered early this time."

"Don't fancy a drive to Baton Rouge to pick them up the morning of the event?" Meredith teased. The sound of a pencil scribbling madly etched through her jollity.

"Not particularly, no." Major winked at her then returned to talking through the number of employees he'd need on the schedule.

At three thirty, the facilities supervisor for Vue de Ceil came in with a copy of the floor plan so they could work out the arrangement of the room—tables, dance floor, and stage.

"Oh! Do you mind if we reset the camera so we can get more of an overhead of y'all working on that?" Alaine piped up for the first time since the meeting started.

Meredith glanced at Major and Orly. Both men shrugged. She nodded at the reporter then returned her attention to the large sheet of paper covering her table. "I don't want it set up just like we did at New Year's. Too many of the same guests are expected, and I want it to look distinctly different."

Orly slid another roll of paper out of the plastic tube he'd brought with him and spread it out on top of the blank one. The heavily notated and revised plan from New Year's. Meredith stood and leaned over the table, resting her right knee on the seat of her chair.

Almost as if someone covered her back with a blanket, she felt Alaine's presence behind her, trying to get a look at the plan. But the reporter didn't interfere, didn't come in closer, didn't say anything. Grudgingly, Meredith admired her restraint.

After quite a bit of discussion, the location of the dance floor was set. Major and Orly started sketching in tables, determining the proper distribution of sizes and the spacing so the servers could easily move around them.

The room went suddenly dim. Meredith, Major, and Orly all stood and turned to see the cameraman taking his equipment apart.

Alaine had the good grace to look apologetic. "I'm sorry. It's four thirty, so he has to get back to the studio."

Meredith checked her watch. "I hadn't realized it was so late. I guess we'll just have to set up another time for that interview?"

"Yes. I'll call you in the morning to schedule it." Alaine helped wrap up cords and pack everything into large canvas bags.

"I can have my assistant call one of the building maintenance staff to help you carry all of that out." Meredith took a few steps toward the door to the outer office.

"Oh no, it's not necessary." The cameraman waved her off. "I've got it."

He did indeed manage to heave everything but one small bag up onto his large shoulders and carry it from the office.

"Do you mind if I come back up and continue taking notes?" Alaine asked. "After I help him take this to his car?"

"That will be fine." Meredith returned to the schematic and pretended to be oblivious to the fact that Major and Orly both watched Alaine leave the room. "Okay, let's see if we can at least get the preliminary layout finished by five o'clock."

When she returned, Alaine stood beside the fourth chair at the table, notepad in hand, making occasional notations while Major and Orly drew in tables, then erased them, then drew them in somewhere else. If Meredith moved just a foot to her right, she might be able to see what Alaine was writing.

"Miss Guidry?" Corie appeared at the main door to the office. "Do you need anything before I go?"

Meredith almost laughed at her assistant's formality. "No, Corie. Thanks. Have a good evening."

"You, too." The young woman grinned and closed the door behind her.

At five fifteen, Orly finally rolled the schematics and stuffed them in the tube. "That's a good start, I b'lieve."

"I think so. Putting the bandstand in front of the east windows will give us a lot more room, even though it means losing the view from that side." Meredith pressed her hands to the small of her back and stretched away the stiffness from two hours' leaning over the table.

"Guests are always happier when there's more room between the tables." Major stacked his papers and files. "And the servers are as well."

"We'll get together again next week to finalize the plan after the board's tasting. I'll e-mail you both to set up a time."

Orly raised the plastic tube in salute. "See y'all later."

"How do you spell his name?" Alaine asked.

"It's actually Orlando Broussard. But he goes by Orly—O-r-l-y." Meredith dropped her stack of work on her desk with a thud.

"Thanks. I really appreciate you letting me do this, Meredith.

This is going to be a great way to publicize the Hearts to HEARTS charity and hopefully raise a lot more money for the hospital."

"I'll do whatever I can to help." Meredith smiled, though dreading the added stress having a reporter and cameraman around all the time would create.

"Mere, I'll bring your take-out box back by on my way out if you're going to be here for a little while." Major hovered near the door.

"Yeah. I have some projects I need to write up for my staff, so I'll be here another half hour or so." She extended her right hand to Alaine. "It was very nice to meet you, and I look forward to working with you."

"Same here. I appreciate everything. Really." That high-wattage smile returned. It seemed much warmer than it had in Mom's office.

Alaine turned to leave. "And Chef, I'm looking forward to seeing a lot more of you soon."

"Why don't you come up to my office, and we can look at my schedule." Major motioned Alaine out the door ahead of him.

Her charitable feelings toward Alaine Delacroix vanished, crushed under a block of ice. Meredith had been right. Major would never feel *that way* about her. Ward seemed to like her, though she couldn't quite figure out why. But how long would that last before he met an Alaine of his own?

CHAPTER 11

"I'm happy you had time in your schedule to meet with me today." Alaine Delacroix finished fiddling with her camera and settled into the guest chair facing Meredith's desk.

"I'm pleased to be able to accommodate you." Meredith clasped her hands atop her desk blotter and tried to force her shoulders to loosen up.

"Chef O'Hara had so many wonderful things to say about you when I interviewed him last week—I couldn't wait to come talk to the miracle worker myself."

"I'm sure he was exaggerating." Meredith didn't know why she always felt the need to deflect compliments rather than just say thank you and move on. "So I take it the interview with him went well?"

"Yes—I aired a twenty-minute segment on today's show as a promo for his cooking segment starting in a couple of weeks. And it made a nice follow-up to the part of the interview I aired on the New Year's Eve Masquerade Ball."

In spite of herself, Meredith returned Alaine's perfect smile. She seemed pretty genuine. Maybe Meredith was overreacting to the reporter's presence and Major's reaction to her. Of course, that shouldn't matter anyway, since she was supposed to be getting over Major.

"Okay—ready?"

"As I'll ever be." Meredith rearranged her hands on her blotter. "Should I look at you or the camera?"

The cycloptic lens stared at her over Alaine's shoulder. "Let's just have a conversation, you and I. Don't think of this as an interview, just think of me as. . .as a potential client who's curious about the event you're working on right now."

Laughter released some of Meredith's nervousness. "I think I can do that."

"Great. Let's start with the history of the Hearts to HEARTS banquet. How did Boudreaux-Guidry Enterprises get involved with a charity to raise money for the cardiac care unit at University Hospital?"

"About five years ago, my father, Lawson Guidry, suffered a heart attack. He was taken first to Bonneterre General, where his condition was misdiagnosed as severe angina, and he was sent home."

Meredith picked up a pen and was about to start twirling it between her fingers until the little red light on the camera caught her attention. She put the pen back down. "Later that night, he passed out during dinner. This time, he was taken to University Hospital and immediately admitted to the cardiac care unit. Dr. Warner personally treated him and attended the surgeon during Dad's bypass surgery. After that, the Warners became like part of our family.

"When Dr. Warner passed away a year later, my parents wanted to do something to honor him and decided the best way was to help raise money for his research foundation, HEARTS."

"Is that an acronym?"

"It is: Heart-disease Education, Awareness, Research, Treatment, and Survival." She grinned, pleased with herself for being able to say the whole thing without having to stop to remember what any of the elements were.

Alaine segued into questions about the actual nuts and bolts of planning the events. Meredith was only too happy to talk about what went into organizing an event like this, being sure to give her event planners and Corie plenty of credit for all of the work they did to help her.

After an hour, Alaine changed her line of questioning. "Tell me a little about yourself, Meredith. How long have you been in this job?"

"I've been the executive director of events and facilities for about six years. Before that, I was an event planner under Anne Hawthorne when she was head of the department."

"Anne Hawthorne—the wedding planner?" Alaine clicked her tongue. "If only I'd known you last year, I might have gotten that interview with her I kept trying for." She laughed. "So Anne Hawthorne worked here before she started Happy Endings, Inc. How long did you work for Anne?"

"About four years. I started working here as soon as I finished grad school."

"Let me guess—MBA?" Alaine grinned.

Meredith shook her head, laughing. "No. Not even close. Art history. My dad wanted me to follow in his footsteps and get my degrees in business, but I chose to go the fine arts route instead."

Alaine's dark eyes glowed from deep within. "I can't believe it! I started out as an art history major—then I took a journalism class for a liberal arts requirement, and I was hooked. But whenever I got a chance, I took art classes to fulfill elective hours."

"What movement did you want to study?" Meredith leaned forward on her elbows, thrilled at the rare opportunity to talk to someone who knew something about art.

"Impressionists. I have Monet and Renoir and Pissaro lithographs all over my townhouse—and a few framed postcards I got at the Louvre several years ago."

"Oh," Meredith half sighed, half groaned. "I've always wanted to go to Europe and tour all the great art museums."

"Have you at least been to the Metropolitan Museum of Art in New York?" Alaine seemed to forget the camera and her notepad, leaning toward Meredith in her interest.

"No. Closest I've been is the National Gallery of Art and the Hirshhorn in Washington, D.C. I've also been to the Art Institute of Chicago."

"What's your movement?"

"Art deco. Everything about the era—the art, the jewelry, the architecture. That's why I jumped at the opportunity to buy a craftsman bungalow a few months ago—even though it did need a complete overhaul inside."

"Really? I'd love to buy an old place and fix it up." Alaine laughed and rolled her eyes. "Well, have my brother fix it up."

"Your brother?"

"Tony. He's a contractor."

A tingle of interest tickled the back of Meredith's neck. Even though she was pretty sure Ward would give her a reasonable offer, having another bid on the work might be good. "A contractor? Here in Bonneterre?"

"Yeah. He actually has his degree in architecture. But he decided he liked getting his hands dirty instead of sitting in an office drawing every day, so he became a contractor instead." Alaine jerked her head then jumped up to turn the camera off. "Sorry. I'll erase all of that personal stuff."

"Not a problem." Meredith stood and walked around to perch on the front edge of her desk while Alaine broke down the camera equipment. "What kind of construction work does your brother do?"

"Home remodeling. Hey, you know what?" Alaine stopped halfway through wrapping up the power cord. "You and Tony would have a lot in common. Would it be weird if. . . ?"

"I'd love to meet him."

"That's great." Alaine gave a little hop of excitement. "I don't usually go around trying to set up the people I'm interviewing with one of my brothers, but I know the two of you would really hit it off."

Meredith's stomach dropped into her left knee. A setup?

"I could give him your phone number or e-mail address and have him get in touch with you." Alaine crouched down to pack everything away in a black canvas bag. "If I can get another one of your business cards, I'll tell him to e-mail you." She caught the tip of her tongue between her teeth when she looked up and wrinkled her nose in a big grin at Meredith.

"I...uh..." How did she expect to end her years of singleness if she passed up opportunities for dates, or get her house finished if she worried that every contractor might ask her out? She swallowed hard and handed Alaine another business card. "Okay."

Meredith walked Alaine out to the main entrance and shook her hand in farewell. Back in the solitude of her office, Meredith allowed the stunned disbelief to swallow her. Had she really agreed to let Alaine Delacroix set her up with her brother?

"Do that later. The movie's starting."

"I'll be there in a second Ma. I can see the TV from here, y'know." Major continued dusting the top of the mirror over his mother's dresser in her studio apartment. A large archway separated the bedroom from what she called the "front parlor"—a sitting area that held her recliner, a loveseat, and a small entertainment center. While Beausoleil Pointe Center sent someone in to clean the bathroom every day and to vacuum once a week, the responsibility of caring for and cleaning any personal furniture items lay solely with the resident. And his mother had never dusted a piece of furniture in her life that Major could remember.

"You just did that last time you were here. It can't be that bad."

"Actually, Ma, I've been here twice since last time I did this. It'll just take a minute." He spritzed window cleaner on the mirror and polished it until all the streaks disappeared. "I take it you haven't changed your bed since last time I dusted either."

Beverly O'Hara waved her hand dismissively. "I don't remember."

Major pulled down the comforter. Yep. Still the same pink-and-yellow-striped sheets he'd put on there two weeks ago. In less than thirty seconds, he had the bed stripped, the linens bundled up and set by the door to take home and run through the laundry—since he was pretty sure that after almost two years here, his mother still didn't know where the laundry room was.

The opening score of *Flying Leathernecks* filled the room. Major hummed along with the melody.

"You're missing it, son!" His mother's voice gained a shrill edge.

"I'm right here. The opening credits are still running, aren't they?" He pulled a clean set of sheets off the top shelf of the closet.

"But this is the one."

"The one what?"

"For heaven sake. If I can remember, you should be able to. The one I named you for."

Major tossed the folded sheets onto the bed and went into the sitting room where he leaned over the back of his mother's chair and pressed his cheek to hers. "Oh, you mean this is the one in which the Duke plays Major Daniel Xavier Kirby, United States Marine Corps."

She pressed her cold hand to his other cheek. He whispered the first few lines of the voice-over introduction in her ear then kissed the top of her head. "Let me finish making the bed. Then I'll put on some coffee, make popcorn, and watch the John Wayne War Movie Marathon with you." He refrained from pointing out that she had the DVDs of all of the films that were going to be shown.

"You'll stay for the whole marathon?"

"I'll stay as long as I can." He returned to the other part of the room and made up the bed with the precision corners his roommate in New York during culinary school—a former army drill sergeant—had taught him.

As promised, before he settled into the cushy loveseat, he'd fixed decaffeinated coffee and microwave popcorn. And Ma was already asleep in her chair. Their typical Sunday afternoon.

"*You've got enough troubles of your own for one man.*" John Wayne said on the TV screen. "*Stop trying to pack everybody else's around.*"

Major had been able to quote nearly every line of this movie since he was a little kid. But that particular line had never hit home with him as it did today. Ever since he'd seen Meredith's date a week ago, he'd given himself indigestion ruminating over whether or not he should tell her about Ma and see if there was any chance to work things out.

The idea of telling Meredith both relieved and frightened him. He couldn't imagine anyone else he'd be more content to spend the rest of his life with. Yet would she understand? Would she be able to accept Ma's condition as a very intrusive and volatile part of their relationship?

Ma snuffled a little in her sleep.

No. He couldn't do this to Meredith. While he'd love to truly become a member of the Guidry family—instead of just an accepted outsider—he couldn't reciprocate and bring Meredith into his family. Guilt gnawed at his stomach, souring the coffee he'd just downed.

"I've got enough troubles of my own."

Meredith, while not a high-maintenance girl like some he'd dated, worked in a high-stress job with long and unusual hours. If a restaurant were to become a success, it would have to be Major's life for the next few years.

Resentment vied with the guilt in curdling the contents of his stomach. He had to make a choice: spend what little free time he would have developing a relationship with Meredith, or spend it with his mother.

"Lord, I don't know how I got myself into this mess. All this time, Ma's been telling me she wants me to meet someone and get married. If only I'd listened to her before now. I've known Meredith for eight years."

The reality of his words sank in. He'd known Meredith for eight years. In the beginning, she'd been like a younger sister. When he'd first started working at B-G, he'd toyed with the idea of finally allowing himself to do something about the crush he'd had on Anne in high school and college. But she'd just gone through the break-up of her first engagement, so he offered a brotherly shoulder for support. It had been only natural that he would treat Meredith the same way when she took over Anne's job—and took the job beyond anything Anne had ever done.

In every respect, she was the ideal companion for someone in the restaurant industry. She understood the late nights, the long hours—because she had the same demands in her own job. She was wonderful with clients. And though he always made sure his numbers were exact and balanced before he turned reports in, he depended on her for many of the business aspects of the catering division.

"She'd never leave an executive director position and come to work at a restaurant. That would be ridiculous."

The movie ended, *The Fighting Seabees* started, and his mother napped on. Major rubbed his eyes hard enough to see stars. Truth be told, if he were going into business with Meredith as his sole partner, he would have signed the papers the day the offer had been made. He'd watched her become MacGyver and fix a broken table with rubber bands, paper clips, and chewing gum; solve any audio-visual problem their equipment could throw at them; make fifty tablecloths work in a room with a hundred tables; and never let on to the client or the rest of the staff that there'd been a problem to begin with.

"She's perfect for me." When he realized he'd spoken aloud, he glanced at Ma, but she hadn't budged. He'd become too accustomed to talking to himself from living alone for so long.

He collected the popcorn bowls and coffee mugs and took them to the kitchenette—one counter along the far wall of the sitting room—to wash. He wished he could find a way to let Meredith know he cared for her, that he'd like nothing better than to be with her forever, but that right now he couldn't.

"Why can't I just bring myself to be honest with her?" He looked over his shoulder to make sure neither the sound of the water nor his voice had awakened his mother. He was starting to get a little concerned—she wasn't usually a deep sleeper like this.

Because if Meredith got wind of the truth—the truth that Major had been concealing his mother and her condition from everyone in his life ever since he returned to Bonneterre eight years ago—she'd never want to talk to him again. And who'd blame her? He deserved to be censured for the shame and resentment he'd allowed to fester in his heart. How would Meredith ever be able to trust him fully?

His watch beeped. Football playoff game started in forty-five minutes. He tidied up the rest of the small apartment. His gut wrenched with what he was about to do. Because his mother had been asleep so long, and because a different movie had come on, he could take his leave without having to make up an excuse—she wouldn't know how long he'd been here.

He almost made up his mind to stay, to salve his conscience. But he had laundry to do tonight, and he had to be at work at five tomorrow morning to cook breakfast for a meeting for some company or another located in Boudreaux Tower.

Promising himself he'd make it up to Ma another Sunday, he leaned over her chair and shook her shoulder.

Her eyes popped open immediately. "You leaving?"

"Yeah. I've got a bunch of stuff I need to do at home tonight, and then it's an early day tomorrow." He kissed her forehead. "You be good, and when they come in here and tell you to turn off John Wayne, don't make a fuss, okay? You have all these movies on DVD and can watch them anytime."

"I know. I promise, I'll be a good little crazy person."

"I'm counting on you. I don't want to get a call in the middle of the night saying you've whacked out on them again. Even if it is fun to scare 'that Nick kid.'"

She laughed, a rusty, rattling sound he didn't hear often enough. "Okay. I tell you what. I'll turn it off at the end of this movie. And I won't raise a fuss."

"Thank you. Love you."

"I know."

He kissed her forehead again. "Good night."

Ma patted the top of his head. "G'night, yourself."

Major's smile faded as soon as he turned his back. How could he just walk out on his mother like this?

"Oh, son?"

He turned around, the fake smile straining every muscle in his face. "Yes, Ma?"

"So who's this Meredith you've been muttering about, and when do I get to meet her?"

CHAPTER 12

"Is she in?" Major paused at Corie's desk Thursday afternoon and nodded toward Meredith's partially closed door.

"Her client meeting ran late, so she isn't back yet. You can go in and put that in the fridge if you want."

"Thanks." Major carried the takeaway box into the office. She'd obviously straightened up yesterday for her meeting with Mrs. Warner after the tasting—making the room feel oddly devoid of any indication it belonged to Meredith. . .with the exception of the soft jazz music permeating the space. The ornate decor bespoke Mairee's taste, not Meredith's.

He stowed the Styrofoam box in the mini-fridge hidden in the credenza, then sat at her desk to leave a note. He went through four green sticky notes before he finally had something he didn't feel embarrassed for her to read:

> Mere—
> Sorry I missed you. Dinner is in your fridge. Enjoy.
> M.

Looking around the office once more, he tried to imagine what it would look like if Meredith had been responsible for decorating it. When arranging events—from the table layout to centerpieces to color schemes—her design skills never failed to impress him. He was curious to see her house once she finished; it was bound to practically ooze with her personality.

He shook himself out of his reverie. If he was going to make it to Forbes's office on time, he needed to get out of here. He waved at Meredith's assistant on the way past.

When he got to the end of the hall, he paused. Leaning casually on the high counter of the reception desk stood Ward Breaux.

The receptionist hung up her phone. "I'm sorry. Apparently Miss Guidry is out of the office right now. Did you have an appointment?"

"Not today, no. I was in the building for another meeting and thought I'd stop by."

"Is there any message—?"

The front door swung open, and Meredith breezed in, drawing everyone's attention. She stopped when she spotted the dark-haired man. "Ward. What are you doing here?"

Molten heat roiled in Major's stomach at the way the contractor's face lit up when he looked at Meredith. Major forced the jealousy aside.

The giant enveloped Meredith's right hand in both of his. He gave the same song and dance about being in the building for another meeting, which Meredith bought hook, line, and sinker.

The flush that bloomed in her cheeks filled Major with dread. She glanced away and looked right at Major. He tried to smile at her, unsure if he succeeded by the slight crease that formed between her brows. She pulled her hand free and motioned Major over.

"Major, you remember Ward Breaux."

Major grudgingly shook hands with the guy.

"The chef, right?" Breaux asked. "Good to see you again."

"Same here."

Meredith glanced at the contractor. "I wasn't really expecting to see you again before tomorrow night."

Tomorrow. . .*night*? Jealousy returned full force. Meredith's going out with this guy once was one thing. But was she seriously considering dating him? A guy who'd picked her up at the hardware store?

"I thought maybe, if you have time this evening, you might let me follow you over to your house so that I can get a better idea of what you're wanting to do with it." Ward grinned at Meredith as if Major weren't standing right there. "And then maybe we could bump up our date to tonight."

"I. . .uh. . ." Meredith, looking more embarrassed than ever, cut her gaze toward Major—then turned and really looked at him. "Major, I thought you were meeting with Forbes this afternoon to talk about. . .that business thing."

The duty of keeping his appointment warred with the desire to stay right here and demand to know what Ward Breaux's intentions toward Meredith were. Duty won. "I put your dinner in the fridge in your office." He gave her shoulder a squeeze on the way past. "I'll see you tomorrow."

"Bye."

Major paused at the front doors, tempted to turn around and look, but a quick glance at his watch spurred him into motion. Wouldn't look good to show up late to the business meeting that could be the first step toward deciding his future. He took the stairs down to the parking garage instead of waiting for the elevator.

He slammed Kirby's door a little harder than he meant to. Okay, he really couldn't walk into the meeting with Forbes to go over all of the legalities of the restaurant deal still upset about Meredith's choice to have a life.

Easing the Jeep out into traffic, Major tried to switch his mind into gear for the upcoming meeting—but the blush on Meredith's cheeks when receiving the compliment from Ward proved too distracting.

Ever since the first time he'd seen Meredith getting ready to go out with Breaux, Meredith had hardly spoken to him about anything other than work stuff.

What kind of name was *Ward* anyway? The only real-life Ward he'd ever heard of was Ward Bond, a character actor who'd been in several of John Wayne's movies.

He slammed on the brakes to keep from running a red light that sneaked up on him. He couldn't compete with someone like Ward Breaux, with his perfect teeth, professional athlete's physique, and a business of his very own. Unlike Ward, Major had always been too cowardly to step out and start a business.

No, not cowardly, just afraid of what might happen to his mother if he gambled everything and lost. Every week he watched a television program in which a celebrity chef went around to failing restaurants and tried to get them back on their feet. No one would come in and do that for Major. He'd always known that if it came to sink or swim, with the added weight of responsibility for his mother, he'd sink. Straight to the bottom.

He pulled into the parking lot of the three-story, red-brick building just as his radio clock flickered over to four o'clock. He grabbed his paperwork, and entered the office of Folse, Landreneau, Maier & Guidry, Attorneys at Law.

Feeling extremely underdressed in his khakis and a denim shirt with the B-G Enterprises logo, Major followed a dark-suited assistant up to the second floor. Everyone they passed wore expensive suits and shoes that looked like they'd just come out of the box, unlike Major's scuffed Top-Siders.

"Mr. O'Hara to see Mr. Guidry," the receptionist told the secretary seated at the desk outside of Forbes's office.

The secretary stood. "Of course. Mr. Guidry is expecting you, Mr. O'Hara."

Major cringed at their formality. It was one thing for his staff to call him Chef—it had become more like a nickname. He was so glad he didn't work at a place where everyone had to go by "Mr." or "Ms."

Forbes stood when Major entered the richly appointed office.

"Come in, Major. Samantha, please hold calls," Forbes said by way of greeting as he shook Major's hand.

"Yes, Mr. Guidry."

"Have a seat, Major." Forbes motioned to a small table on the other side of the large room. Even though he'd been friends with Forbes Guidry since junior high school, Major found himself intimidated by his friend in this setting. He pulled out one of the heavy wooden chairs and sank into it.

Forbes carried a stack of folders over and set them down before sitting. "Now that you've had a couple of weeks to think about my parents' proposal, I'd be interested in knowing your thoughts."

Major quickly recapped the conversation he'd had with Meredith two weeks ago. "I've been spending a lot of time in prayer. And I believe the Lord is telling me this is an opportunity I can't pass up—if all the financial stuff works out."

"I told Mom and Dad that would probably be a concern, since they want you to start off as an investing partner and not just an employee. I believe we've come up with a plan that will work for all parties involved."

From the stack in front of him, Forbes pulled a legal-sized folder with what looked like at least fifty pieces of paper in it. Major swallowed hard. He'd done well in his business law classes in college and culinary school, but that had been so many years ago. This was the part of starting a restaurant that turned him into a blithering idiot.

"According to the start-up plan you gave me to help you with a few months ago"—Forbes pulled it out of the folder—"you proposed to start a restaurant based on an initial investment of $150,000 cash and $600,000 in venture capital. I've presented this to my parents, and they like this plan."

Major's skin tingled, anticipation rising.

"That will make you a 20 percent co-owner in the restaurant. I believe they discussed with you that you will continue to have responsibilities in the catering division of B-G while the restaurant is in start-up phase?"

Major nodded. "Yes, and that I would continue to draw a salary—for a while, at least. I wasn't too sure on that part."

Forbes's gray-blue eyes dropped back to the paperwork in front of him. When he found the document he sought, he passed it across the table to Major. "Here is the five-year buyout plan." He grinned. "This was my idea, actually. It's the plan I came up with for Jenn's restaurant. She was able to buy me out after three years instead of five."

Oh, that Major would be able to do the same. His eyes darted across the numbers and words on the page in front of him, unable to focus on anything.

"Once the restaurant begins to turn a profit—which we know may take at least two years—you will have the opportunity to buy out the 80 percent of the business owned by my parents." Once Forbes started explaining all of the line-items in the spreadsheet, Major could see how it worked—that as he bought the Guidrys out of their investment in the restaurant, his share of the restaurant's proceeds would increase.

The best part was that, even though he'd be taking everything out of savings and cashing out a few investments to buy into this deal, he wouldn't be losing the security of a steady salary in the beginning. He would still be able to pay for his mother's residence at Beausoleil Pointe Center in addition to his own expenses. Of course, he'd be working eighteen to twenty hours a day to get everything done, so he'd never *see* his mother, but in the end, it would all be worthwhile, wouldn't it?

He forced himself to focus while Forbes detailed the rest of the legal and financial arrangements. Mairee and Lawson wanted the restaurant to be Major's—he would be in charge of the menu, the decor, everything. They trusted him to make it a success.

They *trusted* him. They were taking a pretty big risk on him. He would do his best to deserve it and live up to their expectations.

"I know I've hit you with a lot of stuff." Forbes handed the thickest folder to Major. "Take everything home with you, and spend some time reading through everything. Whenever you see something you have questions about, just holler, and I'll explain it to you. I believe my parents told you they don't expect an answer before Easter, right?"

"Right." Which was a good thing. It would take him longer than the eight weeks between now and then to read through everything.

"Let's plan to get together again in a couple of weeks. We can go back through everything, go over any questions that come up, and you can pull together your financial paperwork and the other business applications that are detailed in there." Forbes pointed at the folder.

"Okay."

"Look, Major. We've been friends for a long time. I wouldn't be sitting here talking to you about this if I didn't think it's a solid plan that will be extremely profitable for you in the long run. I also know that you have some concerns about your mom and her health, but I think it's time that you start looking toward your future, start chasing your dream."

Major fanned the edge of the paperwork in the folder with his thumb. The man sitting across the corner of the table from him was his best friend in the world. And even he didn't know the whole truth about Ma—if he did, he'd probably counsel his parents to run, not walk, away from this deal.

He flattened his hands atop the folder. "I'll read through all of this and get back to you."

"That's all we're asking." Forbes stood and returned to his desk, motioning Major to follow.

The chair across from Forbes's desk was much more comfortable than the one at the table. "I appreciate everything you've done."

"It's my pleasure." Forbes loosened his tie and leaned back in his leather executive's chair. "I know that right now, there's no way you'd be able to afford my retainer. Technically, I only represent my parents in this venture. But I want to let you know that if you need anything—*anything*—I'm here for you, pro bono."

"I don't want you having to do that for me. Maybe we can work out some kind of trade agreement—I mean, you've got to have some events for the office, right? Stuff you bring in food for? Special client dinners at restaurants?"

"Yeah—sure, of course. And that'll benefit you, too, because it'll get the restaurant's name out to everyone here."

An unreasonable surge of envy filled Major. How could it be that he and Forbes were the same age—had graduated from high school together twenty years ago—yet here Major was barely starting on his career journey and Forbes was a partner in the largest law firm in town with his own office and his own secretary?

"You're a brave man, Major."

Major blinked a few times, startled. "What do you mean?"

"I mean—to take a step like this. To risk it all on what you've always wanted to do. Not a lot of people would be willing to do this at our age. It's almost like you're getting to start over."

"Start *over*?" He had never thought of it that way. "Up until now, I've always felt like I was waiting to begin my life. Like everything I was doing was just waiting—building up to this."

"You may feel that way, but that's not how it looks on paper. If you were unproven, unknown, do you think my parents would have given you this opportunity? You're a name, brother, a commodity in this town. Sure, part of that comes from your working at B-G for years, but everyone in the business community knows that Mom and Dad don't suffer fools—if you lasted that long with them, you've got what it takes. Plus, just about every one of them has been to one event or another that you've catered."

Forbes's words took a few moments to filter through Major's brain. "Benefits of a city that still has a small-town mentality?"

Forbes laughed. "Something like that. Hey, speaking of small-town mentality, what are you doing for supper?"

"Figured I'd just throw something together at home."

"Not tonight. You ever been to my sister Jenn's restaurant down in Comeaux?"

"The Fishin' Shack? A couple of times. I don't make it down to Comeaux very often."

Forbes removed his tie and reached in his top desk drawer, withdrawing keys and his PDA. "Come on, then. I'm meeting some of my siblings and cousins for our standing Thursday night dinner."

"Okay. . .sure, I'd love to. How about I follow you down there?" Major had heard about this Thursday night family dinner tradition through Anne a few years ago. She'd invited him many times in the beginning, but back then he'd spent almost every evening with his mother. Eventually, the invitations stopped coming; then his mother insisted she didn't want to see him every day.

And if he went, he'd be able to find out if Meredith had foregone bumping up her date with Ward Breaux in favor of her family without having to try to find some way to wheedle it out of her subtly tomorrow.

CHAPTER 13

"You did all this work yourself?"

Meredith leaned against the pillar in the opening between the living room and front foyer while Ward inspected the refinishing she'd done on the built-in cabinets flanking the fireplace.

"I did." She held her breath and followed him around the room with her gaze, praying he wouldn't find fault with any of her work.

He turned and gave her a winsome smile. "Ever considered quitting your job and becoming a subcontractor?"

Only in her dreams. "You can see how much needs to be done if the house is going to be ready for me to move in three months from now."

The toe of his shoe scraped along the row of carpet tacks still stuck in the hardwood near the wall. "For one person, yes, it would be impossible." He continued around the room until he leaned his shoulder against the pillar opposite her. "I'd be very interested in submitting a bid to complete your remodel."

Meredith's face grew hot under Ward's intense gaze. "What will you need me to do so that you can do that?"

"I need to come by some time with my apprentice so we can measure all the rooms and so you can tell me exactly what you want done."

"I'll have to check my schedule at work. With the Valentine's banquet coming up so soon, I'm not sure what my days are going to look like."

His lopsided grin was rather disarming. "That's fine. It means I don't have to make up an excuse to call you tomorrow."

Oh, she shouldn't have skipped lunch today. Her empty stomach knotted and twisted with the rush of pleased embarrassment that blasted through her. Never before had a good-looking, eligible man flirted with her like this.

"I'm sorry. I didn't mean to embarrass you, Meredith. But I just can't seem to help myself whenever I'm around you."

The chirping of his phone saved her from having to think of a response.

He cringed when he looked at the device. "Ooh, I really need to take this. Forgive me?"

"Sure. No problem." She escaped the living room and headed upstairs to make sure the almost constant rain since Christmas hadn't generated any problems.

A few minutes later, footsteps announced Ward's presence on the stairs.

"Meredith?"

"In the guest bathroom." She balanced herself on the edge of the claw-foot tub and ran her hand along the top edge of the wall and around the window casing to check for dampness.

"What are you—"

Her left foot slipped off the narrow edge of the tub. She pitched backward—straight into Ward. He swung her up easily into his muscular arms. Mortification burned every inch of her skin.

"Yes, now I see why you shouldn't be trying to do this renovation all by yourself. What in the world were you trying to do, besides break your neck?"

"There was some damage to the roof in the last big storm. It's been patched, and I was just checking to make sure the patch is holding."

"Well, if you approach everything that way, it's a wonder you haven't broken something—like your neck."

"Speaking of, could you put me down?"

He took a few steps away from the tub and gently set her on the floor, not removing his hands from her waist until she assured him she had gained her balance. He moved around her, bent over, and leaned his weight on the edge of the tub, which promptly began to tip toward him.

"Yeah, that's what I thought: so old the bolts securing it to the floor are either missing or rusted through." He rotated around to face her, returning to his full height. With crossed arms and a frown crinkling his forehead, he could have passed for an avenging angel. "One thing I want you to promise me, whether I get the contract or not."

The back of her neck began to ache from looking up at him in such close quarters. "What's that?"

"You'll follow some basic work site safety guidelines—and you'll make everyone who sets foot on the property do the same. I'd hate for you to get sued because a worker breaks something when he falls off the edge of the tub that isn't secured."

Impressed by his concern not just for her safety, but for anyone else's, she nodded. "I will. And I don't usually do that. It was just expedient tonight."

He grimaced. "And that's how most on-the-job injuries occur. You don't want to start your life in a new home with a huge claim on your insurance, do you?"

Laughter bubbled up and escaped.

"Meredith, I'm serious."

She patted his folded arms. "I know. And I do take safety seriously. I was laughing because you reminded me of my older brother and our mom just then. That's the same lecture either of them would have given me in the same circumstance. When all else fails, appeal to the financial aspect of the situation."

His expression eased, his dark eyes no longer stern, but amused once again. "They sound like very smart people."

"Come on, let me show you the rest of the upstairs."

"Hey, Major!"

At Forbes's younger brother's greeting, the handful of people sitting at the ten-top table turned and greeted Major with the same warmth. Why did he always assume they would see him as an interloper—as an intruder? They'd never treated him with anything but affection and friendship. Most of those present were too young to remember the couple of years that Major worked for Aunt Maggie two decades ago, yet they still acted as if he were a member of the extended family.

"Oh, mercy!" Jennifer Guidry came out of the kitchen. "Now I'm going to feel self-conscious. Forbes, did you have to bring a professional chef to my restaurant?" She winked at him. "Hey, Major."

"Hi, yourself." He looked around with interest at the interior design. "I don't know what you're worried about. I think everything is fantastic. The pirogue is new since the last time I was here." He pointed at the flat-bottomed, pointy-ended boat suspended upside down from the beamed ceiling overhead.

"One of my suppliers down in Jeanerette thought I needed that for some authenticity. So he built it and put it up there a couple of months ago."

Major watched Jenn as she talked with a couple of her siblings or cousins—he could never keep all the relations straight in this clan. He hadn't seen her in at least a year. He used to think that she and Meredith were nearly identical—in fact, when he'd first met them as teenagers, he'd thought they were twins. But Jenn had cool, blue-gray eyes like Forbes's, not wide, nutmeg brown eyes that glowed with an emberlike intensity. Jenn's hair was a little redder, too. She flitted from person to person like a hummingbird. Meredith would have just found a place to sit and observe those around her.

"Chef, we need you in the kitchen."

Major turned along with Jenn—and shook his head at the gut reaction.

"I'll be right back," Jenn called over her shoulder as she followed her employee around the fishing tackle–decorated wall that buffered the dining room from the kitchen. The snap and bustle of working in a restaurant—he missed it.

Sitting beside Forbes, Major found he had a good view of the front door across the large room, because he saw Anne as soon as she entered.

She paused in her confident stride toward the table when she noticed Major. "What—my invitations weren't good enough for you? You had to wait until Forbes invited you to come to family dinner?"

Major stood and greeted her with a handshake. "He's a lawyer—trying to argue with him would just be a losing battle." He held the chair to his right for her.

She glanced around, a frown forming between her brows. "Where's Meredith?"

Finally, someone had voiced the question that had been bouncing around in Major's brain for the last fifteen minutes.

"She's going to try to come later," Forbes said. "She called as I was driving down here to say that something came up, and she made other plans for dinner."

Major's guts melted into a disappointed puddle.

"What do you mean, 'other plans for dinner'?" Anne asked.

Major assisted Anne with the chair and waited to hear how Forbes would answer her question. Jenn returned with a couple of baskets of hush puppies and took the seat on the other side of Anne.

Forbes refilled his glass from the pitcher of tea on the table. "I don't know. I guess something came up at work." He glanced askance at Major.

Major lowered himself into his chair and shrugged. It would serve her right if he told her somewhat meddlesome kin that she wasn't working but was on a date. . .but that would be petty. "I don't know. It could be any of a million things that sidetracked her."

"Well, hopefully she'll be able to get here soon." Anne glanced at the printed list of the day's specials then placed her order. "It would be a shame for her to miss such a historical event as Major O'Hara attending a Guidry family function after so many years."

And to think, if he'd been paying attention and hadn't been so wrapped up in his own little life, he might have recognized his feelings for Meredith soon enough to have actually become part of the Guidry family.

He hardly knew what he was ordering when the waiter came around to him. He could almost hear a game show announcer in his head: *All of this could have been yours, but the price wasn't right.*

As dinner progressed, Major was slowly able to set his thoughts aside, though the self-recrimination remained. But no one could be around this crew for very long and spend any time inside his own skull. Conversations flew fast and furious around the large, round table, ranging from the bizarre case police officer Jason had just worked to the latest plans for Anne's wedding.

On that point, Major could contribute to the discussion, teasing Anne about the lack of extravagance in her menu choices.

"That's our Annie—always suggesting all the frills and frou-frou for everyone else, but never indulging in them for herself." Jenn rolled her eyes.

"I blame it on George—since he's not here to defend himself." Anne's blue eyes twinkled.

"Oh, please." Jenn stood and went to the wait station to refill their pitcher of iced tea. "George would let you do anything you want."

"Well, as brother of the bride, I have to say that I'm glad it's not one of those really over-the-top kind of weddings," Jason Babineaux said.

"Yeah?" Forbes challenged him. "All you have to do is usher. You don't have to stand in front of the hordes of gawkers who are going to be sitting there just waiting for someone to flub up."

"You could always be removed from the list of attendants, Forbes, if the idea bothers you so much." Anne's eyebrows arched up, her expression stern, though she couldn't wipe the smile from her eyes.

"And leave George with only his brother up there with him for moral support? I couldn't do that to the poor sap. Someone's got to commiserate with him on his life as he knows it being over."

Anne turned to Major. "I'm so happy that you could finally come and witness for yourself just how much everyone in this family loves each other." She winked.

Melancholy wrapped around Major's chest. Did the people sitting at this table have any idea just how blessed they were to be part of a family at all? To have what Major had dreamed of his whole life, had imagined when he was a kid?

After everyone had overindulged in Jenn's peach cobbler, people exchanged places at the table as if at a signal. It happened before Major realized it, and suddenly, he found himself not between Anne and Forbes, but next to their young cousin Jodi.

"I'm so glad I was able to get over here to you. I've been hoping to see you again for a while now." Jodi flipped her long, brown hair over her shoulder and gazed at him with wide, dark eyes.

Major straightened and cleared his throat, uncomfortable with what felt like flirtatiousness in the young woman's demeanor. He was certain he was just flattering himself by thinking she was actually interested in him. But when she leaned closer and rested her hand on his arm, a sense of foreboding stole through him.

"What can I do for you, Jodi?"

"Oh, I don't want you to do anything *for* me." She batted long lashes. "It's what I think we can do together."

Meredith leaned against the side of the SUV, her neck starting to ache slightly from looking up at Ward. The in-and-out flow of people from the gourmet deli marked the passing of time as they stood chatting. And while she enjoyed his company and getting to know him better, she couldn't help but think about the fact that, right now, her siblings and cousins were all down at Jenn's restaurant.

When she'd agreed to grab a quick sandwich with Ward, she'd

been proud of herself for the ease with which she'd called Forbes to tell him she wouldn't be there for dinner. But over the past hour, the idea that they were all down there having fun without her kept intruding on her thoughts.

Ward reached out and took her hand. She pressed against the back door of her SUV. He was quite handsome; she couldn't deny it. But the thought that she'd rather be here with Major kept her from enjoying the moment.

"Ward, I hope it won't offend you that I'm going to have at least one other contractor bid the house."

The corners of his eyes crinkled. "I'd think you a fool if you didn't." He rubbed the palm of her hand with his thumb. "But I hope that even if you don't accept my bid, you'll still go out with me."

Come on, heart, flutter! "Of course."

"Good." He looked down when his phone buzzed. "That's my cue to say good night and let you get back to your previous plans." He leaned over and kissed her cheek. "G'night, Meredith."

She blinked twice, stunned that the kiss had been so quick—and so chaste. "Good night, Ward."

He held her door and shut it once she was in with her seat belt fastened. She waited until he'd started the engine of his massive, four-door pickup before pulling out of the lot and heading toward Comeaux.

Though she hated doing it while driving, she pulled out her phone and speed-dialed Anne's cell phone number.

"Hey, Mere." Loud music nearly drowned out Anne's greeting.

"Y'all going to be there awhile longer?"

"Oh, yeah. Karaoke just started, in case you can't tell. Jason just did 'Mack the Knife,' and Forbes and Major are about to get up there and sing 'My Favorite Things.'"

"What—from *The Sound of Music*?" Meredith cautiously but quickly overtook someone piddling around in the left lane. Major was there? And she'd missed it?

"Yeah. Are you on your way? If so, I'll tell Jenn to have them bumped down the list. They've already done a couple—and believe me, you don't want to miss this. They're in rare form tonight."

For the remainder of the twenty-minute drive, Meredith fought the urge to speed. Major was at family dinner, and she'd missed it. How had he—

His meeting with Forbes to go over the details of Mom and Dad's offer on the restaurant. Of course. She'd promised to pray for him before and during the meeting and had completely forgotten.

The gravel crunched and popped under her tires when she pulled in to the overflow lot adjacent to Jenn's restaurant. Yes, indeed, there was Major's green Jeep.

She jogged a few steps then forced herself to slow down. She had no reason to think he'd come because he expected her to be here—only to hope it.

Music spilled out when she pulled open the front door. Though not dark, the houselights had been dimmed to direct attention to the brightly lit stage.

The hostess greeted her by name, as did several servers. Meredith's heart thumped in time with the upbeat country song someone was singing. She skirted the perimeter of the main dining room toward the separated party room at the back.

She strained to see who all was there. Her heart flip-flopped when she saw Major—then almost stopped completely when she saw him with her younger cousin Jodi. Her *much* younger cousin Jodi.

Meredith stopped and watched as Jodi wrote something down on a drink napkin, folded it, and tucked it into Major's shirt pocket.

More clearly than she could see anyone at that table, Meredith could see the choice now standing before her. She could let this bother her, or she could remember that she'd just been taken to dinner—a second time—by a handsome stranger.

She slapped a smile on and approached the table.

"Hey! You're here." Anne pulled out the chair beside her.

Fortunately, everyone else was involved in poring over the lists of available karaoke tracks and barely spared her a glance, much less forced her into hugs and kisses.

Anne leaned close. "So what happened tonight?"

"Oh, it's—" On Anne's other side, Meredith saw Forbes turn his head their direction as if expecting to hear the explanation for her lateness as well. "It's nothing. I'll tell you about it later."

"Hey, Mere, what's this I hear about some guy coming to pick you up at the office a couple of weeks ago?" Rafe called across the table.

So much for her personal life staying private. She tried to laugh it off. "Who told you that?"

"Tonya. She said he was very good-looking and that you were very dressed up."

She'd forgotten Rafe occasionally dated one of the front-desk receptionists. Around the table, everyone focused on Meredith. Except Major, who gazed at Rafe through narrowed eyes.

"Yes. I had a date the other night. What's the big deal?"

Anne squeezed her wrist. "What's the big deal? You had a date, and you didn't even tell me?"

Though feeling bad for not telling Anne immediately, Meredith started getting angry. "It's not announced around the table every time Jenn goes out on a date—or Rafe or Jodi." She flickered her gaze at Major and hoped that pairing would never come to pass. "So why is it worthy of the family grapevine when I have a date?"

"Duh—because you *don't* date. What—did you decide to give up *not* dating as your New Year's resolution?" Rafe teased.

She couldn't look at Major now; in fact, she wasn't sure she'd ever be able to face him again.

"That's enough," Forbes admonished their younger brother. "Meredith deserves to have a personal life that she can keep private if she wants to."

"Aww, come on, Forbes. She hasn't had a date in ten years and—"

Meredith jumped to her feet and grabbed her purse. "I knew this was a mistake," she muttered. "Good night. See y'all later." She almost ran from the restaurant, molten-hot embarrassment propelling her steps.

Halfway across the small, main parking lot, she dug in her purse for the car keys—and promptly dropped them on the pavement.

"Meredith, wait." Major's voice echoed over the dull sound of the music inside the restaurant.

Her eyes tingled and burned, and she had to blink quickly to eliminate the gathering moisture. She picked up the keys and stood—but couldn't face him.

CHAPTER 14

$\mathcal{M}$ajor hesitated when Meredith wouldn't turn around to face him after picking up her keys. He could understand why she might not want to talk to a family member right now, but what had *he* done?

He approached with caution. "Meredith, is everything okay?"

The smile she wore when he got around to where he could see her face was the same one she wore when dealing with difficult clients. "Everything is fine, thank you. I just—it's just been a really long day, and I have a puppy that's been cooped up in my apartment since I ran home to let him out at lunchtime. He's probably destroyed my bathroom, so I really need to get home." She shivered and rubbed her arms.

Without thinking, he shrugged out of his leather jacket and wrapped it around her shoulders.

"Thanks." She clutched the front closed.

He cleared his throat. "May I walk you to your car?"

She shrugged. "Sure."

They walked in silence all the way to her Volvo. After she unlocked it, he opened the front door and looked in to make sure no one waited within to accost her—drawing a real smile from Meredith.

He'd missed seeing that smile from her. "When did things get weird between us?"

The streetlamp illuminated the surprise in her eyes at his question. "I'm not...I don't...." She swallowed hard and licked her lips.

Major's breath caught in his throat. Those perfectly shaped lips.

"Major—I don't know how to say this without coming across sounding stupid and juvenile and potentially making things even more awkward between us." She wrapped his jacket tighter.

He leaned his shoulder against the back window and tried to draw his gaze away from her lips to her eyes. "You know you can say anything to me."

She laughed—but it turned into a groan; her brows puckered, and she shook her head. "I don't think I can. It'll just make things worse between us."

He leaned closer but clasped his hands behind his back to keep from taking her in his arms and declaring his undying love to her. "Whatever it is, I think I'm man enough to handle it."

Tears welled in Meredith's nutmeg eyes, and her breathing increased. "I can't." She swallowed a couple more times, and an odd expression overtook her face. "I didn't realize you knew my cousin Jodi so well."

The sudden change in subject threw him. "What?"

"You. . .and Jodi. I saw you together when I walked in." She reached into the pocket of his shirt. "I saw her give you this."

She pulled out the napkin Jodi had stuffed in there a few minutes ago. He laughed and enclosed Meredith's fisted hand with both of his. "Your cousin told me she'd heard about the restaurant on Alaine's program. She offered to come up with a marketing plan and some materials for me—as part of her portfolio or internship or something for grad school—if the time comes. She doesn't have any business cards, so she wrote her number down for me. I'm supposed to call her when I know what my schedule's going to be like the next couple of weeks."

"Marketing plan?" Meredith's cheeks darkened. "I thought—I mean I didn't think—"

Hope kindled in Major's chest. "You thought Jodi was flirting with me and that I was lapping up the attention of a girl about fifteen years younger than me?"

She nodded, her throat working hard as she swallowed, face as red as a five-hundred-degree oven.

He tried to contain his smile. "So, you were jealous?"

"I—no—I was surprised—"

"You were surprised that someone like Jodi would show interest in me? Or that I would show interest in any woman?" *Other than you.* He wanted her to admit it, to say aloud that she loved him. Of course, he would never be able to act on it, but he really wanted to hear the words.

"It's not quite like that—"

He used the leverage he had by his grasp on her hand and pulled her closer. "Then what is it like?"

Her eyes widened—but not with fear. He leaned his head closer to her, heart thundering.

"Hey, is everything o—" Anne skidded to a stop as she came around the back end of the Volvo. "Oh, dear." She shielded her eyes as if to keep from seeing anything else. "I'm so sorry. I'll just leave now."

"No, it's all right." The breathy huskiness in Meredith's usually smooth voice stirred the smoldering embers in the pit of Major's stomach. She pulled her hand, and he released it, though he didn't want to. "I really need to be getting home anyway."

Major gulped a couple of deep lungfuls of the chilly air to settle his nerves and slow his still-racing heart. Had he really almost just kissed Meredith Guidry?

Meredith was certain she was about to have a heart attack. Unless she was seriously deceiving herself, Major O'Hara had been about to kiss her before Anne interrupted them.

"Oh—okay, well, good night." Anne gave an apologetic grimace and backed away to her own car a few spaces away.

Sweat beaded on Major's upper lip, and he rubbed his forehead with the heel of his hand. "Meredith, I have to tell you something."

The hyperventilating feeling returned to her chest. Would he now declare his feelings for her? Put her out of years of agony? "Yes?"

"I need you to know how I feel about you. . . ." He wiped his hand down his face. "About you and Ward Breaux. I'm—I'm really. . .happy that you've managed to find time to have a life outside of work. You deserve to have some fun and joy in your life, and I hope that you find it."

Nooooo! Emptiness swallowed up all the warm, pleasant feelings she'd had this evening. He wasn't supposed to be happy for her. He was supposed to be jealous, insanely jealous, over the fact she'd gone out on a couple of dates with someone else.

"Thanks, Major. That means. . .a lot to me." She slipped his jacket off her shoulders and handed it back to him—but she'd started shivering before the cold air hit her. "I guess I'll see you at the office tomorrow."

"Ten thirty, right?"

"Ten thirty?"

"The meeting to finalize the Hearts to HEARTS menu?"

"Right. Ten thirty."

"I'll bring coffee and snacks. I'm sure we'll need them." His grin didn't quite deepen his dimples the way it usually did.

"See you then." She climbed into the car, ready for this night to be over. She returned his wave and pulled out of the parking lot.

Meredith was about to give in to the tears that wanted desperately to be released, but her phone rang. She fumbled in her purse for the hands-free earpiece, hooked it over her right ear, and answered.

"Meredith? Antoine Delacroix. I hope it isn't too late."

"No." She grabbed a tissue and dabbed away the moisture from her eyes and nose. "Thank you for calling."

"Of course. My sister has told me some stuff about you. But I have to admit, it confused me. I couldn't tell if she was trying to set us up on a date or if you have a job you want me to bid."

Was Alaine Delacroix the reason Major was happy Meredith had started seeing someone else? "I have a house I'm remodeling, but I've about reached the limit of what I can do on my own—and time is a factor as well."

"Oh. If that's the case, the sooner I come by to evaluate the property, the better, huh?"

"Yes. But I don't have my calendar with me. Can I call you back tomorrow morning once I have it in front of me?"

"I don't really do mornings, so why don't I give you a holler some time tomorrow afternoon?"

A contractor who didn't "do" mornings? "Okay. I'll talk to you tomorrow. Bye."

"Later, dude."

Meredith disconnected with a derisive huff and took the earpiece off. Had he really just called her *dude*? Even the college students they hired to work large events were trained better in customer service than that.

At home she heard the puppy's howls as soon as she opened the back door into her kitchen. She stepped out into the rear hall again at the sound of footsteps on the wooden stairs.

"I was just coming to see what the noise was." Anne hesitated on the bottom step.

"Just the puppy. I'm sure there's a mess to clean up, but come in if you want to." Meredith had no doubt that Anne's visit had nothing to do with the racket the puppy continued to make.

Meredith changed clothes first before daring to open the bathroom door. But surprisingly, the puppy had managed to keep his mess to the newspaper. She still fought retching at the smell as she wadded it up, and she carried it at arm's length out to the large trash bin outside, the puppy doing his best to trip her up.

Anne followed them out, and Meredith joined her on the deck.

"Are you going to keep him?"

Meredith smiled over the dog's antics. "I'd like to. It would be nice to have a dog for some nominal protection once I'm living alone. I just don't have time for him right now."

"What about Jenn? I know she'd love to take him."

"And how does she have more time than I do? She's at the restaurant six days a week. Besides, she double-checked, and the lease she signed doesn't allow pets other than cats, birds, or fish."

"Too bad. He's so cute."

"Yep. But he needs a family with kids who'll play with him every day. I might get a cat, just for the companionship. They sleep twenty hours a day, so it wouldn't care that I'm hardly ever home." She crouched down as the puppy came up the steps, and scooped him into her arms. He lavished her chin, jaw, and neck with kisses.

"I know it's getting late, but I hoped you might want to talk." Anne held open the door.

Wariness settled over Meredith. She trusted Anne implicitly, but how much should she tell her cousin about Major?

"Come in. I'll put some coffee on." Meredith deposited the puppy on the floor, washed her hands, and put on a pot of decaf dark roast. They talked about Anne's wedding plans while the coffee brewed and Meredith fed the dog.

Finally, both cradling Meredith's favorite large green mugs in their hands, they settled in the living room.

"So tell me what's going on."

"It was nothing. We were just talking."

Anne frowned then seemed to understand. "No, we'll get to that in a minute. I mean what's this about your going out on a date for the first time in ten years and not telling me?"

"I'm sorry I didn't talk to you. There's been so much going on in my life the last week, I kind of lost track of what day it is." *And I wanted to have something completely of my own for just once in my life.*

"You know I want all the details: who is he, where'd you meet him? Is he the 'friend' you went to the Savoy with Friday night?"

Meredith told Anne everything. She even pulled up Ward's company Web site to show Anne his picture. Anne seemed duly impressed, but grew silent when they returned to the living room from the second bedroom/office.

"What about Major?" Anne asked.

"What about him?" Meredith picked at a loose thread in the arm of her sofa.

"You've been in love with Major for a very long time."

Meredith got up and went back into the office for a pair of scissors to take care of that pesky thread.

"I didn't really allow myself to recognize it until last year when we were all working on Cliff's wedding reception. I guess being in love myself made me finally recognize it in you."

Meredith really didn't want to delve into the whys and wherefores of her feelings for Major, but if anyone could understand falling in love with someone who didn't return the feelings, it would be Anne. At least, Meredith hadn't been in Anne's position—having to cancel a wedding two days before it took place because the groom chose his career over her. But look how that had turned out for Anne in the long run.

"Yes." Meredith's voice came out wispy. She took a swig of coffee to try to clear away the nervous dryness. "Yes, I have been in love with him for a long time. At least, I thought I was."

"Is that what I interrupted tonight?"

Meredith shook her head. "No. I almost made the mistake of telling him but chickened out at the last minute. Which was a good thing, because he told me that he's happy that I've started to have a personal life, that I've met someone."

"Hmm." Anne's mouth twisted to the side. "Looked to me like he was about to kiss you when I walked up. Do you think maybe he was just trying to hide his own feelings for you because you have started seeing someone else? That maybe he's realized he could possibly lose you to someone else?"

"I doubt it. We've known each other for eight years. If he were interested in me, he'd have told me long before now." Meredith stopped toying with the scissors and put them on the coffee table.

"Mere, I've known him a lot longer than you, and one thing I do know about Major is that he has a really hard time opening up and letting people in. There are things I still don't know about his family and his upbringing."

Meredith's interest piqued. "What do you know?"

153

"Just that he was raised by a single mom, but that on a couple of occasions he was in a foster home. I think the only reason he told me that much is because he knew I'd lost my parents and had been raised by a foster family—even if they are blood relatives. I don't even know if his mom is still alive."

"She is. I heard Forbes ask about her several months ago." Mentally, she made a note to ask her brother about Major's family.

"So can you see why he might not feel like he can express his feelings to you? He got comfortable with the way things were—he knew you'd always be there, that because you gave your full attention to the job, it was like you were giving your full attention to him."

"I think you're reading too much into it." Meredith put her head down on the arm of the sofa. "As far as I'm concerned, Major and I are friends and work colleagues and nothing more. I made a New Year's resolution to get over this crush on him and move on."

Anne sat in thoughtful silence for a moment. "If you think that's the best course of action, I'll support you wholeheartedly."

Meredith pushed herself upright again. "Anne, I'm thirty-four years old—I'll be thirty-five in four months. I want to get married. I'm tired of being alone. I'm afraid that if I don't do something now, I'm going to be alone for the rest of my life."

Anne smiled. "I know exactly how you feel. Of course, I was pushing thirty-six by the time I met George."

"And you had already started trying to meet someone—you were letting Jenn and Forbes set you up on blind dates and introduce you to people."

"Is that what you want—do you want them to start setting you up? Because I'm sure they'd be only too happy." Anne's expression of apprehension was so comical, Meredith had to laugh.

"I don't know about the blind date thing. Especially when it comes to who Jenn might pick out for me. And Forbes is the *last* person I want involved in my dating life." Meredith gave Anne a pointed look.

"I'm right there with you on that one." Anne picked up her mug, looked into it, and set it down again. "I'll keep on the lookout for you. Oh, George's brother, Henry, will be coming to town in a few weeks for a short visit—to get fitted for his tux and meet the family—and it's usually customary for the maid of honor and best man to spend some time getting to know each other. Plus, when we go out while he's here, it'll be nice to have a foursome so Henry doesn't feel like a third wheel."

"As long as it's not the week of the HEARTS banquet, I'll be more than happy to accommodate you."

"No—not that week. I have a huge wedding Valentine's Day. I think it's the week after that." Anne stood and stretched, then carried her coffee cup into the kitchen.

Meredith followed her. "When does George get back from Paris?"

"Not soon enough. He flies into New Orleans next Wednesday, and I'm driving down to meet him—I have a couple of vendors down there I'd like to talk to face-to-face for this Valentine's wedding. We'll spend a few hours down there and then drive back—should be back in time for church that evening."

"That'll make for a long day for you."

"I know, but it'll be worth it once George is with me."

A pang of envy ripped through Meredith's soul at the contentment in her cousin's voice. Yes, coming clean with Anne had been the right thing to do—because now she had the person who specialized in Happy Endings on her side.

CHAPTER 15

*C*ome on, push it. Push it. Push it!"

The only thing Major wanted to push was the stupid trainer out the nearest window. With each impact of his foot on the treadmill, sharp pains shot up through his calves, quads, and hamstrings; and his lungs felt like he was trying to breathe through soggy bread.

When had he gotten this out of shape?

Unfortunately, the personal trainer assigned to take him around and put him through his paces on his first visit to the gym had recognized his name as a former football player at ULB. Though how this whippersnapper could remember someone who played almost twenty years ago was a miracle.

The only thing that kept him from hitting the emergency stop button was the memory of how puffy his face had looked on TV. Sure, no one should trust a skinny chef—but who wanted to look at a pudgy one week in and week out?

He ran as hard as he could to keep from being flung backward off the machine while Mr. Universe called encouragement at him. Finally, the kid reached over and knocked the speed down to three and a half miles per hour.

"Walk it off. Walk it off." He made a notation on the clipboard he carried. "Yeah, I think you can start with running fifteen minutes at. . .seven miles per hour, then walk half an hour at three and a half.

Gradually, you'll work it up so that you're running the entire forty-five minutes."

Major followed him over to the weight machines and spent the next forty-five minutes pretending that he already had more muscle than flab, and planning to decrease the amount of weight on each one next time he came in. If he survived tonight.

After the last apparatus, Major was ready to dissolve into a puddle of melted lard on the floor. Sheer strength of will was the only thing that kept him upright when the trainer smacked his shoulder.

"Good workout, man. Come in four or five times a week and do that, and you'll be back in your playing condition in no time. See ya later!" The trainer jogged away.

Major grabbed the top of the bicep curl machine as the floor wavered beneath him. Sweat dribbled down his spine. . .and his face and his chest and his arms. Why should sweating in the gym feel entirely different from sweating in the heat and humidity of a busy kitchen?

And why had this stupid gym put the locker rooms on the second floor? He stared up the long flight of stairs, trying to talk his legs into carrying him up them.

"Hey—Major O'Hara, right?"

He turned at the man's voice—and groaned inwardly when he recognized Ward Breaux. He knew he should have come in the morning instead of waiting until after work. He wiped his hand on his towel and shook the man's proffered hand. "Yeah, good to see you."

"Didn't know you worked out here."

"Just joined today."

"What'd you think?" Ward started up the stairs two at a time.

Pride—that ghastly beast—refused to allow him to let Breaux leave him behind. Clenching his teeth against the pain, Major ran up the steps to keep up with the contractor. "To be perfectly honest, it kicked my butt. It's been since college that I've made an effort to exercise regularly."

"Yeah? What did you do back then?"

"Played football."

"Really? Me, too. Where'd you play?" Ward nodded at several beautiful young women who smiled and eyed him hungrily when they passed them on the stairs.

None of them noticed Major. "Here, at ULB. Where'd you play?"

"Miami. I guess in your line of work, it's hard to find time to stay fit."

If Major could move his arms, he'd deck the guy. He didn't need someone else to point out to him how out of shape he was. His legs were already screaming that they'd be sore for days to come. "It is. But I figured if I'm about to be on TV every week, I'd better shape up."

"You're going to be on TV?"

Finally, something he had that Breaux didn't. "I'm going to be doing a weekly cooking segment on Alaine Delacroix's show."

Ward's dark brows shot up. He opened the locker room door. "That hot chick who does the midday show on Channel Six?"

"Yeah." Major wasn't sure if he liked the fact that someone who was seeing Meredith had just called another woman a "hot chick."

The contractor let out a low whistle. "No wonder you're here. If I were still unattached and about to be spending that much time with Alaine Delacroix, I'd want to get in shape, too."

If I were still unattached. A little piece of Major's heart died. Things between Meredith and this guy must be more serious than Major originally thought if Breaux considered himself attached to her. Major didn't see any reason to correct Ward's notion that he would be spending time with Alaine, when it had been made pretty clear that it was only the production and camera people he'd see each week on Tuesdays when they came to film.

"Oh, by the way, Meredith told me she'd like to bring you in on planning the kitchen design in her new house. I'd like to pick your brain on that so I can include your ideas in my bid."

Lovely. Just what Major wanted to do. Spend more time with the guy who was stealing Meredith away from him. "Sure. Anytime."

"Great. I'll get your number from Meredith when I see her later. Well, I'll catch you another time." Breaux flung his towel over his shoulder and went around to a different part of the locker room.

Major stuffed everything into his duffel and headed for home before he had to speak to Ward again. The cold air outside turned his sweat to clamminess, and since Kirby's ragtop was more like a colander than a roof, he was shivering by the time he got home a few miles away.

He stood in the shower for a long time, letting the hot water work on his sore muscles and trying to clear his head. But he had to face the truth. He'd lied to Meredith last night. He *wasn't* happy about Meredith and Ward Breaux. He was especially not happy that he'd had the perfect opportunity yesterday to tell her the truth—about Ma, about his feelings—but like a coward, at Anne's untimely interruption, he'd allowed all of his doubts and insecurities to come flooding back.

He couldn't blame Ward Breaux for wanting to have a serious relationship with Meredith. And when he compared himself to the tall, fitness-club-commercial-perfect contractor, he couldn't blame Meredith for choosing Ward over him.

After the shower, he took a couple of aspirin to hopefully head off some of the soreness he was sure would come, pulled on a clean pair of sweats and long-sleeved T-shirt, and went into the kitchen to fix supper. He opened the fridge and bent down to make sure he didn't miss seeing anything in there.

Another Friday night, and here he was at home, alone. Alone, while Meredith was probably at this very instant getting ready for another date with Ward Breaux.

He should win her back.

The thought jerked him upright, and he cracked his head on the bottom of the freezer door. Win her back? He'd never had her to begin with. Had he?

He pulled stuff out of the fridge without really paying attention. The only thing that had kept him from asking her out all these years was fear—fear that once she found out about Ma, she wouldn't want anything to do with him. Once burned...

But Meredith wasn't anything like the other women he'd dated in the distant past. He should give her a chance, tell her the truth, see how she reacted.

He remembered the way the women in the stairwell had looked at Ward. Tossing a package of lemon fish onto the cabinet, he let the fridge door swing shut with a condiment-rattling slam. He couldn't compete with that. He'd only look more like a fool if he tried.

But Major had known Meredith a long time; Ward, only a few weeks. Surely Major could call upon his greater knowledge of Meredith's likes and dislikes to draw her attention back to him.

He loped into the living room and sank—painfully—into the desk chair. The notebook in which he'd been writing his sample menus was on top. He flipped to a clean page and started writing a new menu—a menu of ideas for romancing Meredith away from Ward Breaux.

"I ran into your friend, the cook, at the gym this evening." Ward Breaux held open the door of Palermo's Italian Grill and ushered Meredith in before him.

She tried to think which of the cooks he might have met who would have claimed to be anything but an employee of hers. "Which one?"

"Major O'Hara."

"Oh, he's a chef, not a cook."

Ward chuckled. "Isn't that the same thing?"

"No. The title 'chef' is usually reserved for someone who's been to culinary school."

"And that's a big deal?"

"It would be like me calling someone a contractor who doesn't have a license."

"Yeah—I guess it is a big deal when you put it that way. Anyway,

I saw *Chef* O'Hara at the gym tonight. Told him that you wanted him to be involved in the kitchen design, so I'm going to set up a time to get together with him to get his ideas."

The idea of Ward sitting down one-on-one with Major scared her for some reason. "Let me know when so that I can give you my input as well."

Ward launched into his ideas for the kitchen design. Meredith only half listened as they followed the hostess through the large restaurant to a table near the rear windows overlooking the University Lakes. As usual when in public, the other half of her attention was focused on looking around to see if she knew anyone in the room. It wouldn't do to walk past a former client without at least a greeting— that was one of the first things she'd ever learned from Anne.

Meredith opened the large, leather-like menu and started perusing the many selections. She'd eaten here only a couple of times since they'd open a year ago, and then with the family, so they had ordered the family-sized dishes and shared.

The waitress came to the table, introduced herself, and asked if they wanted drinks and an appetizer.

"Go ahead and bring us a basket of fried mushrooms and two iced teas."

"Actually, make mine Sprite with a twist of orange, please," Meredith hastily corrected, miffed Ward had assumed what she would want.

As soon as the waitress departed, Ward covered her hand with his. "Sorry, I should have asked instead of guessing."

"That's okay. I do usually drink iced tea, but sometimes I get in the mood for something else."

They discussed the menu items, and Meredith wasn't any more ready to order when the waitress came back with their drinks than before.

"Do you need more time, Mere?" Ward looked at her with those heavenly eyes.

She wished her heart would pitter-patter or skip a beat or

something. "Go ahead and order, and I'll make a decision by the time you're finished."

After the waitress finished flirting with Ward with her eyes, Meredith ordered crawfish and shrimp alfredo and gave the waitress her menu along with a warning glance. The girl had the good grace to look apologetic.

Though the tight waistband of Meredith's skirt warned her she shouldn't indulge in the fried mushrooms, once she tasted one with the sweet horseradish dipping sauce, she couldn't help but eat a few of them. She didn't want to go back to the much larger size she'd gotten to in college—turning to food after Brent announced his engagement to her roommate—but she wasn't so concerned about her weight that she wouldn't allow herself to indulge in treats every so often.

As they ate dinner, Ward told stories about his siblings, and Meredith shared a few about hers.

"Do you ever get to a point where, while you still love them, you're just good and sick of your relatives?" Ward asked.

"Yeah, that's what I've been going through for the last two weeks, as a matter of fact."

"Really? What happened?"

"You." Meredith grinned at him.

"Me? Was it because we ran into your brother?"

"Sort of, but it was what you said on our first date—asking me if I ever got away from them. And I realized, I never do. That project house has become something of a refuge for me, and I didn't even realize it until you put it into words. The whole reason I've been so gung ho about doing the renovations myself is because that was the only place I could think of where I could get away from all of them."

"Good for you."

"Yeah, it was amazing—I realized I had no private life with my family, and that I needed to take a stand. I decided not to tell them about you." Meredith kept her face straight—because Ward's was so expressive when she teased him.

"You don't want them to know about me?"

"That's right. Unfortunately, one of my younger brothers occasionally goes out with one of the receptionists at the office, and she told him about you coming to pick me up last week; so he asked me about it in front of a bunch of siblings and cousins last night." And Major. She still cringed at that. But everything had seemed pretty normal during their meeting this morning.

"And what did you tell them?" Ward swirled his tea in his glass. The sugar sludge in the bottom barely budged. She still couldn't decide if it was endearing or just gross that he added sugar to already sweetened tea.

"I didn't have to say anything. Forbes—the brother you met—came to my defense. Of course, that was only after I blasted him Sunday afternoon for prying." And then she'd run out like a child. But he didn't need to know that part.

"Can I interest you two in dessert? Tiramisu or apple crostata or amaretto cheesecake?"

Meredith's mouth watered at the mention of cheesecake, her favorite dessert.

"What do you want, Mere?"

"We have a chocolate Gianduia cake that's to die for."

"I'm not real big on chocolate." It shouldn't be that hard of a decision. "I think I'm going to have to pass. My rule is usually that I can have either appetizers or a dessert, but not both. And since I'm taking half my meal home with me. . ."

"What about this?" Ward reached across the table and took her hand. "Why don't you order whatever you want, and I'll split it with you?"

How could such a completely generous and caring man engender absolutely no emotional response from her other than gratitude and a general liking? "Okay. Do you have a cheesecake that doesn't have almonds or amaretto? I'm allergic."

"We have a mascarpone cheesecake, but it has walnuts in the crust."

KAYE DACUS

"Walnuts are fine. Let's go with that."

"I'll be right back with it."

Meredith liked the warmth of Ward's hand around hers—and the idea that anyone in the restaurant looking at them would think they were really a couple...that she really had feelings for this handsome man, that someone had chosen her.

"You slipped away from me there for a minute." Ward's thumb circled her palm. "Where were you just now?"

"My mind wandered."

He grinned. "Fine, keep your secrets."

"I have to start somewhere. I need the practice." The feel of his thumb rubbing her palm nearly sent her into a trance. She squeezed his hand to get him to stop.

"Do you already have plans for Valentine's Day?"

"I do. I'm working that night. It's one of our biggest events of the year—a charity banquet and auction to benefit the cardiac care unit at University Hospital."

"Let me see if I've got this straight. You work New Year's Eve. You work Valentine's Day. Let me guess...you work the Fourth of July?"

"Not usually. But you did skip Easter."

"Easter?"

"Yes. The multichurch sunrise service followed by the Easter egg hunt in Schuyler Park."

"I thought the mayor's wife did that. That's what they always say on the news."

"I know. The mayor's wife is responsible for leading the events and awarding the prizes. So it's a marquee event for her—show her involvement in the community."

"But you plan and organize all of it?"

She shrugged and nodded. "It's my job. I don't need any special recognition for it."

"Uh, yeah, you do. With all of these events falling within a couple of months, I'm surprised you have time to go out to dinner. Glad, but surprised."

"I have a good team of planners and assistants who work with me. I learned early on in this business to identify people's strengths and delegate responsibility to them." Just as Anne had done with her. She'd zeroed in on Meredith's need to please the people she was working with and put Meredith in charge of working with customers. Learning how to stand her ground with vendors had been a hard-won battle.

"I can tell you don't take enough credit for the amount of work you do and that your coworkers probably take you for granted."

He saw things so clearly—things that until she'd met him, her eyes had been closed to. "Maybe."

"Have you ever considered leaving and doing something totally different?"

Only every time she worked a major event. "Occasionally."

"Like becoming an interior designer—maybe one who works hand in hand with a particular contractor?"

"Why, Ward Breaux—are you offering me a job?" She laughed, but it faded quickly when his expression remained serious.

"I haven't seen your design aesthetic, but I can imagine it's got to be impeccable, just from what I know about you and the work you've done on your house."

The waitress chose that moment to return with the dessert. "Here you go. Enjoy."

Meredith hardly tasted the first bite, still stunned by Ward's offer. Leave B-G and go to work with him? Do the kind of work she'd gone to school for?

"Of course, I know you wouldn't make nearly what you make as an executive director with a huge corporation. But there's something to be said for job satisfaction."

She couldn't let him believe she didn't like her job. "I do have satisfaction in my work." She thought about the happy faces of the people at the New Year's Gala. "I make people happy by giving them the best event possible."

"But is that what you really want to do for the rest of your life? If you say yes, I promise I'll never mention designing again. But if you can't say yes, I want you to think about what I said."

She opened her mouth to answer in the affirmative, but something stopped her tongue from forming the word.

Ward nodded. "I won't pressure you, but I just want you to think about it, 'kay?"

"I don't think I'll have any trouble doing that."

CHAPTER 16

$\mathcal{S}$o, you know what I'm thinking? Concrete floors."

Meredith prepared to laugh, then realized that Antoine Delacroix looked like he really meant what he said. "Concrete floors?"

"Yeah. We rip out all this old wood—it just makes everything dark and closed in—and do painted concrete floors."

The months of lovingly restoring the crown molding, the door and window facings, the built-ins made Meredith's fingers tingle with indignation. "Rip out the wood?"

"Yeah. And I'm thinking a totally modern kitchen—colored, laminated, stainless steel and glass, very streamlined."

Mouth agape, she could only stare as Alaine's brother—her much *younger* brother—wandered from the dining room into the barren kitchen. When he'd shown up—almost an hour late—she'd been surprised that someone as young as he appeared to be was already a licensed contractor. And when he'd handed over his credentials, the recent date on the license had confirmed her suspicions.

"Maybe I didn't explain properly over the phone." Meredith followed him into the kitchen. "I want this house *restored* not *remodeled*."

"Same diff." Antoine waved his hand over his shoulder and continued on into the utility room. "Hey, that den is on the other side of this wall isn't it?" He knocked on the back wall. "We could knock this wall out and put in a kickin' wet bar."

This walk-through couldn't end soon enough. What had Alaine been thinking? If she'd meant to set Meredith up with Antoine romantically, she'd overlooked the fact that Meredith was a good ten to twelve years older than this kid. If she thought Meredith would like Antoine's aesthetic, she'd been sorely mistaken.

She leaned heavily against the back door. "You know, Antoine, what I'm really looking for is someone who can come in and restore the house and keep the historical integrity while bringing the utilities and features, like kitchen and bathrooms, up to date."

The wall-knocking stopped, and he stuck his head out of the utility room. "Really? Most folks I talk to want everything modern these days."

"Well, call me old-fashioned, but I bought a craftsman-style house because I love the craftsman style."

"Dude. You should have told me. I really don't do old stuff."

"I guess there's no reason for me to waste more of your time, then, Antoine. I'll walk you out." Meredith waved him toward the front of the house.

"Yep. You're probably right." He preceded her to the front door. "But you really should think about that wet bar idea. It would be sweet."

"I wouldn't have any use for a wet bar." Besides, Ward had suggested taking away half of the space. And Ward knew an architect who could draw up plans before the end of the week so that he could get started soon and have it finished before Anne and George returned from England at the end of March.

Antoine grabbed the front door's handle but turned before opening it. "So, wanna go out sometime?"

Meredith cleared her throat to mask a chuckle. "While I'm flattered by the offer, I..." Was she really going to turn down an offer for a date? Yes. Yes she was. "I'm seeing someone."

"Cool."

She should be indignant at the relief that showed in his dark eyes, but she couldn't quite conjure it. "Bye."

"Later, dude." He loped down the porch steps and sidewalk to his monster-sized luxury SUV, which dug trenches in the driveway and sprayed gravel everywhere when he gunned the engine backing out.

High-pitched yapping from behind the house caught her attention. She hurried through and out onto the back porch. The fuzzball stood with his forepaws on the trunk of one of the massive oaks, barking his head off at a tabby cat.

Meredith put her fingers to the corners of her mouth and whistled. The puppy—who really needed a name if she was going to keep him any longer—whipped around. Overjoyed to see her, he broke out into his lumbering puppy run, tripping over his too-big feet a couple of times before he reached her.

She brushed off a few dead leaves and scooped him up, holding him low enough that his tongue couldn't reach her face. So he concentrated his kisses on her hands instead.

"Come on, li'l booger. Let's drop you off at home so I can get back to work."

Since the afternoon had turned out somewhat pleasant, Meredith decided she could take the risk of leaving the puppy outside in the small fenced area beyond the swimming pool Anne figured had been set up as a dog run by previous residents.

She put him in it then ran inside to get the kennel she'd borrowed from her parents, the bottom padded with the old towels he'd been sleeping on, along with his water dish.

Anne's cell phone went straight to voicemail—must be with a client—so Meredith left her cousin a message to check on the dog if she wasn't home when Anne got there. She pulled out of the driveway headed north, toward downtown.

Corie was just clearing her desk when Meredith hurried in.

"Hey. Everyone's been looking for you." Corie handed her several sticky notes with messages.

Meredith flipped through them quickly. "I already talked to most of them on the way back here. I'll call this one back tomorrow." She wadded the unnecessary messages and handed them to Corie to throw away. "Any deliveries come while I was out?"

Corie shook her head. "I called them several times. They said the linens were on the truck to be delivered today." The assistant put her satchel down in her chair. "Need me to stay and help out with anything so you're not here all night?"

"No. I've got that meeting in"—Meredith glanced at her watch—"two hours. And then I'm out of here."

"Want me to go pick up something for you to eat?"

"Won't be necessary."

Meredith whirled around at Major's voice. He carried a tray with several dome-covered dishes, a pitcher of tea, and a glass full of ice.

Warm gooiness—like a chocolate chip cookie straight from the oven—stuck to Meredith's insides. "Is that for me?"

"Who else?" He nodded toward her door. "Unless you don't want it."

"Don't be ridiculous." Meredith stepped out of his way and motioned him into her office.

"I remembered you said you had a late meeting tonight, and I figured you might appreciate not having to reheat cold leftovers." Major slid the tray onto her table and began putting out a place-setting, complete with cloth napkin and placemat.

"I guess you're taken care of, then." Corie joined Meredith in the doorway. "Here's all the stuff you'll need for the meeting."

"Thanks." She took the stack of folders. "Have a good night."

Corie's gaze cut toward Major; then she grinned at Meredith. "You, too."

Instead of correcting her assistant's erroneous conclusion, Meredith bade her farewell and carried the thick stack of folders to the table.

"You look like you've gotten some sun." Meredith's voice just over his shoulder startled Major, making him clank the plate cover against the ceramic.

Embarrassment kept him from looking up at her; instead, he concentrated on setting the dishes out just so. "Yeah. Alaine suggested I go to a tanning salon and get a little more color so they don't have to use so much makeup on me tomorrow."

"Oh." Meredith picked up one of the folders she'd just put down. "So, that starts tomorrow, huh?"

"Mmm." Major was so not ready to get in front of the camera again. How had he ever agreed to do this? Oh, yeah, that's right. He hadn't. He'd been *told* he'd agreed to do this.

"Do you know what you're going to cook yet?" Meredith perched on the edge of a chair across the table.

"Alaine suggested starting off with a kitchen basics lesson— talking about different techniques, different utensils that most people will be using at home." He swallowed hard. "We're going to be doing it at my condo."

Meredith's head rocked back slightly, and her eyebrows shot up. "Really?"

"Something about not wanting to intimidate the viewers by showing me only in a professional kitchen." Of course, once they saw his kitchen at home, they'd kick him off as a fraud. No professional chef had anything at home as laughable as what he had. "Then it'll mostly be based on viewers' suggestions and questions as to what I cook each week."

"Sounds like a good idea." Meredith fingered the edge of the folder her arm rested atop. "How is this going to affect your work schedule? I heard the filming is pretty much going to eat up your whole day on Tuesdays."

Major added a last-minute garnish of chopped chives and parsley to the blue cheese mashed potatoes and pulled out the chair for Meredith. Really looking at her for the first time since their meeting last Friday morning, he was surprised by how exhausted she looked.

"Can you stay a few minutes?" she asked before sitting.

"Sure." He sank into the chair she'd just vacated. "I'm not sure yet how this thing is going to impact the work flow. Steven has been pretty much running lunch service upstairs for the past five months, so he's ready to step up as *chef de cuisine* and handle everything. I'm just a little concerned that we only have three and a half weeks until the banquet. Normally, tomorrow would have been my day to start calling vendors and placing orders. I did some of that today, but Monday's a really bad day for getting in touch with anyone in the food industry."

Meredith finished off her Caesar salad quickly and started on the blackened lemon fish with the citrus beurre blanc. At the first bite, she closed her eyes and sighed.

Major relaxed. It had been a favorite of his to prepare in culinary school, but he hadn't made it in years, before Friday night. It was definitely going on the short list for the restaurant menu.

"Is that something Steven can help out with?"

"With vendors for the banquet? I'd rather have him concentrating on lunch service. I'm going to have him do the final inventory and budget this week, as well as have him start ordering for next week. I'm going to work closely with him on it, but it's something he should pick up pretty easily. He's a quick learner."

"He's got a good mentor." Meredith gave him a soft smile.

His insides turned into goo. "Thanks."

"Hey, when are you guys going to sing at church again?" Meredith moved her cleared dinner plate aside and pulled the dish of sliced baked apples forward.

"Forbes said something Thursday night about a few new pieces he'd found for us. It's just a matter of us all having time in our schedule to get together and practice. With Clay working most nights, George off gallivanting all over the world, and Forbes and me working long hours, we hardly cross paths anymore."

"That's too bad. Everyone loves to hear y'all sing. It's the only time we ever get to see Forbes doing something that seems completely out of character for him."

Major laughed. "Yeah, he doesn't seem the southern gospel type. Of course, he's the main reason we dress in suits rather than just making sure we're wearing similar color shirts up there."

Meredith lapsed into silence for a moment, stirring the baked apples around in their sauce. "Major, I don't mean to pry into your personal life, so tell me if I'm overstepping bounds here, but I've always been curious about your family."

Frozen iron settled in Major's gut. "Curious about what?"

"Well, you never talk about them. You know so much about mine—have practically been part of our family for a really long time."

His forearms started twitching from how tightly he gripped his fists. "I don't talk about my family because there really isn't much to say." He should tell her. He would tell her.

Meredith looked over at him, head cocked, a half smile playing about those very inviting lips.

No, he couldn't tell her. He didn't want that open, carefree gaze to be tainted with suspicion, wondering when he was going to go off his rocker, too. "I'm an only child who was raised by a single mom."

"And your mom is. . . ?" She pressed her lips together.

As tempting as it was to let her think his mother had passed away, he couldn't lie to her. "Still living."

"Does she still live in Bonneterre?"

"No." Because technically, Beausoleil Pointe Center was outside the city limits.

"That's too bad. So you probably don't get to see her very often." She looked genuinely sad for him.

Guilt pounded in his head and chest. Why couldn't he just bring himself to tell her the truth? "I see her as often as I can." Like every Wednesday evening and Sunday afternoon.

"Well, if she ever comes in town, let me know. I'd love to meet her and tell her how much I. . .appreciate her son."

Wouldn't Ma love that? Someone to rave about him to. "I'll keep that in mind." He refilled her tea glass. "Want me to leave the pitcher? Jeff and Sandra can pick it up when they come down with the snacks for the meeting."

Meredith's eyes lit up. "Is Sandra making cookies?"

Major stood and started collecting the dinner dishes. "Yes—that's why I only brought you baked apples for dessert." He winked at her.

"You know me too well, Major O'Hara."

But not as well as he'd like—oh, there was no use in entertaining those kinds of thoughts anymore. He'd created the recipe for their relationship; now he had to live with the product.

Meredith rose and stretched, her back audibly popping a couple of times. "Guess I'd better get back to it." She leaned across the table and dragged the pile of folders toward her.

"You'll be careful leaving tonight?" He made sure his expression was as stern as he could make it.

"In addition to my facilities maintenance managers, I'll have all of my security supervisors here. Do you think any of them would let me walk to my car alone?" She laughed. "I'll be okay, you old worrywart."

"If I didn't worry about you—" An all too familiar ring interrupted his retort. His heart sank as the ringtone he'd chosen for Beausoleil Pointe Center's main switchboard trilled into the silent office.

Giving Meredith a tight farewell smile, he hefted the service tray up on one shoulder, grabbed the phone with his free hand, and backed out of her office.

"This is Major O'Hara."

"Danny, it's Ma."

Major hurried down the hall to the executive dining room and through to the kitchen. "Ma, what's wrong?" He slid the tray onto the island and went back to stop the swinging door's flapping.

"Does anything have to be wrong for a mother to call her son?"

"No, but you don't usually call me unless something's happened. So what's wrong?"

"Well, you see, Joan and I were going into the dining room for supper—but they call it dinner around here, and I don't know why. You need to tell them that dinner is lunch and dinner at nighttime is supper."

"Ma, focus. What happened?" Major snapped the lights on,

tucked the phone between shoulder and ear, and set to hand-washing the dishes.

"We'd just gotten our trays, but Gene—he's the one with the daughter I was telling you about, the one that just got married." She paused, obviously expecting a response.

"Yes, Gene with the daughter who just got married."

"Right. Anyway, Gene was behind someone else who stopped right in front of him, and Gene ran into her and both of them spilled their iced tea, see?"

"No, Ma. I don't really see yet. Keep going."

"So, Joan and I were talking and we weren't paying much attention to Gene. You know, all he ever talks about is his daughter who just got married. It's like he's rubbing it in that his kid is married and mine isn't. I want grandchildren, Major."

He needed to bang his head against something hard. "What happened, Ma?"

"I fell."

His hands stilled—but his heart pounded faster. "Fell? Are you hurt?"

"No. But they're trying to make me go to bed. I don't want to go to bed, Danny. Tell them I don't have to go to bed."

Head throbbing, he set the clean dishes on the drain board and found a clean towel to dry his hands on. "Put the doctor on."

"There's no doctor, just that little boy who keeps saying he is one. But I don't think he's old enough. You need to come out here and tell them I don't want to go to bed."

"Give the phone to him, please."

"You're coming, right?"

"Yes, Ma, I'll come. Now give the phone to. . .the little boy."

A bit of fumbling on the line ended with, "This is Nick Sevellier."

"Dr. Sevellier, how bad is she?"

"She's a little banged up and hit her head pretty hard when she fell. But it's not a concussion, so we see no reason to have her taken to the emergency room."

Major'd taken his share of spills, working in kitchens since he was fifteen, and he knew just how dangerous even falling on a wood floor like those at BPC could be. "Was she knocked out?"

"Not at all. But she's developing a pretty good knot on the back of her head."

"And your medical opinion is bed rest?" The kid called himself a doctor, but Major didn't know this kid's credentials.

"My previous rotation was in the emergency room, Mr. O'Hara. I had to deal with a lot of head traumas there. I'm more worried about how sore she's likely to be tomorrow. She wrenched her back a little bit, so I'd like her to lie down and let the nurses give her an ice and heat treatment."

"Okay. Thanks. Put her back on the phone." Major sighed.

"Did you tell him I'm not going to bed?"

"Ma, let them take care of you. I'll be there in a few minutes."

By the time he convinced her, he was back in his office gathering his coat and duffel. "Ma, I've got to go," he said quietly, to avoid Jeff or Sandra hearing him out in the kitchen. "Hang up the phone and let the nurses take you back to your room. I'll be there in about twenty minutes."

"I don't like you very much right now." The line clicked and went dead.

"I love you, too, Ma." Major threw the phone into his bag and turned off the office light.

"Everything okay, boss?" Sandra asked. The cookies she'd just taken from the oven filled the large space with a heavenly aroma.

"Yeah, just fine." He slung his bag over his shoulder. "Jeff, there are some dishes on the drain board down in the executive kitchen. Will you bring those up and run them through the sterilizer with everything else before you leave tonight?"

"Can do, Chef." Jeff didn't look up from the cheese straws he was piping onto a large baking sheet with a pastry bag.

"Meredith is in her office if you need anything."

"Yes, Chef," both cooks responded.

Once in the elevator, Major leaned heavily against the wall, rubbing his forehead. Though he hated keeping secrets from Meredith, tonight's episode with Ma reminded him of why he needed to keep her as far away from Meredith as he could, lest she ruin Meredith's life, too.

CHAPTER 17

$\mathcal{M}$ajor rubbed his dry, burning eyes and looked around the condo one more time, just to make sure he hadn't missed anything. Which he knew he hadn't, since he'd been up at 4:00 a.m. to clean an already spotless apartment.

Maybe he should vacuum one more time.

No. He'd vacuumed twice already. He stepped into the kitchen and caught sight of the clock on the back of the stove. They would be here in less than fifteen minutes, and he wasn't even dressed.

The producer from Alaine's show who'd called yesterday had suggested Major not wear his chef's jacket for the segments. He slid the closet door open and shuffled through his button-down shirts. Solid blue in a variety of shades; blue with stripes and patterns; white with blue stripes of various widths. . .didn't he have anything other than blue? Yes—gray. The producer had wanted him somewhat casual—"weekend wear," she'd called it. Well, he didn't really think that sweats and a ULB T-shirt were appropriate. Instead, he donned a plain white T-shirt, khakis, and a blue-gray waffle-weave pullover that allowed a bit of the white undershirt to show at the neck.

With just a few minutes remaining, he ducked into the bathroom to brush his teeth, again. He should have gotten his hair cut before today. It was going to be flopping down onto his forehead all day. After cleaning the sink and counter with a disinfecting wipe, he straightened the hand towels one more time.

He jumped at the rifle-shot sound of the knock on the front door. When he opened it, a plain woman of indeterminate age wearing a Channel Six–logoed Windbreaker stood on the other side.

She extended her right hand. "Major O'Hara? I'm Pricilla Wilson. We spoke on the phone yesterday."

"Yes. Please come in." He stepped out of the doorway into the space between his living room and dining area.

The cameraman who'd come with Alaine to the tasting last week entered behind her, pushing a cart piled with equipment cases.

"Can I help with anything?"

The cameraman grunted, which Major took as a no, and Major pointed him toward the kitchen.

"While he sets up the lights and cameras, let's sit and discuss the plan for today." Pricilla pulled out one of the chairs and sat at the table, scattering a stack of papers all over it in a matter of seconds. "We've got a lot of stuff to film and not a lot of time to do it."

Eight hours sounded like quite a lot of time to Major.

"The girl doing your hair and makeup will be here in about forty-five minutes—"

"Hey, Priss"—the camera guy came around the corner—"you'd better come look."

Major followed them but stood in the hallway outside the kitchen, since three people wouldn't fit.

Pricilla hit a couple of keys on her phone and pressed it to her ear. "Hey, it's me. We've got no joy here."

Mortification rang in Major's ears and burned every surface of his body.

"Kitchen's way too small for the equipment we need for filming." Pricilla came out of the kitchen to pace the length of the living room. "Of course not. We expected a chef would have at least a decent home kitchen. . . . You want what?"

She brushed past Major again and pulled the phone away from her ear. "Nelson, pack it all up. We're going." Back to the person on the other end of the phone, she said, "Yeah. We'll see you in about twenty minutes."

Major followed her back to the dining table, where she scraped up all her papers—and the placemat.

He reached over and rescued the mat. "What's going on?"

She stuffed the papers into her bag. "We can't shoot here. Your kitchen's too small. So we're taking all this elsewhere."

"Where?"

"Alaine's place."

Major stopped cold. "Where?"

"Alaine Delacroix's place. She thinks her kitchen will work better, so bring what you might need that she may not have, and let's get going. We're on a tight schedule today." Pricilla turned her back on him and made another phone call.

Major had to wait until Nelson got all of his equipment cases out of the kitchen before he could go in. He looked around for what to take with him and grabbed his knife case right away. No chef ever went anywhere without his knives. But what about everything else? Food processor, blender, steamer, butane warmers...

The whole point of what they were doing today was to familiarize people with stuff they already had in their home kitchens. What better way to do that than in the kitchen of someone who didn't have professional-quality products? He tucked his knife case into his duffel bag and joined the production assistant and cameraman at the door.

"I'll follow you over there." He locked the door behind them and trailed them out to the parking lot where, this time, Nelson accepted his help in loading all of the equipment back into their van.

The van headed toward Old Towne and into an older part of the townhouse development where Forbes lived. Major had looked at a couple of units here when he'd moved back to town, but even though he'd much preferred the kitchens, the price on his condo had been more palatable.

He parked one space away from the van to give them room

for taking equipment out, just as a small, sporty Mazda with dark windows pulled into the driveway at the townhouse across the roadway.

Alaine sprang out of the little black car—but if Major hadn't known she was meeting them here, he might not have recognized her. Dressed in jeans and a black sweater, she wore her hair pulled up at the back of her head haphazardly as if done on the fly, and she didn't have any makeup on, making her look pale and wan.

"I had a great idea on the way over here." Alaine jogged across the street to help with equipment. "Hey, Major."

"Hi, Alaine."

"What's this idea?" Pricilla asked.

"Were you working at the Food Network when Gordon Elliott did that show where he went around and dropped in on people and made a meal from whatever they had in their kitchens?"

"That was before my time, but I watched it pretty regularly." Pricilla heaved a large case onto the cart. "You want him to do something like that?"

Major loved being talked about as if he weren't standing right there with them.

"Similar idea. What if he were to fix a meal just from whatever I have on hand in my kitchen? He could explain what he's doing but also go ahead and give recipes and tips and a cooking demonstration along the way." Alaine finally turned to acknowledge his presence. "What do you think?"

Considering he hadn't wanted to do this in the first place? "Sounds like it would be better than me trying to demonstrate how different things work or explain what they're used for."

"Try to use as much of the stuff that I have in my kitchen as you can—there are a bunch of things in there that I don't even know what they are. My mom gives me stuff for my kitchen every year on my birthday and at Christmas. I guess she hopes I'll eventually stop hating to cook and start using all of it." She wrinkled her nose like Samantha on *Bewitched* when she grinned.

He couldn't help but laugh. Why did everyone he know hate to cook? "I'll see what I can do. But if you don't like cooking, am I going to have any ingredients to work with?"

"I went to the grocery store last night. I always have the greatest intentions, but I never follow through. Fortunately, Mama likes my kitchen better than her own, so she usually comes over one night during the week and cooks up a bunch of meals for me."

Oh, to have a mother who could do stuff like that without burning down the building. "Great. Let's go see what you have, and I'll come up with a menu."

He followed Alaine through the one-car garage—which was empty, so it looked as if she actually used it for her car—up several steps, and into a utility room/pantry. He stopped and looked at the dry goods on the shelves. Flour, sugar, baking powder and soda, spices, dried herbs, canned vegetables and fruits, and cereal—lots of cereal.

Alaine's cheeks were red when he finished his perusal. "I'm a big cereal-for-supper girl. And breakfast."

Meredith had been that way, too, until he'd stepped in and started making sure she had decent meals to take home with her every day. "Show me to your kitchen."

Jealousy struck instantly when he stepped out of the utility room and into the main part of the house. Though not huge, the fact that the kitchen was completely open to the living and dining rooms made it feel huge. And she had upgraded stainless appliances, including a gas stove built into the eat-at island that divided the kitchen from the rest of the space.

"So, Chef, tell me what you think." Pride laced Alaine's voice.

"It's great. I didn't know any of these units had kitchens like this. The ones I looked at were much smaller and more closed off—they just had pass-through windows."

"The people who owned this before me completely renovated it based on something they saw on TV. The colors were hideous—tomato red walls and a green tile backsplash so it looked like Christmas all the time—but that was a pretty easy fix. And I got the place for a song—I mean, most buyers can't stand the fact that the front overlooks a bunch of old, dilapidated warehouses across the highway."

"But you don't care about the view?"

Alaine turned slowly around, her arms extended. "When I could have this?"

"I see your point."

She looked at her watch and sighed. "While I'd love to stay and watch you work, I've got to get back to the station and finish writing some stories for today's show. Have fun, and leave me some leftovers." She winked and left.

Pricilla and Nelson brought in the equipment and went to work setting it all up while Major explored Alaine's kitchen. At first, he felt odd going through all the drawers and cabinets, until he started seeing the quality of her cookware and small appliances. Not quite professional quality, but definitely top of the line.

Once familiar with where everything was, he pulled his spiral notebook out of his duffel and went to the fridge. Inventorying its contents, he started writing down ideas for dishes that were moderately simple and quick, that pretty much anyone could cook if given the right instruction. The freezer offered up even more ideas, especially once he saw the lamb shoulder steaks and artichoke hearts. He took them out, filled half the sink with cold water, and put the plastic-bagged meat in it to start thawing.

The makeup gal, Charla, arrived and had Major sit on one of the stools from the island, which had been moved into the middle of the living room. She tucked paper towels around his collar and went to work. Pricilla took the opportunity to wire him up with a lapel microphone—which she had to run up under his shirt from the battery pack clipped to the back of his belt. As he could throughout the process, he wrote recipe ideas, trying to figure out exactly how to explain the processes and eliminating several ideas as too complicated to explain.

"Have you ever thought about getting your teeth whitened?" Charla asked.

"No. Can't say as I have." What—were his teeth *that* bad?

"Hmm." Charla shrugged and made a face as if to say, *Your funeral.*

Great, one more thing to be self-conscious about. Pudgy face, check. Bad hair, check. Hideously discolored teeth, check. He'd hit the trifecta.

He held his breath to keep from sneezing when Charla dusted powder over his whole face. "Now, whatever you do, don't touch your face. Don't scratch your nose or rub your eyes."

Immediately, his entire face started itching. "I'll do my best. What about sweating?"

"This makeup can withstand a lot of moisture, but try not to sweat too much. If you feel like you're going to need it, turn the thermostat down or open some windows to cool off." She closed up her makeup kit—which looked like a fishing tackle box—and shrugged into a coat with a huge furry collar. "I'll be in and out all day for touch-ups."

"Thanks."

"Keep those paper towels in your collar except when you're filming. I guess they didn't tell you not to wear white up on your neck."

"No. Sorry."

"That's okay. Just try to keep your head up at all times so your makeup doesn't rub onto the white shirt."

Great. Now everyone involved in this project was frustrated with him. "Will do."

"Chef, we're ready to get some test shots of you," Pricilla called.

They'd set the tripod camera up across the island from the cooktop, and Nelson had another one on his shoulder.

"Here's the deal." Pricilla pulled one of the stools over beside the tripod and set her clipboard down on the seat. "This is the camera you're going to talk into, and I'm going to be running it. Nelson is going to be getting shots from more of an over-your-shoulder perspective. We may have to run through some of the steps a couple of times so that he can get close-ups of what you're doing."

"Did I hear Alaine say you used to work at the Food Network?"

"I did two internships there as an undergrad and as a graduate student and then worked there a couple of years after college." Pricilla smiled for the first time this morning. "Having a cooking segment on Alaine's show was my suggestion."

Now he knew whom to blame for this entire fiasco. He went around to the stove. Pricilla adjusted the fixed camera's angle. "Move around as if you're cooking—go to the sink and the fridge, move to the side of the stove where you'll chop vegetables. . . ."

Major moved around the kitchen as directed, doing his best not to be freaked out that a big guy with a large camera on his shoulder was following his every move. The lights they'd put up in every corner of the triangular kitchen were really heating up the place, and he hadn't even turned on the stove or oven yet.

"You good, Nelson?" Pricilla asked.

"Yep."

"Let's go through your menu, Chef, and figure out the best order for doing this. We want it to be real time as much as possible— meaning that if someone was really making this for a meal, they'd have to be working on multiple projects all at once. We aren't just going to do a dish at a time."

Forty-five minutes later, he pulled the paper towels out of his collar and began explaining to the camera how to thaw frozen meat safely.

"Let me stop you for a second, Chef." Pricilla came out from behind her camera.

His heart pounded, and he really needed a bottle of water from the case he'd seen in the pantry. "What's wrong?"

"First, you need to remember to breathe. You're talking way too fast."

"Right. Breathe. What else?" He took a couple of gulps of air to prove he could do what she said.

"Don't say *all right* at the beginning of each sentence and end each sentence with *okay*, okay?" She nodded her head.

"Right. No *all rights* or *okays*."

"Ready to go again?"

He gave her a thumbs-up. "Ready." He launched into his explanation of defrosting meat again, trying to slow down the words tumbling out of his mouth and stumbling each time he was about to say the no-no words.

"Let me stop you again, Chef." Pricilla sounded a little more frustrated this time. Major knew just how she felt.

"Still too fast?"

"A little bit. But the problem is that you don't sound like you're talking to a person. You sound like you're talking to a camera. Forget that it's a piece of equipment. Pretend that there's someone you know really well, who doesn't know how to cook, sitting right here across from you. Talk to that *person*. In your head, carry on a conversation with them. Imagine their reactions to what you're saying. Can you do that?"

"Imagine a person, right." A person. A person who didn't know how to cook. Slowly, a grin split his lips. Meredith. Of course. The one person he'd love to spend time with in the kitchen more than anyone else. Imagine Meredith sitting here, taking cooking lessons from him. Imagine this was his kitchen and Meredith was here with him, lending her moral support and gazing on him affectionately with those wonderfully expressive brown eyes.

"Let's try it again." Pricilla made another notation on her clipboard and moved back behind the camera.

For the next six hours, Major talked to Meredith—through the camera—and created dishes he knew she would be able to recreate if she put her mind to it. Finally, at four o'clock after Nelson got close-up shots of the plated dishes, Pricilla called it a wrap.

Having cleaned as he went—as he'd been taught to do by Aunt Maggie—Major didn't have much cleanup to finish, so he immediately set to it, eager to run up to the office to find out how everything had gone today.

"Now, when you come in Thursday to do the voice-over—"

He whipped around at Pricilla's words. "What? Where am I supposed to go Thursday?"

"Didn't I tell you we'd need you to come in and do some voice-overs for where we've edited the segment down?" The corner of her mouth pulled down in a sheepish expression.

"No. I wasn't told I'd have to do more than just filming on Tuesdays. How much time do you think it'll take?" He couldn't afford any more time away from work. And if he started the restaurant, he'd need every hour he could get.

"An hour, maybe ninety minutes. You'll get to watch the edited segment through and write out what to say to bridge where we've condensed. Remember, this is fitting into a fifteen-minute segment. It's just too bad that everyone at the studio won't get a chance to taste it, because just what you fixed us for lunch was fabulous."

"Thanks." Yeah, having to cater lunch for all of Alaine's co-workers would be the cherry on top of this hot-stress sundae. He rummaged around in her cabinets for storage containers. He separated all the food out into single serving sizes and labeled everything with the masking tape and marker he found in one of the drawers. Too bad he hadn't thought to bring a disposable takeaway box so that he'd have something to take back to Meredith.

He hummed as he worked, enjoying the sense of accomplishment that washing the last few dishes gave him. By the time Alaine's kitchen was as spotless as it had been when he'd walked in, Pricilla and Nelson had finished loading their equipment in the van.

Pricilla came back in and closed the garage door then ushered Major out the front, locking the door behind them. She gave Major a funny look as they walked down the steps.

"What?"

"You're going to want to wash that makeup off as soon as you get home. Most people complain that their faces break out pretty bad if they wear it for more than a couple of hours."

His face suddenly started itching again. "Thanks. I'll do that." He had to go right past his complex on his way to the office, so he might as well stop and do it there.

"See you Thursday," Pricilla called, swinging up into the passenger seat of the van.

He waved and climbed into Kirby. As he drove home, he reviewed the day. Thank goodness Pricilla had the idea to tell him to imagine talking to someone. He'd be forever indebted to Meredith for helping him make it through his first day of filming. Maybe one day he'd really have the chance to spend that much time with her one-on-one.

He just hoped it wasn't so she could cook for Ward Breaux or any other man.

Chapter 18

As the weeks dwindled down to days and then hours before the Hearts to HEARTS banquet, Meredith began to realize just how hard her New Year's resolution was going to be to fulfill. Though she had been asked out twice since Antoine's invitation, and had even gone out with one of the guys, she just couldn't seem to find anyone she wanted to spend a whole evening with, let alone the rest of her life. And while she enjoyed Ward's company, she couldn't force herself to fall in love with him.

She stared out over the city from the glass-front elevator. Truth of the matter was, no matter how hard she tried to get over Major, each man she met seemed to reinforce just how deep her feelings for him ran.

Fat lotta good being in love with him would do for her, though. That he was falling for Alaine Delacroix couldn't be any more apparent—from the tanning to the teeth whitening to going to the gym and losing weight, he seemed to be doing everything he could to make himself fit the image of a man someone like Alaine would deign to be seen with.

Shame tingled on her skin. Alaine had never been anything but friendly with Meredith, and she couldn't allow her own jealousy to shine an unflattering and untrue light on the reporter.

The elevator doors slid open on the twenty-third floor. Speaking of Alaine...

The facilities staff swarmed the enormous floor space of Vue de Ceil, with a cameraman and his spotter hustling around in the chaos getting shots of the setup. Meredith jinked and dodged through the mayhem to get to the service corridor on the other side. She wished she could stop and enjoy the way the red and orange sunset made the banquet facility glow, but she did at least spare it a moment's glance, hoping tomorrow's sunset would be just as spectacular.

The pandemonium in the kitchen wasn't at quite the fevered pitch of the banquet hall, though the presence of another cameraman and spotter, along with Alaine and her producer, did make it feel much more crowded than usual.

"Hey, Meredith." Alaine waved in greeting.

Meredith slipped through the busy cooks and porters to join her. "How long have y'all been here?"

"Since nine this morning. Well, not me, because I had to do my show. But Pricilla and Nelson were here at nine to start filming prep. I brought everyone else with me after the show wrapped. Good thing this was Major's regular day for filming and that the banquet is our feature for his segment this week."

Meredith moved out of the way as a prep cook came out of the walk-in refrigerator behind them with a crate of pears. "My mother said something to me about Major and me meeting you at the studio Friday?"

"Yes—didn't my intern call you?" Alaine shook her head, her plump curls bouncing around her shoulders. "I'll have to have a word with him. You and Major are my featured guests on the show Friday."

"On the show—*on* the *show*?" Meredith's legs wanted to give out on her.

"Yes. It's going to be clips of the event—and all of the stuff we've filmed up until now—interspersed with live chat with the two of you about it. Don't worry; you'll be fine. You did great in our interview."

"Yeah, well, that was just the two of us in my office. I'm sure you've got a bunch of people in the studio watching when you do your show." She stuffed her hands into her pants pockets to keep from wiping the sweat on the ivory fabric.

Alaine patted her shoulder. "It'll be okay; I promise." She glanced over at the prep cook who was in the process of peeling and coring the pears. "What are those for?"

"Poached pears with ginger crumble. One of the three dessert choices the diners were given." She was particularly glad Mrs. Warner and the board had stayed away from the two desserts containing tropical fruit. Though she trusted Major's staff to be cautious about cross-contamination of foods such as raw meats, most prep cooks didn't worry about cleaning and sanitizing a work surface between cutting up different types of fruit. And if someone who'd been working on the tropical fruit touched something else that then touched something Meredith might eat that night. . .

She shuddered. The memory of the last time she'd eaten something that had been cut on the same surface as kiwi wasn't pleasant. Her throat had been sore from the breathing tube for nearly a week afterward. But at least it'd kept her from suffocating when the swelling from the allergic reaction nearly closed her windpipe.

"How did that whole thing work? I know you and Mrs. Warner narrowed down the choices from what was presented to the board a few weeks ago." Alaine pulled her pen from behind her ear, ready to write on the steno pad in her left hand.

"Once we narrowed that down, I had menus made up giving each banquet attendee a choice of starter salad, protein—from red meat, poultry, seafood, or vegetarian—and dessert. The menus will be at each place, and the wait staff will take the guests' orders as they serve beverages." Meredith glanced around for Major but didn't see him. She didn't really need to talk to him, but coming up to ask Alaine about Friday had been all the excuse she'd needed for an opportunity to bump into Major.

"But all of the meals are served at the same time?" Alaine scribbled on her notepad.

"Yes. Dinner service is at seven o'clock sharp."

"How do you know how many of each dish to prepare?"

"Based on the percentages of how many chose similar dishes last year," Major said, and Meredith turned, heart thrumming. "Hey, there."

"Hi." She wanted to think that the warmth of his smile, the soft expression in his eyes were for her—but who was she kidding? No man in his right mind would look at her like that when she was standing next to someone like Alaine. Just as she'd only seen that kind of expression in men's faces whenever she was with Jenn.

"What brings you up to the kitchen? Everything okay?" Though he looked at Meredith, his attention was most definitely divided between her and what was going on in his domain.

"I needed to ask Alaine a question about Friday."

"Yeah." He crossed his arms as his gaze wandered over his staff. "That sort of took me by surprise, too. But it'll be easier to do it together."

"Chef!"

"Gotta go." He squeezed Meredith's shoulder and disappeared into the intricate ballet dance of a frenzied kitchen.

"I guess I'd better head back downstairs and get back to work myself." Meredith sighed.

"What are you working on today?" Alaine looked as if she wanted to follow Meredith back to her office, which was the last thing she needed.

"All of the last-minute details—confirming all vendors and deliveries for items not arriving until late tonight or tomorrow, coordinating with all departments involved to make sure the work is getting done"—her cell phone started ringing— "and fielding lots of phone calls."

Alaine grimaced. "I won't keep you, then. See you around."

"See you." Meredith answered the phone as soon as she stepped out into the nominally quieter hallway. "This is Meredith."

"Mere, it's Corie. You'd better get down here. I've got the florist on the phone—he says it's urgent."

"I'll be there in a minute." Instead of risking the stop-and-go pace of the main elevators, Meredith opted for the freight elevator across from her, which let her off just across the hall from the executive kitchen on the fifth floor. She swiped her security card and dashed through the dim kitchen and dining room to her office.

"Which line?" Three of them flashed, signaling they were on hold. "Two."

Meredith took a deep breath. "This is Meredith Guidry."

What had sounded like an emergency turned out only to be a glitch with the schedule for delivery of the centerpieces. She dealt with it and moved on to the uniform supplier on line one and the symphony director on line three, who wanted to inform her she was getting four violins and two violas instead of three and three as originally planned.

In a brief respite between phone calls, Meredith finally took the aspirin she'd been thinking about taking for her headache all afternoon.

Corie knocked on her open door and stepped inside the office. "I just got off the phone with Giovanni's. The pizza is on its way."

"Great. Thanks for handling that." Meredith picked up the phone and dialed the extension for the Vue de Ciel kitchen.

"Catering division, Steven LeBlanc speaking."

"Steven, it's Meredith. Is Major easily accessible?"

"Sure. Hold on just a second." The freight-train sound of the busy kitchen was replaced by soft classical music for a moment until Major picked up.

"Hey, Mere. What's up?"

"The pizza's on the way here. How do you want to handle sending folks down to eat?"

"Let's send the facilities staff down first. It'll be easier for them just to stop what they're doing and take a dinner break. Once they're fed, I'll have my crew come down as they get to stopping points. I'll send a couple of porters down with the ice chests of sodas, but other than that, the executive dining room should be set up for buffet service."

"Mind if I keep your porters and have them help sort pizzas and get everything organized?"

"I figured you would. They'll be down in a minute."

Meredith rubbed the back of her neck. "Remind me why we decided against canceling lunch service today?"

"We?" He chuckled. "I thought that command came down from on high."

"Hmm. Yeah, I guess you're right."

"See you in a bit."

"Bye." Her hand lingered on the receiver for a few seconds after she hung up. How would she do this without him? She almost snorted at the irony. Maybe if he did decide to start the restaurant, she should take Ward up on his offer to work as his interior designer so she didn't have to find out how horrible this kind of event would be without Major at her right hand.

She leaned back in her chair and let her eyes wander over the features of her office—wrecked though it was currently. Seeing Corie, Pam, and Lori bustling around in the outer office warmed the cockles of her heart. And though right now it seemed crazy, she was actually excited about the banquet tomorrow night. She couldn't wait to see the looks on the board members' faces when they walked in and saw how the thousands of candles sparkled off the glass walls and ceiling.

She thought about Easter in the Park and the library fund-raiser in May. She couldn't think of anyone her parents might hire to replace her who would put heart and soul into those events the way she would. She pressed her thumbs and forefingers to the corners of her eyes.

Truth of the matter was—she liked her job. Despite the fact her parents had little respect for her position, doing her job gave her pleasure. And even with as much as she enjoyed working on her house for the past couple of months, she knew she wouldn't get as much pleasure from remodeling and redecorating houses as she got from planning events. God had given her the heart, mind, and soul to be doing exactly what she was doing.

And there was always the slight possibility that Major might not take her parents' offer.

Around seven o'clock, Major went to each station in the kitchen and told his people to go down to eat as soon as they got to a point where they could stop.

Steven returned from his quick dinner break, allowing Major the opportunity to go grab a bite. Out in the main room, the facilities staff were just getting back to work, and Alaine stood over to one side, talking to her people as they packed up equipment.

He detoured over to them. "Calling it a night?"

"They are. I'm going to stick around awhile longer if that's okay with you." Alaine pulled her hair back into a ponytail.

"That's fine. Why don't y'all come down and grab some pizza before you go." He nodded toward the freight elevator. "This one takes us practically right to where the food is set up."

Only one of the camera assistants didn't want to stay. Major led the rest of them down to the fifth floor. Most of his kitchen staff sat around the carved mahogany tables in the executive dining room—a place none of them had probably ever dreamed of eating a meal, even though the pizza was served on paper plates.

The two event planners, Pam and Lori, along with Meredith's assistant, sat with pastry chefs Sandra and Jeff, having what looked like a very entertaining discussion. Major glanced around the room again. He hadn't been mistaken—no Meredith.

Corie got up and came over to him. "She's still in her office. Maybe you might have better luck convincing her to take a break and come get something to eat."

"I'll give it a shot." He went across the hall to Meredith's office. Her door was half shut. He knocked lightly and pushed it open.

Meredith and Mairee looked up from the large piece of paper they were leaning over, spread on Meredith's table.

"Everything okay?" Meredith asked, her eyes begging him to say yes.

"I was just getting ready to ask you the same question." He nodded toward the table-layout schematic.

Meredith rubbed the back of her neck. "Just a few last-minute RSVP changes, so we're having to rearrange some of the seating assignments."

"Additions?" He joined them at the table.

"Yes." Meredith pointed to an eight-top table she'd penciled in. "But it works here. Remember how you and Orly kept saying that side of the room looked unbalanced? Well, now it's balanced."

He nodded. "I reviewed the original with Jana this afternoon for server assignments, so I'll be sure to inform her of the change tomorrow before the staff arrive so she can adjust coverage if she needs to."

"Well, I'm going to leave this in your more-than-capable hands." Mairee put her hand to the small of Meredith's back. "Meredith and Major, you've done a wonderful job on the preparation, and I know tomorrow night is going to be spectacular." With a smile trailing behind her, she turned toward her own office, her gait a bit stiff.

Meredith left the floor plan on the table and went around to collapse in her desk chair.

Major followed and grabbed her hands. "Nope, come on. You need something to eat."

"I'm too exhausted to eat." She resisted his gentle tugging for a few seconds, then, with a sigh, got back out of her chair. "All right. I'm coming."

It was all Major could do to let go of her once she was back on her feet. Her hands fit perfectly in his, felt just right clasped there. He tried not to think about Ward Breaux, with his big catcher's mitts, holding Meredith's hands.

Corie passed them on their way into the dining room, and she grinned at him. "See, I told you that you would have better luck convincing her."

Meredith didn't seem to hear—or care about—what her assistant said. "Corie, do you mind staying until I get back? I'd hate to think what would happen if someone else calls and I'm not there to answer it."

"I already told you I can stay as late as you need me."

The fatigue in Meredith's face vanished when she smiled. "Thanks. You're sweet as a Georgia peach."

"And twice as sassy." Corie cocked an eyebrow and laughed.

Meredith went over to talk to Pam and Lori, so Major fixed plates and grabbed sodas for both of them. He chose a table a little bit away from where the few remaining kitchen staff sat, wanting to give Meredith a few minutes' peace before she dived back into work.

On her way to join him, she made a full tour of the room, speaking to everyone, including Alaine and her camera crew. Compared to Alaine, on whom the toll of the long day was evident, Meredith looked as if she were just starting her day—shoulder-length hair perfectly in place, cream-colored pantsuit not in the least rumpled or wrinkled, skin as luminous as ever. Alaine, on the other hand, with her hair pulled back in a limp ponytail, looked like she'd been through the wringer. She'd slung her suit coat across the back of her chair, kicked her shoes off under the table, and rolled her shirtsleeves up. But it was in her face, in the dark circles beneath her eyes and the slight downward turn of her mouth, that her fatigue showed the most.

His chest tightened with pride in Meredith and how she thrived in a whirlwind like tonight. Finally, she joined him. He asked a blessing, and they launched into eating.

After her third slice of pizza, Meredith leaned back, popped open a second can of Diet Coke, and took a long swig of the soda. "Ah. I needed that. Thanks for making me come eat."

Major weighed the pleasure of a fourth slice against the pain of the extra running he'd have to do on the treadmill later on. The pizza won. "Want some more?"

"Some apple dessert pizza would be great." She handed him her plate.

197

After getting her dessert and his fourth slice, he turned to see Alaine had joined Meredith at the table. He grimaced. He'd hoped to have Meredith to himself for at least a few more minutes before he had to get back up to the kitchen.

"Major, I've been wondering something," Alaine said before he could regain his seat.

"What's that?" He handed Meredith a fork to go along with her dessert.

"I was a little surprised to see that you actually wear your chef's jacket to cook in. I always thought those were just for show—you know, something you put on before you come out of the kitchen to take a bow. Hardly any of the chefs on TV wear one."

Every muscle in his body cringed. He hated it when people compared what he did to what the celebrity chefs did on TV. Wait a minute—*he* was now one of those TV chefs. Oh, the irony. "The jacket is actually a very practical piece of the kitchen uniform in addition to looking good. It's double-breasted to protect from burns, but also, if something gets spilled, it can be rebuttoned with the other side out to hide the stain." He went on for another minute or two on the design and proper usage of the chef's jacket.

"So, would it be better if we had you wear one in your segment?" Alaine propped her elbow on the table and rested her cheek against her fist.

"Probably not. Since I'm supposed to be preparing what people can do in their home kitchens, it would probably look pretentious if I started wearing it after I've already been on the show for two weeks without it." He ate a few bites of the pizza before he realized he wasn't hungry anymore.

"Yeah, that probably wouldn't go over very well." Alaine raised her hand to cover her yawn. "Sorry, I've been up since five this morning."

Major caught Meredith's eye—they'd walked in together from the parking garage at a quarter of six this morning. The corner of Meredith's lips quirked up, but she turned her attention to her apple pizza.

"I've been meaning to tell you, though, that the feedback we've

198

been getting from viewers has been overwhelmingly positive. You're a big hit with my viewers, Chef O'Hara." A little bit of the glimmer returned to Alaine's dark eyes.

"That's good to know. I'd hate to think I was tanking and taking your show down with me." Actually, he'd tried not to think of it, because he knew finding out wouldn't be good for maintaining a healthy level of ego.

"The feedback we get most often, from our female viewers of course, is that they feel like you're talking straight to them. Some of them were afraid that you might do stuff that was way over their heads or too fancy or that you would use terminology or techniques they didn't understand. But they say they feel like you're just a friend who's come into their kitchens to give them a one-on-one cooking lesson." Alaine stifled another yawn. "Which is exactly what we were hoping for."

This time, Major didn't risk looking at Meredith. If only Alaine knew to whom he was really talking when he explained what he was doing. If only Meredith knew that he sometimes imagined she was there with him, sharing and participating in his favorite thing to do.

Lord, I love Meredith. I want to marry her. Please, show me what to do.

CHAPTER 19

When the first guests arrived at six thirty, Meredith breathed a relieved sigh, thankful they'd never know how frantic Vue de Ceil had been mere moments ago. But now, all of the tables were set, candles lit, place cards where they were supposed to be. In their white tuxedo shirts, black bow ties, and black pants, several servers waited with her near the elevator foyer to show guests to their seats.

"Good evening, Mr. and Mrs. d'Arcement. Good to see you again. You are at table twenty-three. Jeremy will take you. I hope you have a wonderful evening." Meredith glanced down at her list to double-check that the d'Arcements were indeed at table twenty-three. She had to keep reminding herself there had been too many last-minute changes to rely totally on her visual memory of the seating chart.

After more than half of the three hundred expected guests had arrived, one of the newer workers looked at Meredith in awe. "Wow. You know everybody. You haven't once had to ask anyone's name."

"I've been doing this a very long time, and most of the people who are coming tonight have come to this event every year since we started. A lot of them come to most of the events we do." She looked over as two of the elevators opened at the same time. Her parents and several other couples came toward them.

Meredith greeted everyone by name and handily sent them with

200

servers to their tables. She stepped away from the service staff to speak with her parents, while still keeping an ear out for the chime that indicated an arriving elevator.

"How's it looking?" her father asked, craning his neck to glance around the venue.

"We'll have a few latecomers as usual, but it looks like the majority have chosen to show up on time this year. It really helped to put on all of the mailers they received that dinner would be served *at* seven o'clock." Her gaze caught on the black-clad cameraman and his spotter in the corner near the orchestra. She was glad she'd won the battle, insisting on one stationary camera out of the main line of sight of the guests rather than the two or three cameramen wandering around in the room Alaine had wanted, their bright lights interfering with the mood set by the thousands of candles now reflecting off the walls and ceiling.

Mom, instead of looking around the room, scrutinized Meredith. "You look gorgeous tonight, Mere. Is that new?"

Meredith looked down at the wine-colored gown. "I picked it up at a consignment store down in Baton Rouge last time I was there."

"The color's perfect on you. I know you get tired of hearing this, but I do so prefer to see you dressed up than in those torn-up, paint-splattered clothes you like to wear on the weekends." Mom reached out as if to touch Meredith's cheek but lowered her hand again. "Forbes told us that you were feeling like we don't respect you or your position in the company."

Meredith closed her eyes and rasped her breath in the back of her throat. "He shouldn't have said anything. It wasn't his place."

"No. It was yours. Why didn't you ever say anything?" Instead of looking affronted, sadness filled her mother's expression.

"I guess because I thought that you'd eventually realize you were riding roughshod over me. I thought if I put up with it long enough, you'd see that you treat me differently than any of the other executive directors." Meredith wished she hadn't taken her jacket off. Chill bumps danced up and down her arms.

"You're right." Dad rested his hand on her shoulder. "We have been taking advantage of the fact that you're our daughter. And we promise that's going to stop."

"But you have to make us a promise in return." Mom smiled. "You have to promise that you'll come to us and talk about these things before they make you so mad that you take it out on other members of the family. Okay?"

Leave it to Forbes and Jenn to make it all about them. "Okay."

The elevator chimed, saving her from more awkward parental attention. They moved on to take their seats, and Meredith returned to her post.

The room buzzed with voices, the twelve-piece orchestra barely discernible above the din. Meredith couldn't wipe the smile from her face. Though the lead-up to tonight had been anything but easy, seeing their guests—dressed in their glittering best—talking and laughing and enjoying themselves was one of the moments she lived for.

A Bible verse strayed through her thoughts: *Give her the product of her hands, and let her works praise her in the gates.*

She hoped her parents meant what they said about showing her more respect from now on, but if not, she would learn how to be content with knowing that by creating a good "product" through hard work and dedication, God would reward her with fulfillment and the pleasure she could take in the praise of her guests' enjoyment.

A burst of static startled her. "It's five till seven." Major's voice came over her earpiece. "Jana, please send the rest of the service staff into the kitchen."

Meredith pressed the talk button on her module. "I'll let my father know to get things rolling."

He must have checked his watch, because before she could leave her post, Dad glanced over at her with raised brows. She nodded, and he stepped up onto the stage. To the side of the platform, the sound tech gave him a thumbs-up.

"Good evening, friends." Dad's voice boomed over the crowd,

which immediately quieted. "Happy Valentine's Day and welcome to the Eleventh Annual Hearts to HEARTS Banquet and Charity Auction to raise funds for the Warner Cardiac Unit at University Hospital. I hope you came prepared to enjoy a wonderful dinner...and to spend lots of money at the auction. I've been told that we have some fabulous items that you're all going to want to bid on. Now join with me in asking the Lord's blessing on the meal."

While her father prayed, Meredith moved around the perimeter of the room to the opening of the service hall leading to the kitchen. As soon as he said, "Amen," she motioned the servers to disperse throughout the dining hall, not envying them the trays they carried, piled with covered dishes. She would never have survived in that job.

Major brought up the rear of the line of servers and joined her. "Sounds like everything's going well."

"It is now. I wasn't so sure there about forty-five minutes ago. But once Manny figured out that the elevator system hadn't been reset since the fire alarm went off this afternoon, things have been flowing just fine."

"Yeah, getting this many guests up twenty-three flights without elevators wouldn't have been pretty." Major's phone rang—she'd heard that ringtone once before, and that time Major had paled and left her office immediately. Now he grimaced. "If you'll excuse me." He disappeared down the hall and into the kitchen.

She sighed. By now she should be accustomed to his shutting her out of anything remotely personal, no matter how much she really wanted to get to know what was going on in his life outside of this place.

Major shut his office door before answering the phone. "Major O'Hara, here."

"Where are you?" His mother's voice was shrill and sharp.

"I told you five times today already that I have to work tonight,

Ma." His jaw ached from grinding his teeth a little harder every time she'd called tonight.

"But it's Wednesday night. You always come on Wednesday night."

"I know, but as I already explained, I have to work tonight. I'll be out there tomorrow night. It's just one day, Ma." *Lord, please help her understand so that I can get through this evening without any more interruptions.* "Isn't this the night that the chef teaches cooking lessons? Don't you usually do that before I come?"

"I don't want to do that. I want to see you."

"Then why don't you put on a John Wayne movie. What about *Without Reservations* or *The Quiet Man?*"

"I don't want to watch John Wayne. I want you to come like you're supposed to."

Frustration throbbed behind his eyes. "I can't come, Ma. I have to get off the phone now. I have to work tonight. But I will see you tomorrow, okay? So don't call again tonight unless it's an emergency."

The line clicked and went dead. He closed the cell phone and pressed his forehead and nose against his desktop. "God, I don't know how much more of this I can deal with."

But he didn't have time to wallow in his problem. He dropped the cell phone in his pants pocket and returned to the kitchen, allowing the controlled chaos to calm his frazzled nerves.

Plating the main course and sides continued apace. He stepped in and assisted where necessary when garnishes didn't suit his taste or when a plate was unnecessarily messy. But he had a good team of well-trained and -educated chefs and cooks, so not much coaching was required.

Fifteen minutes after service began, servers returned with trays stacked with mostly empty salad plates. As soon as the servers divested themselves of the empties, they reviewed the lists of requested meals for their assigned tables and worked with the kitchen staff to get the appropriate dishes. Thankfully, Meredith had managed to convince Mrs. Warner that everyone should have the same side dishes—

roasted baby veggies and garden risotto—instead of giving guests a choice there, too.

More than half of the mains had gone out when Major's phone started ringing again. He almost ignored it. But knowing his mother, she'd just keep calling until he answered. He couldn't step away from the kitchen right now, though.

"Major O'Hara." He inspected the dishes on a tray and nodded his approval.

"Mr. O'Hara, this is Gideon Thibodeaux, facility director of Beausoleil Pointe Center. I'm calling regarding your mother."

A wave of nausea struck so forcefully, Major wavered. "What's she done now?"

"She had an accident and started a little fire in the kitchen."

Horrible memories and visions from his childhood assailed him. "Was anyone else hurt?"

"No one but her. She has at least second- and possibly third-degree burns on both arms. We've called for an ambulance to take her to the emergency room. I suggest you meet her there instead of trying to come all the way out here."

Major pressed his thumb and fingers to the outside corners of his eyes. "I'll be there as soon as I can." He closed the phone and released a heated, angry breath.

"Boss, is everything okay?" Steven approached with trepidation in his steps.

"I've had a. . .situation come up. I have to go to the emergency room. I need you to take over and make sure that desserts get served right at eight o'clock. Jana knows, but because of the schedule with the auction, it can't be any later than eight, even if some of the guests aren't finished with mains yet. Okay?"

"Yes, Chef." But Steven's brow remained furrowed.

Major didn't have time to stay and try to alleviate his sous chef's concerns. He grabbed his keys from his office and dashed out of the kitchen, hitting the call button for the freight elevator.

No, he couldn't leave without telling Meredith. But what would he tell her? He tapped the talk button on the earpiece he'd forgotten to take off. "Meredith, I need to see you in the service corridor, please."

"I'll be there in a second."

Many seconds later—but not long enough—the perfect vision that was Meredith materialized in the hallway, worry written all over her face. "What's up?"

"I. . .I have to leave. I have to go to the hospital."

Her eyes widened, and shock replaced the worry. She reached over and touched his arm. "Are you okay? Do you need someone to drive you?"

"No. It's not—" He swallowed convulsively and pulled away from her, though it was one of the most difficult things he'd ever done in his life. "I have to go. Steven knows what needs to be done. I'll try to make it back here if I can." The freight elevator arrived. "I'm sorry."

The last glimpse he got of Meredith before the doors closed was of a woman who was both upset and confused by his actions.

He braced his forearms against the elevator wall and rested his head against his fists. "God, why does my mother have to ruin *everything*? She's done it all my life, and she's doing it again."

The fire had been no accident. It was her way of punishing him. She'd always been fascinated by flames but had started setting fires just for the joy of it when he was in junior high. Whenever he did something she didn't like or forced her to take her meds, she started fires. He'd tried to make it hard on her—getting rid of all matches and lighters. But she always got more.

He'd been pulled out of class when he was fifteen, a sophomore in high school, after she'd set a fire that quickly got out of control, destroyed their apartment, and damaged several adjoining units. Fortunately, no one had been hurt—that time. The state had committed her for thirty days, and Major had been sent to live with a foster family. A foster family who owned a restaurant. He continued to work for them even after he went back to live with his mom.

The fire she'd set eight years ago that led to his returning from

New York had severely injured several other residents of the apartment complex.

Maybe it was time to discuss with her doctor a change in her medication levels, especially since it seemed as if her episodes were becoming more frequent. Either that, or it was time to look into having her committed to a full-time nursing facility.

He stopped halfway across the garage to Kirby. If he had her committed, it would mean he'd finally given up on her. And even with as much anger as he had toward her at this very moment, he wasn't sure he was ready to do that.

But he sure wasn't going to be able to forgive her anytime soon.

The tires squealed when he pulled out of the garage. He turned off the southern gospel music he'd been listening to on his way to work. But not before it reminded him what he'd been thinking—dreaming—about on the drive: the restaurant.

His head spun. At a restaurant, he'd never be able to walk away from a dinner service the way he'd just walked away from the banquet. And if his mother did this based on his missing one night's visit with her, what would she do when he wouldn't have time for weeks or months at a stretch to go out to visit her?

He shook with impotent rage. He'd already given up everything for her—his childhood, New York. . .and Meredith. And would Ma ever appreciate it? No. Of course not. He refused to give up his dream of opening a restaurant.

He trudged into the emergency room lobby and went straight to the information desk.

The woman in khakis and a pink sweater looked up over the rim of bejeweled reading glasses. "How can I help you, Mr. O'Hara?"

He frowned at her use of his name. She smiled and pointed at his left shoulder; he looked down and read his name, upside-down, on his coat.

"My mother, Beverly O'Hara, was being brought here by ambulance from Beausoleil Pointe Center." He unbuttoned the jacket.

"Let me call back to the nurses' station and see if she's ready for visitors. In the meantime, you can have a seat there." She pointed behind him.

"Yeah, I know the drill. Thanks." He slumped into one of the stiff upholstered chairs, his back to the few other people in the waiting room.

A few minutes later, the admissions nurse called him over to her window to answer the standard payment and insurance questions.

He turned at the sound of rubber soles squeaking on the tile floor. A vaguely familiar young man ran to the information desk. "I need to see Beverly O'Hara."

"Are you a relative?"

"No—I'm from the center. I was there—it's my fault she got hurt, you see, and I need to make sure she's going to be okay."

Major turned to the admissions nurse. "Do you need anything else from me?"

"No, sir, I think I've got everything."

"Thanks." He went back over to the information desk. "Excuse me. You said you're from the Pointe?"

The younger man turned. "I'm Patrick. . . ." His eyes flickered down to Major's coat. "Oh, Mr.—I mean, Chef O'Hara. I am so sorry about what happened to your mother. It was all my fault. I only turned my back for a second. . . ."

Major led him over to a semisecluded area of the waiting room and forced him to sit with a hand on his shoulder. "Start from the beginning and tell me what happened."

"She came in late, after the cooking class had started. She comes every week and has always done very well—owing to you, I'm sure."

"Go on." Major crossed his arms, displeased with the kid's attempt at flattery.

"Well, I asked her if she would remove a pot from the stove. I warned her it would be hot and to use a towel wrapped around the handle to move it. But I forgot to tell her to turn the burner off first. She must have dragged the tail of the towel in the flame. That's all I can figure."

"But how did it burn both of her arms?"

"Oh, that wasn't what burned her. She jumped back and the pasta water splashed all over her."

"I see." Major rubbed his eyes. Guilty sympathy chiseled away his anger. Burns from liquid could be almost as bad as from oil or open flame. He should know—he'd suffered his share of them.

"O'Hara family?"

He looked over at the nurse standing in the door that led back to the ER.

"May I come with you?" Patrick stood with him. "I want to apologize to her."

"Sure." A short corridor connected the lobby to the actual emergency room facility. As soon as they passed through the door on the other end, he could hear his mother's shrill cries.

All anger toward her forgotten, Major sped up and bypassed the nurse the last few yards to the room where he could hear her.

"Ma?" He pushed the privacy curtain aside. Two orderlies were trying to hold her shoulders down on the bed, while a nurse held a syringe, trying to give her a shot in her upper arm.

"Major, make them stop!" For someone so frail looking, she sure was strong. His throat tightened. No matter what she'd done, she was his mother. For that reason alone, she deserved his respect and love.

He stepped over and pulled the orderly closest to him away, then looked at the one on the other side and nodded. "I'm here, now, Ma."

Huge crystalline tears coursed down her cheeks. "It hurts."

"I know it does. But they're trying to make it better. Let the nurse give you a shot, and it won't hurt as much anymore." He looked around and found a box of tissues on the counter beside the small sink. He grabbed several and dried his mother's face, which was turned away from the nurse with the needle.

"What is that?" He nodded toward the syringe.

"Demerol—a pain killer."

A man in a suit entered the room. "It's all right, Mr. O'Hara. I've already briefed them on your mother's condition and the medications she's on." He nodded at the nurse, who couldn't mask the fear in her eyes when she approached and gave the shot.

Major continued wiping at his mother's tears. "And you are?" He glanced over his shoulder at the man.

"I'm Gideon Thibodeaux."

"I don't know him, Danny." Ma's blue eyes opened and showed that the pain medication was already taking effect.

Major had never met BPC's new director. "He's the manager at the Pointe, Ma."

"Patrick, may I speak with you outside?" Mr. Thibodeaux's grave expression told Major that Patrick might no longer be employed by the center in a few minutes.

"Can I. . . ?" Patrick looked at Major, then at Ma.

"Yeah." Major stepped back and let the kid have his place beside Ma.

"Ms. O'Hara, it's me, Patrick. I'm so sorry about what happened. I hope you're better soon."

Ma's glazed eyes tried to fix on the young man. "I had fun. But you need to go back and make sure the macaroni and cheese isn't burning. I won't eat it if it's burned on the bottom."

Patrick relaxed a bit. "I'll do that. But you don't worry about that. You just worry about healing, okay?"

" 'Kay." She closed her eyes. "Major Kirby, don't leave me."

"I'm staying right here." He pulled over a stool. "I'll never leave you, Ma." Even though it would mean sacrificing everything he wanted in life. He would do his duty.

210

CHAPTER 20

"You'll come tomorrow?"

Major pulled the covers up under his mother's arms. "I'll come tomorrow." He set two pillows beside her. "You can put your hands down now."

Gingerly, Ma settled her arms down on top of the pillows. "What if my shoulders get cold?"

He went to the closet and pulled a small lap blanket down from the shelf. He unfolded it and tucked it in around her shoulders. "There. All snug?"

She wiggled farther down into the nest created by the pillows and covers. "All snug." Each time she blinked, it took a little longer for her eyes to open. The emergency room doctor had said she would probably sleep through the night and most of the day tomorrow. And Mr. Thibodeaux had arranged for around-the-clock nursing attention for the next week or so until the bandages came off.

"A nurse is going to be coming in every so often to check on you during the night." He held up a little speaker. "And they're going to be monitoring you, so if you wake up and you're in pain or you need to go to the bathroom, just say something and they'll come help you."

" 'Kay." Her eyes drifted closed.

He leaned over the bed, careful not to bump her arm, and kissed her forehead. "Good night, Ma. I love you. I'll see you tomorrow."

"Me, too."

He stopped and talked to the floor nurse on the way out to make sure they called him in case anything happened. Then with heavy steps, he walked out into the chill night air to his Jeep. He glanced at the clock on the radio as he pulled out of the parking lot. Three o'clock in the morning. In two hours, he needed to be at work to prepare food for Mr. Guidry's Thursday morning prayer breakfast. So that everyone could sleep in and recover from their late night working the banquet before they had to report to prepare for lunch service, he hadn't scheduled a subordinate to assist.

At home he collapsed on the bed without even bothering to undress—but did make sure the alarm clock feature on his phone was set for four thirty. He'd barely closed his eyes when the alarm sounded, it seemed.

More tired than he'd ever been in his life, he dragged himself to the shower and managed, somehow, to get ready for a full day of work and then a full evening out at the Pointe with Ma.

As executive chef and co-owner of a restaurant, he could expect to put in these kinds of hours on a regular basis in the beginning.

He stuffed anything he might possibly need into his black duffel and walked out the front door, then went right back inside for his knife case—remembering after five minutes of wandering all over the condo looking for it that he'd left it at work last night.

At five o'clock in the morning, Bonneterre still slept. Only a hint of pink tinged the sky on the other side of the river. He had to sit through red lights at a couple of vacant intersections and fight falling asleep before they changed to green.

The parking garage security attendant greeted him with a wave and a stifled yawn. Major had to swipe his card twice—the second time making sure the magnetic tape was actually facing the right direction.

His shoes seemed to be made out of concrete. Every step sapped him of a little more of his precious energy reserve. Finally, he made it to his office. Someone—probably Steven—had thoughtfully cleaned and repacked his knives and put the soft-sided case on his desk. He steeled himself against the temptation of collapsing into his chair and closing his eyes for a few minutes, pulled his burgundy jacket out of the armoire, and went down to the executive kitchen to get to work.

By the time Mr. Guidry's breakfast meeting broke up, Major had come to a decision. He gave Lawson a few minutes to get back to his office before following him. He knocked on the open office door.

Lawson looked up from his computer and pulled his glasses off. "Come in, come in."

"Do you have a few minutes, sir?"

"Of course. Have a seat."

"Thank you." Major forced his body to fold itself down onto one of the leather chairs facing Lawson's massive desk.

"Meredith said you had an emergency last night and had to go to the emergency room. I hope you're all right."

"Yes, sir. It wasn't me. It was my mother. Which is why I wanted to talk to you." The nausea that had started with the doctor's call last night returned full force. Good thing he hadn't eaten in more than twelve hours.

"If you're worried that there will be any negative repercussions from us because you left to take care of your ailing mother, don't."

Major wanted to get up to pace but wrapped his hands around the wooden arms of the chair instead. "That wasn't really what I'm here about. But it does bear on what I need to tell you."

Lawson leaned back in his chair and tapped his glasses against his chin. "Am I correct in assuming this is about the restaurant deal, then?"

"Yes, sir." Major swallowed twice, trying to eliminate the bitter acidity in the back of his throat. "After a lot of thought and prayer, I am going to have to say no. I know y'all proposed the partnership based on the plan I gave Forbes to look at for me. And I really appreciate the belief you and Mrs. Guidry showed in me by coming up with the proposal—you have no idea how much I appreciate it.

But the truth of the matter is that I can't commit the kind of time that opening a restaurant requires—my mother needs me too much. These last two accidents with her have also shown me that I can't take everything that I have and invest it in a business that might not turn a profit for eighteen months or longer. I need the safety net just in case something else happens."

The words had spilled out in a monotone, his eyes glued to the front edge of Mr. Guidry's desk. But now he dared to look up at his would-be benefactor.

Lawson's expression hadn't changed—still slightly smiling and warm. "I am sorry you feel that way, son. But I understand your desire to want to be sure you can take care of your mother. I was afraid it might come to that. I don't suppose the fact that groundbreaking has been delayed six months would change your decision?"

Six months? Major went over all the numbers and scenarios in his head. The pit of his stomach gnarled. "No, sir. Six months probably won't make a significant difference in the amount of time I will need to spend with my mother, nor in my financial situation." The words *I'm sorry* tripped to the end of his tongue, but a recurring line from *She Wore a Yellow Ribbon*, the John Wayne movie he'd watched with Ma on Sunday, zipped through his mind: *"Never apologize. . . . It's a sign of weakness."*

"It's disappointing. We want to see you chasing your dream of owning a restaurant. But if anyone understands family obligations, we do." Lawson stood and extended his right hand. "We'll look for another opportunity with you in the future."

Major sprang to his feet and shook Meredith's father's hand. "Thank you for the offer, sir. And you can trust that I'll be working extra hard to get to a place where I can do something like this."

"And we'll do whatever we can to help."

Over lunch Thursday, Meredith filled Anne in on the details of everything that happened at the banquet the night before. Their check arrived right as Meredith got to the part about Major.

Anne's pen stopped halfway through her signature on her receipt. "What happened? Was he okay?"

Meredith slipped her signed receipt into the black folder and tried to remember if the pen was hers or the restaurant's. "I think so. Apparently, he fixed breakfast for Daddy's prayer group this morning."

"Who told you that? You haven't been calling in and checking on work on your day off, have you?" Anne took her sunglasses out of her purse and slipped them over the top of her head.

Meredith tried to look innocent, then grinned as she slid out of the booth seat. "Okay, just the one time. Corie told me she saw Major go in to Dad's office after the prayer group broke up."

"What do you think that was about?"

Meredith shrugged and followed her cousin out of the restaurant. "I don't know, and I'm tired of speculating. If Major wanted me to know what's going on in his life, he'd tell me. Since he hasn't, I have to operate under the assumption that he's perfectly happy with our relationship just the way it is. I can't live my life hung up on every little thing he does."

"That's probably wise." A mischievous grin appeared on Anne's face. "So whom are you going to ask as your date to the wedding?"

"I'm in the wedding. I don't need a date. Forbes'll be my date." Meredith feigned interest in the display of handmade soaps in the store window they were passing.

"Forbes has already asked someone."

She stopped. "Really? He's asked someone to be his date to your wedding?"

"That's what he told me yesterday. But he wouldn't tell me who she is."

"Wow. Forbes is actually bringing a date to a family function."

"Speaking of, I think you should ask this Ward fella." Anne hooked her arm through Meredith's and got her moving again.

"Ask Ward?"

"Yeah—you are still seeing him, aren't you?"

"Not in the last couple of weeks—I've been too busy." And even though he'd called and asked her out a few times, she'd told him she was too busy simply because it was easier than admitting to herself that, while she really liked him as a person and enjoyed spending time with him, she had no romantic feelings toward him whatsoever.

Anne let go of Meredith's arm to unlock the front door of her office, located in one of the converted Victorian row houses lining Town Square. "Well, Jenn already has dibs on Henry, so it's looking like Ward's your only option."

"All right, I'll ask him." It took a moment for Meredith's eyes to adjust to the dim interior of the office from the bright sunlight outside. When she could finally see clearly, she saw Anne looking at her expectantly from behind her desk. "What?"

"You have a phone, don't you? If not, you can use mine." She pushed her desk phone closer to Meredith.

"You want me to call him right now?"

"Yes, now. Because if I leave it up to you, you won't call."

How well Anne knew her. Reluctantly, Meredith pulled out her phone. "What should I say?"

"Oh, for mercy's sake. You've known the guy for almost two months now. You'll think of something."

Meredith quick-dialed Ward's cell number, praying he wouldn't answ—

"Hey, pretty girl."

Instead of warmth or tingles, all Meredith felt was embarrassed. "Hey, yourself."

"What's up? Calling to check progress on your house? Right now, we're on schedule to be finished about a week early."

"That's good to know, but it isn't why I'm calling."

Across the desk from her, Anne's expression of encouragement was anything but helpful. Meredith averted her gaze.

"So to what do I owe the honor of a phone call from Meredith Guidry?" The laughter in his voice conjured a vivid image of Ward's handsome good looks in Meredith's mind.

"I. . ." She forced herself to breathe. She'd never asked a guy out before. "My cousin Anne is getting married a week from Saturday."

"I know. You're the maid of honor."

The fact that he was humoring her made what she needed to do a little easier. "Right. But I was wondering. . .thinking maybe you might like to come as my 'and guest.'"

Anne sighed loudly; Meredith gave her a dirty look.

"I'd love to be your 'and guest' at your cousin's wedding. It's in the evening, right?"

"The ceremony starts at five o'clock."

"Good. I can still go to the hospital, then."

Taken aback, Meredith glanced at Anne. "The hospital?"

"Didn't I tell you? I volunteer in the pediatric cancer unit on Saturday mornings."

Could this guy be any more perfect? He was going to make someone a great husband someday. "No, you never told me. What led you to do that?"

"I've been doing it since I was fifteen and my youngest brother was diagnosed with leukemia." Someone yelled his name in the background. "I'll have to call you back, Mere."

"Okay. I'll talk to you later. Bye." She closed the phone and dropped it in her purse.

"The hospital?"

Meredith told her.

"He sounds like a keeper." Even though Anne leaned over to pull out the binder of her wedding plans from under the desk, it wasn't quick enough to keep Meredith from seeing her amused smile.

"For someone else, maybe."

Anne snapped upright. "What?"

"I just don't feel that way about him."

"Not everyone falls in love right away. Sometimes it needs a chance to grow. I've planned plenty of weddings for people who were friends for years before they fell in love with each other."

Friends for eight years before falling in love? Meredith shook her head. "I'm giving it a chance—it's not like I have a lot of other options at this point in time."

"You know I've been praying for you about this, right?" Leaving the binder on her desk, Anne came around to sit in the chair beside Meredith.

Emotion lumped up in Meredith's throat, forcing her to nod as her only reply.

"Have you been praying about it?"

She nodded again.

"More than just, 'Please, God, send me a husband'?" Anne's blue eyes twinkled.

Meredith laughed. "Sometimes. But most of the time it's, 'Please, God, let me get over Major so I can fall in love with someone else.'"

"Oh, I can so relate." Anne sighed. "Before I found out George wasn't the one marrying Courtney Landry, that was my almost hourly mantra—'Lord, please don't let me be falling in love with a client.'"

"But he turned out not to be the one getting married, and he fell in love with you."

"Right. But what I'm saying is that God did answer my prayer—granted in a rather roundabout fashion, but He answered. You have to trust that God will answer your prayer. . .just maybe not in the way you expect or on your timeline."

Meredith groaned and slumped down in the chair to rest her head against the top of it. "Maybe I should pray instead that He'll take away my desire to get married. Then it won't matter if the man I'm in love with doesn't return my feelings."

"Maybe you should pray for the patience to hold on until Major realizes what he's missing." Anne stood and picked up the binder.

"Right. And let God make me wait another eight years? I know what His sense of humor is like. No way I'm praying that!" She let Anne pull her out of the chair and followed her cousin to the small table in the bay window overlooking Town Square in the front of the building.

"Then I guess you'll just have to muddle through."

"Thanks. You're tons of help." Meredith stuck her tongue out at the woman who'd been her best friend since before she could remember.

"Well, you could always just talk to him."

"Who?"

"Major—I thought that's who we were talking about."

"Talk to him?"

"About how you feel."

"No way. Call me old-fashioned, but I firmly believe that a man should make the first move." Meredith pulled her own folder of information for Anne's wedding out of her bag. "Can we focus on you now, instead of me? You are getting married in a week, you know."

"Nine days."

"Right. Nine days. And there's still lots to do, so let's get to it." Meredith pulled out her to-do list and started reviewing everything they'd accomplished since their last war-room briefing.

But she couldn't put Anne's words out of her head. Talk to Major about her feelings? What if he once and for all told her he could never feel that way toward her?

No, she'd rather live with the pain of unrequited—but hopeful—love than to know for sure that she would never have a chance at love with Major O'Hara.

CHAPTER 21

$\mathcal{F}$orbes, I saved you a seat." Meredith waved at her big brother, who'd just entered The Fishin' Shack.

"Thanks, Sis." Forbes looked somewhat frazzled, which served as partial explanation as to why he was so late for the Thursday night cousins dinner. He walked around and greeted everyone at the table before taking the chair between Meredith and George.

"Tough day?" Meredith moved her purse from the table to the floor.

"Somewhat. But I'm no longer at work, so I refuse to think about it further. How was your day off? Did you and Anne get everything done you wanted to do today?" Forbes poured himself a glass of iced tea and doctored it with three packs of sweetener.

"There are still a few loose strings, but Anne will have everything tuned up and ready to go by the time we get to church for the rehearsal Friday evening."

"I'm sure she will. I just hope we can all live up to her exacting expectations."

"Hey—I heard that!" Anne leaned around behind George and poked Forbes's shoulder.

"What? Anne's here?" Forbes winked at their cousin.

Once the subject of the wedding had been brought up, it consumed quite a bit of attention around the table. Certain that no one was paying any attention to her or Forbes, Meredith leaned closer to him.

"What do you know about Major's family?" she asked softly.

"Excuse me?" Forbes looked startled.

Maybe she should have figured out a better way to broach the subject, but she wasn't sure how much time she would have before they were drawn back into the general conversation. "Major's family. What do you know about them?"

"He was raised by a single mom."

"I know that. But do you know anything more specific? I mean, you two are pretty close friends." She twisted her napkin in her lap.

The little upside-down Y formed between Forbes's brows. "I think that's something you should ask Major."

She sighed in frustration. "I have asked him, and he won't tell me much more than what you just did."

"Then I can't believe you're going around behind his back asking me to divulge whatever he may have told me in confidence. Really, Mere, I thought you had higher principles than that." Though his words came across as angry, all she could see in his eyes was discomfort.

"I'm just worried about him. He had to leave the banquet early last night—some kind of an emergency. I wanted to make sure everything's okay, and if not, to see if there's anything I can do to help."

With meticulous movements, Forbes unfolded his napkin and draped it across his lap. "As I said, it's something you'll have to ask him." He turned his attention to the wedding talk, effectively cutting off any further questions from Meredith by the angle of his body.

Eventually, the discussion of Anne's wedding waned. Across the table, Rafe said, "Hey, Mere, how's the work on your house going?"

"Great. I talked to my contractor this afternoon, and he said it's looking like they might be done early."

Rafe's left brow shot upward. "Your *contractor*? Would that be the *contractor* you've been dating?"

"I'm not dating him." Her pulse quickened—she hated being the source of her siblings' amusement. "We're just friends."

"Really? What would you call it when you go out to romantic restaurants for meals alone with him?" Jenn joined in on the teasing.

"I've only been out with him a couple of times. We're still just getting to know each other." Meredith glanced at Anne for help, but her cousin was listening to something George was whispering in her ear.

Rafe laughed. "You met him on New Year's Day, right? Jenn would be practically engaged if she'd met someone six or seven weeks ago who'd asked her out."

"Take it back!" Jenn laughed and punched their younger brother in the arm.

Meredith laughed, too, glad not to be the sole recipient of the ribbing.

"Hey, did y'all know Meredith's going to be on TV tomorrow?" Jenn turned a saucy smile toward Meredith.

So much for not being the sole focus of her teasing-prone family.

The next morning, Meredith's desk was piled with messages and paperwork, as it was every time she took a day off—only today it was compounded by the fact they'd had a massive, midweek event.

"Corie?"

Her assistant appeared in the door, still in her jacket with her backpack hanging from one shoulder. "Yes?"

"What time do I have to be at the TV studio?"

"Let me check the e-mail." She disappeared for a couple of minutes then reappeared sans coat and bag. "It says you should plan to arrive no later than ten o'clock."

Meredith glanced at the clock in the lower right corner of her computer monitor. Seven forty-five. "Can you give me a heads-up at nine thirty if it looks like I'm not paying attention to the clock?"

"Will do. Want to go over the stuff from yesterday so we can get started on reports?"

Not really. "Sure. But give me a minute to get some coffee."

"I'll come with." Corie grabbed her big, hand-painted ceramic mug from her desk and walked with Meredith to the executive kitchen. "How was your day off?"

"Fun. Anne and I got a lot of last-minute stuff done for the wedding." She told her assistant some of the details of what they'd accomplished.

Her mother's executive assistant greeted them in the dining room, coming from the kitchen with three mugs of coffee. Meredith waited until the kitchen door closed behind them then turned and grinned at Corie.

"I guess I'm not letting you live up to your title of executive assistant."

"You know I really wouldn't mind getting your coffee for you."

"Not to demean the other executive assistants, but you're more valuable to me than just someone to fetch and carry at my whims." Meredith pulled out the coffee carafe and poured Corie's coffee first. "In case I haven't said it recently, you're a vital part of this team; and at your annual appraisal in April, we're going to be discussing moving you into a junior event planner position."

Corie's brown eyes lit up.

"Now, I can't promise that will happen. You of all people know what the approval process is like around here. But I think I can make a pretty convincing case on your behalf."

They doctored their coffee with flavored creamers and sweeteners and returned to Meredith's office. Over their morning caffeine fix, Corie reviewed the messages she'd taken on Thursday, as well as everything she'd handled on her own.

Once Meredith was up to date on everything that happened in her absence, Corie went back to her desk with the folder of receipts and invoices Meredith had worked on organizing last night after she got home from dinner. She e-mailed the rough spreadsheet to Corie, who would work some kind of magic on it to generate all kinds of comparisons and charts and departmental breakdowns of how much money Meredith had spent on behalf of B-G on the banquet. Thank goodness someone from the HEARTS Foundation board handled everything connected with the money from the auction. One less thing for Meredith to have to deal with on the back side of the event.

She spent the morning returning phone calls from yesterday—as well as answering those coming in—and was about to go get a second cup of coffee when Major knocked on the open office door.

The sight of him was enough to make her bite the inside of her cheek to keep from telling him how much she wished he wouldn't keep her at arm's length, that he would let her into his life, even just a little bit.

"You ready to go?" He wore his burgundy jacket—the one that made his eyes look almost purple.

She glanced at her watch. "Oh, mercy. I didn't realize it was nine thirty already." She jumped up from her desk then leaned back down to get her purse out of the bottom drawer. She stood slowly. "Are we going together?"

"I figured we could—save gas, you know."

"Oh. I just didn't know if you had to be there longer or something." She shrugged into her suit coat and grabbed her planner from her briefcase—the planner where she had all of the notes she'd written down, things Alaine had asked her to think about so she'd know what to say about the event when Alaine asked her questions live on air. "I'll drive."

He grinned at her. "Don't feel like arriving windblown?"

She returned the smile. "Not particularly."

"Did you have a good day off yesterday?" Major asked as she pulled out of the parking garage.

As she had with everyone else, she talked about what she'd done yesterday. But that filled only enough time to get them halfway to the studio.

Now or never. "Major, I wanted to ask you about Wednesday night—about why you left. Is everything okay?" She glanced at him from the corner of her eye.

He'd gone all stiff. "Everything's fine. I just—something came up that I had to go handle."

"At the emergency room?"

"It was. . ." He swallowed hard. "It was my mom. She got hurt, and I had to meet her at the emergency room."

Finally—something about his mother. "Is she okay?"

"She will be. She burned herself—cooking, actually. Splashed scalding hot water on her arms." Tension pulled in tight lines around his mouth.

"I thought you said she didn't live here—but you met her at the emergency room?"

"She doesn't live in town, but the hospital here is closest. Careful—don't want to miss our turn."

His discomfort with the subject couldn't be any plainer. And though it hurt Meredith that he didn't trust her enough to tell her the truth about his mother—whatever that might be—she was determined to figure out a way to convince him to confide in her. Because she was starting to feel like this secret was the only thing standing between her and a happily-ever-after ending with Major.

Major hoped his tension from the time they got out of the SUV at the TV studio until the cameras turned off would appear to Meredith as nothing more than nerves over being on the live broadcast. But her fishing expedition in the car, trying to find out what had happened with Ma, had sent him into a state of near panic, afraid he might have to lie to her or tell her the truth, both of which would ruin everything.

On the way back to the office from the studio, he talked about the great job Alaine's team had done at putting together the documentary-style footage on all of the preparation leading up to the banquet as well as the event itself. And he'd been right—doing the live broadcast had been much easier to bear with Meredith sitting beside him.

He kept up a steady stream of inane chatter until they got on the elevator to go back to their offices.

"Can you have your reports to me by the end of the day?" Meredith's voice sounded tired.

"To you or to Corie?"

"To me. I've got to take everything home with me to work on this weekend."

"You work too hard." His arms itched to hug her, so instead, he took a step back and leaned against the bumper rail at the back of the elevator car.

"I know, but it's part and parcel of the job of being the executive director of a department. I knew that when I accepted the position."

He wanted to say more, but her cell phone rang. The tension drained from her face when she put the thing to her ear. "Hey, Ward."

He hated the softness, the warmth in her tone.

"Tonight? Well, I have a lot of work to do. . . . Sure, I could do something quick." Meredith waved her farewell when the elevator doors opened at the fifth floor.

Major crossed his arms and stared out the window on the rest of the ride up to the top floor. He deserved every bit of the awful, gut-wrenching pain now ripping apart his insides at the idea of Meredith falling in love with and possibly marrying someone else. He deserved it because he'd brought it upon himself by pushing her away.

The kitchen crew was just finishing lunch service cleanup. He wished them all a happy weekend then cloistered himself in his office for the remainder of the afternoon. Just before five o'clock, he e-mailed his reports to Meredith, then gathered up all of his receipts and invoices in a folder.

Down in the corporate offices, the interior door that connected Corie's office to Meredith's was partially closed.

Corie looked up from her computer when he walked in. "She's on the phone."

Meredith's laugh floated out through the narrow opening.

"I brought these for her. She said she wanted to take this stuff home to work on over the weekend." He handed Corie the folder and tried to smile.

"I'll make sure she gets it."

"Thanks." He couldn't torture himself by standing here listening to the happy tone of her voice any longer. "Have a great weekend."

"You, too."

When he got to the parking garage, he realized he'd forgotten to bring jeans to change into. Oh well. The guys would just have to put up with him in his black-and-white checked pants and the limp New York City T-shirt he'd been wearing under his jacket all day. He pointed Kirby toward church and tried to keep his mind from returning to the ride with Meredith to the TV studio. The look on her face when he wouldn't tell her why he'd had to disappear from the party last night. . .

A light drizzle started as Major pulled into the parking lot. He grabbed his folder of music and jogged in through the side door by the church offices.

George sat at the piano practicing the new piece they'd chosen to sing Sunday. He stopped, stood, and extended his hand. "Hullo."

"Hey. I figured I'd be the last one here."

"No. Forbes and Clay both called to say they're running late."

"Oh. Okay. That's good, actually. I could use a few minutes' downtime before we start singing." Major tossed his folder into a chair and collapsed onto the floor, stretching out flat on his back.

"Nice pants," George chuckled.

"Yeah, they're all the rage in New York," Major shot back. He did some of the stretches he'd learned in physical therapy after tearing his trapezius, ending his college football career. They almost always worked to ease the deep muscle spasms between his shoulder blades he'd been plagued with since then. Recently, though, nothing seemed to work. Every time he saw Meredith and the insane urge struck to tell her everything—about Ma, about his jealousy over Ward Breaux—he would clamp his mouth shut, his shoulders would tense, and the sharp pain would worsen.

He sat up and eyed George, who'd gone back to playing.

George must have sensed the scrutiny, because he looked up, and the music stopped. "What?"

Major hooked his arms around his bent knees. "I need to ask you something really personal. And if you don't want to answer, I'll understand."

"Go on." George turned to straddle the piano bench and leaned over to brace his elbows on his knees.

"When you met Anne and you couldn't tell her the truth about who you were and whose wedding she was really planning, how did you handle it? How did you keep from just blurting out the whole truth?"

George registered no expression of surprise or offense—or any reaction at all—over the question. The man should be a professional poker player.

"I wanted to every day." George rubbed his chin. "Many times I came close to slipping up and saying things that would have shattered my cover story. It was a wrench, I'll tell you, especially once I started falling in love with her."

Major could completely understand that. "But how did you make yourself keep the secret?"

"Because I was foolish enough to believe that the contract I signed was more important. But when I finally realized that it was not only wrong but would hurt Anne more the longer I waited to tell her, I gained permission to at least tell her I wasn't the groom, just his stand-in."

Major rocked back and forth. "So you wish you'd told her everything from the very beginning?"

"Of course." George eyed Major speculatively. "Is there someone you're keeping a secret from that's vital to your relationship?"

Vital to their relationship? "No—yes. I guess so. It's something about me—about my. . .family that very few people in the world know. And I've kept it that way to protect myself from undue scrutiny and judgment."

"But it's something that will affect the person you want to have a relationship with?" Deep lines formed in George's forehead when he raised his brows like that.

"Yeah—it could. It probably will." Major collapsed down onto his back again, covering his eyes with his left arm.

"You must tell her, then. Even if you are not dating currently, putting off the telling of your secret will only serve to make it worse when the truth becomes known later."

The choir room door swung open, and Forbes entered looking like Cary Grant or Gregory Peck in his dark gray, tailored suit and overcoat.

"Still waiting on Clay?" Forbes shook hands with George.

"I imagine he'll be along shortly." George turned back square to the keyboard and began playing again.

"In that case, Major, can I have a word with you? Privately." Forbes motioned to the door leading into the men's robe room.

Major nodded and followed, hoping this conversation wasn't about what he was afraid it would be about. He leaned against the metal storage cabinet in the small room.

Forbes stood in the middle of the room and turned to face him, unbuttoning his suit coat. "I know you don't want to hear this, but you have to tell Meredith about your mom."

Yep. That was what he'd hoped this conversation *wouldn't* be about. "What makes you say that?"

"She asked me about your family last night. She was very concerned about something that happened Wednesday night—you had to leave the banquet?"

"Ma spilled hot water during a cooking lesson and burned her arms. I had to meet her at the emergency room." Major crossed his arms then uncrossed them—he couldn't protect himself from Forbes's penetrating gaze no matter where his arms were.

"Look, I went along with you when you decided not to tell anyone but my parents about your mother's medical condition, but aside from the fact that Meredith is your boss, she's a person who cares a lot about you—I have a feeling more than either of us wants to admit—and you're only hurting her by not telling her the truth."

Major ran his tongue along the backs of his teeth. Twice within five minutes. It couldn't have been any clearer if God had taken a cast-iron skillet and smashed him over the head with it. "I promise, I will tell her the truth." As soon as the right moment presented itself.

CHAPTER 22

"Meredith, you're going to wrinkle your gown if you keep holding it up like that."

At Anne's soft words, Meredith released her death grip on the layers of purple chiffon and satin. "Isn't the bride supposed to be the nervous wreck and the maid of honor the one reassuring her?"

Anne paused in her circuit around the room, ensuring each person knew what to do as soon as they left the bridal room.

Melancholic joy filled Meredith's throat until she thought it might burst. She was overjoyed for her cousin yet at the same time felt as if she were losing her.

"Don't start," Anne warned, her smile wavering. "You know if you lose it, I will, too."

"I know—" Meredith's phone chimed and saved her from dissolving into the unwanted tears. She dug her purse out of her satchel and read the new text message. She deleted it, tossed the phone back in her bag, and turned to Anne. "Ward's here. Do you mind. . . ?"

"We have a few minutes. Go on."

Meredith avoided grabbing the front of her dress to lift the skirt. She didn't need to for walking. She was just used to long skirts that were straighter than this A-line, flared thing. She was also used to being much more covered up on top. Though the straight-cut bodice provided modesty, the spaghetti-straps left her shoulders feeling very bare.

She nodded and smiled in greeting at the guests milling in the vestibule.

Ward's dark, curly head towered above everyone else. Her pulse gave a halfhearted flutter at the sight of him. Dressed in the tailored charcoal suit he'd worn on their first date, he drew the admiring attention of every female near him.

Why, then, couldn't Meredith muster even an ounce of attraction for him? She'd hoped that by bringing him as her date to such a romantic affair as a wedding she might be able to jump-start an interest in him as something more than just a friend.

"Meredith Guidry." Her name came out as almost a low growl when Ward finally noticed her. "You look gorgeous. I'm afraid I'll break you if I hug you."

She rested her hand on his chest as he squeezed her bare shoulders and kissed her cheek. "Thanks. You clean up pretty well yourself."

"When you told me this was going to be a big wedding, I had no idea you meant everyone who's anyone in Bonneterre would be here. I think I saw the mayor arriving as I pulled in the parking lot."

"Anne's worked with him on several events." As had Meredith. "That's why the reception is invitation only—and even still, we expect almost three hundred guests there." She turned and glanced into the sanctuary. The room that seated more than one thousand looked like it was getting pretty full.

"I should probably go in and find a seat, huh?" Ward came up behind her and rested his hands on her waist.

By turning around to face him again, she dislodged his hands, uncomfortable with such a possessive touch from someone she wasn't sure she liked *that way*. "Yeah, I'd better get back to Anne."

Ward gave her a cocky grin. "At least I know I'll be able to find you easily in all this crowd. You're the prettiest girl here."

She tried so hard to get her heart to flutter or her stomach to flip-flop at his flirting, but. . .nothing. "Aww, just what every maid of honor needs to hear." She patted his arm. "Now, go. I've already been gone too long, I'm sure." She grabbed her skirt and hurried back to the bridal suite.

Anne directed Meredith to join the rest of the women for photos, discussing them with the photographer as if she were the wedding planner, not the bride. Everyone laughed when the photographer had to remind Anne that she needed to be in the picture.

After a few posed shots as well as several candid shots of them all laughing again, Anne sent Mamere and Aunt Maggie out to be seated.

Meredith shifted her weight from foot to foot as Anne calmly made one final check to ensure everything was ready. Certainly with just Meredith and Jenn as attendants, she didn't have much to organize. But an aura of peace surrounded her, no doubt from her years of experience planning other people's weddings. Meredith hoped if she ever got married, she could be so annoyingly serene.

A knock on the door jarred all three of them. Uncle Errol stuck his head in. "You girls ready?"

Meredith's throat tried to swell closed again. Anne retrieved her bouquet and a large silver picture frame. Meredith took a few deep breaths and followed Jenn down the hall and back into the lobbylike foyer behind the sanctuary. Jason was just taking Aunt Maggie, the foster mother of the bride, down the aisle.

One tear escaped and trailed down Meredith's cheek when Anne handed the framed photo of her parents to Whitt, her oldest foster brother, to carry down the aisle and place on the pew beside Aunt Maggie.

Jason and Whitt came back to man the doors. Anne motioned a red-eyed, sniffling Jenn to go down the aisle.

Meredith turned to Anne. "I'm so happy for you that I think my heart might explode."

Anne blinked rapidly a few times, and her lips quivered. "Please don't do that—it'll make such a mess." They both laughed. "And thank you. But you need to go, now. And don't walk as slowly as you did last night, please."

"All right, all right. Good grief, I'm going." Meredith winked at her cousin, grateful that Anne had lightened the mood.

Though more than a thousand people crowded the sanctuary, Meredith had never felt more alone, walking down that aisle. At the other end stood George; his brother, Henry; and Forbes. But though Forbes nodded at her, they weren't waiting for her. They were waiting for Anne.

Then she saw him. As soon as she got to the front and turned to face the crowd, his face was the only one she could clearly see. In the back row, on an outside aisle, Major O'Hara smiled and gave her a quick thumbs-up.

Meredith couldn't help grinning like a fool—but fortunately, the doors at the back opened, the organ fanfare at the beginning of the march Anne had chosen started, and the congregation stood to watch Anne Hawthorne come down the aisle on her uncle's arm.

The wedding planner's wedding.

Across from Meredith, George Laurence's brown eyes stayed glued to his bride, his sharp but handsome profile reflecting the joy on Anne's face.

The happiness Meredith had been afraid would burst her heart did—and flooded her entire being with joy that made her want to sit down and weep. Her gaze broke away from Anne and George, now separated only by Uncle Errol, as the pastor began the ceremony in prayer.

Before she closed her eyes and bowed her head, Meredith stole one more glance at Major and witnessed him sneaking out the side door. No doubt to go back over to Lafitte's Landing to finish everything for the reception.

Meredith joined everyone else in a prayer posture. *Father God, I hate to sound selfish on Anne's day, but You know how much I want to get married. Please change my heart toward Major so I can fall in love with Ward—or anyone who'll love me back.*

Major sneaked one last glance through the small, cross-shaped window in the door at the back of the sanctuary. Meredith stood in profile to him, looking at her cousin with such emotion, Major wanted to charge up there and beg Pastor Kinnard to make it a double wedding.

But Major hadn't missed the sight of Ward Breaux greeting Meredith in this very foyer before the ceremony. Major had had his doubts about how serious Meredith was getting with the contractor, but wasn't inviting someone to a wedding a sure sign that things were going beyond the "seeing each other" stage? He backed away from the door, needing to get to Lafitte's Landing to finish setup—and needing to get away from Meredith.

He shrugged out of his suit coat and removed his tie and tossed them in the passenger seat. He grabbed his phone and quick-dialed Steven.

"Anything I need to pick up on my way back?" he asked his second-in-command.

"No, Chef. But you are on your way back?" Steven's harried tone set off warning bells for Major.

"Yeah. I'm headed that way now."

Ten minutes later, he pulled into the narrow service lot behind Lafitte's. Once inside, he changed into his utilitarian work smock. He'd put his presentation jacket on after the cooking was finished and when he would step out of the kitchen to watch his friend and colleague cut her wedding cake—which his staff had picked up from Aunt Maggie's house that morning along with the chocolate groom's cake frosted and decorated to resemble George's omnipresent PDA.

"Why hasn't plating started yet?" Major called over the din of work in the large kitchen. He walked over to Steven, the only one from whom he expected an answer.

"The trays all had to be rewashed, Chef. They're drying them now."

Major glanced at his watch, then looked around, knowing he'd drawn everyone's attention upon his entrance. "The wedding ceremony will end in less than ten minutes, which means we can expect guests to start arriving in about twenty to thirty. I want cold hors d'oeuvres and canapés on the buffet tables in no more than fifteen minutes; passed hot hors d'oeuvres ready for the servers in twenty."

"Yes, Chef," his staff called.

"This is Anne Hawthorne's wedding reception, folks. I know most of you weren't working here when she was the event planner for B-G, but you do know how much business she brings the company—and that she's Mr. and Mrs. Guidry's niece. So let's make this perfect beyond her expectations."

"Yes, Chef!"

He slipped into the staff break room off the kitchen and changed shirts, then plugged in the earpiece that connected him with everything happening outside the kitchen.

"Lori, this is Major. I'm back. How's everything front-side?"

"Fine. Two of my staff showed up late, so we got off to a later start than I wanted, but everything's fine now."

"Good. First guests should be here in about fifteen. Did you and Jana brief the servers?"

"We did. No one is to approach Mr. Ballantine any differently than any other guest—no asking for autographs and stuff like that."

"Okay, thanks." He released the TALK button and returned to the kitchen.

Could it really have been nine months since Major had prepared the food for mega–movie star—and Anne's one-time fiancé—Cliff Ballantine's engagement party in this very kitchen? Ironic that Anne would have chosen to have her wedding reception in the place where she learned George had been keeping Cliff's identity secret from her for weeks.

"Chef, taste," called one of the cooks. He crossed to the station and tasted the cheese grits.

"Needs more pepper." Major tossed his spoon into the sink and went to the meat station. "How's the prime rib coming?"

"It'll be perfect just in time to set up the carving posts."

Major ran down the list at each station, pleased that everything had been timed just right.

"Chef," came Lori's voice through the earpiece, "guests are arriving."

He pressed the TALK button. "Thanks." He clanged a ladle against an empty metal bowl. "Cold trays out now. Hot trays in five." He spoke into the earpiece again. "Jana, send in the servers, please."

Meredith managed to make it through the ceremony with only a couple of tears escaping—sighing over George's British accent as he recited his vows, giggling with Jenn when the kiss lasted a little too long.

"Ladies and gentlemen, please join me in congratulating Mr. and Mrs. George Laurence." The pastor's voice was nearly drowned out by the applause from the wedding guests.

Meredith handed Anne's bouquet back to her, leaned over to adjust Anne's train, then took Henry Laurence's arm to be escorted to the vestibule behind Anne and George. She hugged her cousin and new cousin-in-law as soon as they reached the foyer. Inside the auditorium, the pastor invited everyone to stay while photos were being taken.

Meredith groaned.

"I know—you hate the idea of people watching you while we're taking pictures," Anne said. "But it was either that or a receiving line, since most of these people aren't invited to the reception."

"I guess feeling like a monkey in the zoo is a little better than standing there for two hours—and then still having to get my picture taken." She followed Anne down the side hall to reenter the sanctuary near the front.

For all that everyone had been invited to stay, not many did. Meredith smiled at Ward as warmly as she could when he joined them at the front, while Anne and the photographer discussed the best way to get the shots Anne wanted.

"You looked stunning up there—like a princess." Ward pulled Meredith into a hug.

She sighed, disappointed that Major had never hugged her like this. "Thanks."

When she stepped back from his embrace, she caught a glimpse of her sister hovering nearby. Meredith looked around for Henry Laurence—ah, he and George were deep in a private discussion.

"Ward, I don't believe you've met my sister yet." She introduced Jenn. Was it her imagination or did his gaze linger, his handshake last just a little longer than necessary when he greeted Jenn? Well, even if it had, it wouldn't matter. Jenn had had eyes for no one but Henry from the moment George's youngest brother set foot off the plane.

With Anne's guidance, the photos were finished in short order.

Meredith, Jenn, Forbes, and Henry climbed into the first of the two limousines waiting outside the church. Forbes and Henry sat toward the middle of the stretch vehicle, while Meredith and Jenn—not wanting to trip on and possibly damage their skirts—sat in the back.

"You never told me Ward is so good-looking," Jenn whispered, stealing a glance at Henry to ensure he and Forbes were still in deep discussion about the differences between practicing law in the States and in Australia.

"Didn't I?" Meredith closed her eyes against the inevitable. She'd seen the glaze overtake Ward's eyes when she introduced him to Jenn.

"And if you two aren't dating, as you keep protesting, remind me why you asked him to be your date for the wedding."

"Anne told me I should. And yes, we were sort of dating."

"Meredith! You denied it all this time? After all this time you finally get a boyfriend, and you pretend like it's nothing—what do you mean you *were* dating?"

"I mean I'm going to tell him that I don't think things are going to work out between us."

"Are you crazy?" Jenn smiled at Forbes and Henry when they looked over at her shouted question. She leaned closer and lowered her voice. "Are you crazy? He's gorgeous."

Would it do any good to try to explain? "Yes, he is very handsome. And he's a wonderfully charming guy. But after seeing him for almost two months, I don't feel anything for him but friendship."

"Try."

Meredith groaned in frustration. "I *have* tried. I've prayed, begging God to let me stop being in love with—" She clapped both hands over her mouth.

Jenn's eyes grew huge. "In love with who? Meredith Emmanuelle Guidry, you have to tell me. I'm your sister. I tell you everything."

Whether I want you to or not. She might as well go ahead and spill the whole can of worms now that it was open. Jenn would never leave her alone otherwise.

"Major."

Jenn stared at her for a few seconds. "Major. . .O'Hara?" she whispered, shock obvious.

"Yes, Major O'Hara. Who works for me—well, for Mom and Dad, but he reports to me."

"Major O'Hara?" Jenn looked as if she was going to laugh, but Meredith quelled her with a withering glance.

"You have to promise you won't say anything to anyone, Jenn."

"But if you're in love with Major, why are you dating Ward Breaux?"

"Because I made a promise to myself that this year I'm going to finally get over this thing I have for Major and not spend next New Year's alone."

"What do you mean 'finally'? How long have you harbored feelings for him?"

"Jenn—"

"No. I want the truth."

"Oh, all right." Meredith huffed, but a sense of release seeped in around her frustration with her sister. It actually felt good to finally tell someone other than Anne. "Eight years."

Jenn's mouth dropped open. "Eight *years?*"

"Yes. Ever since he started working at B-G."

"So if you're not interested in Ward Breaux, can I. . . ?" Jenn tipped her head to one side and waggled her eyebrows.

Meredith snorted. "What about Henry?"

Jenn looked over at George's handsome younger brother. "He's a lot of fun for right now, but he will be returning to Australia day after tomorrow. Ward lives right here in Bonneterre."

While Meredith wished she could be jealous over the idea of Ward turning his very romantic attention onto her sister, the thought brought profound relief—especially since she'd always hoped her sister would find a man as wonderful as Ward.

"Yes, by all means, go for it. . .him."

The limo rolled to a stop in front of Lafitte's Landing. Meredith scrambled out as soon as the door opened, allowing one of the boys taking invitations at the entrance to assist her out of the car.

"Wow, Miss Meredith, you look great."

"Thanks, Jeremy."

Lori met them inside the front door.

"Anne and George's limo pulled up just behind ours," Meredith told her. "Let the kitchen know and go give the DJ the heads-up—" She stopped with an apologetic smile. "Sorry. Old habits."

The veteran event planner shrugged her shoulders. "I was getting ready to defer to you, so I guess we're both operating on old habits." She stepped away from them to do just what Meredith had instructed and rejoined them as Anne and George came in. "Everyone is ready. Bridal party, if you'll come with me."

Meredith reminded Jennifer with one look that as maid of honor it was she, not Jenn, who should be escorted in by Henry Laurence.

It was going to be a long night.

CHAPTER 23

"Ladies and gentlemen, please join me in welcoming Mr. and Mrs. George Laurence."

Meredith applauded with the other three hundred people in the room, emotion once again trying to get the better of her at the sight of how happy Anne was.

"Miss Meredith?"

She turned. One of their longtime servers stood behind her, a tray of champagne flutes filled with Major's secret recipe fruit tea. Meredith gratefully took a glass.

Henry looked at the beverage contemplatively. "Unlike my brother, I've yet to grow accustomed to the idea of cold, sweetened tea."

"Ah, yes, then you'll want. . ." Meredith touched his arm for balance as she raised up on tiptoe to look around for a server with a different option. She caught the eye of one and motioned him over.

"What's this?" Henry took a glass of the clear, fizzy liquid.

"Sparkling water. George's choice."

"Excellent."

Jenn joined them and slipped her arm through Henry's. "I can't believe you left me at the mercy of Great-Aunt Edith, Mere. You know how much she likes to harp on me because I'm not married yet." Jenn batted her lashes at Henry.

"Why do you think I escaped?" Meredith winked at her sister.

241

On more than one occasion, Edith had offered to set Meredith up with some "fine young man" she knew. She considered that a moment. Edith herself had married quite well—Great-Uncle Rodney had been handsome and wealthy.

If things got dire, maybe she'd take Edith up on her offer. She laughed to herself.

"Here you are." Ward encircled Meredith's waist with one arm and kissed her temple.

Meredith introduced him to Henry and then to Forbes, again, who materialized out of the crowd of people trying to greet Anne and George. "But Forbes, where's your date?"

His eyes scanned the crowd, but his face looked a bit redder than normal. "She. . .she had something come up at the last minute and couldn't come."

"Something?" Jenn cocked her head and gave him a speculative stare.

"She got engaged last night."

Meredith and Jenn both groaned.

"Not another one who agreed to go out with you just to make her longtime boyfriend jealous?" If Meredith could ever figure this dating thing out, she'd have to teach Forbes how to do it, too.

"Yeah, something like that." He shook himself slightly, as if trying to dislodge his embarrassment. "Hey, what are we supposed to be doing right now?"

"This is technically what's considered to be the cocktail hour. At seven, the DJ will announce dinner; once everyone's seated, Reverend Kinnard will say the blessing before food service begins. At seven forty-five, the toasts begin—Henry, then me, then Uncle Errol and Aunt Maggie."

Meredith visualized the list in her head. "At eight o'clock is the first dance—Anne and George. Then Anne will dance with Uncle Errol, and George will dance with Aunt Maggie since his mom couldn't be here, and the attendants will join on that one—me with Henry, Jenn with Forbes. Then the floor's open to everyone for dancing."

Around her, Jenn, Forbes, Henry, and Ward all looked at her in astonishment.

"What?"

"Pray, continue," Henry said. "I had no idea all of this would be happening."

Heat rushed into her face at her ability to be a dork no matter what circumstance she was in. "Well, at nine o'clock, they'll cut the cake. Dancing will resume. And at nine thirty, Jenn, Aunt Maggie, and I will go with Anne to help her change out of her dress into her going-away outfit, and at ten o'clock, they'll leave. Forbes, you'll need to make sure we get out of here with George's tux so we can take it with Anne's dress to the dry cleaner on Monday."

"I'll be sure to do that." Forbes nodded.

"Meredith Guidry, there you are!"

She turned at the somewhat shrill female voice. "Hello, Mrs. McCord." She let the mayor's wife take her hands and kiss her cheek—well, kiss the air with her cheek pressed to Meredith's.

"I tried to find you after the banquet to tell you that it was absolutely the most wonderful event I've ever attended. You outdid yourself, young lady."

"Thank you very much, Mrs. McCord."

"And you looked positively darling on TV afterward. You're so photogenic. And that Major O'Hara—if he isn't just the yummiest thing I've ever laid eyes on. How long have the two of you been together?"

"We've worked together for a little over eight years now."

The mayor's wife simpered. "No, dear, I mean how long have you been dating?"

Meredith was acutely aware of Ward standing right beside her. "I'm not dating Major. We're colleagues, nothing more."

"Well, then you must be blind to the way that boy looks at you— as if you hung the moon and stars. I'm sure everyone watching that program thought the same thing I did, that your wedding would be the next one we'd see announced in the paper."

"Mrs. McCord, may I introduce you to my date, Ward Breaux?" Meredith moved a little sideways to pull Ward into the conversation.

"Oh—my." The older woman looked like she might attempt a swoon after taking her time to drag her gaze up Ward's striking figure to his handsome face.

"Ward, this is Mrs. McCord, first lady of Bonneterre."

He shook the woman's hand and answered her questions about his family and what he did for a living. As it turned out, Mrs. McCord and Ward's mother had been in the same sorority together in college.

Mrs. McCord turned to Meredith. "That means your mother would know Ward's mother as well, Meredith, as Mairee and I pledged Tri-Delt together our freshman year. If I recall, Ward, your mother was two years ahead of us."

"Really?" Meredith exchanged a raised-brow look with Ward. "I'll have to ask her later if she remembers Ward's mom."

"You do that." Mrs. McCord waved at someone beyond Meredith. "I've got to run—oh, but I will be calling you Monday to set up a time to come in and talk about Easter in the Park. It's time we get *in the hunt* on that." Her laughter trailed behind her after she walked away.

"Was that supposed to be funny?" Jenn asked when Meredith and Ward turned to rejoin the group.

"Hunt—the Easter egg hunt. Get it?"

"Oh. Ha-ha." Jenn smirked. "So, Ward, Meredith hasn't told us much about you." Even hanging on to Henry's arm, Jenn seemed to have no shame in flirting with someone else.

Ward talked a little about his family and his business. Meredith allowed her gaze to wander around the room, catching details that most attendees at this soiree would never notice—Lori talking to the DJ, the number of black-and-white-clad servers walking around with the trays of hot hors d'oeuvres, the little knot of servers gathered at the mouth of the hall leading to the kitchen.

Without really thinking about what she was doing, Meredith

excused herself and crossed the room to the service hallway. By the time she got over there, the servers had dispersed. But now that she was this close to the kitchen, she might as well stick her head in and see how everything was going.

She'd barely pushed the door open when the nearest person yelled, "Civilian in the kitchen."

Though on a smaller scale, the frenetic pace of the kitchen was very much like what it had been on Valentine's Day.

"May I help—oh, it's you." Major wiped his hands on a towel and draped it over his shoulder. "You look beautiful, Meredith."

She was pretty sure even her shoulders were blushing. "Thanks. How's everything going in here?"

"Is it my imagination, or are you supposed to be *not* working tonight?" The dimple appeared in his left cheek, though he tried to keep his expression stern.

"I just. . ." She shrugged. "Busted."

"Since you are a *guest* and not part of the staff tonight, I have to order you out of the kitchen." He pressed his fingertips to his earpiece. "Especially since I just got the five-minute warning until salad service. So," he reached behind her and pushed the door open, "please vacate the service area of the premises."

She caught the tip of her tongue between her teeth—he was so close to her. All she had to do was raise up on her toes and she'd be within a millimeter of kissing him.

She took a deep breath and swallowed hard. "Yes, Chef." Her voice squeaked, and she turned and fled the kitchen.

She was halfway through her Chateaubriand before her heart returned to a normal rate and she stopped imagining what would have happened if she hadn't backed away and practically run from the kitchen. Major would have been mortified if she'd kissed him in front of his staff, and possibly offended.

Mrs. McCord's words had wrecked Meredith's ability to ignore her romantic thoughts about Major. And even if Major did feel something for her, she couldn't do anything until she had a conversation with

Ward to tell him the truth about her feelings toward him.

"And now, the bride and groom will share their first dance."

George led Anne out to the open space in the middle of the room to the guests' soft applause. Out of the three songs Anne had narrowed the choices to, "True Love" had been Meredith's favorite. And she was really glad that Anne had been able to find the recording of Bing Crosby and Grace Kelly singing it, because it was a little slower, more romantic, than the Dean Martin version Anne had played for her a few weeks ago.

As soon as that song ended, the DJ invited Errol, Maggie, and the attendants to join Anne and George on the dance floor. When the first notes of "That's Amore" started playing, Meredith giggled, nerves pressing at her throat. Even though Anne had taught her several different steps, Meredith was by no means comfortable with the task of dancing, especially since Henry was so graceful it made her feel like an elephant trying to balance on a tightrope.

Thankfully, it was a short song. Meredith was just about to escape when Ward stopped her.

"May I?" He extended his hand.

She shook her head. "I'm not really a dancer."

"You looked wonderful out there." He took her hand and led her back onto the dance floor. "If you're truly awful, we'll stop, I promise."

Not only was Ward good, but he also softly sang along with "It Had to Be You" as he whisked Meredith around the floor. But two dances were enough for Meredith. She went and sat down with Forbes while Ward partnered up with Jenn.

"Do you think Jenn's seriously interested in Henry, or is it just because he's new and different?" Forbes asked.

"New and different. She's got her eye on Ward now, too." And from the way Ward was looking at Jenn while they slow-danced to a song Meredith had never heard before, he might not mind spending some time with Jenn.

"You don't think she'd try to steal him away from you?" Forbes leaned forward, concern evident in his slate blue eyes.

"It won't be stealing." She leaned across the table to retrieve her glass of tea.

"I see." Forbes resumed his more relaxed posture. "You've already told Jenn that?"

"Yeah. But I need to tell Ward."

"Best do it now." Forbes nodded at the two of them coming toward the table together.

She'd hoped to put it off as long as possible, but she could see the struggle in Ward's eyes when he sat down beside her.

Forbes sighed and stood. "Come on, Jenn. Dance with your decrepit old brother."

Ward reached over and took Meredith's hand. "You don't look like you're enjoying yourself."

"Ward...there's something I need to tell you."

"Sounds serious." He rubbed his thumb against the palm of her hand.

"It is." She pulled her hand out of his and rested it on her lap. "It's something I should have told you awhile back, but I've been putting it off, hoping things would change."

He leaned forward and braced his hands on his knees. "Hoping *things* would change—as in the way you feel about me?"

"Yeah." She drew the word out. "I have had so much fun going out with you, and I have never felt more cherished and admired than I have since I met you."

"But you aren't falling in love with me." Kindness permeated his voice and soft smile. "Would it surprise you to learn that I'm not in love with you either?"

Breathing came a little easier. "A little. Why keep asking me out if. . . ?"

"Because I *wanted* to fall in love with you. On paper, Meredith Guidry is the perfect woman for me."

"But I'm not the same person in real life that I am on paper?"

"No, that's not what I mean. I mean that every quality that I've ever dreamed of finding in a woman, I found in you."

"But the spark isn't there." She began to relax, understanding that he really did feel the same way she did.

"Exactly."

"I was seeing definite sparks between you and Jenn." She grinned at his surprise. "Henry leaves day after tomorrow, and while she's having fun flirting with him, when I told her I was going to break up with you, she wanted to know if that meant you were fair game. So I'm giving you the same blessing I gave her: go for it."

And he did. As soon as Jenn came off the dance floor with Forbes, Ward took her right back out and relinquished her to Henry only twice.

"I'm proud of you, Mere."

"Hmm?" Meredith hadn't caught all of what Forbes said. She was too caught up in watching Major make his way around the room. It must be almost time for the cake cutting, since he'd said he was going to make an appearance for that.

A sudden welling of emotion took Meredith by surprise. She'd wished, wanted, hoped, desired, prayed for so long that what Mrs. McCord had said would come true—that she would marry Major O'Hara. The desire to melt into a heap of tears, in private, drew her to her feet, but before she could disappear and give into the temptation, Anne waved her over to the table where the enormous cake Aunt Maggie had created stood.

As soon as Anne and George had finished feeding cake to each other and the servers had taken over cutting the masterpiece into pieces for the guests, Meredith slipped out the front door and followed the wraparound porch to the place overlooking the lake that lay between Lafitte's and the university campus.

She immediately wished she'd stopped to get her wrap as the cool, damp air prickled her arms and cheeks. But she didn't feel like going back inside to get it. She'd come out here to feel miserable, and being cold only added to her self-pity.

Leaning against one of the pillars, she wrapped her arms around her middle and gave into the tears that had been building for weeks, months, years. Tonight she'd lost Anne and Ward. Though Anne would never cease being her cousin and friend, their relationship would never be the same again—she'd seen the hints of that over the past six months since Anne and George met. And even though she hadn't been in love with Ward, at least she'd had the appearance and comfort of having a boyfriend for a couple of months.

"Lord, what's wrong with me? Why doesn't anyone want me? Are You trying to show me that I'm going to be alone for the rest of my life?"

She wasn't really sure she expected an answer. For years, she'd been praying the same prayer in different ways, but basically asking for one thing: a husband. Someone, as the song said, to watch over her. The one person who would not only flatter her vanity and make her feel cherished, the way Ward had, but who stirred the very embers of her soul, the way Major did.

But maybe Anne had been right. Maybe she should be praying for something other than for Major to come to his senses. She closed her eyes. "Lord, I've been begging for You to make Major return my feelings for a long time now. And I've never once prayed to ask You to show me Your will in my relationship with him—or any relationships. Father, please help me to be content with where I am and what I have in my life, and to be looking for the ways in which I can make myself a better person and serve You better."

The muscles in her shoulders cramped with the cold, and she shivered violently. But she couldn't go back inside. Not yet. Not until she got all the tears out of her system. She hoped God would start giving her that contentment soon, because right now, all she had was a great big, empty, gaping hole of loneliness.

"You know, you really shouldn't be out here without a coat."

Warmth enveloped Meredith's shoulders—and the scent that was unmistakably Major's. She snuggled into his leather jacket even as she tried to wipe away any evidence she'd been crying.

"How'd you know where to find me?" Hoping her supposedly

waterproof eye makeup hadn't run, she turned, her heart wrenching at the familiar and beloved sight of him in his pristine white chef's jacket.

He reached over and pulled the collar of the jacket closed under her chin. "I always try to make sure I know where you are."

The gruffness in his voice nearly keeled her over. "Oh."

"Meredith, I—" He swallowed a couple of times. "I'm sorry Ward Breaux hurt you the way he did tonight. I couldn't believe it when I saw him blatantly and openly flirting with Jenn right in front of you."

A sob-laugh burst from Meredith's throat. "He didn't hurt me. I told him tonight that I don't have any feelings for him—not romantically anyway—and I gave him and Jenn both my blessing."

"Your blessing?" Major moved closer, clasping her shoulders, his eyes midnight blue in the faint moonlight. "You're saying you're not in love with Ward Breaux?"

"Yes, I'm—"

Major's lips pressed to hers in a kiss that buckled Meredith's knees. She kissed him back with all the intensity eight years of hoping for this moment had built inside of her.

When the kiss finally ended, Major pulled her into his arms and pressed his cheek to her hair. "I love you, Meredith. I have for a very long time."

She laughed. God hadn't taken very long in answering her prayer for contentment.

CHAPTER 24

I still can't believe you laughed at me when I told you I love you."

"You're so cute when you're disgruntled."

Major couldn't help smiling back at Meredith. When he'd seen Ward Breaux dancing with Jenn last night, he'd been ready to call the guy out—forget the fact that Breaux had the advantage of at least four inches and a couple tons more muscle. And at that moment, Major knew he couldn't live one more day without letting Meredith know he loved her.

"Are you sure that coming to Sunday dinner with my entire extended family isn't going to be awkward for you? No one knows about us."

"Um, I think they can see us sitting here together." Major looked around the sanctuary and back at Meredith. He wanted to go with her, to have her show her family that they were together, that they loved each other. And as long as this family meal didn't last three or four hours, he would be able to get out to BPC before Ma started wondering where he was—though she had been a lot better since the trip to the emergency room a week and a half ago.

Meredith half turned on the pew to face him. "Major, you know how I feel about you."

He grinned. "Yeah. You've been in love with me since we first started working together." He'd been both surprised and humbled when she'd told him that last night.

"Right. But even though we've worked together for a long time and I love you for who you are as a person, before we can move forward with our relationship, there's something you're going to have to do for me."

The organ music started, and around them, everyone rose to sing the call to worship.

Heart throbbing with guilt, knowing what she was about to ask him, Major stood and opened the hymnal. He leaned over and whispered, "We have plenty of time to talk about our relationship. Let's just take things slowly."

He did have a lot he needed to tell her. She didn't even know yet that he'd turned down her parents' offer to open the restaurant. And then there was Ma. He prayed for wisdom.

It shouldn't have surprised him that Meredith had a special journal in which she took notes on the sermon. The few times he'd attended the late service when the quartet sang, he hadn't taken the time to notice how studiously she paid attention and wrote down ideas sparked by Reverend Kinnard's sermon.

He also found it interesting that Meredith had chosen to sit across the sanctuary from where most of her family were. But as soon as the service ended, Forbes appeared—almost as if magically and instantaneously transported across the large room.

"You don't usually come to this service." Forbes extended his hand to Major, speculation practically dripping from his gaze.

"It was a late night last night." Major glanced at Meredith.

"Forbes, I've invited Major to come to Sunday dinner today."

His friend's speculation disappeared into a knowing smile. "I see. I thought last night things might be moving in that direction."

Meredith leaned left to look around her brother. "Why don't we go on and head over to Maggie and Errol's?" She looked up at Major, a slight nervousness in her smile.

He looked beyond Forbes, too. Jenn, Rafe, and a few others of Meredith's siblings and cousins were heading in their direction.

Forbes glanced over his shoulder. "You'll have to deal with them one way or another."

"I'd rather deal with them in a less public setting, thanks very much." She shooed Major out of the pew, and he obediently led the way.

"Do you want to ride over with me?" Meredith slid her sunglasses on when they reached the brightness outside.

"I think I'm closer to home at Maggie and Errol's than from here, so why don't I just follow you over there." Guilt nibbled at his conscience like ravenous piranhas.

"Oh, okay. But I thought maybe we could drive out to my house afterward so you can see the progress Ward has made on the kitchen, since you did help him design it."

And when he'd talked on the phone with Ward about the things he would want to see in a home kitchen, Major had experienced jealousy unlike anything he'd ever want to go through again. Not just for the fact he was talking to the man he thought Meredith was falling for, but because he couldn't foresee ever being able to afford a kitchen like that for himself. But now. . .

The drive to Maggie and Errol's sprawling mini-mansion didn't take long, and he and Meredith were among the first to arrive.

"Do my eyes deceive me, or is that Major O'Hara?" Maggie Babineaux stopped stirring the contents of a pot on the stove and came across the ginormous kitchen to hug him. He could understand Maggie's having a kitchen like this—after all, she'd been a caterer and cake decorator for years—but he still didn't quite understand why Meredith, who didn't cook at all, wanted a gourmet-quality kitchen.

"It's good to see you, Maggie."

"I'm glad one of our girls finally wised up and brought you around." Maggie winked at him. "The first time I met you, I knew you were destined to become part of this family."

He endured the ebullient greetings from the rest of Meredith's aunts—and the more reserved welcome from her grandmother. The only outward sign of surprise Mairee gave when she entered a few minutes later was the slight lifting of one eyebrow.

While he'd had an intellectual understanding of just how large Meredith's extended family was, to experience it in reality soon became almost overwhelming. The table in the cavernous dining room seated all the adults, while teens sat at the long central island in the kitchen, and children, at tables set up on the sunporch.

"Anne called before their flight left Atlanta," Maggie announced after Meredith's grandfather asked the blessing and food began making the rounds of the table.

"Did she sound like she was coping okay?" Meredith passed him the bowl of mashed potatoes.

"She admitted she had gotten sick to her stomach before they boarded the plane here, but since the flight to Atlanta was smooth, she's feeling okay about the flight to New York. Still, I could tell she's worrying about the flight to London."

"It's a miracle she's flying at all." Rafe shook his head. "If it hadn't been for George, she might never have had the motivation to get on a plane again."

"Well, she asked everyone to pray that she doesn't have a panic attack along the way, because she doesn't want to ruin this trip for George."

Though the food was what most French-trained chefs would consider "rustic," Major loved every morsel that passed his lips, from the fall-apart-tender roast beef with rich gravy, to the corn pudding, to the mustard greens that had been cooked with a ham hock. Every family should have a meal like this once a week.

After dinner was finished, the women cleared the dishes and returned from the kitchen with thick slices of cake garnished with fresh berries, which they served to everyone at the table. Meredith set Major's in front of him, and he immediately recognized the cake.

"There was this much wedding cake left over? I'm surprised there was any."

"Aunt Maggie made an extra tier that she ended up not using. So now we get to have it for dessert." Meredith scraped a thick swirl of frosting off her piece with her fork and ate it, closing her eyes with a sigh.

Major wasn't a big fan of cake, but Maggie's creations were in a class by themselves. He enjoyed every bite but wished he could take a piece to his mother, who loved cake and never got a chance to eat any but the dry, grocery store cakes that they occasionally served at BPC for someone's birthday.

As soon as the last crumb was eaten, the last dollop of frosting scraped off the plates, the men all stood and collected the dishes. Forbes indicated with a nod of his head over his shoulder for Major to join them. He took his and Meredith's plates and followed Forbes into the kitchen.

Led by Errol, the men scraped and rinsed all of the dinner dishes and put them into the three dishwashers hidden behind panels that matched the cabinet doors.

"Major, how long have you known our Meredith?" her grandfather asked as he scraped the few spoonfuls of mashed potatoes from the serving dish into a plastic container.

"Eight years, sir."

"And it's taken that long for her to invite you to Sunday dinner?" The old gentleman's brown eyes twinkled—just like Meredith's did when she teased him.

"I'm a slow learner."

The head of the Guidry clan threw his head back and laughed. The self-deprecating humor seemed to be all the men in Meredith's family needed to accept him as one of their own, as no one else questioned his presence and what it meant.

But as soon as the dishwashers hummed and swished in the background, Major approached Lawson Guidry. "May I have a word with you, sir?"

"I hoped you might want to." Lawson cuffed his shoulder and led him to a study beyond the kitchen. He closed the door then motioned for Major to take one of the wingback chairs that flanked the fireplace.

Major had occasionally imagined the day when he would sit down with the father of the woman he loved and confess his feelings and ask for the father's blessing. Now that it was here, he wasn't exactly sure where to start.

"Mairee and I cannot thank you enough for the exemplary job you and your staff did at Anne's reception last night. I know Anne appreciated every effort you made on her behalf."

"Thank you, sir. It was my pleasure to give her the best of everything." He wiped his hands on the knees of his slacks. "Mr. Guidry, I'm in love with your daughter."

"Which one? I have four." The corner of his mouth twitched.

Major stopped fidgeting, Lawson's humor breaking the tension in the room. "You mean, I can have my pick?"

Lawson finally gave in and smiled. "I've been aware that Meredith has carried a torch for you for a while now. We were quite surprised when we learned she had started seeing someone else. And when you told me two weeks ago that you couldn't take the restaurant deal due to your need to tend to your mother, I almost wanted to tell you then that Meredith would be the perfect helpmate."

Major swallowed hard. "I haven't told her about my mother just yet."

The humor seeped out of Lawson's face. "Why not?"

Because I'm chicken. "The right opportunity hasn't presented itself yet. But I will tell her, soon."

"See that you do. Honesty is of the utmost importance in any relationship."

"I will."

"Good. Now, if that's all." Lawson rose.

Major stood as well.

Meredith's father extended his right hand. "Welcome to the Guidry family, Major."

His stomach flip-flopped. "Thank you, sir." Following Lawson out of the study, Major looked at his watch. One thirty. Not too bad. As long as he made it out to BPC by three o'clock, Ma should be okay.

When he walked into the dining room with Forbes, Rafe, Kevin, and Jonathan, Meredith's face was beet red. The intrusion of men into the room broke up the hen party, and couples started discussing getting their kids home for naps or homework.

Meredith jumped up from her seat. "Major, are you ready to go see the house?"

"Sure, if you are." He had the distinct impression that her aunts, cousins, and sisters had been giving her a hard time about him, thus her eagerness to escape.

"Let's go, then." She bade a hasty and general farewell to her relatives and practically dragged him from the house, muttering. He caught random words, such as "meddling" and "privacy," which confirmed his suspicions.

She didn't slow down until they arrived at her SUV. "Are you following again or riding?"

"I might as well just follow you over there." Because he could go straight out to BPC instead of taking the time to come all the way back over here.

Meredith's house sat deep within the Plantation Grove area of town, where the lots were enormous and the houses no newer than seventy or eighty years old.

From the street, the craftsman bungalow was half hidden by the two huge oak trees in the front yard. Azalea bushes, which were starting to show hints that they'd be blooming soon, lined the base of the porch on either side of the wide steps. From the outside, the house appeared in perfect condition—until the driveway took him around to the back. A large Dumpster blocked access to the carport and detached garage, and construction detritus littered the side yard.

Meredith climbed out of her SUV and held her arms open wide. "Welcome to my house, such as it is."

"It's great." He pocketed his keys and met her at the gate to the backyard. A high-pitched bark seemed to be coming from nearby. "Is there a dog here?"

"I dropped my puppy off over here this morning before church, since I knew I'd be coming by this afternoon to check on the progress." A much larger puppy than Major had pictured trundled over. Meredith bent down to scoop it up—then apparently changed her mind. "Your feet are muddy."

Major crouched down beside her, drawing the little guy's attention—and muddy paw prints on his pant leg. He scratched behind the floppy ears, then on the tubby tummy when the pup rolled onto his back. "What's his name?"

"I haven't named him yet."

"How long have you had him?"

"Since January first. I found him under the back porch."

"You've had him almost two months and you haven't named him?"

Meredith stood and started for the raised deck. "I don't really have the time to commit to a puppy—housebreaking, obedience training, and paying attention to him in general."

Major rocked back onto his heels. If she didn't think she would have time for a puppy, how could she have time to deal with his mother if he needed her to? But a puppy and a person were different, and her priorities would probably change in that case. "If you were going to keep him, what would you name him?" He joined her on the porch.

"Duke." She had to jiggle the key in the knob to get it to unlatch. She swung the door open and closed a couple of times. "Good. They rehung this door so it doesn't scrape the floor anymore."

"Duke—any special significance?" He followed her into the house.

"It was John Wayne's nickname." She flipped a couple of switches, and light flooded the room they were in—the kitchen.

But for the moment, Major had no attention for anything other than what she'd just said. "John Wayne?"

"I know. I'm a weirdo for liking John Wayne movies. But he's my favorite, and I refuse to apologize for it." She faced him, arms crossed as if daring him to contradict or tease her.

"Have I ever told you my full name?" He bit the sides of his tongue to keep from smiling.

She frowned, appearing uncertain as to the seemingly random change of subject. "No."

"Major Daniel Xavier Kirby O'Hara."

She repeated the name slowly. And a second time. Then understanding flickered in her nutmeg eyes. "Major Dan Kirby. . .the character Duke played in *Flying Leathernecks*?"

"None other. I like John Wayne movies, too. But I am partial to the war movies."

She braced her hands on the edge of her kitchen island. "I knew there was something I liked about you. But I have to disagree—I like his westerns best."

How could he ever have doubted that God meant for the two of them to be together? Once he could drag his gaze away from her, he finally took in the sight that surrounded him, and it quickened his heart. The cherry cabinets had been stained to exactly match the original woodwork of the window casings and crown molding. The grayish green granite countertops needed a good cleaning but looked exactly how he'd imagined. All the room lacked were the appliances—the six-burner, commercial-grade stove with double oven; the stainless-steel refrigerator and dishwasher; and the hood with the warming shelf built in.

Oh, yes, he could create the perfect romantic meals for the two of them in this kitchen. As a matter of fact, that would be a great way to celebrate the completion of this room, as well as a perfect time for him to tell Meredith all about Ma.

It would mean talking to Ward Breaux to find out when construction would be finished—and he wondered if Alaine's crew would mind shooting a segment here, since she said she'd like to get him in some home kitchens every so often.

Meredith toured him through the rest of the house, but Major's mind was occupied with creating the perfect romantic menu—one that would hopefully make up for the fact he'd been keeping a pretty big secret from her.

"Oh, for heaven's sake." Meredith's words drew him out of his thoughts. "See, this is why I don't want to deal with owning a dog. I hate cleaning up messes."

Duke had indeed messed on the protective paper covering the kitchen floor.

"I'll take care of that if you want to put him outside." Major tore the paper in a large square around the little pile, pulled the corners up, and carried it out to the Dumpster in the driveway.

Meredith's attitude about the responsibility of having a puppy niggled him. If she felt so strongly about something as simple as dog poo, how was she ever going to be able to cope with Ma?

CHAPTER 25

*S*he said it would be seven o'clock before she'd be able to get here." Ward leaned against the edge of the island.

Major finished emptying the grocery bags. "That's perfect. She doesn't suspect anything even with me here filming today?"

"Just that there's something wrong with the house." Ward crossed his arms and glared at Nelson. The unflappable cameraman continued placing lights around the freshly painted, stained, and polished kitchen.

Pricilla came in with more equipment cases. "I can see why you wanted to film here, Major. Sorry we had to put it off a day."

He introduced her to Ward. "He's the man responsible for all this." Major turned, his hands held out in front of him. "In fact, one of the caveats Meredith gave for allowing us to film here today was to make sure that Ward gets recognition for creating this kitchen. So I'd like to open with a little bit of me talking to him."

"Whoa—you never said anything about me being on camera."

"Think of the free publicity," Major said in a low voice.

Pricilla shrugged. "No problem. The rest of your script is staying the same though, right?"

If one could call the rough outline of what he was going to say a script. "Yes. Want to go over your notes on it?"

He spent the next fifteen minutes going over the plan for the day's

261

filming while Charla did his makeup and Nelson tested the lighting. Once they finished those tasks, Major rehearsed the blocking of his movements around the unfamiliar space, using Nelson's guidance to choose where to place the pans, dishes, utensils, and small appliances he'd brought from home and the executive kitchen.

Major spent the first few minutes of filming talking to Ward about the features of Meredith's kitchen and things homeowners could do to increase the efficiency of their cooking and food-prep spaces. When they finished, Major shook hands with his former rival and invited him to stay and watch, but Ward excused himself, promising to return later.

Nelson did some close-ups of different areas of the kitchen while Major set out his mise en place, carefully arranging all of the utensils, dishes, and food items he would need in the order he would use them.

"Ready?" Pricilla asked from behind the stationary camera diagonally across the island from him. This would be a little harder than usual, since the stove was over to his right instead of behind him, as in the executive kitchen—or in the island, as at Alaine's place. But it would work.

"Ready."

Pricilla gave the take number then pointed at Major to start.

"I'm Chef Major O'Hara, executive chef for Boudreaux-Guidry Enterprises' catering division. Today we're going to be making braised beef short ribs; cheesy potato casserole; sautéed broccoli rabe with lemon and garlic; and for dessert, an easy, rich, flourless chocolate cake."

He got started cooking. Every time he looked into the camera lens, he got a little tickle in his stomach, imagining Meredith on the other side instead of Pricilla. In just a few hours, Meredith would be here, eating the food he was cooking.

At three o'clock, Major designed the presentation plate for Nelson to shoot.

"You were really on a roll today." Pricilla started wrapping up cords.

"It seems to be getting easier every week."

"Let the homeowner know that we're grateful for the chance to film here—and that I'm jealous over this house."

"I'll be sure to tell her." He pitched in and helped break down the equipment and load it in the van. Even though he could use some of what he cooked for the segment, he had quite a bit of work to do before he could run out to see Ma and still get back in time to surprise Meredith.

He grabbed his phone and called Ma's direct line.

"Yes?"

"It's me, Ma."

"Why are you calling? You're coming tonight, aren't you?" A tinge of panic laced his mother's voice.

"I'm coming early for my visit tonight. I should be there around five o'clock." That should give him enough time to do a quick clean of her room and let her tell him everything that had happened to her since Sunday.

"Oh. Okay. But you'll have to leave by six, because that's when we have dinner."

He'd have plenty of time to get back here and sauté a fresh batch of the broccoli rabe, put last minute touches on everything else, and change clothes before Meredith arrived. "I'll see you in a little while, Ma. And I'll be sure to leave by six."

" 'Kay. Bye." She hung up.

He dialed Ward's number.

"Is the coast clear?" Ward said by way of greeting.

"Yeah. Did you get the table and chairs?"

"I did. I'm headed that way with them now."

"Thanks. See you in a few, then." He closed the phone and turned his attention to the romantic dinner for Meredith. He marveled at the irony that in the short span of two weeks, Ward Breaux had gone from enemy to Major's greatest ally.

Twenty minutes later, he slid the pan of hash-brown casserole back into the smaller warming oven to reheat. Tires crunched on the gravel drive. After a moment's panic that Meredith had come early, Major went out to help Ward carry in the table Major had found at a secondhand furniture shop. If she protested his buying it for her, he'd insist it was a housewarming gift, especially since he'd overheard her telling Corie how much she wanted to find a drop-leaf table to put on the newly screened-in back porch.

Major pulled out the tablecloth, candles, and flowers he'd brought. Ward returned with the two chairs.

"You're sure you don't mind staying while I run a last-minute errand?" Major placed the matchbook on the table so he could light the candles as soon as Meredith drove up.

"So long as I don't have to do anything with the food." Ward glanced nervously over his shoulder at the kitchen.

"Nope. Everything's either warming or chilling or braising, so it's good to go until I get back to finish it off. I should only be gone about an hour. Hopefully, she won't come early."

The morning's slight drizzle had turned into a steady rain. He hoped it wouldn't cause any problems. The last thing he needed was to get stuck in a traffic jam trying to get back before Meredith arrived.

Meredith groaned when the radio DJ announced that traffic in midtown was still in a snarl because of a major accident at University Avenue and Spring Street—the most direct route to get to the house from the office. She picked up her phone and quick-dialed Ward's number.

"Hey, pretty girl."

She laughed at his continued use of the endearment. "Hey, yourself. I'm calling to let you know that it looks like it may be seven fifteen or later before I can get there. Traffic through town is bad, so I'm going to have to go around the long way."

"Not a problem. Drive carefully."

"I will. See you in a bit." She ended the call and set the phone in the closest cup holder. She made a U-turn to head north instead of south out of downtown.

But even the winding country roads that led to the back entrance to Plantation Grove were packed with cars barely crawling along. She breathed a huge sigh of relief when she turned into the subdivision and traffic instantly thinned out.

Tension ebbed from her shoulders at the warm, beckoning light shining through the front windows of her house. Almost thirty minutes late, she hoped whatever it was that Ward needed to show her wouldn't take very long.

Pulling her jacket over her head, she dashed up the sidewalk to the front porch. The beveled glass in the top of the door glittered and sent glittering rainbows across the porch and floor when it swung open.

The heavenly aroma of food greeted her. She drew in a deep breath and sighed—then laughed. Best not get used to the smell of food cooking in this house. At least, not in the near future. But maybe someday. . .

She nipped that thought in the bud. Until Major told her everything about himself—about his family—she'd promised herself she wouldn't let their relationship progress past its current stage.

He was supposed to have finished filming several hours ago—so why did it smell like the food was cooking now?

She followed the scent toward the back of the house—and stopped just inside the dining room door. A table with flowers and unlit candles as a centerpiece, formally set for a meal, sat in the middle of the large room. Her heart jumped. Could this be for her? Or something left over from the TV segment?

A noise in the kitchen motivated her to move. "Hello?"

Ward appeared in the doorway to the kitchen.

Her heart dropped. Had he changed his mind? Was this an attempt to win her back?

"Hi, Meredith."

"What. . .what is all this?" She stopped at the table and gripped the spindle back of a chair.

"Uh. . .well, you know that Major was over here today, shooting his TV show. You see, it's like this: He wanted to surprise you with a romantic dinner, so he asked me to call you to come over tonight."

"Oh." Drat the way her voice went all high and squeaky when she was excited. "Is he in the kitchen?" She started around the table.

"No-o-o." Ward's forehead became a washboard of frown lines. "Truth is, I don't know where he is. The only reason I'm here is because he had to run an errand. He said he'd be back around six, but I haven't heard from him since he left."

Meredith looked at her watch. "It's almost a quarter of eight." She reached for her phone but then remembered it was still in the cup holder in her car.

Ward extended his phone. "Here."

She dialed Major's cell phone number from memory. It rang four times; then his voicemail picked up. She dialed it again. It rang twice, then—

A woman's voice answered. "Hello? Who is this, please?"

Meredith's heart pounded. "Meredith Guidry. I'm looking for Major O'Hara. Have I dialed the wrong number?"

"No, ma'am. Are you a relative of Mr. O'Hara's?"

Her knees buckled. Ward grabbed her shoulders to keep her from falling and pulled out the closest chair for her to sit. "I'm. . ." What was she to him? "I'm his. . .his boss."

"Oh. I'm Alison Rihsab, a nurse in the emergency room at University Hospital. We couldn't find any emergency contact information on Mr. O'Hara."

Meredith's head spun, and she doubled over to keep from passing out. "Emergency room? What happened?"

"He was in a car accident."

"How bad is it?"

"I'm sorry, I can't give that information over the phone. Do you have any contact information for an emergency contact for him?"

"I'm his emergency contact, and I'll be there as soon as I can get there." She ended the call and tried to jump up from the chair, but Ward wouldn't let her.

"Slow down. Tell me what happened."

She repeated what the nurse had told her. "So I have to go. I don't think he has anyone else to be with him."

"Fine. But you're not driving in this condition unless you want to end up in the hospital bed right next to him." He held out his hand. "Give me your keys. You're parked behind me, so it'll be faster to take your truck than mine."

She dropped her keys into his large palm.

"Now, you just sit here and take some deep breaths while I do something about that food."

Meredith's head started spinning again, so she leaned over, arms wrapped around her stomach. "Oh, Lord, let him be okay. Let him be okay. I can't lose him now." She repeated the words like a mantra until she started feeling calmer.

After a lot of clanking and clattering, Ward reappeared. "Come on. Let's go."

"I think I'm okay to drive."

"Are you sure?"

"I'll probably be out there most of the night—you know how slow things move in the ER. I don't want you tied up out there with me when you don't have to be."

"Do you want me to follow you out there, just to make sure you get there okay?"

She reached over and squeezed his hand. "Thanks for the offer, but really, I promise I'll drive carefully."

He handed the keys back to her. "You call me when you get there and find out what happened, okay? No matter how late it is."

"I will."

"And be sure to let me know if there's anything I can do." He walked her to the front door.

"Just pray."

"I already am."

Meredith ran to her SUV and was about to punch the accelerator to get to the hospital as fast as she could—then remembered where she was going and why. No point in getting into an accident herself by speeding on the wet roads. With both hands in a death grip around the steering wheel, she headed for the sprawling medical park that surrounded the largest hospital in town.

She prayed the entire way, never getting beyond *Please let him be okay*.

Trying to figure out where to park to get to the emergency room frustrated her almost to the point of tears. She eventually found the designated lot and pulled into a space, not caring that her right wheels were over the line.

Her heels tapped on the tile floor in a quick staccato as she half walked, half jogged to the information desk.

"May I help you?" the woman behind the glass asked.

"Yes. I'm here for Major O'Hara. He was in a car accident. I talked to a nurse—" Oh, what had her name been? "Amanda or Abigail or. . .Alison! I talked to Nurse Alison, who answered his phone when I called it."

"And your name is?"

"Meredith Guidry."

"Please have a seat, Ms. Guidry."

"But—"

The woman slid the glass closed.

Defeated by worry, Meredith perched on the edge of the nearest chair and dug in her purse for a piece of gum or candy or something. She found a peppermint that had been in there forever and put it in her mouth, tapping her back teeth on its hard surface.

The sitcom on the TV hanging off the wall twenty feet away ended, and another show started. Meredith couldn't sit still any longer. So she paced.

Surely after so many years and so much time wasted, God wouldn't take Major away from her like this.

CHAPTER 26

Major tried to concentrate on what was going on around him, but the shot they'd given him in the ambulance made his stomach woozy and his head feel like it was stuffed with cabbage. He couldn't move. They had him strapped to a board.

But he needed to get to Ma. She would be frantic when he didn't show up at the time he said he would. She'd have an episode—and she'd caused so much trouble recently that it might be the last straw. He didn't want to have to find another place for her to live.

"I need my phone." He watched as they put another shot of something into his IV.

"Mr. O'Hara, we need to get X-rays of your neck and spine. If those come out okay, we'll unstrap you from the board. Is there someone we can call for you?"

"My mother—she's at Beausoleil Pointe Center. She's expecting me. But if I don't come—I think I'm going to throw up."

The medical staff scrambled to turn him onto his side and stuck a plastic tray under the side of his face. After a few long seconds, the wave of nausea abated.

"I'm okay now." But he wasn't really. His vision started going dark around the edges. Maybe if he just closed his eyes for a minute, everything would be okay when he opened them again.

Painful pressure on his chest woke him.

"Mr. O'Hara, don't go to sleep on us now."

"Won't." But the drifting feeling tempted him, because to follow it meant he didn't have to experience the reality of the severe pain in his left leg or the sharp stabbing in his left side every time he breathed.

"Mr. O'Hara, there's a Meredith Guidry here to see you."

"Meredith? Where?"

"Is it okay if she comes back? She said she's your emergency contact."

"Yes." He closed his eyes. He answered yes or no to the nurses' questions about his medical history. They finally removed the neck brace and back board.

"Major?"

He opened his eyes to the most beautiful sight he'd ever beheld. "Meredith. I love you. Will you marry me?"

Tears dripped from her eyes. "I think that's something we should probably talk about sometime when you aren't doped up on morphine."

"Okay. I need to get out of here. I've got to go—get to Ma." Strong hands pressed his shoulders back against the bed.

"You just need to stay here and let them fix you up." Meredith's fingers grazed his forehead, pushing his hair back.

"We need to take him up to get an MRI on his leg before surgery." A nurse appeared beside Meredith with a plastic bag. "These are his personal effects—his clothes, shoes, wallet, phone... everything he had on him."

"Surgery?"

"For the compound fracture in his leg. I'll take you upstairs to the waiting room near where they'll be doing the procedure."

"Thank you."

Major heard a familiar sounding tune. Ma's song. It was his phone. Ma was calling. But the sound grew fainter, and the ceiling tiles whizzing by overhead were making him sick to his stomach again.

Meredith wiped the moisture from her face and followed Alison to a different set of elevators than the ones they'd taken Major away in.

"The pain killers they gave him were making him say things that he probably didn't mean," Alison said.

"You mean when he asked me to marry him?"

The nurse nodded.

"I told you I'm his boss, but we're also sort of dating."

"Oh, so he might have meant it, then." The elevator doors opened, and Alison motioned Meredith to follow her.

Major's phone started to ring again with that peculiar ringtone she'd noticed on other occasions.

"Whoever that is has called a couple of times already. Once we talked to you as his emergency contact, we didn't want to answer it."

Before Meredith could dig the phone out of the bottom of the big plastic bag, it stopped. "Well, if they call back, I'll answer it, just in case it's something important."

They stopped at the nurses' station for the surgical unit, and Meredith gave them her name and cell phone number.

"You realize he's going to be in pre-op and surgery for a few hours, right?" the nurse asked when Meredith told her she planned on staying around.

"Someone needs to be here for him, and as far as I know, I'm the only someone he's got." Pressure built in her throat. Even though she'd seen him with her own eyes and Alison had assured her he'd be okay, fear laid claim to her soul. Something could still go wrong.

"All right. But it'll be a long evening. If you'd like, the cafeteria is down on the second floor. They serve dinner until nine o'clock, and the coffee shop is open all night."

The heavy plastic bag started digging into Meredith's fingers. "I think I'll go put his stuff in my car—oh, I'm parked in the ER visitor lot. Should I move it to another parking area?"

"Your car should be fine where it is." Alison touched Meredith's arm. "I'll be praying for your. . .friend."

"Thank you." Meredith briefly pressed her hand on top of Alison's.

"I'll take you back down to the ER—that'll be the easiest way to get to your car."

Meredith did her best to pay attention to their route so she could find her way back through the labyrinthine building when she came back. Alison showed her where to go from the emergency room lobby to get back upstairs. Meredith thanked her again then stepped out into the chill March air.

Only when Major's phone started ringing again did Meredith remember to dig it out of the bottom of the bag.

BPC flashed on the screen. It took her a couple of tries to find the correct button to answer. "Hello?"

A slight rustling came over the line then a click and dead air.

"Hmm." Meredith looked at the screen again. CALL ENDED. Well, that was odd.

She'd just gotten onto the elevator when the phone rang again. "Hello? This is Meredith Guidry answering for Major O'Hara."

A slight pause. Then, "Major—I need to talk to him." The voice was low and hoarse enough that Meredith couldn't tell if it was male or female.

"He can't come to the phone right now."

"I need to talk to him." Urgency made the voice sound female.

"I understand, but he's. . .he's been in a car accident, and the doctors are looking at him right now. Is this—are you his mother?"

Dead air was the only response she received. She looked at the screen, but the call timer kept ticking the seconds away. They hadn't been disconnected.

"Hello?"

Nothing.

She kept the phone to her ear and made her way down a myriad of corridors until she found the correct surgical waiting room.

"Hello? Are you still there?"

Silence came back to her.

After another few minutes, she tried again, but to no avail. She disconnected and stared at the screen a moment. What did *BPC* mean? She scrolled through his contacts to find it. Taking a deep breath, not knowing who would answer, she hit SEND.

The line rang twice, then a click. "Hello. You have reached the main switchboard at Beausoleil Pointe Center. Our hours of operation are 7:00 a.m. to 6:00 p.m. If you know your party's extension, please dial it at any time. If this is an emergency, press 6 to page the on-call physician."

Meredith hung up. On-call physician? What was this place?

She went back into his contacts list and scrolled down to the *Ms*. She got a slight smile seeing her name with all of her contact phone numbers listed, but kept scrolling. No *Mom* or *Mother* listed. Closing the phone, she sighed. She'd just have to wait for the woman to call back.

She flipped through a couple of old magazines, called her parents, tried to watch the news program on the overhead TV, called Forbes, paced, sat, called Ward, paced some more, and prayed—prayed hard. The more time dragged on, the more frustrated and worried she became.

"Ms. Guidry?"

She practically ran to the nurses' station. "Yes?"

A male nurse dressed in green scrubs leaned against the counter. "Mr. O'Hara is in the pre-op area. The doctor said you can go back and see him for a minute if you'd like."

"Definitely."

He spotted the cell phone in her hand. "You'll have to turn that off. You can't use it back there anyway."

"Okay." She pressed and held the END button, hoping it worked just like hers. Blessedly, it did, and she dropped it into her jacket pocket. Flipping her phone open, she did the same to it.

Major was the only patient in the pre-op area. Her breath caught. The entire left side of his face looked bruised, with tiny cuts across

273

his forehead, cheek, and jaw. His broken leg, the sight of which had nearly made her ill downstairs, was covered with a sheet.

The anesthesiologist who hovered near the head of the bed introduced himself. "I thought I'd wait until you had a chance to talk to him before I gave him the sedative."

"I appreciate it." She approached the other side of the gurney. "Major?"

His eyelids raised to half-mast to reveal glazed eyes. He blinked a couple of times, and his gaze became a little clearer. "Meredith." He reached toward her.

She grabbed his hand with both of hers. "It'll be okay."

"Will you pray for me?"

"Of course. I have been praying for you." She lifted his hand and pressed it to her cheek.

"I mean right now."

"Miss, I really need to administer this." The anesthesiologist raised a hypodermic needle.

"Major, I'll pray for you while the doctor gives you the sedative." She looked up at the anesthesiologist. At his nod, she leaned closer to Major, keeping one hand wrapped around his and resting the other on top of his head.

"Lord God, I bow before You right now so thankful that You chose to spare Major's life. Father, I pray for the doctors and nurses who will be performing the surgery. Steady their hands, give them strength and wisdom and clarity of mind. And I pray especially for Major, someone I know is precious in Your sight. Watch over him and protect him while he's in surgery, and then we ask for a quick recovery afterward. Amen."

"Amen," the nurse who'd brought her in repeated.

Major grunted, and his head lolled to the side.

The anesthesiologist removed the needle from the port on Major's IV. "It works pretty quickly."

"It's time, Ms. Guidry. We have to take him to surgery now."

She nodded, fighting more tears. Placing her hands on Major's cheeks, she turned his head until he looked at her. "I love you, Major O'Hara, and I'm not giving you up without a fight."

"Love you." Slurred though his words were, they still sounded sweet to Meredith.

She followed them out into the hall, but they went the opposite direction from the door that would lead her back to the waiting area. After standing in the middle of the corridor for a few long moments after they disappeared, Meredith returned to what she was quickly coming to think of as *her* chair.

But she couldn't just sit here all night. Maybe she should go down and get something to eat. The memory of the heavenly aroma of the meal Major had cooked for her in her new house brought the tightness back to her throat, but she ignored it. There would be other romantic dinners in that house.

She let the nurse know where she was going—just in case—and took the elevators down three floors. She took a few wrong turns but eventually found the large cafeteria.

The puppy!

Someone needed to go over to her apartment and let him out—and probably hose down the bathroom. She pulled out her phone—and remembered that she hadn't turned either hers or Major's back on, which she quickly rectified.

She started to call Forbes, but her dear older brother didn't really do well with pets and their messes. She called Rafe instead, but he'd just flown back in and would be at the airport filling out paperwork for a while. So she called her brother Kevin, who was only too glad to help her out.

No sooner did she hang up with him than Major's phone started ringing again. At last, she might finally get to the bottom of the mystery calls.

"Hello?"

"This is Gideon Thibodeaux from Beausoleil Pointe Center. With whom am I speaking?"

Hearing a strong male voice when she'd expected the weak one of the previous call, took her by surprise. "Meredith Guidry."

"Ms. Guidry, I am trying to get in touch with Major O'Hara."

She stepped out of the traffic pattern, though there were few enough people trying to get to the buffet of food. "Mr. Thibodeaux, Major has been in a car accident. He just went into surgery. Is there something I can do?"

"Are you a relative?"

"No. I don't think he has any relatives. Except his mother."

"It's his mother I'm calling about."

Meredith staggered into the closest chair. "His mother?"

"She's having an episode. We don't want to sedate her, but the other residents are starting to get agitated. We need someone to come out and try to calm her down so that we don't have to take extreme measures."

Mouth completely dry, Meredith worked her tongue back and forth to try to form words. "An episode?"

"Yes. We are an assisted-living facility for the psychologically challenged, not a psychiatric hospital. If no one can come and manage her, get her to calm down, we may have to call the state mental hospital and get them to come take her."

Meredith shivered. Was this the kind of call Major had gotten the night of the banquet? No wonder he'd dropped everything.

"I'll come. But I need directions how to get there." Digging a pen out of her purse, she grabbed a napkin from the dispenser on the table and wrote down what the director told her.

She dashed back upstairs to leave word at the nurses' station that she would be leaving the hospital for a while, then out to her car.

The facility lay outside the city on the north side of town. In daylight, it must be lovely. But at night in the rain, the winding drive from the main road kept Meredith's foot hovering over the brake pedal so she didn't accidentally miss a sharp curve and drive off the road.

Finally, the lane widened into an almost empty parking lot, with the hulking, shadowy mass of a large building beyond. Leaving everything but her own cell phone in the car, she ran in through the rain. Mr. Thibodeaux had said to head up to the second floor and follow the main corridor.

She jogged up the stairs and hurried down the wide central hall, the sounds of a major commotion spurring her on. The hall ended at a large room furnished with many cushy-looking sofas and chairs, game tables, and a couple of entertainment centers with big TVs. But rather than enjoying all that, about a dozen people stood in a semicircle while a woman with thin white hair paced, yelling and crying.

Meredith watched, dumbfounded. The woman screamed if anyone got within five feet of her. She banged her fists against her temples, muttering to herself, shouting occasional random words.

Could this be Major's mother?

"Are you Ms. Guidry?" A tall, middle-aged man in a suit approached Meredith.

"I am. Is that. . .is that Mrs. O'Hara?"

"Gideon Thibodeaux. Do you see why we needed you to come?"

She nodded then shook her head. "I don't know what I'm going to be able to do to help if no one else can get close to her."

"You have to try. It's not good for her to be in a state like this."

"Do you know what triggered it?" Focusing on Mrs. O'Hara, Meredith wracked her brain to come up with something, anything, she could do to help Major's mother.

"She was upset that her son hadn't shown up to see her when he said he'd be here at a certain time. Then she started acting like this. I can only assume the hospital found her phone number in Mr. O'Hara's personal effects and called her and revealed he'd been injured."

Stomach sinking, Meredith looked at Mr. Thibodeaux again. "Actually, I think that's my fault, then. She called Major's cell phone, and I answered and told her."

"Don't blame yourself. Positive energy is what's needed."

"What should I do?"

"Try talking to her. Sometimes, as with babies, a soothing, steady stream of words can lull them into a calmer state of mind."

Right. Just like that. "What should I talk about?"

"See if you can recognize anything she's saying. Get her to focus on one thing and talk to her about it—ask her questions, tell a story together, whatever it takes."

Hands and heart trembling, Meredith took a deep breath. She'd created this mess; she had to fix it. "I'll do what I can."

CHAPTER 27

$\mathcal{M}$eredith made her way through the people standing around Major's mother until she stood in the neutral zone between them. With a closer view of the woman, Meredith revised her idea of how old she was—her white hair and the gauntness of her face had aged her prematurely. She might be younger than Meredith's own mother.

"Mrs. O'Hara?"

Major's mom didn't stop pacing or muttering.

"Mrs. O'Hara, I'm Meredith. I'm a friend of Major's."

Mrs. O'Hara raised her voice, and Meredith caught the words, "Asked her why. . ." before the muttering became incoherent again.

"Who did you ask, Mrs. O'Hara?"

"Custer is dead."

Meredith shook her head, not sure if she'd heard the woman correctly. "Custer—General Custer? Yes, he's been dead a long time."

"Two hundred twelve officers of men. . ."

"Mrs. O'Hara, I don't understand what you mean. Are you talking about Custer's last stand at Little Big Horn?" Meredith took a cautious step forward.

"No—don't come closer. Where's Major? I want my son! I'll leave here and go find him myself." As suddenly as she started screaming, she stopped and returned to muttering. " 'Ten thousand Indians under Sitting Bull and Crazy Horse. . .uniting in a common war against the United States Cavalry.' No one understands. No one knows. Where's my son?"

Meredith moved closer. "Wait—Mrs. O'Hara, what were you saying about Sitting Bull and Crazy Horse? I've heard that before." She stilled when Mrs. O'Hara turned and looked directly at her.

" 'The Sioux and Cheyenne are on the warpath.' "

"I'm going to call the state mental hospital." Meredith hadn't noticed the director coming up behind her. "She's making no sense at all."

"No!" Mrs. O'Hara's arm whipped out, and her bony fingers wrapped around Meredith's wrist. "Don't let them take me away. They can't take me away from Danny. They took him away from me before and put me in the loony bin, and they can't do that to me again. Where's my son? Take me to my son."

Before Meredith could respond, Mrs. O'Hara collapsed on the floor and began wailing, yelling Major's name over and over.

Meredith turned to Mr. Thibodeaux. "Don't call yet. I think I know what she was talking about." She knelt on the floor by the rocking, keening woman. "Mrs. O'Hara, were you quoting lines from *She Wore a Yellow Ribbon*?"

" 'Round her neck she wore a yellow ribbon. . . .' " Mrs. O'Hara sang.

Tears of relief sprang to Meredith eyes. She gingerly rested her hands on the distraught woman's shoulders and sang the next line of the song.

" 'When I asked her why. . .when I asked her. . .' " Mrs. O'Hara looked up at Meredith through the fingers she held over her face.

Meredith continued singing. When she got to the chorus, Mrs. O'Hara repeated "cavalry" along with her each time she sang it. Meredith moved from kneeling to sit beside Major's mother and put her arm around the woman's shoulders.

After what must have been at least ten minutes of singing the movie's short theme song over and over and over, Meredith felt Mrs. O'Hara's taught muscles suddenly relax. She leaned into Meredith's side.

Without the ranting and screaming to entertain them, most of the people who'd been standing around this whole time dispersed.

" 'M tired. Want to go back to my room now."

Meredith helped her to her feet. "I'll go with you to your room."

Major's mother looked at Meredith as if she hadn't seen her before. "Mary Kate?"

"No. I'm Meredith."

"Meredith—Mary Kate." She grasped Meredith's arm. "Come back to my apartment, Mary Kate."

Meredith corrected her twice more but then gave up and answered to Mary Kate, letting Mrs. O'Hara lead her down a couple of halls until they stopped at room number 267.

Mrs. O'Hara pointed to the number. "Twenty-six seven. John Wayne was born on May 26, 1907."

"Was he?" Meredith figured the easiest thing to do right now was just humor her until she was certain the woman would stay calm.

"Such a sad day when he died. Danny was just a little boy."

"Danny? Is that Major's brother?" Perhaps pumping Mrs. O'Hara for information on Major's family wasn't the most honorable thing to do, but she never could get it out of him.

"No. Danny is Major. Major Daniel Kirby Xavier. . .Major Xavier Kirby. . ." Mrs. O'Hara frowned and looked like she was building up again.

"Major Daniel Xavier Kirby O'Hara."

"You know Danny?"

Meredith's forearms were going to be bruised where Mrs. O'Hara kept grabbing her. "I work with Major. I've known him a long time."

"Come on, Mary Kate, I want to show you my apartment." Mrs. O'Hara shoved the door open.

As soon as Meredith entered the room, she finally understood where the seemingly random references to John Wayne stemmed from. Framed movie posters lined the walls of the small studio apartment—*Stagecoach* and *Fort Apache* and *Sands of Iwo Jima* and *Flying Leathernecks*.

But Mrs. O'Hara crossed into the bedroom and pointed to one hanging over her vanity table.

"Mary Kate." She pointed at the poster.

"Of course." Meredith took in the illustrated image of John Wayne with Maureen O'Hara in his arms. "*The Quiet Man.* Maureen O'Hara played Mary Kate Danaher."

"You look like her." She grabbed Meredith's sore arm again and took her around to look at each of the posters.

Finally, Major's mother collapsed into the plush recliner in the small sitting area, which included a TV, DVD player, and a rack full of what looked like just about every movie John Wayne had ever been in.

"Take me to see Danny."

The sadness in his mother's voice broke Meredith's heart. "I'll have to ask Mr. Thibodeaux if I can take you. But Major's going to need to sleep for a long time after he comes out of surgery."

"I want to see him." Large tears dripped from Mrs. O'Hara's faded blue eyes.

"I understand. Let me go ask." She glanced around the apartment. Would Mrs. O'Hara stay here quietly if Meredith left to track down the director? "Do you want me to put a movie on for you?"

Mrs. O'Hara nodded.

"How about *She Wore a Yellow Ribbon*?" Meredith reached for the case.

"No. *Donovan's Reef.*"

"Good choice." Hopefully the comedy would get her into a better frame of mind. Meredith put the disc in, and by the time she turned around, Mrs. O'Hara had a remote control in each hand. "You got this?"

"Yes."

"I'll be back in a few minutes, okay?"

" 'Kay."

"You'll be here waiting for me when I come back?"

"Go."

Startled, Meredith did as bade and left the apartment. She didn't have far to look for the facility's director. He came down the hall toward her.

"Sorry I abandoned you. I had to make sure everyone else was okay." He rubbed his left temple. "You did a great job with her. I can't believe you recognized that she was quoting lines from a movie. I've never even heard of that film."

"It's one of John Wayne's westerns—and one of my favorite movies." Meredith turned to walk back to Mrs. O'Hara's apartment with him. "She asked me to take her over to the hospital to see her son."

He shook his head. "After that episode, it'll be better if she stays here. One of our psychiatrists is on the way here. He'll give her something to help her sleep through the night so she doesn't relapse."

Meredith cringed. "I thought you said you didn't want to give her something to knock her out."

"That would have been different. We would have been giving her a powerful antipsychotic drug. Instead, it'll be a mild sleeping pill along with her other medications. It'll keep her from suffering adverse affects from the episode." He knocked then opened Mrs. O'Hara's door. "Hi, Beverly. May I come in?"

"Where's Mary Kate?" Beverly O'Hara asked without turning away from John Wayne on the small TV screen.

Meredith resigned herself to answering to the character's name. "I'm here, too."

"Okay, you can come in then."

She followed the doctor in and sat on the edge of the loveseat.

"Beverly, I don't think it's a good idea for you to go to the hospital to see your son. You wore yourself out tonight. And he's going to need his rest, too. So it'll probably be better for you to stay here and for your son to come see you when he gets out of the hospital."

Beverly looked at Meredith, worry crinkling the papery skin of her forehead and around her eyes.

"Mrs. O'Hara, I think it's a good idea. I promise I will bring Major out here to see you as soon as he's released. But just so you know, that may be a couple of days."

Major's mother chewed her thin lips. "But what if I need him before that?"

"How about this?" The director spoke before Meredith could respond. "I'll ask Ms. Guidry to leave her phone number for you—but only if you promise that you won't call her unless it's an emergency. Can you promise to do that, Beverly?"

Her gaze flickered back to the TV—and after a little while, it seemed as if she'd forgotten anyone else was in the room. Meredith looked askance at the director, who shrugged.

"I agree. I'll only call if it's an emergency." Beverly reached into the end table beside her chair and pulled out a marker and a pad of sticky notes. "Major uses these to write down things I need to remember."

Meredith wrote her cell phone number in large, clear numerals and handed the pad back to Beverly. "Mrs. O'Hara, I will call you with an update on Major in the morning."

"Promise?"

"I promise."

All three turned at a knock on the door. A nurse came in with a young man in a white doctor's coat.

"Hi, Mrs. O'Hara. I came to talk to you about what happened earlier." The kid-doctor offered Meredith a nod and smile of acknowledgment before scooting past her to sit on the loveseat.

Meredith stood. "Maybe I should go—"

Whip fast, Beverly grabbed Meredith's arm again.

"Why don't you stay," Dr. Sevellier said.

Meredith extracted her arm then held Beverly's hand loosely in hers and sat down.

For the next half hour, the young psychiatrist managed to impress Meredith with the way he drew information out of Major's mother until the woman was speaking coherently. Finally, Dr. Sevellier stood, had a whispered conversation with the nurse, and moved beside the recliner.

Meredith released Beverly's hand and scooted back in her seat to allow him room.

"The nurse is going to bring your meds. And I'm having her add a sleeping pill so you can get some rest and recover from your ordeal." Dr. Sevellier patted Beverly's shoulder and moved toward the door.

Beverly reached for Meredith's hand again. "They're going to put me to sleep. Don't let them put me to sleep. I want to watch the movie. Don't let them take me away from the movie."

Meredith moved back up to the edge of the sofa so her shoulder wasn't in danger of being pulled out of its socket. "Mrs. O'Hara, would it help if I stay until you fall asleep? We can keep the movie on so you can see it from the bed."

Beverly agreed and took all the pills the nurse brought. The director, doctor, and nurse left. Meredith helped Beverly change into her nightgown and took over the task of brushing the baby-fine white hair when Beverly complained that her arms were too heavy to continue.

"Will you sing it for me?" Beverly stretched out and pulled the covers up to her chin.

"Sing what?"

The older lady yawned. "Yellow ribbon song." Her eyelids drooped.

By the time Meredith made it all the way through the tune, Beverly O'Hara was sound asleep. As quietly as she could, Meredith turned off the lamp on the bedside table and straightened up the room, putting Beverly's clothes into the hamper, wiping the water and dripped toothpaste off the sink in the small bathroom, and turning off the TV and video player, returning the DVD to its case and the case to its original spot on the shelf.

"Cavalry. . ."

Meredith jumped at Beverly's muzzy singsong voice. But Beverly didn't move and didn't say anything else. Meredith released her held breath and let herself out of the apartment, releasing the doorknob a smidgen at a time until the latch softly clicked into place.

The director met her in the lobby and got her contact information, then walked her to the front doors.

"Thank you for coming tonight, Ms. Guidry. I'm certain Beverly and her son appreciate it, as well."

"I'm glad I could help." Meredith shook hands with him then headed out to her car. She sat for a moment, fingers steepled over her nose and mouth. *Lord, what did I just step into the middle of?* And why had Major never told her about his mother? He had a lot of explaining to do.

Awareness dawned at about the same speed it took a watched pot to boil. Major became vaguely aware of odd little sounds that he'd never heard in his condo before. A rhythmic beep. A plastic rustle and slight whoosh of air every time he moved. Though there were times when he woke up sore the morning after a hard workout, breathing had never hurt as much as it did this morning. The back of his right hand was killing him, too.

He opened his eyes, and in the dimness, his surroundings took a minute to resolve. He wasn't at home. He was in a hospital room. And then he remembered—

The car in front of him had slammed on its brakes for no apparent reason. He'd lost control of the Jeep on the wet pavement. Kirby had rolled over a few times. After that, he only remembered bits and snatches. The emergency room. Being told he needed surgery on his leg. And Meredith. . .

The beeping sound increased. When she'd appeared at his side in the emergency room, all he could think of was wanting to make sure she never left him again. He'd said. . .he'd said. . .

His face burned. Though he did want to propose to Meredith *eventually*, hopefully she understood that he'd been under the influence of heavy-duty painkillers.

An insistent buzzing sound caught his ear, followed by rustling from the dark corner of the room.

"Hello?" A whispered voice. "No, Beverly, he's still sleeping. I promise, I'll call you as soon as he wakes up so you can talk to him.... Okay. Bye."

Nausea churned Major's empty stomach. "Meredith?"

"You're awake?" Her figure materialized out of the darkness and came over to the bed.

"Was that—were you just talking to my mother?"

A neutral expression masked her face. "I was. I had to go out to Beausoleil Pointe Center last night because she had an episode when you didn't show up to see her."

He groaned.

"Why didn't you ever tell me about her?"

"How am I supposed to explain her? 'Oh, by the way, I have a crazy mother'?" Anger came to his defense against the tears forming in Meredith's eyes. "I learned a long time ago that if I didn't want people wondering when I was going to lose my mind, I couldn't tell them about Ma."

Meredith was silent for a while. "I'm trying to see this from your point of view, but I can only come up with two explanations of why you basically lied to me about your mother—either you don't trust me, or you're ashamed of her."

He was ashamed all right—of himself. "Mere, you don't understand...."

"Then help me to understand. I've known you, worked beside you, for eight years. *Eight years*. And unless I'm remembering incorrectly, a couple of weeks ago, you told me you love me. Yet the next day, when I tried to ask you about your family again, you shut me down, putting me off once again. Were you ever going to tell me?"

He sighed. This was exactly why he hadn't told her. "Last night, over dinner. I was going to tell you then."

"If you didn't chicken out first."

Her words cut like his sharpest knife. She knew him too well. But he'd been right about her, as well. "All I can say is, I'm sorry. This is exactly why I've been trying to keep away from you, to stop myself

287

from falling in love with you. Because I knew once you found out about her, you wouldn't want to have anything to do with either of us. I mean, you're the one who told me you didn't want to take the time to deal with training a puppy. How would you possibly want to take the time to deal with my schizophrenic mother?"

Meredith stood silent for a long time. The only indication she hadn't turned to a statue was her deep, ragged breathing.

He fought the guilt that tried to drown him over the words that had just come out of his mouth. He'd only lashed out at her because he was angry with himself. But he was doing this for her protection. In the long run, she'd thank him for saving her from his fate.

"I'm sorry you feel that way. I think your mother is a lovely woman who has done the best she can do while fighting a terrible affliction, and she's someone I would be proud to know better." Meredith took a few more gulping breaths.

He couldn't look at her anymore, couldn't bear to see the hurt in her eyes—those beautiful eyes he loved so much. *Never apologize. . . . It's a sign of weakness.* And he had to be strong if he was going to let her walk away.

She cleared her throat, but her voice remained heavy with emotion when she spoke again. "I'll let Mom and Dad know it'll be awhile before you're able to return to work. When you are ready, let me know, and we'll discuss your duties and what you can and can't do until you're on your feet again."

Turning her back on him, she returned to the chair in the corner of the room to gather up her things. "Forbes is planning to come out after work tonight. You should arrange with him about getting a ride home when you're released." She flipped the strap of her briefcase over her shoulder and came back to his bedside.

The words of apology, of begging her forgiveness, of pleading with her to stay, nearly tore his throat asunder. He clenched his teeth together to keep from speaking. He had to let her walk away.

She held his phone out toward him. "Call your mother. She's worried about you."

CHAPTER 28

$\mathcal{M}$eredith fought fatigue the remainder of the day—and angry tears every time someone stopped by her office to find out how Major was doing. Her only saving grace was the amount of work she needed to do to make sure Easter in the Park and the Easter brunch at Lafitte's Landing went off without a hitch on Sunday.

Around three o'clock, she was startled out of a stupor by a knock. Steven LeBlanc stood in the doorway, a Styrofoam box in his hands.

He cleared his throat. "When I talked to Chef earlier about what I'll need to do for Sunday, he told me I should bring you a boxed lunch this afternoon."

The lump of emotion that she'd fought all day tightened into a fist in her throat. "Thanks." She met him halfway across the office to take the box then waved him toward one of the guest chairs facing her desk. She put the box in the small fridge in her credenza and tried to compose herself before she turned back around.

Taking a deep breath, she clasped her hands on top of the pile of paperwork on her desktop and smiled at Major's second in command. "Where are we since we talked this morning?"

"Jana was able to get all the servers she'll need for the number of RSVPs we have. I got with Orly and arranged for the steam tables to be taken over to Lafitte's. I double-checked with all the food vendors to make sure we're still on track for everything to be delivered tomorrow—to Lafitte's. And the pastry chefs guaranteed me that they have everything they'll need to make the doughnuts and stuff for the event in the park."

"I've also talked with Orly," Meredith noted, "and he's arranged for drivers to transport the food out to the park early Sunday morning. Are there some kitchen porters on the schedule to help with loading and unloading and setup once it all gets there?"

"Yes."

"Thanks for stepping up and handling everything, Steven. I guess it's good practice for when Major leaves to start his restaurant, huh?" Meredith shivered. She might be mad at him right now, but that didn't keep her from wanting to continue working with him.

"But he's not—" Steven shook his head. "He told me he'd turned down your parents' offer to start a restaurant."

Did she need more proof of Major's distrust of her? "Oh. That's interesting." Her phone rang. "I guess that's all. I'll call you if I have any other questions."

She waited to pick up the phone until Steven left. "Facilities and Events. This is Meredith."

"Hey, Mere. It's me."

"Hey, Jenn. What's up?"

"I just heard about Major's accident. Is he okay?"

Meredith ground the heel of her hand into her forehead, trying to will away the dull, throbbing headache. "He had to have surgery on a compound fracture in his left leg last night, and he has a couple of cracked ribs and some bumps and bruises."

"Whoa. Sounds rough. He's still in the hospital?"

"Until tomorrow or Saturday. I'm not sure which."

"I guess you'll be spending your evening out there tonight instead of coming for family dinner?"

She hadn't thought about today's being Thursday. "Actually, I've got a ton of work to do for this weekend, and then I'm going home to crash. I didn't really get any sleep last night."

"Let me know what day Major is released, and I'll send some meals over for him."

"Forbes is going to take care of getting him home from the hospital."

Jenn didn't say anything for a long time. "What's going on?"

"It's—it's private. I can't talk about it." But she needed to talk to someone. Why did Anne have to be gone for ten more days?

"Look, I know I'm just your younger sister, and that you've always chosen to confide in Anne about these things; but I *am* your sister, and I am a grown-up who can keep things confidential."

Before she could think twice, Meredith blurted out everything that had happened yesterday—from the dinner-that-wasn't, to meeting Major's mother, to Major's reaction this morning when he learned she'd discovered his secret.

"I had no idea." Jenn whistled. "It's pretty rotten that he didn't tell you a long time ago."

"It's not rotten. He was just protecting himself, I'm sure." With several hours' distance from their encounter, Meredith's anger began to abate.

"There's protecting yourself, and then there's flat-out lying."

Jenn's vehement defense of her brought Meredith's first real smile of the day. "You know, I've replayed every conversation I've tried to have with him about his family, and he's never actually lied to me. He's always just hedged, changed the subject, or told me part of the truth."

"You're going to stick up for him?"

The image of Major lying there in the hospital bed, bruised, scratched, and utterly distraught brought Meredith around full circle. "I love him, Jenn. Yeah, I'm upset that he didn't trust me enough to tell me the whole truth, but it's something we can work through."

"I still think he's a jerk for not telling you."

"Let me ask you this: Do you tell the guys you date everything about our family when you start dating them?" Meredith picked up a pen and started doodling in the margin of her notepad.

"Are you kidding me? If I told guys I'm one of eight kids, they'd immediately think that all I want is to marry them as fast as I can and start popping out babies." She paused. "Oh. I see what you mean."

"Major said he learned a long time ago not to tell people about his mother, or they thought he might have problems, too. I imagine that some of the people that happened with were women he dated. I've heard that some forms of mental illness are genetic."

"Yeah, that's what I've heard, too. Hold on." A rustling sound followed by tapping came through Jenn's end of the line. "What did you say his mom has? Paranoia?"

"Schizophrenia."

"Hold on." More clicks. "How do you spell that?"

Meredith spelled it for her.

"Okay, this Web site—which shows that it was written by a panel of psychiatrists—says that there's only a 10 percent chance that a child can inherit schizophrenia from a parent with the disease. . . condition." Jenn paused for a long time.

The lull gave Meredith time to think—and to listen to her heart. Her shoulder muscles began to relax; her head stopped throbbing.

"It says here that if someone has schizophrenia, they start having problems by their teens or early twenties. So Major's, like, *way* past the age for you to be worried about him having it."

Meredith laughed. "That was never really a concern for me."

"Just the lying part."

"Right—even though he didn't lie to me." She tapped her pen against her chin. "The truth of the matter is that I love him. I've loved him for a very long time. I'm not going to let something as simple as the fact his mother is. . .a little different from ours, scare me off."

Major looked up from the old copy of *Gourmet* magazine one of the nurses had scrounged up for him. "Hey, Forbes."

Dressed in his expensive suit, Forbes looked every inch the lawyer. "How're you feeling?"

"Better now that most of the anesthesia has worn off."

Forbes shrugged out of his coat and started loosening his tie. "Pain?"

"Some. Actually, my ribs hurt worse than my leg right now. But they tell me that won't last long." Using his arms for leverage, Major pushed himself into a more upright position—and grunted at the pain that wrapped around his chest.

"Have they told you yet when they're going to release you?"

"Tomorrow morning, if all goes well."

Forbes pulled one of the visitor's chairs closer to the bed. "You're going to come stay with me until you're up and about."

"No, I can't—"

"How long have we been friends?" Forbes removed his cufflinks and rolled his sleeves up to mid-forearm.

"Since high school." Major narrowed his eyes, pretty sure he knew where this was going.

"More than twenty years. And in all that time have you ever known me to back down or not do something I say I'm going to do?"

"No. But in all that time have you ever known me to rely on anyone but myself?"

"No, but I've always thought you should every once in a while." Forbes waved his hand dismissively. "Besides, the doctors have already told you that you shouldn't be home alone until you can get along on crutches by yourself, haven't they?"

"Let me guess—you talked to the doctor before you came in here."

"Fraternity brother."

Major rolled his eyes. "Fine. I'll come stay. But you can't make me like it."

Forbes's booming laugh filled the room. "I won't try to make you. Did you ever get in touch with your health insurance company this afternoon?"

Major told him everything he'd managed to do since their earlier phone conversation. "What I want to know is how am I supposed to get the ambulance, emergency room visit, and surgery preapproved? I mean, come on!"

Brows raised, Forbes leaned forward. "Are they refusing coverage?"

"No, I just had to go over the head of the gal who answered the phone and talk to someone who wasn't just reading off a script."

"If you have any more trouble with them, just tell them your lawyer will be calling." He relaxed again.

"I will. Now, I'm tired of wallowing in my own issues. Tell me about an interesting case you're working on or something. I've spent too much time in my own head today."

Forbes obliged. Major zoned out a bit, listening to the ramifications of some statute or other that was keeping Mairee and Lawson from moving forward with getting the area around the old warehouse district declared eminent domain, or something to that effect.

"Your dad told me that the groundbreaking had been pushed back six months. Is that why?" Major readjusted his pillow.

"Yes. Apparently some of the property owners out there are putting up a fight."

"I thought you didn't represent your parents—that everything for B-G was handled by one of the senior partners."

"I don't. But I keep up with everything that's going on—because my folks expect me to know about it. Speaking of, Dad told me you turned down the restaurant deal."

Major told him about his mother's accident the night of the Hearts to HEARTS banquet. "It made me realize that as long as my mother's around, I'll never be free to do something like that."

Forbes crossed his arms, his expression hardening. "Did you ever tell Meredith about your mother?"

And here they were—on the very subject Major had hoped wouldn't come up tonight. But if he was going to be staying with Meredith's brother, he'd have to tell him sooner or later. "I was going to tell her last night. I cooked dinner for her at her house but was running out to the Pointe to see Ma when I got in the accident. Apparently Ma had an episode when I didn't show up. Meredith answered my phone and went out to try to get Ma to calm down."

"I see." Forbes's jaw worked back and forth. "I would imagine she was pretty upset finding out that way."

"I wouldn't be surprised if she doesn't want anything to do with me again."

A flicker of anger twitched Forbes's expression. "Once again, you're underestimating my sister."

"You didn't see how mad she was."

"I don't have to. I know her. . .better than you do."

Anger—at himself, at Meredith, at Forbes, at Ma—boiled in Major's chest. "Look, I appreciate your concern for Meredith. I really do. But this isn't any of your business. It's between me and Meredith and no one else."

"If you had a sister, you'd understand why I can't let this go, why it is my responsibility to make sure she isn't hurt."

"Like it was your responsibility to get George Laurence to lie to Anne for weeks about his real identity?" Sure, it was a low blow, but Major wasn't going to be the only one in this room being accused of not treating someone fairly.

"You don't know anything about what happened. Besides, that's a totally different situation." Forbes raked his fingers through his hair. "I think the real issue here isn't Meredith. It's you."

"What's that supposed to mean?"

"I mean you're a coward." Forbes stood, posture stiff.

Major tried to push himself into a straighter position and ignored the sharp pain in his side. "I beg your pardon?"

"You never told Meredith about your mother because you're a coward—you were afraid that if you told her, she might not love you anymore just because of your mother's condition."

No words came to mind with which Major could defend himself.

"I've known you, watched you, listened to you talk about your mother for more than half our lives. The truth is that you're ashamed of her. You didn't keep her a secret from everyone—especially

Meredith—because you were protecting her from them. You kept her a secret because you're embarrassed by her condition, mortified that someone might think that you're the same way she is."

Guilt pelted Major like hot grease splattering from a fryer.

"If that's the way you truly feel, you are not the kind of man I want my sister spending the rest of her life with." Forbes gathered his coat and tie and started toward the door.

Through the overwhelming pressure in his chest, Major caught his breath. "Wait."

Forbes stopped, arms crossed. "Well?"

"You—you're right. I am embarrassed by my mother. I always have been. But you don't understand what it was like growing up with a mom who might throw a tantrum in the middle of Sears with everyone watching. You don't know what it's like to be called out of Algebra class and told that your mother set fire to your apartment and she's being taken to the state mental hospital and you're being put into foster care. You don't know what it's been like to have every woman you've ever dated break up with you as soon as they find out about your mom because they're too scared to listen to the facts and find out that I'm *not* going to be like her."

Forbes came back around the bed and sat down.

"You don't know what it's like to give up everything—football, New York, the restaurant, Meredith—because she's had another breakdown, set another fire, had another episode. I've had to live with that my whole life, have had to deal with it with no help from anyone else for thirty-eight years. And I'm tired of it."

As quickly as his anger had flared, it waned. "But mostly, I'm ashamed of myself."

"Why?"

"Because ever since I moved back here from New York, every time something happens with her, it makes me wish she weren't around." His voice cracked, and he tried to clear the pressure out of his throat. "Can you imagine that? My mother, who raised me by herself, who loves me, who did the best she could. And I wish she didn't exist, because I feel like she's ruining my life."

"How do you think your life would be better if she didn't exist?"

Major closed his eyes and leaned his head back. "I don't know. . . . Maybe I'd still be in New York, executive chef in a high-end restaurant in Manhattan."

"Why did you go to New York in the first place?"

He looked at his friend, wondering if he'd really forgotten. "For culinary school."

Forbes stood up again and began pacing the length of the bed. "What made you decide to go to culinary school?"

"I'd been working in food service since I was fifteen." He now knew what a witness on the stand felt like under Forbes's cross-examination.

"You were fifteen?" Forbes paused and raised his brows.

"Yes—you know this already."

"What happened when you were fifteen that led you to taking a job in a kitchen?" The attorney resumed pacing.

"I—" Major clamped his mouth shut.

Forbes stopped and turned to look at him again, his gaze piercing.

Frustration pushed out a big sigh. "The foster family I was placed with when Ma was put into the state institution owned a restaurant, and everyone in the family pitched in."

"But when you went back to living with your mom, you kept working at the restaurant?"

"I needed some kind of stability. Some assurance I could take care of myself." He was starting to see the point of Forbes's probing. He never would have thought of working in a restaurant if he hadn't lived with that foster family for a month. He wouldn't have fallen in love with the industry, wouldn't have gone to work for Maggie Babineaux in her catering business.

"So you admit that it is because of your mother that you entered the food service industry."

"Yes. I'll admit that."

Switching out of lawyer mode, Forbes flopped back into the chair. "And you got to go to college, where you played football until you injured your back, if I recall, not because of your mother."

Okay, yes, he'd used his mother as an excuse as to why he'd had to give up playing. "Yes. I got to do that."

"And you lived in New York for how long?"

"Two years in Hyde Park for culinary school and six years in Manhattan."

"How often did you come back to visit during those eight years?"

Major swallowed hard. "A couple of times—but I was working in restaurants, trying to build my credentials."

"And your mother was doing what during that time?"

This exercise in chastisement was starting to chafe. "Living here alone, doing her best to take care of herself so I could go off and do what I wanted to do."

"How were things going for you in New York?" Forbes looked smugly superior.

"Are you going to make me say it?"

"Yes."

"Fine. I was struggling to make ends meet, living in a rundown apartment with three other guys, working at least two jobs, and making myself sick because I never slept."

"And since you've been back here?"

Major wanted to punch his friend in the face but couldn't reach that far. "I was hired by your parents to be the executive chef and manager of the catering division of Boudreaux-Guidry Enterprises." He crossed his arms—then wished he hadn't when he elbowed his own cracked ribs. "I see what you're getting at. If it hadn't been for my mother, I wouldn't be where I am today."

"Then don't you think it's time you do what the Bible says?"

Wracking his brain, Major couldn't easily come up with whatever Forbes was referencing. "Ask her forgiveness?"

"That's part of it. I'm talking about honoring your mother."

Major nodded. "Tomorrow when we get out of here, I want you to take me to BPC. I've got a lot of years of dishonoring her to make up for."

CHAPTER 29

"You sure you got it?"

Major glared at his friend but quickly returned his focus to keeping his balance on his right foot while turning to lower himself into the wheelchair.

The wheelchair was bad enough, but not being able to maneuver himself around in it because of his stupid cracked ribs made his embarrassment complete.

Forbes closed the door of the sleek black Jaguar, then pushed Major across the parking lot and in through the sliding glass doors of Beausoleil Pointe Center. Major directed him to the elevators then through the halls to his mother's apartment. Forbes reached to knock on the door, but Major caught his wrist.

"I can knock for myself, thank you very much."

"No need to get tetchy."

"No need to laugh at me." The good mood Major had woken up with at the thought of being released from the hospital hadn't lasted long when he realized how much he *wasn't* going to be able to do for himself for quite some time to come.

"So are you going to knock?" Amusement laced Forbes's voice.

Major glared at him then leaned forward to knock, ignoring the shooting pain the movement caused in his chest and leg.

A few seconds later, the door flew open. "Danny!" Ma put her hands on his cheeks and pulled his head forward to kiss the top of it, bumping his heavily splinted and bandaged leg in the process.

He drew his breath in through clenched teeth. "Careful, Ma."

"We've been waiting for you." She squeezed out the door around him and pushed Forbes away. She grunted with the effort of getting the chair started on the carpet, but once rolling, she had an easier time.

"We?"

"The girls and me. We're having lunch on the terrace. Everyone's been talking about you, and no one wanted to start without you." She stopped at the door to the back stairwell. "Oh. Guess we can't go down that way."

Forbes coughed.

Major glanced over his shoulder, trying to put as much warning in his expression as he could.

"Well, it looks like you're in very capable hands. So, I'll just wait for you to call me when you're ready for me to come back and pick you up, shall I?" Forbes twirled his keys on his index finger.

"Yeah, yeah. *Ooph*, easy there, Ma." Major pressed his hand to his ribs, which had just hit the side of the chair when his mother jerked it around with strength he didn't know she possessed. He glared at Forbes as Ma pushed the wheelchair past him. "I'll call you when I'm ready to go."

Whistling, Forbes waved. "Bye, Mrs. O'Hara. It was good to see you again."

"Uh-huh." Ma didn't turn, just kept pushing Major toward the elevators. The top of Forbes's head hadn't disappeared down the main front staircase before she said, "I don't like him, Danny."

"Forbes? He's my best friend, Ma."

"He's too...pretty. He's like Gregory Peck in *Roman Holiday*. You look at him, and you know he's up to no good."

Major laughed. "He's one of the best guys I know. I trust him with my life." Even though he hadn't always trusted him with the whole truth of everything going on in his life.

"Well, don't trust him to throw him."

Now Major was the one who coughed to cover a laugh.

Ma whacked him between the shoulders. "You're not coming down with something are you? You can't be here if you're sick."

"Ow. I'm not sick, Ma."

"You know that most people come out of the hospital sicker than they were when they went in? I saw a program about that on TV. How people pick up all kinds of germs in the hospital when they're suspectable."

"Susceptible."

"You could have picked up meningitis or strep or herpes and not even know it until you keel over and die." She shoved the wheelchair out of the elevator and through the main receiving room.

"Thanks for those cheerful thoughts, Ma." He held his hands out to try to keep his leg from bumping chairs, plants, tables, the corner of the wall as they entered the back hallway. . . . The pain in his ribs to wheel himself around might be worth saving himself the stress of his mother's driving skills.

One of the staffers met them at the door to the flagstone terrace. "You should have called one of us, Mrs. O'Hara. You shouldn't be pushing this by yourself." The young woman took over and pushed Major behind his mother toward one of the farthest-away tables.

He loved being referred to as *this*, as if he were nothing more than a roasted turkey or sack of flour.

Ma's card-playing friends all came over to examine the cuts and bruises on Major's face, to poke at the ACE bandages covering the lower portion of his left leg, and to beg him to lift his T-shirt to show them the wrapping around his chest. Okay. Being called *this* wasn't so bad, comparatively.

The chicken salad on croissants, fruit, and potato salad were a bit cliché for a springtime alfresco meal; but after the bland food at the hospital for the past two days, nothing had tasted better to him in a long time.

After everyone finished eating and dispersed to different activities, Ma pushed him over to a separate, somewhat secluded area of the patio, partially shaded by a pergola and magnolia trees at three corners. With a fireplace and the privacy the surrounding raised planters gave it from the terrace, he could almost pretend they were at a park instead of an assisted-living facility for the psychologically challenged.

Ma sat at one of the two small tables and fanned herself with a lace hankie. He flashed back to his childhood. For as long as he could remember, she'd always carried a handkerchief instead of disposable tissues. It was more ladylike to use a hankie than a piece of flimsy paper, she'd explained to him when he'd asked about it at age eleven.

"How did you do it all those years?" He manipulated the wheels of the chair until he faced her squarely.

"Do what, Danny?"

"Raise me. Put up with me. Support us. Hold yourself together until I was old enough to take care of both of us." Emotion shredded his voice into hoarse shards.

She shrugged. "I just had to. You were a little boy." She patted her forehead with her fingertips. "I had to think about things because you couldn't do it and because I knew they'd take you away from me. That was the worst time, when they took you away from me." Her eyes filled with tears. "I didn't mean to set the fire, Danny. I didn't mean to."

He stroked her arm until she started to calm down. "I know you didn't. You couldn't help it. Flame has always fascinated you. Like a moth." He grinned. "You can't stay away from it."

"But I was supposed to because you could be hurt in a fire, and I don't want to hurt you."

"Of course not. You've always protected me, Ma. And I've never told you how much that means to me. How much I love you for that."

"Fssh." She waved her hand. "You tell me you love me all the time."

"I may say the words, but I don't always show it. I'm sorry I left you on your own when I went to New York, that I didn't make more of an effort to get back down here and see you."

She pushed wisps of white hair back from her cheek. "You were doing important work. That's what I told all my friends at my jobs I had while you were gone. You were in New York becoming a famous chef. They were all jealous of me because my son was a famous chef in Manhattan and none of their children ever did anything important like that."

"I wasn't famous, Ma. I worked long hours in menial positions so that I could try to get better hours in less menial positions."

Her eyes clearer than he'd seen them in a long time, she patted his hand where it still rested on her arm. "I didn't want you to have to come back here. I wanted you to get out of this town, out of this state. I wanted you to have a better life than what you could have here. I wanted you to go away so you didn't have to watch me become this crazy old lady who drools and doesn't know what she's saying half the time."

He swallowed hard. "You don't drool."

"That's how little you know." She smiled vaguely.

They sat like that for a while, touching but not speaking, the warm spring breeze bringing the scents of early blooming flowers. Major used the time to compose his emotions. If there was one thing that sent his mother over the edge faster than anything, it was to see him in anything but a completely cool and collected state.

"This is a romantic spot, don't you think?" Ma asked.

"It is."

"You should bring her here sometime."

"Who?"

"Mary Kate."

He frowned, digging deep into the recesses of his mind for anyone by that name. "Ma, I don't know anyone called Mary Kate."

"Mary Kate—you know her. Mary Kate." She frowned, her confusion and consternation clear. "Mary Kate—*The Quiet Man*, like the poster."

He shook his head. She must have decided that if he wasn't going to bring a real woman here, she'd set him up with someone from one of the Duke's movies. "I don't think that's possible, Ma."

She shrugged. "She'd come if you asked her."

"I don't think I can ask her."

She patted his hand. "Never mind. I'll ask her."

"...which leads me to my final point."

Meredith took Pastor Kinnard's words as her cue and slipped out of the back row of folding chairs. The Easter Sunday worship service had gone off without a hitch—she again sent up a prayer of thanks that the forecast rain never materialized. Now for the hard part of her day.

She checked in with Pam to make sure the senior event planner had everything under control to start the Easter egg–related activities immediately after the worship service ended. Mrs. McCord hadn't been too happy when she'd learned Meredith would have to be gone for the beginning of the event, but had changed her tune when Meredith told her of Major's accident and her need to be at Lafitte's to make sure that Easter brunch ran smoothly.

Meredith drove as fast as she dared over to the property just off the college campus but slowed when she reached the drive up to Lafitte's Landing. The azalea bushes lining the road exploded with color—mostly deep fuchsia, but some white and some pale pink—which made springtime in Louisiana her favorite season of all. Though when the crepe myrtle trees that shared the sides of the road with the azaleas were in bloom in the late summer and early fall, they were pretty spectacular, too.

Under the tachometer, the SUV's clock showed 10:30 a.m. when Meredith pulled into a space in the shade of one of the heavy-limbed oak trees surrounding the parking lot. Half an hour until they would begin seating guests. Hopefully by eleven thirty, she'd be able to leave and go back to the park to check on activities there. With Major unable to work and Lori on vacation for the holiday weekend, Meredith's supervisory responsibilities had increased tenfold, but she thrived on it. She just needed to keep telling herself that.

The porters and facilities staff greeted her when she walked into the cool interior of the converted and expanded antebellum mansion.

"Everything looks wonderful, y'all. Keep up the good work," she called, crossing the ballroom to the kitchen in the back.

As she'd hoped, she was greeted by a dull roar of activity in the large room.

"Civilian in the kitchen." The line cook greeted her even as he announced her presence.

"Oh, good. You're here." For the first time since he'd worked for B-G, Steven's appearance betrayed his stress—his cheeks red, his jacket damp with sweat, his usually spiked hair limp and lifeless.

"What's wrong?" Meredith dropped her keys and phone into her suit coat pocket, then stripped the jacket off and stepped into the staff room to lay it over the back of a chair.

"Nothing's wrong. I just wanted to go over everything with you to make sure it meets with your approval." He brushed past her into the room to where several large sheets of paper were spread out on a battered table. "Here's my diagram of where I want to put everything on the steam tables and buffet tables."

Meredith ducked her head down to look at the sketches to hide her amusement from the overeager young chef. And just so she didn't appear to be humoring him, she asked him questions about his decision to place the trays of sausage patties and bacon before the eggs, and if he had made labels for the two different types of quiche listed.

"I asked someone to do that. I'll check to make sure it got done."

"Great. Everything looks fine to me. You've done a good job taking over and making sure this stayed organized and on schedule. I'll be writing an official commendation for your personnel file."

He grinned at her. "Thanks!" He swept up his diagrams and swaggered out of the room.

Though still sticky and hot from the early spring heat wave outside, Meredith put her jacket back on before guests began arriving. Even though the sleeveless sheath dress looked fine, there was something about bare arms that didn't feel professional to her.

By eleven thirty, everyone who'd RSVP'd and prepaid for the first seating had arrived, been greeted, and were now happily filling their plates at the tables lining the long back wall of the ballroom. Jana handled checking names off the reservations list while Meredith assumed the role of hostess, greeting guests before passing them off to a server to be shown to their tables.

Jana confirmed every name checked off.

Meredith came out of her jacket again. "Let Steven known that I've gone back over to the park and that I'll be back before the one o'clock seating begins. But y'all can call me if you need me before then."

By the time Meredith got back out to the park, Pam had already handled getting the hamburger and hotdog grilling under way, and more than half the crowd looked as if they were almost finished eating.

"Cooking's going a little slower than we expected," Pam said, breathless after scurrying over to greet Meredith as soon as she got out of her car. "But everyone seems to be understanding about it, so long as we keep the activities for the kids going."

Meredith couldn't find anything to do at the park but walk around and talk to VIPs, former clients, and family friends she'd known her whole life. Before she left, she reviewed everything about cleanup with Pam who, as Meredith had with Steven earlier, humored her.

"Enjoy your day off tomorrow," Meredith told Pam and waved at the rest of the staff on her way to the car.

Back at Lafitte's, she went through almost the same routine as before, but this time powwowing with Jana and Steven to see how first service had gone and agreeing to their suggestions for how to make second service run more smoothly.

By two o'clock, tired of making small talk and shaking hands,

Meredith leaned against the edge of the old table in the staff room, enjoying a piece of spinach-artichoke quiche, not having eaten anything else all day but a bowl of cereal at four this morning.

"You look like you could use a nap." Steven slung a towel over his shoulder and stopped about five feet from her, hands clasped behind his back.

"I could. And that is exactly what I'm about to go do." Though most of the staff had been off Friday or would be off tomorrow to make up for having to work this weekend, as the boss, Meredith didn't have any such luxury. And with the mayor's dinner to honor the top students from all the high schools coming up in a few weeks, as well as the Spring Debutante Cotillion the first weekend in May, followed by the library fund-raiser and three of the high schools' proms at B-G properties after that, she'd be lucky to get a Saturday off to move before the summer wedding and event season hit full force. Of course, once Mom and Dad approved the new third event planner position and she officially promoted Corie, she might be able to get a little more time for things like Saturdays off and naps on Sunday afternoons.

"I think Jana and I can wrap things up if you'd like to go ahead and get out of here." His eager blue eyes begged her to say yes.

"Since we don't have anything scheduled here before week after next, it's okay if not everything gets done this afternoon. We can always send facilities guys over to finish—put tables and chairs up or bring the steam tables back to downtown—sometime this week when we're not having to pay them double time for working on a holiday."

"We'll take care of it." He reached for her empty plate and coffee mug.

"Call me if—"

"We know. Call you if we need anything." He swept his arm toward the door. "If you please."

"You've been hanging around your boss too much." But she obliged and departed.

No more than five minutes after she drove away, her phone's hands-free earpiece beeped. With a sigh, she pressed the button on the side. "This is Meredith."

"Mary Kate," came Beverly O'Hara's singsong voice.

"Hi, Beverly." She had to laugh. Major's mom had taken to calling her at the oddest times the past few days—usually when Meredith was at her most stressed and needed a reminder that her life wasn't nearly as hard as it seemed at the moment. "What's going on?"

"Can you come today?"

"You want me to come out and visit you today?" She pulled to a stop at a red light. Forbes had told her earlier that Major had spent most of the day yesterday at the center with his mother, and that he'd been pretty drained when Forbes picked him up last night. He must have told Beverly he didn't plan to come today, and she was bored.

"Yes. For tea. Iced tea. Not hot tea. I don't like hot tea. Do you know I burned my mouth on hot tea at a restaurant once? Major would never have served it that hot, because he knows that I don't like hot things."

Meredith stifled her laughter. Bless Beverly for keeping her entertained this stressful weekend. She wanted to go home and nap, but she wanted to get to know Major's mom better, too. Still, a shower and a change of clothes were a necessity. "It will probably be around four o'clock before I could get there. Is that okay?"

"Four—today, right?"

"Four today—about two hours from now."

" 'Kay. See you at four."

CHAPTER 30

$\mathcal{M}$eredith opened her eyes and glanced at the clock—blinked away the bleariness and glanced again.

"Oh, mercy!" She scrambled up from her prone position on the sofa and darted to her bedroom. She'd only meant to close her eyes for a few minutes after her quick shower; she'd never meant to sleep for almost an hour and a half. Now she had less than ten minutes before she was supposed to be at Beausoleil Pointe Center for tea—iced tea—with Beverly.

At her closet, she let her hand rest wistfully for a moment on the stack of folded, soft, much-worn T-shirts—the ones that had been neglected for far too long in recent months. But this wasn't a time to dress down. Beverly deserved more respect than that. Meredith exchanged her comfy robe for her best pair of trouser jeans, a sleeveless wine-colored shell, and a three-quarter sleeve, lightweight brown cardigan.

Lastly, she stepped into brown ballet flats before making a mad dash for the car. "Lord, please don't let her have an episode because I'm fifteen or twenty minutes late."

At 4:05, by the clock in the dashboard, her cell phone rang.

"Hello, Beverly. I am on my way out to see you right now."

"You're still coming?"

Meredith wasn't familiar enough with Beverly yet to know if her tone carried panic or excitement. "I'll be there in about ten minutes."

" 'Kay." The click and silence that followed were apparently the hallmark ending of a phone conversation with Beverly O'Hara.

When she arrived at the center, she had to park at the back end of the parking lot. No doubt most of the residents received regular visits from their families on Sundays. Would she ever become part of Beverly's family?

She shook off the thought. Plenty of time to deal with Major later.

Cool air whooshed out the sliding front doors. Meredith started the stairs two at a time but slowed her pace halfway up when she got winded. She really needed to start exercising again.

She took two wrong turns but eventually found Beverly's room. She knocked. And waited. Odd. She knocked again. No answer.

Returning to the lobby, she approached what looked like a concierge station. The young lady behind the high counter—whose name tag included the initials R.N. after her name—smiled up at her. "May I help you?"

"I'm here to see Beverly O'Hara, but she's not answering her door."

"Is she expecting you?"

Meredith nodded. "I just talked to her on the phone about ten minutes ago."

"You're looking for Beverly?" Another nurse approached the desk.

"Yes. I'm supposed to be having tea with her." Saying it renewed Meredith's amusement at how Beverly had described it.

"I think I saw her go out onto the back terrace. If you go down those stairs there"—she pointed to a door with an illuminated EXIT sign over it—"you'll come out right by the back doors."

"Thanks." Meredith entered the stairwell and stopped just beyond the door at the bottom to get her bearings. She was in a hallway that looked very much like the one above, except to her right was a large glass door leading onto a patio.

Two women who looked about Beverly's age stood just inside the door. Meredith smiled at them, and they giggled, putting their heads together and whispering as she passed.

Outside, she slid her sunglasses down from the top of her head and looked around. The large flagstone paved area looked like an outdoor café, and most of the tables were filled with residents and their family members—most still dressed in their Easter Sunday finery.

But she didn't see Beverly anywhere. She was just about to head inside when she heard someone calling, "Excuse me, excuse me, are you Mary Kate?"

"I'm—yes, I'm Mary Kate." At least she hoped in this instance she was.

The elderly lady grinned, showing dentures that looked too big for her mouth. "Come this way. Beverly is waiting for you."

"Oh." Meredith released a relieved breath. "Good."

The woman took Meredith's hand and practically dragged her through the maze of tables and down a little path leading away from the main patio. Behind a large magnolia tree, they came upon a second patio—much smaller, covered with a wood pergola. It had only two tables, at one of which sat Beverly. . .and Major.

Meredith's heart pounded. She hadn't seen or spoken with him since Thursday, that awful morning. She sent up one last prayer that he hadn't really meant most of the hurtful things he'd said to her.

Beverly looked up, and a smile transformed her face from gaunt to angelic. "Mary Kate."

Major whipped his head around. Had Ma truly lost it this time?

But instead of the fictitious Mary Kate Danaher from *The Quiet Man*, Meredith Guidry stood framed by the entrance to the gazebo, looking once again like an exquisite dish of chocolate and strawberries with the way her brown sweater brought out the red tones in her hair. He wished he could stand up, go to her, pull her into his arms, and beg her forgiveness for the way he'd spoken to her the other morning. But he couldn't.

As she came around to greet his mother, Meredith touched his shoulder. Fleeting and light, the contact told him enough. She'd already forgiven him. But he still needed to say the words to her.

"I was just telling Danny yesterday how romantic I thought this place was. He was too scared to ask you to come, so I called you myself."

Heat tweaked Major's cheeks.

"I'm glad you did call, Beverly."

His mother grabbed Meredith's forearm and practically forced her into the chair next to him. "You two wait right there." She skipped away with her friend.

Major stared after her.

"What's wrong?"

"I haven't heard her giggle like that in. . .ever." He summoned his courage to face Meredith again. "Since she met you, she's been happier than I've seen her in more years than I care to remember."

"I think she's a wonderful person."

"She is a wonderful person. And I'm. . ." He swallowed back years of following John Wayne's character's advice. "I'm sorry I never told you about her."

"You were trying to protect her."

"No. I was trying to protect me. I was embarrassed by her, ashamed to admit I have a mother with schizophrenia, scared to see how people reacted to that knowledge."

"You *were* embarrassed?" Hope shone in Meredith's brown eyes.

"Was. Past tense." Rustling noises and women's whispers and giggles caught his ear. "There's just one more thing I need to do to make it right."

Ma and her friend returned carrying plates, with two other women behind them holding glasses of iced tea.

"A romantic spot calls for a romantic meal." Ma's forehead creased. "I had to make due with what I had in my apartment."

The plates went down in front of Major and Meredith. Tuna on wheat with a side of Cheetos and a Twinkie for dessert. He had to clear his throat a couple of times before he trusted himself to speak without bursting out laughing.

"Thanks, Ma. This is wonderful."

"You two lovebirds enjoy this." Ma started to leave with her friends, but Major caught her by the hand before she disappeared.

"Wait. I have something I need to say to you, something Meredith needs to hear me say."

"But this is your romantic dinner, and I'm not supposed to be here."

"It'll just take a minute, Ma. Sit down, please." He waited until she pulled over a chair from the other table and sat beside him.

"Ma, yesterday we talked about how much I love you and how sorry I am that I didn't come home more from New York, remember."

"Of course I remember. I'm not an idiot."

No way was she going to get a rise out of him today. "Well, there's more that I need to say. And that's to ask your forgiveness, Ma. You see, all my life I've been embarrassed to tell anyone about you, to let them know what a wonderful mother I have."

"Danny, I'd be embarrassed by me, too." Ma stroked the side of his face with her dry, papery fingertips.

"You have nothing to be embarrassed about. You are my mother, the only one I have. You've done the best you can to give me a wonderful life—which, I've recently been reminded in a very painful way, is precious to me." He pressed his hand to his cracked ribs. "I don't want to think about how bleak and empty my life would be without you in it. So will you forgive me for being an ungrateful son?"

Ma wrapped her arms around his neck and kissed his cheek. "You are my son, and I'll take you any way I can get you. But before I forgive you, there's something you have to do for me."

"Name it."

"Marry Mary Kate."

Molten lava melted his insides. The volcanic heat flared into his face, but he took a deep breath, disentangled himself from Ma's hug, and managed to turn his wheelchair so that he was parallel with

Meredith's chair, facing her.

"I had the perfect romantic menu planned and wanted to do this at a time when I could do it right and get down on one knee." He took both of Meredith's hands in his. "I haven't even gotten you a ring yet."

Moisture filled Meredith's eyes, and her breath seemed shallow. But her smile was all the encouragement he needed.

"Meredith will you—"

"Can't find it. Can't find it. Can't find it." Beverly stood up, her hands flapping around her as if she were beating off bees. "Can't find it."

Major cringed but reminded himself that his mother couldn't help the way she was.

Ma took off toward the building. With a sigh, Major looked at Meredith. "It's always something."

"Should we follow her?" Meredith's fine brows knit together.

"Yes. Do you mind?"

Her frown disappeared into a radiant smile. "Of course not." She pushed him back into the building and all the way to his mother's apartment.

But he didn't see her when they entered. "Ma?"

"Where is it? Can't find it." Around the side of the bed, Ma hunkered down on hands and knees, digging for something under the bed. "Ah." She came back up with a shoe box, removed the lid, and dumped the contents in the middle of the bed.

Fascinated, Major wheeled himself closer.

Ma rummaged through thimbles, paper clips, clothing tags, pennies, and other trinkets—and Major understood. This was her collection. The little things she picked up here and there that, somehow in her mind, connected her to memories and coherency.

Finally, she picked up an item, blew on it, wiped it on her shirttail, and handed it to Major. He looked down at the object in his hand. Love unlike anything he'd felt for her before overwhelmed him.

"Thanks, Ma." He turned the wheelchair around to face Meredith. "As I was saying. Will you—"

"Not here! You have to do it over the romantic dinner on the patio."

Meredith laughed and wiped her damp cheeks with the back of her hand.

"I guess we need to go back outside then," Major said.

Once back out on the secluded patio, Beverly instructed Meredith to resume her seat and pushed Major's chair so he was just where she thought he'd been before.

"Can I ask now, Ma?" He glanced over his shoulder at her.

"What are you waiting for?" She waved her hand then went to hide behind the pillar at the entrance.

"As I was saying before, I had this romantic dinner all planned out. . . ."

Meredith squeezed his hand. "You should have known me long enough by now to know that I'm not one for fancy dinners or gourmet food. Tuna and Cheetos is a romantic enough menu for me."

"Why have I wasted so much time?"

"Because you're crazy!" Ma called.

He and Meredith laughed. "I guess I'd better get on with this before she comes over here and does it for me." Taking her left hand, he slipped the object Ma had given him, his grandmother's engagement ring, onto her finger. "Meredith Guidry, will you marry me?"

She never broke eye contact with him. "On one condition."

His heart stopped. "What's that?"

"You'll go back to my father and tell him you've changed your mind about the restaurant deal."

"How did you—?"

She pressed her free hand to his lips. "That doesn't matter. What matters is that I'm pretty sure your mother is the reason you turned him down. And if I agree to marry you, she's going to be my mother, too, which means I can share in the responsibility of taking care of her while you work at the restaurant."

"But what about your job and your hours?"

"I'm promoting Corie into a new planner position to take some of the pressure off me so that maybe I can go back to just a fifty- or sixty-hour work week." She grinned. "So will you?"

He would never deserve her. "Will you agree to keep the puppy and name him Duke?"

"You'll help out with training?"

"Naturally."

"Then, yes, I'll keep the puppy."

"Good. Now, you haven't answered my other question. Will you marry me?"

"Yes, she will." Beverly's whisper carried to them.

Meredith laughed then leaned forward and kissed him. "Yes, Chef. I'll marry you."

KAYE DACUS is a graduate of Seton Hill University's Master of Arts in Writing Popular Fiction program. She is an active member and former vice president of American Christian Fiction Writers (ACFW). Her novel *Stand-In Groom* took second place in the 2006 ACFW Genesis writing competition.

If you enjoyed

MENU FOR ROMANCE

then read

STAND-IN GROOM

by KAYE DACUS